'They say so much about the sins of the fathers, but they never mention the mothers! I'm beginning to feel as if the sins of this mother will be visited on the fourth and fifth generations . . .'

From the day she was widowed, pregnant with her only child, Marged Richmond had only one man in her life – her son Henry. Throughout his childhood she schemed and worked to turn her modest inheritance into a thriving business and Henry into a gentleman. Her plans centred round founding a dynasty of Richmonds who would conquer the commercial world – but she never predicted what she would do if Henry fell in love with the wrong girl . . .

*Also by Merle Jones*

Mademoiselle

# Kingmaker

## Merle Jones

**HEADLINE**

Typeset in 10/12½ pt English
by Colset Private Limited, Singapore

Printed and bound in Great Britain by
Collins, Glasgow

HEADLINE BOOK PUBLISHING PLC
Headline House
79 Great Titchfield Street
London W1P 7FN

For Andy Creed-Miles,
who set the ball rolling

# PART ONE

# Sovereign Lord

# Chapter One

## North Wales, 1858

The Welsh witch warned Henry Richmond that her potions would change the lives of his children's children and send them across a great ocean to remake the family fortunes. He was less interested in her prophecy than in the spell she cast over him.

Not that there was anything mystical behind that particular enchantment. It lay in the sly inviting look in her light blue eyes, startling against her mane of black hair; in the erotic round weight of her breasts beneath the thin stuff of her workaday dress; and in the sinuous movement of her hips as she slid past him into the dim recesses of her little shop.

At the age of eighteen he found such magic infinitely stronger than talk of his children. They were unlooked-for dreams as yet. She was here and now and he could imagine nothing he wanted more than to possess her. He wondered if he dared try . . . after all, however dim it was here inside the herbalist's den, it was a bright sunny market day outside, with half the inhabitants of Llangefni parading through the streets minding their own and other people's business. And Uncle Idris would be looking for him. Idris would never let him live it down if he were to walk in and catch his young nephew compromised with Myfanwy Owen.

The girl had drifted away, far into the back of the shop, leaving a trail of some exotic scent to remind him of the invitation in her eyes and her walk. It was too good to miss . . . certainly too good to throw away just on the chance that his uncle would catch him at it. After all, he'd never tell Mother, would he? But Marged Richmond was a woman of such fearsome presence that the very thought of her discovering his interest in Myfanwy killed Henry's desire instantly. He started backing out of the shop, away from the pulsing reality of the girl's allure and towards the God-fearing commonplace world of his virtuous mother.

'I – er – I have to go, now, Myfanwy . . . business, see. Some – some other time . . . soon . . . that is . . .'

His tone sounded weak and strained even to his own ears. To this strange young seductress it must have been little more than the wail of a disappointed child, wanting to steal apples from a forbidden orchard but afraid to climb the wall and get them. Only silence answered him out of the dimness. Irritation, then anger began to replace his nervous regret. All right, if that was the way she wanted it, he'd go. There were plenty of other willing girls around, more than happy to entertain a young man with prospects like his. But not another Myfanwy Owen, a mocking satyr voice murmured inside his mind. Henry stopped once more, half way out of the little shop now, his hand on the peculiar brass door handle, reluctant finally to relinquish the prize that had so nearly been his . . .

He glanced outside and saw his uncle striding along the narrow street, deep in conversation with a farmer.

The sight was enough to propel him back into the shop at an undignified trot. He was in no state to face his family at the moment.

There was still no sign of Myfanwy. He hesitated momentarily, then pushed through the bead curtain across the doorway behind the counter. Beyond it was another, thicker curtain. He pushed through that, too, beset by a feeling that he was entering a different world, remote from the prosaic existence of Llangefni. Now he was in a long, narrow room which was a caricature of an alchemist's laboratory. There was even a little stuffed crocodile hanging by wires from a hook in the shadowed ceiling. The remnant of Myfanwy's scent curled through more sinister odours of formaldehyde and pickling spices. Henry shuddered, but the girl's dark allure and his own reluctance to be discovered here by his uncle drove him further into the back of the shop.

'I was beginning to think that old crocodile had got you.'

The voice was smoky, infinitely promising, with an alien tone underlying the Welsh singsong.

Henry hoped that his laugh sounded cynical and dismissive and that she wouldn't mistake its lightness for mounting panic.

'Myfanwy, where are you? What are – oh, Christ, you've got nothing on!'

'Well, what with you undressing me with your eyes out there, I thought I'd make your wish come true. Haven't you ever seen a girl like this before?'

Suddenly the panic subsided as he looked in wonder at the figure in front of him. The room was done up as a sort of gimcrack gypsy's caravan interior. If there were any windows, they were obliterated by the heavy cloth hangings which swathed the place from ceiling to floor. Myfanwy had been behind a tall, painted screen when he came in. A couple of vivid Paisley shawls hung casually over it. The floor was covered with rag rugs and huge, fat cushions. Indeed, they seemed to comprise the only furniture apart from the screen. One glance told him he had better not look more closely at the engravings which hung on the wall among the swathed hangings. Even in the lamplit gloom, the people they portrayed appeared to be doing things he had never suspected were possible.

And in the middle of all this imitation opulence stood the one genuine jewel in the place: this beautiful, beautiful girl. Henry's sense of reality was slipping away fast. Her scent swirled around him again, although she did not appear to have moved towards him. He stepped forward and suddenly her arms were around him and he was engulfed by the scent and by the soft resilience of her breasts. He surfaced from her long kiss, gasping like a drowning man, and her faery eyes slanted up at him, seeming to mock him.

'Too much for you, am I? Still got some growing up to do?'

Henry kissed her again, desire surging through him, and he knew that far from being too much for him, she was everything he wanted. Her skin, velvety under his fingers, seemed to singe him. The spicy, ancient odour of her scent gusted from the loosened skeins of blue-black hair. He would drown in it, and never go home . . .

'Henry, come on, we haven't got all day!' He was turned to stone. Uncle Idris!

The panic returned, strengthened a thousandfold.

'Myfanwy, what can I do? How can I . . .?'

There was contempt in the wide-awake smile that had instantly replaced the heavy-lidded passion in her expression. 'Afraid of the grown-ups, are you? Never mind – your Aunty Van will protect you, little boy. Only there's a price. Remember, boy, there's always a price.'

She turned away from him and drew aside the wall hanging. Behind it was a very ordinary door. 'It goes straight into the yard,' she said. 'Only blank walls – no spying windows to overlook it. Just go through the gate over the other side and double back down the outside passage. You'll come out two doors up from the shop front. Come back soon, mind. I haven't finished with you yet.'

The thought appalled as much as thrilled him. He scrabbled out through the low door, undignified in his haste, and it clicked shut behind him with a smoothness that suggested frequent use. The latch of the little gate was oiled and it, too, slipped open and shut almost noiselessly. He turned back along the dank stone-floored passageway between two buildings and moments later almost fell out into the brilliant sunshine of the spring morning. He had time to resume a less frantic air in the few paces which brought him up behind Idris Richmond, who was just closing the front door of the herbalist's shop in considerable perplexity.

'So there you are at last, man! Surely you've no need of herbal remedies at your age?'

'What are you talking about, Uncle? I was next door. Haven't been in there.'

Damn, that settled it! Uncle Idris had seen him. Now there was definitely no going back. Henry struggled to conceal the fury that rose within him. It was Idris's fault he'd got into such a state. If he had been alone he would have had the courage to live the adventure with that glorious girl. Alone, he would not have feared a telltale whisper in Mam's ear. Alone he would have put Don Juan in the shade . . .

His Uncle Idris kept up a stream of chatter which he knew was passing over Henry unheard. Idris didn't mind; as usual, he was absorbed in contemplation of this startling youth who was so unlike the rest of the family. Sometimes he had difficulty in believing that the boy shared his blood.

The Richmonds were middlemen in the food supply business – buyers of produce from the Anglesey farms to provision the small shopkeepers of the huge industrial heartland around Manchester and Liverpool. Idris's brother Rhys had died before he ever got the chance to capitalise on the good dowry brought by his young bride Marged Lewis, leaving her a pregnant widow at just eighteen. Idris had promised to take care of the girl and her child, to help manage the small but useful inheritance, and to bring the boy up fit to make his way in the world. Now eighteen more years had passed. Young Henry seemed quite capable of fending for himself – shrewd, cool-headed, never one to act impulsively and live to rue it. But occasionally you looked at him and it seemed there was a devil inside, raging to escape.

Idris wondered why the lad gave that impression. He had never seen Henry throw a tantrum or encourage companions of whom his mother would disapprove, or known him to break his word. And yet there was that

8

peculiar air of self-containment, that feeling that the world saw only what the boy wanted it to see. And what had he been doing in the herbalist's? By his high colour and the flustered look of him, Idris guessed that for once Henry had cast caution to the winds. But surely he couldn't be setting his cap for that little gypsy Myfanwy Owen? Why, that girl had been born old. She'd even taught Idris a thing or two, and that had been a couple of years back, before he realised he wasn't her only romantic interest . . . which was why Idris was leading young Henry away from her lair and deliberately acting the middle-aged innocent about his nephew's presence there.

'Henry – listen to me now. I've done most of what I came for, no thanks to you, mind. Thought we might have time for a glass of beer and some bread and cheese before we start back.'

Henry brightened. Until now his mind had been in the exotic dark shop with Myfanwy, not with the boring commonplaces of his uncle's provision buying. But the opportunity for a drink and a bite in manly surroundings cheered him. His uncle's arrival had killed his desire instantly. The public house would give him time to collect himself. Anyway, he had precious few opportunities to enjoy such places with his mother always demanding attention and obedience.

'Right, then. The Bull, is it?'

'Where else? All the best scandal there. If the right people are there we may even get a bit of game for the pot.'

The Bull Hotel was a grim building of mock Elizabethan structure calculated to add dignity to the little market square. It was the only hostelry in Llangefni which could claim the status of an hotel, with its English-style choice of bars, a smoking room and a proper dining room. The other inns around the town settled for serving food on rough-hewn tables at one end of the big one-room bar and sometimes offered a few spartan bedrooms for travellers who could not rise to the cost of a room at the Bull. Many of them were merely ale houses, with neither food nor sleeping accommodation. Llangefni was rapidly overhauling Beaumaris as capital of the island county, but it was a very modest county.

Idris was not interested in the dining room where a few of the more prosperous farmers were already sitting down to their roast mutton. He walked through to the saloon bar, where he knew he would find plenty of familiar faces. Henry followed eagerly, warmed by the place's air of masculine companionability, disturbing memories of Myfanwy fading with every step. Public house though it was, no females ever strayed in here. In London, certain sorts of women were known to venture into such establishments, but the Isle of Anglesey was almost three hundred miles from London and a hundred years behind it in time. Even disreputable females were not permitted to cross the threshold of the Bull.

Marged Richmond had lived half her life in Bangor with-out really becoming part of the community. Pressed to explain her isolation, the locals would have said it was because she came from outside. But the real reason was that she wanted to remain separate. Married at seven-teen, a pregnant widow at eighteen, her life had seemed to hold little promise. Marged saw it otherwise. She knew what she wanted and it was a long way removed from middle-class respectability in a tiny provincial town. Her ambitions were enormous – so grand that she accepted she might never live to see them fulfilled. But she had no intention of dying until she had laid the foundations of a dynasty which would impress the whole world. Her son Henry embodied all Marged's hopes and desires. She loved him more than anyone else she had known, and beyond him her imagination saw a line of descendants stretching forward into a golden future which she, little Marged Lewis the merchant's daughter, had set in motion.

Marged knew about Myfanwy Owen. She had known about the girl for a long time – since she had almost seduced Idris, whom Marged regarded more as a personal possession than a brother-in-law. Marged had put a spoke in that little wheel by letting Idris know, indirectly, of course, that he was only the latest in a long line of Myfanwy's moonstruck victims. His pride devastated, Idris had withdrawn, as Marged had known he would. But she had not engineered the parting out of jealousy. She was a realist. She didn't mind Idris fumbling with a maidservant on a remote farm, or even building his desire into a business transaction and going to visit the professional tarts in Manchester or Liverpool. In Myfanwy she recognised a rival whose talents were potentially at least a match for her own. Idris today, Henry tomorrow, her instinct had said. Now she had been proved right – but in such a manner that she yearned to have been mistaken.

It was a perfect summer morning and she had received Idris in the first-floor drawing room of her house overlooking the Menai Straits. Beneath her window lay a view to rival the coasts of Italy, but Marged was blind to it. She was concentrating her entire attention, and fury, on Idris.

'You knew! You knew at Easter and you did nothing about it! Were you temporarily soft in the head or did you hope the little trollop would save a few crumbs for you after he'd had his fill of her?'

'Marged . . . Marged, please . . . it's hardly a subject for a lady.'

'In that case, I'm no lady, if that's what it takes to make you discuss this. I don't think you have the faintest idea of what this could do to Henry's future. Rather than see her drag him down, I'll discuss anything, however sordid it might be, so you'd better get used to hearing unladylike words from my lips, Idris Richmond!'

Cornered, Idris reluctantly accepted her challenge. 'It seemed so harmless, Marged. The boy had to sow some wild oats some time, somewhere, and he certainly wouldn't have any chance in that English boarding school of his. I thought you'd disapprove less if it happened this way than if he – well – visited one of those places in London or Bristol. The girl may not be respectable, but at least she's clean.'

Marged cut him off. 'You're more of a fool than I thought. Try and get your eyes up out of the sty for a moment and take a look around you! I wasn't thinking of the physical side of things – of course I knew that was bound to happen one day. Can't you see, Idris? Even when she nearly trapped you, can't you see she has a lot more than carnal attractions? She's clever, she's ambitious, and she has no more intention of spending the rest

12

of her life on the island than I have of letting Henry do so!'

Idris was stung into retaliation. 'Oh, you're dramatising it, girl! Of course she's ambitious, but she'd never be daft enough to think Henry would make an honest woman of her. One of the Llanddona witches? Not in a thousand years!'

Marged had become ominously calm as he spoke. Now she advanced on him, as though intent on physical attack. 'You seem to forget that I've devoted a large portion of my dowry to making sure Henry grows up far away from anyone who'll tell him about the Llanddona witches, or any of the other primitive nonsense those Anglesey peasants believe. By now she knows that, too, and she probably thinks it's her best chance of hooking a good catch. After all, it'd be brave local man who'd share his life with one of them. Henry would just wave the whole thing away as silly superstition and carry on with her regardless. If we were only talking about a few wild oats, I'd almost encourage it, but we're not. Once she really gets to work on him, it will be for life. I hope to God I've found out soon enough to put a stop to it, that's all.'

'Marged, Marged, you're putting too much on this. I don't know what you've heard, but I can assure you the boy didn't have a chance to get up to any real mischief the time I almost caught them together. He just disappeared for twenty minutes or so and I saw him coming out of that little shop of hers in Llangefni. What with the shop open and all she'd have to be a lot cleverer than even you think she is to make a man of him that day. And a week later he was off back to school for the summer.

13

Nothing could have happened, I tell you.'

'You're as far behind the times as this bloody town!'

He was really troubled now. Never before had he heard Marged or any other woman of her kind swear. But before Idris had time to protest she was off again.

'That was just the day she planted the seed in his mind. He had the whole summer term shut up at Warwick with all those boys, dreaming about whatever little bits of heaven she'd shown him, imagining how exciting it would be to go back for more . . . Dear God, it would have been better if she'd gone all the way with him. At least he'd have had to day-dream about reality then, not about some wonderful pleasure still to come. By the time he came home he was ripe for the plucking – straight off to Llangefni the first excuse he got, and I let him go without a second thought because you hadn't told me where he'd be going!'

Idris was abashed. 'Oh, so he's been back already.'

'Been back? Been back, the man says! He's been in and out of that shop so often everyone must think he's a helpless invalid after a miracle cure! That girl probably imagines she's got him half way up the aisle already. Well, it's stopping now and I'll see to it. If I trust you to look after things, you'll be helping him put the ring on her finger next!'

Idris felt terribly sorry for young Henry. The boy had no idea what was awaiting him. Still, it was beyond his power to help. Marged would take him apart if she ever had reason to think he had even warned Henry of her suspicions. Unable to reason with his sister-in-law, he allowed the rest of her tirade to flow over him and lapsed into private contemplation of his nephew's exploits, and

Marged's powers of detection. It was amazing, really. The woman had very few friends and insisted herself that she had no acquaintances. Most outsiders learned nothing of the interior life of this closed community. And yet she had an infallible nose for any goings-on which affected her family: woe betide them if those goings-on were guilty secrets!

Henry, meanwhile, blissfully unaware of what awaited him at home, was on his way to meet Myfanwy Owen. He had seen her even more often than his mother suspected during the three weeks since his return from school. Marvellous, really, he thought, how a girl with as few advantages as Myfanwy could grow up so accomplished, so clever – and so beautiful. Dress her up in expensive clothes and you could mistake her for a lady, any day . . . Well, if you worked on her accent for a little while, you could. And in the meantime, it had a delightful ring to it.

According to the tale he had told Marged, he was driving the family pony and trap over to the island in order to look at some prehistoric ruins. In reality he was heading for a meeting with Myfanwy. He could not be expected to know that a member of the Cathedral Ladies' Guild which his mother attended was a patron of Myfanwy's little shop. The woman had been there on his last two visits. Subsequently, at a Guild meeting, she had yielded to the temptation to deflate the stuck-up Mrs Richmond. Her highly-coloured version of the encounters between the young lovers concentrated on their whispered endearments, and she even hinted that they were more intimate than delicacy permitted. Now

Nemesis, in the shape of a raging mother, awaited Henry back at the house in Menai View.

His years at public school had given him a veneer of sophistication that most local boys of his age lacked; but it was only a veneer. Inside he was as green as any of them, although his native shrewdness saved him from a lot of scrapes. Unfortunately it was of little use in guiding him through the thickets of first love.

He had blinded himself to the fact that Myfanwy was four years older than he; that she was from a lower social class than his own (indeed, even the humblest Anglesey labourers regarded the Llanddona witches as inferior); and, most of all, that he was barely eighteen, with a bright future already planned by his domineering mother. Marged Richmond's worst fears were well founded. Henry was not day-dreaming about a quick sexual liaison, but about marriage.

In the back of the trap he carried a picnic basket, made up that morning by the cook at Menai View for whom Master Henry's whim was law. It contained pieces of cold chicken, a big meat and potato pie on a plate, two peaches, a wedge of cheese, freshly-baked bread and a fruit cake. Mrs.Davies was Temperance, so the liquid refreshment comprised two bottles of ginger beer. She had packed enough for him to entertain a small army. The child in him hoped Myfanwy would be impressed.

After a term of fantasising about his new love goddess, Henry had hurried to Llangefni the first time he could escape his mother after coming home. He had left Warwick for good this year, and Marged was making a deliberate effort to let him feel he had more freedom to come and go unquestioned now he was on the threshold

16

of manhood. Nevertheless it took a long time to get to Llangefni and back by pony and trap, and Myfanwy had to keep the shop going. As a result, the lovers' meetings so eagerly spied on and reported to his mother had been little more than bouts of harmless flirting. Henry had begun to get desperate and perhaps Myfanwy sensed this for on his last visit, three days earlier, she had told him that if he came for her before noon on Tuesday, she would close the shop and come out with him for the afternoon. He had been counting the minutes ever since.

New love had made Henry too rash to think of secrecy. He drew up in the street outside the herbalist's and, with the promise of a penny, left the rig in the care of a small boy. Minutes later he was handing Myfanwy up into the passenger seat, paying off his young helper and setting off at a stylish canter. Their departure was universally noticed.

They stopped a short distance out of town, beside the water mill at Bodffordd. It was both beautiful and peaceful in the secluded clearing up the lane from the miller's house. Myfanwy knew no one would disturb them because the miller always went off to deliver sacks of flour on Tuesday afternoons.

It was a hot day. Henry removed his jacket, then started laying out his picnic feast on a cloth that Mrs Davies had packed at the top of the basket. He did not get very far. Myfanwy lay back on the woollen rug he had spread for them to sit on, and spoke his name very softly. Henry turned to look at her and could not look away. The sunlight fell dappled through leaves and played on the girl's perfect skin and hair. Mutely she raised her arms to him and he went to her.

Once more that softness, the scent . . . and this time there was nothing to hold him back. Her open-mouthed kiss seemed to drown him. His hands moved over her pliant body with a confidence that sprang from his intense desire for her. Myfanwy possessed the seductress's priceless talent of being able to manipulate her lover so that he thought the initiative was all his. Her demure dress fastened up the front to a lace-trimmed high neckline. Somehow, now, the buttons were undone, and it seemed perfectly natural to find her breasts bare beneath the outer garment. His mouth moved down across her chin and neck, finally, deliciously, finding the red nipples which hardened as his lips touched them. Her own small hands were inside his shirt, the nails trailing with maddening effect across his muscular chest and belly. Practised fingers unfastened his belt and slid downward. Writhing with desire, Henry began to raise her skirt, then started back with a gasp of surprise.

'There's – you've nothing on down there, either!'

She stirred dreamily. 'Didn't think you'd want me to dress up special for a picnic . . . thought it was go as you please –' she drew his hand up between her thighs – 'and this is how I please.'

Things became rather vague after that. Henry found himself thrust into a world of pure sensation, where colour and touch and scent and noise all surged together into a crashing, glorious mêlée with Myfanwy at its centre. Finally, racked by ecstatic sobs, he felt his whole being pitch forward into her and begin to fall so wonderfully that he never wanted to reach the bottom.

When reality returned it was almost as good as what had gone before. She had discarded her dress altogether

18

and was crouching over him, tickling his chest with a feathery stalk of grass. Henry seemed to be wearing only his shirt; he had no memory of removing his other clothes. Desire kindling again, he began to reach for her, but she laughed and dodged his grasp, dancing backwards the tranquil millpond.

'Oh, no you don't – not till after we've had our food, anyway! Come on, let's have a wash first!'

As she spoke he had started up towards her and now, catching him slightly off balance, she grabbed his wrist and twisted them both into the water. It was tingling cold and wonderfully refreshing. Shocked by his sudden immersion, Henry bobbed out of the water, shuddering and yelling until his flesh adjusted. A few feet away, Myfanwy was splashing about like some mythical water nymph. He turned and surged towards her.

'Just you wait, madam – I'll make you pay for that!' They splashed each other like children for a few minutes before he hauled her out on to the bank.

'Now what d'you suggest we do, you mad thing? We'll never be dry enough to put our clothes back on!'

'Of course we will. Anyway, I like to come prepared. Look in my picnic bag. You'll find the right stuff there.'

He had assumed that the bag she brought with her from the shop contained things she had bought in Llangefni. Instead, he found two bath sheets, a brush and a comb.

'There you are!' Myfanwy was smug. 'What more could you want? Now, let's 'ave something to eat and after, as a special treat, you can do my hair.'

They did full justice to the food, and after they had finished Myfanwy undid her thick braid of hair. It flopped wetly around her shoulders and she handed the brush to Henry. 'There you are, boy, a little extra bit of pleasure for you.'

As he brushed the thick black mane, Henry began to feel it had a life of its own. By the time it was smooth and untangled, it covered the girl like a cloak. 'You look like some lovely magic thing that just appeared out of the water,' he told her wonderingly.

'Maybe I am. You know that some people say I'm a witch?'

'Oh, no! What idiots people are. Just because you're a herbalist, I suppose.'

She gave him a strange, sidelong look. 'Maybe . . . maybe not. P'raps the witch came first and the shop came after, did you ever think of that?'

In these surroundings, looking as she did, it was easy enough to believe. Henry determinedly shook off the faint sense of unease that crept over him.

'Come on, Van – surely it's superstition? You know what these old-fashioned country people are like.'

The girl laughed, but there was no humour in it. 'Oh yes, I know what these country people are like – none better. Haven't your mam ever told you about the Llanddona witches, even if only to warn you?'

'No, honestly. Of course I've heard the term before. Everyone around here uses it. But nobody ever told me what they meant by it and I suppose if I ever thought about it at all, I imagined it was just a way of referring to anyone from Llanddona.'

'Not quite, boy. We'm special. The ordinary farming folk down our way don't get called it. Just us.'

'Who's "us"? You talk as if you were foreigners, but

20

your name's far more Welsh than mine.'

'Well, it would be, wouldn't it? Seeing how my dada was one of those good farm boys who was a Llanddona Welshman pure and simple. Ieuan Owen would 'ave run a mile from my mam if he'd known how being married to her would destroy him. But by the time he found out it was too late, and he was as much an outsider as we were. Silly, really, all of it. In the beginning all we were was newcomers who didn't speak the language.'

'But other English people have managed all right. Why not you?'

'English? We was no more English than my dada! Our people came from Ireland and the only tongue they spoke at first was the old Irish language. It was long, long ago, Henry, a hundred years back, but folk round here have long memories. The ones who ruled in Ireland, they had a fancy punishment for smugglers. Used to stick them in open boats, without sails or oars, and just a little bit of fresh water and a bit of bread. Then they pushed the boat out into the Irish Sea and waved good-bye to the criminals. Their white English hands were clean of our blood, but none of us would ever come back to trouble them again. I expect most of the poor souls died on the high seas – it's one of the roughest passages of all, they say. But two boatloads that were pushed off together were lucky in a funny sort of way. A big storm took the boats and swept them across the sea, then blew them around the northern tip of Anglesey and down into the estuary east of Pentraeth. When they were washed ashore, they had to tramp further south to secure the one boat – the other had broken up – and by the time they'd done that the tide had cut them off from the estuary. You

21

must have been to Llanddona some time, and seen the road.'

'Oh yes – Uncle Idris took me there a couple of times. Told me all the heavy goods have to be taken in and out by boat because the road down to the beach is so steep.'

'That's right. Well, there were my people, all trapped down there on that beach, wringing wet and without any food. But there was woods and marshes backing on to the sand, and a good fresh stream running down, so pretty soon they got game and fresh water and made sort of shelters for themselves. When the local people first saw them and tried talking to them in Welsh, then English, all they got was these words that they could nearly understand but not quite. And they didn't know where we come from. So they said we was witches, conjured up out of the storm.

'In the beginning they left well alone because you can imagine how this bunch of wild Irish smugglers scared them. But then they started bearing us a grudge because we was trapping on the marsh and making a living from the fishing. They tried to drive us out. I suppose it was a mix-up of their fear and our wildness but when they attacked, our men and women howled and pointed and cursed in Irish – not that they thought it would work, but because they didn't have anything else to fight back with. It frightened the farmers stupid and that taught our lot a lesson. If you look as if you can do magic, often you can.

'From then on they were left more or less in peace. After a few years they were on their feet enough to come up off the shore and start selling fish and game in the markets, along with the herbal remedies they had to rely

22

on for everything from cleaning clothes to nursing the sick. The local people found they charged decent prices and in the end the witches started to scratch a living. But of course, they were still outsiders, and after a bit the bad ones among the Welsh started trying to do them down.

'The witches still didn't have any weapons worth the name and when one of them was caught by a bunch of ruffians, he played a trick he'd been told about in an old fairy tale. He put his hand in his pocket, groped about, then pulled it out and threw a handful of nothing at the gang, shouting that the witches' curse and the evil eye was on them. I don't know whether it was a convulsion or a heart attack or something from the shock, but one of the bullies fell down on the ground, writhed around in agony and then lost consciousness. I don't know if he died, but some say he did. After that, no one tried to interfere with us – they was all too frightened! But now we weren't just poor, we were evil as well. This all happened before my time, but by the time I was born, they hated us and were scared of us. They looked down on us, as well, mind, because we were so poor.

'It's funny, though, if people believe you have powers, after a while, perhaps you get them from somewhere. My mam could cure sick animals by laying her hands on them,' here she paused and looked darkly at him, 'and she could kill healthy people much the same way, though I don't expect a city boy like you to believe that. And she could see ahead in time, too –' another pause – 'and so can I, Henry boy. That's why I know so surely that our children's children will make a great family fortune across the seas. That's why I know we're meant for each other . . .'

She fell silent and he stared at her for a while, mesmerised by the feeling of stillness and darkness which had enwrapped them as the girl told her story. He believed all she had said. She had spoken with such conviction that it never occurred to him to do otherwise. But, obsessed as he was with Myfanwy, he was beginning to feel uneasy about what it might mean to be locked together with her for life. After all, by her own admission it had been the ruin of Ieuan Owen. Would Henry Richmond fare any better? Eventually he spoke, in a small, lost voice, striving to impose the everyday on her odd account.

'What about the rest of your people? You must be quite a crowd by now.'

Myfanwy shook her head. 'Oh, no. Somehow they seemed to be doomed. It was as if they'd been turned loose to wander forever on the face of the earth and Anglesey was just a place where they rested for a while. It was a terribly hard life and a lot of women died. From the start there weren't as many women as men, anyhow. Then some of the younger men started drifting away, once they'd taken to trading in the island markets. It was as if they knew they could disappear if they moved to crowded places where they wouldn't show up so much. My mam only stayed because she was married to Dada by then, and as his family had disowned him for it, she had to stick by him.'

'What happened to them?'

'Dada died very young. Just seemed to fade away, probably because he couldn't cope with being pushed out of his family. Of course, they said Mam had bewitched him to death. He left her with a little farm. She sold most of the land except a couple of acres around the house, and opened the herbalist's shop with what she got. She knew I wouldn't be able to run the farm by myself. It was as if she was only hanging on until she'd taught me all about her people's herbal remedies, and got the shop going. Just after I passed sixteen, she went off with our little boat one summer night – said she wanted to go fishing for mackerel. The boat was washed up back on Llanddona beach next morning. Her body came up at Black Point on the next tide. She didn't look a bit frightened – more happy, really. Afterwards, my father's one decent relative, his younger sister, took pity on me. But really she's been my only friend in hard times. Apart from her, I haven't got nobody.'

Henry squeezed her hand silently. He knew he should have reassured her that she had him now, but somehow the words choked him. Myfanwy watched him for a few moments, her face troubled. Then she sighed and stood up, breaking the spell. 'Maybe I shouldn't have told you today. It's spoiled our lovely picnic.'

His protests were hollow. They made themselves respectable, then he put the pony in the shafts once more and they headed back towards Llangefni in the golden early evening sunshine.

At the top of the hill that led into the town, Myfanwy asked him to stop. 'If you let me off here, I can easily walk the rest and you'll get back home sooner. I'm staying at the shop tonight, not going back to Llanddona.'

Henry helped her to the ground, and stood looking down at her lovely face. He was still troubled by her story. She smiled, trying to break his sombre mood.

'Come on, now, where's my happy boy? When will I see you next?'

What could he say? She still drew him like a magnet, but there was a nervousness there now which had not intruded before. 'I . . . er . . . that is . . . it's a bit difficult getting out here, I'm afraid. You know, the trap and all that . . .'

'No need to worry about that! You go mackerel fishing some nights, you've told me you do. Have you got your own boat?'

'Yes, of course. I was thinking of going out one night soon.'

'Good. I lock up on Friday and go back to Llanddona 'til Monday. If you go out fishing Saturday night, you could come round the Black Point to Llanddona in less time than it takes to bring a pony and trap to Llangefni. We could have some time together and then you could go back about dawn.'

'I – I can't promise. Don't know yet if I can get away.'

'Don't worry – I'm not going anywhere. I'll be down on the shore with a little fire from eleven on Saturday night. There's a full moon, too, so you'll have no trouble. Come to me then. If you can't manage it, no harm done.'

Henry clasped her hands in his and nodded, trying to pump some enthusiasm into his expression. 'Until Saturday, then. Take care, Van, and think of me . . .'

Her face was solemn, full of unasked questions. For a moment he thought she would speak, but she remained silent, merely reaching up to touch his cheek fleetingly before setting off down the hill into town.

# Chapter Two

Marged knew how to manipulate men. Her outburst of rage with Idris had been genuine, but she had no intention of railing at Henry over his involvement with Myfanwy Owen. That would merely drive him further into the girl's arms. Having relieved her true feelings at her brother-in-law's expense, she was determined to wear a mask of sweet reason before her son.

She was out when he arrived home from his afternoon with Myfanwy. Marged knew he went to Anglesey for only one reason these days, and she preferred to leave him to his own devices afterwards in case she betrayed her anger. Thus Henry was pleasantly surprised to find a quiet house and a note in the hall to tell him that Mrs Davies had left hot soup in a *bain-marie* in the kitchen, and a cold meal laid in the dining room. Marged herself was at a church meeting that might end late, so he should not wait up if he was tired after his day out.

Henry felt a little like a small boy who has just successfully raided an orchard and escaped undetected. He had returned home more than half convinced that Marged would know intuitively what he had been up to. Relieved to have avoided a confrontation, he ate his meal hurriedly and went to his room. When he saw his mother at breakfast next day, she was serene and affectionate. He began to relax. She made her opening move as he was pouring a second cup of coffee.

'I hope you're not planning to go off anywhere today, Henry. I think it's time we made some plans and it will take all morning at least.'

'Plans? Wh-what for?' Momentarily he had a panicky suspicion that Marged was about to bring his romance out into the open and start discussing a possible marriage. For some reason the thought disturbed more than pleased him.

His mother appeared to be thinking of something else entirely. 'Silly boy! Your future, of course. You can't think you are just going to drift along like this forever. We have to discuss bringing you into the business – and that's hardly a matter to be dismissed in five minutes.'

'But shouldn't Uncle Idris be here? I mean . . . I know it's not strictly his line, but he is, sort of, responsible for things, isn't he?'

There was a faintly malicious edge to her smile. 'Not really, my boy. At the end of the day, the responsibility is all mine – and after that, yours, of course. Now come along, we can't talk business over the remains of the bacon and eggs. We'll use the small parlour.'

The drawing room in Menai View was on the first floor, where the spectacular panorama of the Straits made a superb backdrop. On the ground floor were the dining room, the morning room, where they had eaten breakfast, and a small front room referred to as the parlour, which in fact was Marged's office. Henry seldom ventured into the room. It was not forbidden territory; he simply had no interest in whatever his mother got up to in there. Without conscious thought, he had always assumed Idris looked after the business affairs of the shop as an extension of his own wholesaling concern. If he considered the matter at all, he thought Marged spent her time in the parlour dealing with Church voluntary work and writing letters. She disillusioned him quickly.

'Now, Henry, tell me what you know about the shop. Don't look so suspicious – I'm not trying to trap you. If, as I suspect, the answer is nothing, that's my fault as much as yours. Well?'

'Well . . . not quite nothing, Mother, but not much more. We sell provisions from the shop in the High Street and about half-a-dozen people work for us there. It's our main source of income, but there are some investments, too. Is that right?'

Marged sighed. 'As far as it goes, I suppose. Really, it's time I took you in hand. I thought you'd have picked up at least a little more than that. Don't you ever think about it?'

'No – should I? It earns us a living. What more do I need to know?'

In spite of herself, Marged was growing exasperated. 'Presumably you expect to earn your own living now that you've left school? You must have something in mind, and I assumed it would be the shop.'

Henry laughed. 'What on earth would I do in the shop? You've got a perfectly good manager in Mr Beynon. You've never worked there yourself and we've lived well enough in spite of that. What could I possibly do to improve matters by going to work there?'

'Now you really are being stupid, boy! Just because I

29

don't live in the shop, it doesn't mean I have nothing to do with it. I work almost as many hours as Mr Beynon each week – certainly as many as Idris does in his business. There's more to running a prosperous grocer's shop than shifting sacks of sugar and cutting up cheese!'

She got up and went over to the built-in bookshelves which lined the back of the room. The bottom shelf was full of cumbersome box files. Marged took one out and brought it back to the big desk where they were sitting.

'Who d'you think deals with all this? Buying stock, submitting accounts, chasing the bad payers, seeing the housekeepers from the big estates get their proper tips on time – George Beynon couldn't keep up with all that to save his life. Anyway, to be fair to the man, we're doing so well that he's got both hands full just weighing and packing and filling shelves, with one eye on the assistants and the other on the stockroom.'

Henry was naively astonished. 'But you never seemed busy! When did you have the time?'

She smiled tolerantly. 'How would you know whether I was busy? You've been away at school for more than half the year ever since you were eight, learning to be a gentleman. In the holidays I always tried to give you most of my time. But even then, I'm out quite a lot. Where did you think I was?'

'I always thought you were doing something or other at the Cathedral.'

'Really, Henry, I'd be a religious fanatic if I was at that place as often as you imagine! I can see I've kept you away from getting your hands dirty for far too long. You've got a lot of catching up to do. But before we go into that, you never did tell me what you expected to do for a living.'

30

'Oh – I somehow assumed I'd go in with Uncle Idris. In fact, I thought that was why he hauled me off around the markets and farms every time I came home on holiday.'

Marged shook her head. 'What petty ambitions you have, my son! Start aiming a bit higher. You should be thinking about Idris's business and our own – that's where the future lies, one pair of hands running the lot. Do it well and there's a fortune to be made. But it'll take hard work, training and talent. I'll have to leave the talent to you and Providence, but I can do something about the training and hard work. Come on – we're going out.'

Without further explanation she was up and bustling off in search of shawl and bonnet. He heard her in the hall, telling Mrs Davies to get the garden boy to bring round the pony and trap.

When they arrived at the shop, George Beynon was sweeping the doorstep. Henry was outraged. 'After all you've spent on my education, surely you're not planning to turn me into a glorified crossing sweeper?'

Before Marged could retort, Beynon turned to a boy who had been standing watching him. 'There you are, Ellis, now you do it again – and proper, this time, mind. Long, wide sweeps, remember, to keep the dust down and not flying all over the place. Off you go.'

Henry's mother permitted herself a smug smile. 'You should learn a bit of patience, Henry, then you wouldn't make yourself look silly so often. Mr Beynon is very good at training the apprentices – and he believes in showing, not telling, however humble the job may be.'

Henry flushed. What a start! He was still wondering how to react to his mother's plan, and was unsure whether to tell her he already had some profession or other in mind, or insist he wanted a few months more to consider the matter. The one thing he was sure of was that he didn't want to start his adult life as a counter-jumper in some obscure country store. But he was shrewd enough to know he would do nothing for his case if he made stupid blunders in his attempts to evade her plans for him.

Inside the shop, Henry took a good look at his inheritance for the first time since his childhood. He seldom went there because, until today, he had never thought its day-to-day operation would concern him.

'I have a few things to do before we discuss your career,' Marged said. 'George, will you show Mr Henry everything? I think he knows even less about the workings of a well-ordered provision shop than most of your lady customers!' She departed, her expression just like the one his history master would assume on saying 'Questions will be asked . . .' after setting some reading.

'Right, Mr Henry, where d'you want to start – front or back?'

'I'm entirely in your hands, George.' Henry used the man's first name with some hesitation. He still secretly thought of himself as a small boy and Beynon as a grown-up. But the manager seemed not to notice anything amiss. 'I must confess I don't know one end of the place from the other.'

'We shall 'ave to do something about that double quick then, shan't we, Mr Henry?' The tone was suspiciously sharp and Henry glanced at the man's face, expecting to detect resentment. But all he saw was a helpful smile.

Afterwards, Henry always said it was the smell that captivated him first. It came curling seductively from the stockrooms behind the shop, a wonderful mixture of tea, coffee, spices, cheese and bacon, each component retaining its own identity while magically combining with the rest to conjure an atmosphere of plenty and quality.

'I'd forgotten how wonderful it always smells,' he told George Beynon.

'Aye,' George nodded. 'I've been in the trade nearly twenty years now and it still makes me sniff the air every time I open up. Better than a glass of wine, isn't it? We'll start out the back. Then you'll see why it do smell so powerful.'

The rear stock rooms could have been the provision depot for a small army. In one, chests of tea were ranged along the wall, stacks of small blue and red paper bags next to them, waiting for George to blend and package them. Gunpowder Green, Oolong, Yunnan to one side; Darjeeling, Assam, Nuwara Eliya to the other. The names alone were like a voyage of exploration. A wide table in the same room was piled with loaf sugar, in the process of being chopped into lumps or pounded into powder form for different domestic uses. The stock was completed by a bench and bins of coffee opposite the tea chests. Here the green beans were toasted to rich dark brown each morning, so that customers could drink their coffee freshly roasted. The enormous commercial grinder was supplemented by a smaller one.

'Some of the ladies don't have their own at home and it's wasteful to put half a pound through the big grinder, so I do it with that,' George explained. 'We're making some changes in this department soon. Your mam gets some bright ideas on the quiet and she do reckon the ladies like the smell of the roasting coffee so much, it's worth doing it out in the front of the shop. So we're putting the roaster out there from next week – and the small grinder, too. Creates a bit of extra interest, see.'

Henry was becoming perplexed. 'You know, I've probably been back here some time, but it must have been when I was too young to remember. I never realised all this was going on. It's like a factory!'

'Of course it is, Mr Henry. How d'you think we stock the shop?'

'I've never really thought about it. I knew you portioned up all the butter and cheese, because I've seen the way Uncle Idris buys it in bulk from the farmers. But I never realised everything came like that.'

'It's a highly skilled trade, and serving the customers isn't the half of it,' said Beynon. 'You saw young Ellis out there by the step? He've just started his apprenticeship. He's twelve now, and even if he's really good he'll still be learning until he's seventeen. If he's only so-so, he'll be nearly twenty before he's considered really experienced.'

'Is that how you learned the trade?'

'Certainly is, Mr Henry – the only way, too, if you don't mind my saying. I had the advantage of doing it in Liverpool. My grandad was a ship's master out of there and when the time come for me to start work, Mam apprenticed me up there near him and Granny. Not that

34

it mattered that much, of course, 'cos I was living in all through the apprenticeship. They'd never let you go home o' nights then. Some apprentice boys I knew had to sleep down behind the counter in the shop, but I was luckier than that.'

'What was so special about being in Liverpool?'

'Oh, stands to reason, any seaport with a good East India trade gets the tea. My master always used to say you can teach everything in the trade by example except the tea. You got to teach that by taste. That's why I never smoked tobacco. Spoils the palate. We sell the best teas in North Wales from this shop, and it's all thanks to what I learned in Liverpool in the thirties. I make a couple of trips up there every year and taste and choose the basic types we want. Then I have them sent down here in bulk and blend them as we need them. There are other grocers around Bangor but none of them in our class, and it's all down to the tea. They just buy a couple of chests now and again and as long as the tea's got a dark colour and a bit of strength, they couldn't care less about the taste. Well that's all right if you're only catering for a bunch of farmers, but Richmond's is patronised by all the gentry from Caernarfon to Conway, and they know their onions – or rather, their tea!' He stopped chattering momentarily to chuckle at his small joke.

Henry was astonished by the change that had come over the man as they went round the shop. At their few previous meetings – usually at the house when Beynon came to see Marged on business – the manager was polite but withdrawn, with nothing to say beyond a greeting and a stock remark about the weather. Now, unleashed on his speciality, he was positively garrulous.

35

They moved on to the next room, the central section of the warehouse premises. Doors opened from it to the other two store rooms and at the rear was a loading bay for delivery of supplies and despatch of customers' orders. At present a load of dairy produce and bacon had arrived by carrier's cart from Anglesey – their share of Idris's latest purchases.

Beynon was off again. 'Ah, another innovation – well, at least, a bit of a trial. We cure our own hams and bacon, of course. But if we're going to keep our standard high, we can't produce enough. Trade is coming on very nicely but it can be a bit embarrassing when you haven't got the stock to satisfy the demand. So Mr Richmond has bought in a couple of sides of best bacon and two hams, just for us to try in comparison to our own, see.'

'If it does, will we stop curing our own?'

'Goodness, no, Mr Henry! Our reputation depends on our good bacon nearly as much as it do on the tea. No, we'll tell our customers we've got two different sorts now and ask them to see which they prefer.' He glanced around as if expecting a spy to emerge from the carrier's cart. 'As it happens I'm going to try a little experiment – see if I can't persuade people by *showing* them which they should like best . . .'

He was positively twinkling now. Henry was totally absorbed by the little man's enthusiasm. 'Come on, tell me what you have in mind!' He knew he should have felt silly to be participating in such parish-pump matters, but Beynon's enthusiasm was contagious.

'Well, we have about a dozen really well-off customers – housekeepers to the bigger landowners, you know the sort – so I'll send each of them a pound of bacon and half a pound of ham from the farm purchases, with Richmond's compliments, and ask them to compare it with their usual order of our own. It will cost us a ham and a side of bacon, but I think it will be worth the outlay. Then we'll offer the farm product to them at a lower price than our own – making sure they realise the difference, of course. If my little idea works out, we'll end up with the best customers using up all our own cure and the rest buying the farm stuff because it costs that much less. I wouldn't be at all surprised if we didn't end up selling a lot more, because the snobbish ones will soon get to know that Lord and Lady So-and-So's house-keeper takes Richmond's special cure and they'll buy a couple of slices at the higher price, on top of the full amount of cheaper stuff, just to be able to say they keep the same sort of table as the grand folk.'

Henry's admiration was quite genuine. He had never realised there might be such scope for original thinking in a trade as prosaic as food supply. This might prove more interesting than he had thought.

'I might even volunteer to come round and help you slice up the first orders, George.'

Smiling, Beynon shook his head. 'Oh, no, Mr Henry, not for a long time yet. It takes practice to cut a proper slice of bacon. Now, what can I show you next?'

They moved on into a high, airy stillroom, where cheese, butter and eggs were kept cool until the last min-ute before they went on sale. 'No one ever gets rancid butter that's been out in the sunlight from Richmond's,' said George primly. They looked into the smokery, where the celebrated own-label hams and sides of bacon hung in fragrant semi-darkness, and finished up in the larder section. Here were rank upon rank of tins, jars and bottles.

When they re-entered the shop's sales area, Henry saw it with new eyes. Now it was a sort of treasure house, displaying riches from all over the world, little mouthfuls of the best of everything. It was a double shop unit, with black and white tiled floor, mahogany shelves lining the walls, and counters on three sides. The counters down one side were topped with fine white marble. This was where the bacon, eggs and dairy produce were served. The rest were mahogany to match the shelving. Sturdy chairs were set on the customer's side of the counters at regular intervals. Provision shopping could be a lengthy affair and the customers preferred to do it in comfort.

In contrast to the cornucopia in the store rooms, food was not greatly in evidence here. 'Too much dust coming in off the street,' said George. 'We keep a few hams and sides of bacon hanging up out here; they're all right because they've already been exposed to the smoke and the cure, but we do keep all the delicate fresh stuff tucked up proper out the back. Your mam always says it's worth wasting the bit of butter and things we put in the window display, to keep our reputation up. We never sell any of that –' his voice dropped to an ostentatious stage whisper – 'we do pack it up into food parcels to distribute to the needy.'

Henry winced. By the sound of that, the needy paid a high price in terms of lost dignity to get their supplies. Still, it was probably better than starving.

George Beynon was prattling happily on, unaware of

the discordant note he had struck with the younger man. 'Now, you'll probably be asking yourself what's in all them little drawers with their brass handles? That's all the delicate spices and special flavourings – things like nutmegs and vanilla pods and such like, see?' He tugged the brass knob on a little drawer and it slid out silently. Inside lay rows of dry black vanilla pods, lined up like ranks of discarded snake skins.

This really impressed Henry. 'Don't we carry a huge range of things? I'd never have thought there was much call for bits and pieces like that.'

'It's what makes us, Mr Henry. There's not another grocer west of Chester or north of Swansea as do keep special stocks up to this level. But your mam do know what she's doing. Some of the ladies who shop here will test us by deliberately asking for something out-of-the-way. It's a matter of pride with your mother that we've usually got it. But it's good business as well. You do that often enough on a sixpenny item and the customers wouldn't think of spending their sovereigns anywhere else, let alone their pennies!'

And so it went on. By the end of the morning, Henry saw not only the business but his mother in a entirely new light. She was far more than the lovable but tyrannical domestic figure he had always known. She was a talented entrepreneur and he knew without being told that she wasn't going to stop with a High Street grocery shop in Bangor.

At one o'clock Marged arrived back at the shop. The pony and trap were brought round to the front door and mother and son drove home together. One look at his enthusiastic face was enough to tell Marged she had won the first battle, if not the whole war. But she tucked away her triumph and turned to him with a polite enquiry.

'Enjoyable, or a waste of time?'

'I never dreamed trade would be so much fun! Why – it's hardly like work at all!'

She was sceptical. 'Hmm, we'll see whether you continue to hold that opinion when you're turning out on black winter mornings to get the shop open before the first delivery men arrive! Still, though, I take it you were impressed.'

'I can't think why you didn't introduce me to it all years ago!'

'Maybe I didn't think you were ready until now.'

'Well, at least it's relieved me of the problem of a five or seven year apprenticeship! I think that would have palled fairly quickly.'

'Don't imagine that because you're eighteen and a gentleman, I'm letting you get out of that.' She smiled and calmed him with a restraining touch of her hand as he began to expostulate about the indignities of sweeping up. 'Now don't go off half cocked, either, man! I was about to say that your apprenticeship will last a lot longer than five years, but only a very small part of it will be spent behind the counter. There – how does that sound?'

'Interesting enough for me to want to know more.'

'Right. Mrs Davies will have to swallow her Temperance principles today. We're going back to an adult luncheon with some good wine and I'll tell you my plans. If you like them, we'll go on from there. Does that suit you?'

He beamed, once again feeling very adult. 'Admirably, Mama – admirably.'

Poor little Llanddona witch, Marged thought, I hope you haven't done anything foolish, because this one is mine and he's staying that way.

In the drawing room after luncheon, she gave Henry his first glimpse of her grand strategy, drawing him into it by asking his views and tacking on news of her own plans.

'Not quite the little back street emporium you've always had in your mind, is it?' she asked.

'I must admit it seemed bigger and much grander than I remember from when I was a little boy.'

'That's because it *is* bigger. I doubled the selling area five years ago when the draper next door went out of business.'

'Oh dear, and I never knew. Hardly the conscientious son, am I?'

She laughed. 'No point in forcing an unwilling horse to water, Henry. And as I recall, that was the very time when you began to feel rather ashamed that your family was in trade.'

'Did I let it show?'

'At thirteen? Show me the child who isn't transparent at that age and I'll show you a monster. Of course it showed! But it was really my fault you were growing up like that. No one made me send you to a school for gentlemen, did they? Anyway, that's in the past. What do you think of the family business now?'

This time it was Henry who laughed, with some embarrassment. 'I'm surprised at myself. I loved everything about it – the smell, the look of the place, all those faint traces of romantic places far away, with little humble reminders of home and farms and green fields tucked

41

in higgledy piggledy. If I had the necessary skill, I could go to work there tomorrow and be a happy man –' he broke off and raised a cautionary hand here – 'but don't imagine that means I'm ready to settle down as a shopkeeper. I'm not prepared to be a glorified errand boy for the years it takes to learn, and I know that, much as it attracts me now, I'd grow bored and discontented once I knew all the tricks. I need to spread my wings outside Bangor – outside North Wales for that matter. And that hardly helps any plans you might have for my running things, does it?'

'Oh, I wouldn't say that, Henry. I wouldn't say that at all . . . George Beynon is a very capable manager here. What if I wanted to spread my wings too, and what if it meant taking the business far beyond Wales? Maybe that would be more interesting.'

'I don't understand. How could you do that?'

'For a start I could set up Richmond Quality Provisions branches all over the north-west of England and North Wales. If I can build a business that keeps us in reasonable comfort in this remote spot, think what I could do if I had thousands more customers to play with!'

Henry regarded his mother with a new respect that bordered on awe. 'But – but it would mean starting from nothing in a completely unknown territory – and if there's money to be made, surely local tradesmen will be making it?'

'Small shopkeepers stay small because they have no sense of adventure.' Marged's voice dripped contempt. 'Expansion means risk and they stay inside their little nests, afraid to chance a few twigs to win a whole tree!

I'm prepared to try, but it's your future too and I must know you're with me.'

Instinctively Henry knew his reaction was vitally important. His immediate impulse was to say 'What are we waiting for?' but somehow he knew it was not what she wanted to hear. He pondered the question for a moment, then said: 'First tell me why we're going to succeed. It must be more than willingness to risk everything.'

She nodded her approval. 'Bravo, Henry! You're growing up. Let me turn things around a little. Why do you think we might not make it?'

Again he hesitated. 'I . . . I feel a bit of a fool, handing down my views like this. I'm a complete beginner and all my opinions may be wrong – probably are when you consider what a blinkered view I had of our own shop.'

'No assumed humility, young man –' Marged's tone was irritable now – 'I value your intelligence and you've obviously picked up some ideas, or you wouldn't be acting like a coy girl over them. Come on, out with it!'

'I'm not sure there are enough people with the sort of money we'd need to make. I realise I've no experience of the shops, but George made it clear today that his prize customers are the big estates – in the person of the housekeepers, of course. I gathered that the rest are local businessmen's wives, with less money to spend but still quite prosperous. Once you've counted them, though, that's the end of the story. The quarrymen and the farm labourers can't afford our prices; the farmers' wives won't pay them, even if they can afford it. I see them around Llangefni market when I go there with Uncle Idris, haggling down the price of a dozen eggs or a cheap

43

cut of cheese. The working people will take second-rate goods because they can't afford the best. The farmers are practically self-sufficient and when they have to buy they always prefer to haggle at the market than to cough up a fixed rate in a shop.'

He had not spelled out this opinion before, even in his mind. Now he was doing so, he realised it made a lot of sense, and grew increasingly disconsolate as he contemplated its possible effect on his mother's plans.

But she seemed not at all put out. 'If that's all you're worried about, you can stop now, although I'm very pleased that you can think sensibly about it. What you see around here is yesterday, Henry. I'm talking about tomorrow. We live in one of the most backward parts of the country – even the fashions in house-building up here are fifty years behind other places. In the outside world there's a lot more new money than North Wales will ever see. Forget the poor – you're right there, they don't have enough to keep us in business. But I've been reading about a sort of association that working people are forming for themselves to buy and re-sell cheap food. I think if we went in with Idris, we could copy some of those ideas and start selling to the better-off classes with the advantages of clever buying. How about that for an idea?'

'You're going too fast for me, Mother. What is this association?'

'They started a few years ago in Rochdale. Groups of people form a Co-operative Retail Association based on their town, and open shops there to sell groceries. Because it's not just one small family shop with a few customers, they can buy in bulk, the way Idris does for his retailers. But because they run the wholesaling side and the retail business, they have far more control over their profits. Or at least, they would if they used them as profits. They share out any savings between the members of the association.

'If we were running such a concern, all that would be money in our pockets. Of course, they concentrate on the cheapest stuff they can get, so apart from developing their idea, we wouldn't be trespassing on their territory at all. We'd be buying a far higher quality and selling it through a lot of shops like Richmond's in Bangor. The crucial difference between what we have now and what we'd have then is that we'd be able to buy the quality we sell in Bangor at a fraction of the price we pay now, because we'd be placing such big orders with our suppliers. We could reduce our prices enough to capture all the potential customers who are just getting prosperous, but still keep them high enough to maintain our exclusive reputation. The extra profits would either make us very rich straight away, or go into a fund for starting more and more branches, which would make us even richer if we were prepared to wait a while. How do you like that idea?'

'I think it's brilliant. But how does Uncle Idris like it?'

'Your guess is as good as mine.'

'You mean you haven't asked him yet?'

She laughed scornfully. 'Henry, Idris is all right as far as he goes - but you'll soon find out that's not very far unless he's led by the nose. Now I can lead him part of the way, but beyond that point, I need the help of a big strong man. I can wind him around my little finger on most things, but he's far too old-fashioned to accept that a woman might know more than he does about business. If you agree, I'm going to tell him you're coming into the family business. Then, after a decent interval, I'll go to him all a-flutter with anxiety because you've had this wonderful idea but I don't know whether it will work. If he thinks it comes from another man, even one as young and inexperienced as you, I'll wager he'll be happy to go along with it. If I suggest it as my own idea, he'll run a mile!'

She sat back, as though breathless with the enormity of what she had been putting over. Henry looked at her for a long time, wondering how he could have been so blind to her talents. Why, if she'd been a man, she'd be rich and famous by now!

'Mother, I think you're wonderful. But why are you taking me into your confidence? What if I had reacted as you expect Idris to?'

'Not you, my son! I know you better than you know yourself. If you don't understand my thinking, it's not worth going on, so I've lost nothing by telling you. But you do understand, don't you?'

'I most certainly do. When do we start?'

'Slow down – remember, poor old Idris still thinks he's a one-man wholesale business! We'll have to take it quietly. Will you trust me to guide you?'

'Of course – you've more brains than I'll ever have. Just tell me what you want me to do.'

'Well, as far as Idris is concerned – and George Beynon, for that matter – you'll start a sort of concentrated apprenticeship at the Bangor shop in a week or so. Leave it to me, and I'll introduce the idea to him gently. By the time you're ready to move, he'll be like a lamb to the slaughter. Now, I think you've earned a glass of port, even if one really shouldn't at lunch-time!'

She poured the wine and they raised their glasses ceremoniously to each other. As they finished the toast, she said in a low voice, 'Just one more thing, Henry. This will absorb all your time and attention for a few years. There's no time or place for romance in your life for a while. It will come soon enough, but not yet. Do you understand me?'

He returned her look steadily. 'Yes, Mother. I understand you perfectly.'

Idris spent most of the week in Liverpool and Manchester, calling on his customers, taking new orders and finding out whether the shopkeepers were happy with the quality and price of the latest deliveries. In the past he had often resented these business trips because they took him away from his adored Marged. But this time he was relieved to be away. He shuddered every time he thought of the wrath she would hurl down on young Henry.

By Friday he was back, and had no excuse to refuse Marged's dinner invitation. Anyway, by then he was missing her enough to brave the chilly welcome he expected.

The reality could not have been further from his imaginings. Marged was elegant, smooth and regal as usual. Henry was bubbling over with some unspoken enthusiasm which made him seem even younger than his eighteen years. Idris itched to know what had happened, but he could hardly raise the matter in front of the boy. He need not have worried. Henry was planning to go fishing the following night and wanted to check on the condition of the boat before it got dark. As soon as they had finished dinner he said goodnight and went off down to the harbour.

Idris was bursting with curiosity. 'What on earth have you said to him, Marged? He looks more like your devoted lifelong slave than a chastened black sheep!'

'I suppose you've spent the week imagining me boiling him in oil!' Her scornful tone was mixed with affection. She remembered as well as he did the intensity of her fury the day she had rounded on Idris about her son's girl.

'I admit I half expected to find him in little pieces. But he seems . . . well . . . radiant, almost!'

'I always found treacle a more useful bait than brimstone. My apologies for taking it out on you – but you really were asking for it. As for Henry . . . well, when I calmed down I decided that since it was bound to end in tears, I should try to avoid giving him extra cause for grief.'

If only she wasn't so lovely, I'd be able to work out the weakness in that theory, thought Idris, but I just look at her and nothing else seems important . . . Nevertheless a small reasonable voice inside him murmured that it was bound to end in tears only because Marged Richmond did not want it to continue. The mere fact that she was being decent to the boy didn't mean she was treating him with any justice.

Still, in the nineteen years he'd known her, Idris had never been able to find fault with Marged for more than a moment. Henry would have to learn, just like every other man, that if you gave your heart too readily you were likely to get it back in fragments. It was unthinkable

48

that his boyish whims should be allowed to thwart Marged. He relaxed as she poured him a glass of brandy, and enjoyed a brief fantasy which cast her as his beloved wife and Henry as their son. If only life had turned out a little differently . . .

On Saturday night there was a full moon; not that there were many dark hours for it to illumine at this time of year. It was not completely dark until ten o'clock and the sky would be light again by four in the morning. The light south-westerly breeze was perfect. Soon after nine that evening, Henry set sail up the Straits with the remains of a spectacular sunset behind him and headed for his rendezvous with Myfanwy. For form's sake he set a line and caught some mackerel. The water was alive with them and it was almost possible to pick the fish out by hand. As long as he had a string of fresh fish to take home, no one would question the purpose of his outing.

His small boat skimmed past the picturebook seaside town of Beaumaris, the candy colours of its seafront houses looking like a town in a child's story. An hour later he had reached the easterly extremity of the Isle of Anglesey. Off its tip floated Ynys Seiriol, the islet where primitive monks had cut themselves off from the world of fleshly needs. Now there were no holy men left, just seals, puffins and moonlight.

Henry set his vessel between Ynys Seiriol and the small lighthouse on Black Point, where a bell tolled dolefully to warn sailors of the fearsome rocks around the shore. He doubled back north-westward. The moon had not risen above Ynys Seiriol yet and ahead of him was a great blackness, slightly translucent where the land mass gave way to the sea. Low cliffs humped their backs for a while before falling away to reveal the beginning of a huge inlet which always seemed too big for the humble stream that flowed into the sea here. As he rounded the point, a spark relieved the blackness of Llanddona beach. Myfanwy's fire! There was something magical about it – a tiny glint of warmth and love in all this velvet blackness.

As he headed inshore, the moon swung clear of the horizon and hung in brilliant splendour over the sea. He gasped in wonder, momentarily forgetting everything in appreciation of the perfect beauty around him. The sky was darkest blue, so intense that it seemed to have its own dimensions. He felt that if he tried, he could plunge his arm into that sky and it would immerse itself in the deep blueness as if in water . . . The pure silver disk cast itself free and sailed forth, towing one brilliant star. What a night for love! What a night for forgetting about anything except the white arms encircling your neck and the red lips engulfing you in their sweetness . . . If only the breeze would pick up a little – it would bring him to her that much sooner!

But he was there soon enough. His little witch stood at the tideline, the moonlight adding mystery to her exotic face. She helped him to beach the boat then stood just above the water's edge, waiting for his kiss.

The strange reluctance which had come upon him at the millpond had faded quickly after he left her on Tuesday. Now it started to trickle back. Something had changed . . . what was it? Until this week he had been mad for her and she had held him off, encouraging and mocking him at the same time. She had been a mature

woman and he merely a schoolboy. Now she seemed to be the eager one and he the one who held back; moreover he felt much older and she seemed far younger. But as they kissed, her old magic began working on him and Henry sighed with the ecstatic pleasure of a man who has found a great prize.

It was a wonderful night. The dark glassy sky was peppered with brilliant stars and the air was as warm as afternoon. Myfanwy led him up the beach to where her fire crackled, sheltered by low dunes behind. She had spread a blanket beside it and now stretched herself on it like a little cat. 'Come to me, Henry, I've missed you.'

Fully under her spell, he sank down beside her and took her in his arms. Her young, firm flesh pressed back against his caressing fingers. Her hair poured around her shoulders like liquid black light. 'My God, when I'm not with you, I forget how beautiful you are!' he murmured.

Neither of them was wearing much and they soon lay naked together. The closeness of her smooth body was suddenly too much for him and he would have killed to possess her, now and always. Myfanwy sensed his urgency and whispered, 'Come on, then, quickly now. Under the moon – make our son!'

He was too excited to pay much attention to her words then. All he wanted was to make love to her and never to stop. The moon, sea, sand and her lovely flesh all melted into one image in his mind as he entered her, and he let out a great cry in which loss, passion and fulfilment seemed tangled together. Then, as the tide of his excitement receded, he vaguely recalled what she had said. What if he had made their son here on this night? What if . . .? He shook his head. The images that followed were too painful to contemplate on a night like this.

They lay quietly together on the blanket for a while, half waking, half sleeping. Then Myfanwy sat up and tugged at his arm. 'Come on – let's swim to the moon!'

'What? What are you talking about? That's nonsense – where are you going?'

'You'll see. Come on, I mean it!'

She ran down the beach, still naked and seemingly a natural part of the ethereal landscape. Grumbling but intrigued, Henry followed. At the water's edge she stopped and pointed out to sea.

'There – told you I meant it. We can swim to the moon!'

It certainly appeared possible. The sea was flat calm, hardly raising a ripple even when it broke against the gently-shelving beach. The great white moon hung over it and the surface of the water reflected back a silver highway that led out towards the sky. Myfanwy seemed bewitched by it.

'Just watch,' she said breathlessly, and stepped forward into the moon-stained water. As she moved, the multi-faceted drops showered liquid sparks around her. Henry could not resist following her. They swam out along the moon path and finally paused, far out of their depth, treading water together and laughing with pleasure at the beauty of the night. Suddenly she became solemn.

'Sometimes I think this would be the way to end all our sorrows. Swim out along the moonbeams and then, when it got good and deep, just . . . stop . . . swimming.'

Even as a fantasy, the thought filled Henry with

horror. 'Don't ever think like that!' he said, his voice suddenly high and thin. 'There's everything to live for – everything to achieve!'

'Are you sure? For both of us?' Her eyes met his, there in the white moonlight, and for a moment he knew she was aware his plans had never really included her. But how could she think that? A week ago, he himself would have been the first to deny it. All he wanted then was to be with Myfanwy forever.

But that was a week ago, and since then his mother had opened up an irresistible future which beckoned through the door of a modest small-town shop. His new dream had no place for a strange Welsh-Irish misfit who saw visions and swam naked along the path of the moon. Henry shook his head, simultaneously showering sea water from his hair and might-have-beens from his mind.

'Come on,' he said, 'time to go back.'

He turned and began swimming towards the shore. He had taken a dozen strokes before he realised she was not with him. He felt cold for a moment, then forced himself to turn and look back. She was still there, a dark shape silhouetted against the silver water. A seal or a mermaid – or a forsaken lover.

'Henry,' she called, 'please don't go. Please stay a minute!'

He swam back. 'Come on, Van, we really have to go ashore. I know the water feels marvellous, but we'll get cold quickly and neither of us would have a chance this far out if that happened.'

He reached for her and she turned with him, linking her hand in his so that they both swam as one person.

When they reached the beach, she was shivering. 'Hold me close, Henry. I can't stop shaking.'

He pressed her into his arms. 'We shouldn't have stayed out there so long. Come on, try to run up the beach and then we'll roll you up in the blanket.'

Her teeth were chattering now. 'Not cold – frightened. Oh, Henry, I'm so frightened!'

He chose to ignore the half-spoken plea for reassurance and hustled her up the beach. 'No need to take up that blanket,' she said. 'I brought another.' A sob quivered in her voice. 'I thought it would be handy if you decided to stay here with me tonight.'

'Oh, Van, you knew I couldn't do that! I have to be back home by dawn or not long after. People don't go fishing and just stay out all night.'

She was still shivering. 'Y-Yes they do. Th-they do when they're with the ones they l-love!' And she burst into low, muffled sobs.

He drew her down on to the groundsheet blanket, cuddling her in the spare one to get her warm again, murmuring nonsense words to comfort her. Eventually her little body stopped shaking and the sobs diminished to an occasional sniffle.

'Now,' he said, 'let's talk. Why on earth are you in such a state? What's happened to you all of a sudden?'

'You don't want me. You're going to leave me.' He had feared she would start weeping again, but she seemed calm enough.

'I do want you, Myfanwy. I've never felt like this about a girl before. But I haven't promised you anything, and as far as I know you haven't asked for anything. I'd never done anything like . . . like this before – his gesture

54

managed to cover their whole relationship, not merely the midnight swim – 'I wouldn't have known how to start if you hadn't encouraged me. Surely you're not trying to say I seduced you?' He was trying desperately to be kind without misleading her. He was as sure as he ever would be that his future did not lie with Myfanwy Owen. But why had she seemed so certain that it did?

She raised small hands to his face and held it steady as she stared deep into his eyes. 'No, of course not, boy. I'm used to going all out for what I want and I did with you. It's not you, it's my Sight. I saw us – or our children's children, anyway – using my skill to make a fortune in a far country across the sea. It's always been right before. How can it be wrong now?'

Henry's sympathy was fading fast. All this fanciful talk about foreseeing the future! It might frighten the life out of the yokels, but it cut no ice with him! It was too conveniently close to what Myfanwy might have *hoped* the future held in store. He fought to keep his tone kind and loving.

'It was a dream, Van, only a dream. Perhaps you mixed it up with your second sight. Look, are you feeling a bit better now? Because the moon has gone and the sky is already getting light. Even with a bit of a breeze, I'm going to take a while getting back. I really should be going.'

Her hands slipped away from his face and she turned aside. 'Yes, you must go.' Her voice was toneless. 'Mind the rocks around Black Point. They're deceptive when the tide is up.'

Henry put more wood on the dying fire, then finished getting dressed. 'Perhaps I should see you home before I go. I'm still not sure you'll be all right.'

She smiled bleakly. 'The farm is only just over these

dunes, along the lane. Nothing worse will happen to me tonight. You go.'

Wrapped in her blanket, she walked across the sand with him to where they had beached the boat. The tide was coming in fast now and he had to push the vessel only a few yards to re-launch it.

He unshipped the oars and started heading out to sea. She waved forlornly, the dawn wind catching her long hair and teasing it out around her head and shoulders. 'Goodbye, Henry. Please come back and see me again.'

'Of course – I'll be in Llangefni as soon as I can!' Henry forced a bright tone into his voice but they both knew it would be a long time before he set foot inside her shop again.

Back at Menai View, Marged was wide awake. She had guessed his destination the previous evening and, although confident of victory, had been anxious enough to pass a troubled night. At half past five she heard him come in at the back of the house. She remained silent as the small noises continued, then said, 'Oh, to hell with it!' threw back the covers and got up. Moments later, clad in her dressing gown, she was with Henry in the kitchen.

'Mother! What brings you down so early? I hope I didn't wake you.'

He was as confused as a child caught stealing. She gave him a bright smile. 'I wasn't asleep. How would you like some breakfast?

'But Mrs Davies doesn't come in until eight – it's Sunday.'

'I haven't lived through thirty-six years without know-ing how to make a hearty breakfast, you ninny! Come on, now, we could have your mackerel or ham and eggs. Which d'you prefer?'

Marged was a great one for portents and she was reassured to see him eye the sparkling-fresh fish with distaste. 'I don't know why, Mother, but somehow I don't fancy them. Ham and eggs sounds wonderful!'

'Put the fish in the cold larder and Mrs Davies can take them home. She'll be happy you thought of her. And now, for once I'm going to eat a man's breakfast, too.'

He sat watching her as she bustled about the kitchen, admiring her with a mixture of filial affection and an almost objective appreciation.

Marged was at the peak of her beauty – a bit of a waste, she often thought, as Idris was the only man around to appreciate it. Her chestnut hair had never been cut. By day it was twined into a neat chignon, but this morning it still hung down her back, a braid almost as thick as a man's wrist, and even plaited it reached her hips. Her skin was creamy and she had large, bright-brown eyes. Henry had often wished his own eyes were that colour, because they commanded instant attention and he had noticed no one broke his mother's gaze. Other people were always the first to look away, and he was willing to bet that they never forgot the colour of her eyes. She had strong, well-defined features: a wide fore-head, a long, high-bridged nose and high cheekbones. It was a long, thin face, the cheeks lacking fullness after the prominence of the bones. A queen's face, he thought, not the face of a grocer's widow. She was very slim with-out appearing skinny. Her long-limbed frame was so stately that she appeared slender rather than thin. Her hands were lovely. Henry's earliest memory of his mother was of those hands, their pale perfection; their skill in motion; their tranquillity at rest.

Although he had always appreciated her good looks, he had never thought of her as girlish. But this morning she was more like his sister than his mother. Or was it a sweetheart she reminded him of?

Confused, he hastily set the thought aside. But before he did so, he briefly glimpsed a truth which was about to mould his future: Myfanwy could not compete with this female dynamo.

Marged brewed a pot of strong Indian tea. She cut two slices off a pink ham and set them to sizzle in clarified chicken fat in the big black frying pan on the kitchen range. Halved black puddings and quartered field mushrooms swiftly followed. In another pan she fried slices of yesterday's bread until they were crisp and golden. Within moments it was all assembled on two warm porcelain plates. As a finishing touch she slipped four fresh eggs into the pan, spooning scalding fat over them to cook the tops without hardening the yolks. They sat down together and plunged into the early-morning feast, Henry regarding Marged with wonder as she put away as much food as he did.

'Mother, I've never seen you eat like this in my life!'

'You've never seen me let myself go, that's why. I'm usually more disciplined than this. But today I feel like celebrating my son's arrival in the world of commerce!'

She poured tea for them both and for a while they ate in silence. Eventually Henry pushed away his plate with a sigh of satisfaction.

'Mama, that was perfect. I'd say "I'll never eat again",

but I have a suspicion I'll be ready to tuck in again at luncheon.'

'At your age I'd be worried if you didn't. Now, have another cup of tea and then go to bed for a couple of hours. You'll be tired out.'

His eyes slid away. 'Yes. I went rather further than I intended . . .'

'I bet you did.' It was out before she could stop it.

He looked directly at her again. 'Perhaps I'd better tell you.'

'Only if you want to. I'm not trying to pry, but nothing you might wish to say will make me angry or cruel. If it helps you, I'll be pleased to listen.'

Inside her head, all was turmoil. But, above all, Marged was a strategist. If she listened sympathetically now, there would never be a barrier between them again.

Having come this far, he seemed lost for words. Treading carefully, Marged led the way. 'It's a girl, is it?'

He reddened, but beneath the embarrassment there was obvious relief. 'Oh God, Mother, I'm so confused!' And then he told her. All of it.

Marged Richmond was an exceptional woman. Females of her age and background were raised to regard any discussion of sensuality as unthinkable, even between husband and wife. But she sat calmly and listened as her son blunderingly sought words to describe his emotions and actions in the first serious physical love affair of his life. It was harder than anything she had done before but she managed it, and in doing so enslaved him for life.

When he had finished his tale, Henry was almost in tears.

With a considerable effort, Marged remained impassive. Eventually she said: 'You left out something very important. You've told me what happened. You haven't told me how you felt – how you feel now, for that matter – and obviously that's the part that gives you trouble.'

He nodded, still silent, then the dam broke and he started sobbing. Marged got up and moved around the table to her son, and cradled his head in her arms.

'Oh, Mother, I feel so guilty – so dirty!' he finally managed to say. 'I know she led me on, but then . . . then she seemed to get terribly keen on me, too, but she started to frighten me. There's something so strange about her – almost as if those stories about her people were true. She's like flames. They're so pretty you want to touch them, and once you do, they burn you. After that, you still know they're lovely but you don't want to touch them again . . .'

He made a visible effort to regain control. 'I know that sounds fanciful, but it's the closest I can get to how I feel. A week or two ago I wanted to spend my life with her. Now I want to keep away, but I feel that I've done her wrong.' Anticipating what Marged would say, he shushed her. 'No, Mother, you can't fob me off by saying it was her fault for leading me astray. You know very well it takes two to do what we did.'

To his confusion, Marged burst out laughing. 'It would be news to me if it didn't, boy! Dear God, all this emotion is making me sound quite Welsh. Idris would be proud of the way I say it, even if he dropped dead with shock at what I'm saying! I'd be the last one to tell you that you could desert her with a clear conscience. If that were true, I'd be saying that you're not grown up yet, and you are. But that just means you take responsibility for your actions. It doesn't mean you have to suffer all your life for one indiscretion. If you're willing to trust me, you can stop worrying.'

'Of course I trust you, but it's not your affair. How can you change things?'

'By seeing she doesn't suffer as a consequence of what you and she did. I want you to promise you won't try to contact the girl again, and I'll see to it that you're not around Llangefni in future. In return, I'll promise you that Myfanwy Owen will be properly looked after, whatever happens. Does that make sense to you?'

'Mother, there can't be another like you on this earth. I'm a very lucky man.'

'Just you remember that when you want to tell me to clear off out of it – because you will want to one day, believe me.'

'Never!'

'I might hold you to that, my son. Now, away with us both. It's nearly half past seven. I'm tired now, too. We'll both creep off to our beds. When Mrs Davies sees the dirty dishes, she'll just think you had someone with you on the fishing trip and brought them back.'

'I suppose I did, in a way – a guardian angel.'

She gave him a scathing look. 'That is pure sentimental slush. I'll put it down to exhaustion. Off you go!'

He kissed her resoundingly on both cheeks and departed for bed. Marged stood in the kitchen for a while, gazing at nothing. Finally she smiled and said, 'There you are, my girl, you never know what you can do until you try!'

She stacked the breakfast plates and cups in the deep slate-lined sink and went off to bed.

# Chapter Three

Henry began work in the family business the following Monday with the sort of zeal more usually found in religious converts. George Beynon watched him closely for a week, vigilant for signs of the emergence of the amateur dabbler he privately thought Henry must be. But he quickly recognised he had misjudged the younger man. Instead, Henry was eager to learn, quick to acquire skills, and never resorted to reminding George that he was the owner's son.

At boarding school, the Welsh boy had been an outsider among his English classmates. It had been necessary to adapt or remain one throughout his stay at Warwick. Henry had adapted, fast, and in doing so had learned to be a natural observer of other people's behaviour. It was an aptitude which served him well for the rest of his life. Now he took care to study George Beynon, learning from him even when the manager was not consciously teaching, and also quickly understanding what sort of behaviour George liked and what put him off. Within a couple of weeks they were friends, as well as being master and trainee.

Ellis Williams, the young apprentice Henry had seen learning to sweep the step, would normally have lived in at the High Street shop. But he was the only child of a widow who had been ill for years. Both Marged and George Beynon were reasonable employers and they had agreed that Ellis should live at his own home while his mother's condition was so delicate. In any case, it was less important for Richmond's to have a live-in apprentice, because George and his young wife lived in the rooms over the shop. If anything went wrong, the manager was always near at hand.

George's wife was expecting their first child. It was born in the apartment above the shop a couple of weeks after Henry started work in Richmond's. The baby was a healthy boy, but Siân Beynon was weakened by the birth and the doctor said it might take her a month or more to regain her strength. Within a few days, Henry suggested to his mother that they should offer George some help.

He raised the matter with Marged one evening after supper. 'Mother, George would be furious if he knew I was telling you this, but I think he needs someone to back him up after hours while his wife is getting better.'

'Why – is his work falling off?'

'Oh, come on, Mother, you know George. He'd die of exhaustion before that happened. Anyway, aren't I rather green to be able to pass judgement?'

'You seem to be passing judgement about something!' Marged tended to be prickly if anyone else noted a weak point in her business that she had not already seen.

'He's as conscientious as ever. But he looks tired out, and when the carters arrive with a load, or when the boy wants the orders checked over before going off to deliver, he sometimes lets out a sigh that would tear you apart. I asked him about it yesterday and he said while Siân is so helpless, he gets up at night with little Albert. You know his normal working day is nearer sixteen hours than twelve, so that extra strain of not getting enough sleep must be dreadful.'

Having spoken his piece, Henry fell silent to let his mother consider the matter. He knew better than to attempt to apply pressure.

'Mmm . . . it must be hard for him, certainly, but it won't last forever and I can't see any way around it. Can you?'

'That's just it, there's one obvious way. If Ellis Williams lived in, none of this would matter. So as I'm the nearest thing we have to an apprentice apart from young Ellis, how about me living in for a month or so?'

'Henry, that's ridiculous! Why, there's – there's no room for you, for one thing!'

'Oh yes there is, and you know it. What about the little box room with the truckle bed between the smokery and the dry goods store? George told me the apprentice boys always used to sleep there before Ellis started.'

'Yes, they did. But – but they were just working boys – often they only had straw-filled mattresses at home. It wasn't any hardship for them . . .' Marged stopped herself. 'You're right. I'm just being selfish. I'd like to keep you here with me, so I'm thinking up a dozen silly reasons for stopping you. It's an excellent idea. It won't be for too long, it will take the pressure off George, and it will teach you more about the business in less time than anything else. I almost wish I'd thought of it myself!' She even managed a forced smile as she secretly wondered how she would feel when the time came for Henry really to leave home.

The day after the new arrangement started, Beynon took Henry aside. 'I know you want me to think this was your mother's idea, but I've got to say thank you, Mr Henry. I must admit I didn't think you had it in you. I hope you'll forgive me for that.'

Henry grinned at him. 'Of course I do, George. And since you're my boss, don't you think I should prove my good faith by asking you to drop that "Mr Henry" nonsense? I'm Henry from now on, all right?'

Beynon smiled happily back and shook his hand. 'Right. Henry it is, Mr Henry.' The two men stared at each other for a moment then roared with laughter. Henry slapped him on the back. 'Come on, proud father, time to give me my day's orders!'

So Henry embarked on a short interlude of harder work than he had known so far. He set up and opened the shop each morning, which included being awake and dressed at dawn to take delivery of the perishables which came in every day. Then he put out the sides of bacon and hams which hung outside the shop; swept the tiled floor and scattered fresh sawdust on wet days to ensure that customers did not slip; replaced any stale-looking items in the window display of fresh foods and packed the removed goods into charity parcels. ('We could do them later,' George had said, 'but I'd only worry they might get mixed in with the fresh goods for sale. Better get them out of the the way.') After that, all the cooked meats and cheeses had to be brought out of the cold larder and placed on display under glass on the dairy counter. Finally it was time to pull out the striped green and white awning which shaded the shop front from sun and rain, and to open the front door.

In the evening a similar process took place in reverse order, with the sweeping-up of the soiled sawdust the last task after the perishable foods had been replaced in the cold larder.

'Sometimes I feel like just leaving it all in place,' he told George on the third day. 'I wonder whether anyone would notice.'

George smiled knowingly. 'Not the individual things at first, maybe, but they would after a while. That's why we're the best grocer in town – and why a couple of the less particular traders have gone out of business. For a while their stuff will look as good as ours, except the customers get stomach upsets a bit too often and start wondering about tainted food. Give it a bit longer, and it don't even look right. I don't think there is a proper word to describe that stale look, but in my mind I always call it furry. You know, as if it had a sort of pile on it, like a carpet. *Ach y fi!* If you're not too tired one night, you just go down the High Street and look in them windows. You can see into the back of the shops and tell if the cold meats and cheese don't get put away. And if you can see that, so can the customers. When they do look in this shop, all they see is the empty display counter. That don't do us no harm at all.'

Then there was the cooking, something Henry had never imagined having to handle. 'Nothing to it, boy,' George assured him. 'My God, I've been doing it this five years and I wouldn't know how to make supper for the family even now. It's not what you'd call home cooking like high tea, see.'

It turned out to be one of Henry's favourite jobs, and involved the preparation of the cooked meats they sold.

67

Beef, pork and ox tongues were cured in different sorts of brine. They matured in big crocks on the floor of the cold larder for anything up to ten days, after which they were boiled in the copper in a bakehouse outside the loading bay, or oven-baked in the wood-fired range, where the hams were basted with honey and orange juice and the pork with cider. After they had cooled in their cooking liquids, they were pressed or drained and coated with aspic, decorated and put on display. The hams were skinned and then rolled in toasted breadcrumbs before being placed on tall white porcelain stands. Richmond's did their cooking every two weeks, so there were always cuts either pickling in the larder or bubbling on the stove.

'You can thank your lucky stars it's not November, Henry, or we'd be up to our armpits in spiced goose and cold roast turkey as well. Always likes a good choice of cooked meats, does your mam.'

Now and then Henry would be roused from sleep because some carter bringing produce from a remote spot would arrive at the wrong time. When that happened he had to show the new arrival to the stables at the back, find forage for the horse and something for the man.

The other out-of-hours job was making up the orders, and that usually took care of the whole of Thursday evening after closing time. The delivery boy took out the goods all day on Friday, so they had to be packed and ready for him first thing in the morning. These orders varied from enormous monthly consignments of provisions for the great houses in the area – delivered by cart because the boy could never have managed them – to a dozen or so small items required by someone too frail to carry them home herself, or too socially insecure to accept that a lady might carry her own purchases. Whatever the size of the order, it involved dashing back and forth to assemble tins, bottles and waxed-paper parcels of loose merchandise, before putting them all neatly into a box or basket with the recipient's name, address and bill attached on top. Whenever Henry did this job, he felt that any pleasure he derived from cooking the meats was paid for tenfold in his dislike of this other essential task.

After his second frustrating week of assembling the deliveries, George discussed it with him. 'I was wondering whether Mrs Richmond would consider us taking someone on special to do them orders, Henry. You've seen for yourself, now, how much time it do take to do them proper. Only one item missed out and you've lost a good customer, isn't it?'

Henry agreed. 'Haven't you mentioned it to Mother before?'

'Well, no. It do sound so trivial, don't it, unless you've had to do it. Put together a few bags of groceries? Certainly, madam, be with you this minute. But when you do it yourself, you know it do take hours. Now if we had a good reliable lady from town to do it, maybe one afternoon or one full day a week . . .'

'A woman, not a man or an apprentice?'

'Well, I've got this theory that if we had a nice middle-aged lady who'd been stocking up her own larder all her life, she'd be more conscientious, you know? She'd understand what it would mean if the sugar got left out or there wasn't enough tea put in.'

'Hmm, good idea. I suppose in a way, women might be better than us at all sorts of jobs in the shop, because they're used to keeping their households straight.'

George exaggeratedly pressed his finger to his lips. 'Shh! Don't let your mam hear that, or we'll both be out of a job!' They laughed at the idea, but Henry remained convinced it had a lot going for it.

What happened next renewed Marged's faith in divine providence.

Henry had been sleeping at the shop for nearly a month. He came home from mid-day Saturday, when Richmond's closed, until late Sunday evening, but otherwise she did not see him unless she visited the shop. Missing him, she was sleeping badly, and that led to her getting wind of a potentially dangerous situation early enough to nip it in the bud.

It was the night of the first full moon after Henry's romantic fishing trip. Wide awake after midnight, Marged rose and walked over to her bedroom window, which overlooked the Menai Straits. As always the view calmed her, particularly in its magical moonlit setting. Then she was distracted by a movement closer at hand. She glanced down into the deep shadows across the road from the house. There, almost invisible beneath a great oak tree, was a woman. Marged knew she herself had not been seen. She slid back behind the concealment of heavy curtains, and watched. The figure emerged fully and crossed the road, standing for some minutes by the front gate of Menai View, as if trying to decide on a course of action. It was Myfanwy Owen.

Marged had not seen the girl before, but she did not need to be told it was she. Myfanwy was gazing at the house, obviously held back only by uncertainty as to which window was Henry's. She stood thus undecided for at least fifteen minutes, then retreated, reluctance apparent in every movement. Marged stood as though turned to stone for some time, as if her own stillness might keep the girl at bay. Eventually she stirred and went back to bed. But she did not sleep at all that night.

The next night was just the same. This time, though, Marged had put on a dress, shoes and stockings. She was determined to see whence this girl came and where she was going. After a similar vigil to the previous night's, Myfanwy turned and moved away, down the narrow tree-lined lane that led to the harbour. Marged gave her five minutes, then followed.

She did not need to be too close, because, given the girl's general direction, she could have only one destination. Marged gave her a good lead, knowing instinctively that Myfanwy would easily spot someone following her close. By the time Marged reached the dark harbour, a small boat was putting out across the Straits, heading north-east. She could just make out a female silhouette against the moonlit clarity of the water. The Llanddona witch was on her way home, empty-handed . . . this time.

Marged hurried back to Menai View, let herself in and poured herself a large brandy before going back upstairs. Dear God, if she hadn't permitted Henry to go and live in the shop, he might have been looking out of his own window tonight. He might have seen the girl and run down to her. And if she was preparing to say what Marged suspected, perhaps he wouldn't be back in a hurry . . .

She was sure Myfanwy had not come here before this week, and equally certain she would come again. As the girl realised her lover did not plan to return, she would grow bolder. Eventually she would not hesitate at the

71

gate. She might not even wait until after dark. If Marged was to protect Henry's future, decisive action was necessary now.

Idris owned a small grocery shop, although it could not be compared with Marged's business. He had taken it over in settlement of a bad debt and was soft-hearted enough to allow the defaulting debtor to stay on as manager. The shopkeeper's drunken wife had died a couple of years later and since then the little store had at least broken even. But Idris was glad when the man came to him with the news that he was too old to continue. His daughter had done quite well for herself and now wanted him to retire and move in with her family. Idris accepted the news with relief. Now, at least he was free to close or sell the place if he wished. So far it had been more liability than asset.

It was located on a street corner in a working-class backwater of Manchester. The single, small-paned window displayed only tinned goods. This was not an area where fresh foods could be risked in the hope of realising bigger profits. The customers were poor and mark-ups therefore minimal. In a rural area they would have shopped at open air markets. They still bought vegetables and such meat as they could afford in the big covered markets of the city, but could seldom afford enough to last the week. When they ran out, unable to spare the time or money needed to get into the centre again, they used the corner shop. No credit was allowed and people rarely bought more than the minimum necessary to keep body and soul together. The idea of door-to-door deliveries or home-cooked meats was derisory. Corned beef was the one cooked meat on sale here, slapped out of an enormous

72

square tin and sold by the paper-thin slice to give body to a potato soup or to make up the meat-and-bread meal the wage-earner took with him to the factory.

As she agonised over what to do with Henry, a vision of the dingy shop rose in Marged's mind. Why, that might be perfect! Henry would have to see the drab side of the business if they were to expand as she hoped. Nothing like jumping in at the deep end. If it went under, Idris would not really care. It could scarcely do worse than it had to date. And if it succeeded, he would probably be all the more amenable to a merger between their interests. Whatever it did or didn't do, one thing was certain: Myfanwy Owen would never find him there.

Idris was a push-over. He still felt guilty of negligence in allowing Henry to become involved with Myfanwy, and Marged knew it. She had only to remind him of his unconscious complicity to have him begging to help mend the situation. And when he reached that stage she struck.

'Have you decided yet what to do with that awful little shop in Manchester?'

'Well, almost . . . there's no real future in it. I'll sell up. I'd never have got involved in the retail side in the first place if it hadn't been for that bad debt. No good ever came of it. But we were talking about Henry. What does the shop have to do with him?'

'At present the farthest place I can think of to send Henry where we could still keep an eye on him is Manchester. If you've already written off the shop, he can't do it any harm, can he? And if the reports I get from George Beynon are true, he may even bring the place to life.'

'I don't think the Holy Ghost could breathe life into that place!'

'Don't blaspheme, Idris. If you're not godly, remember some of us are!'

'All right, girl, but it's true just the same. A wasteland, that. I know old Smith's wife drank away their living, but even if she hadn't, there wasn't enough profit there to keep a gnat alive.'

'Maybe not, but while Henry is finding out, he'll learn a lot more about the business. And in the end, you'll not lose by it. I'll see to that.'

'Oh, Marged, Marged, you got a terrible cruel tongue on you sometimes. When would I ever ask you to dib in for a loss like that? It would be a privilege to help you. I'm just anxious not to see the boy get disheartened, that's all.'

She was suddenly all soft womanhood. 'You're a very kind man, Idris. Sometimes I wonder whether Henry and I would have survived these long weary years without you there in the background.'

Instantly he was upon her, moving gingerly along the sofa where they were sitting, his big awkward hand covering hers.

'It was nothing, Marged. If only you'd let me do more . . . I could do so much for you. Why, I've never wanted anything but to keep you safe and happy. You only have to say the word and I'd make you my wife.'

Hell and damnation, she thought, I didn't mean to encourage him that far!

Applying a tiny lace handkerchief to completely dry eyes, she turned away. 'Don't make me abuse your generosity and friendship, Idris! I love you like a brother but even after all these years, Rhys would always be there between us. I – I'm so sorry . . .' She managed a couple of ladylike sobs, reflecting as she did so that she had long ago forgotten her dead husband's face.

Contrition seized him. 'Oh, please forgive me, *cariad*! I just got carried away. You must have known all these years how deep my feelings were. I'd never have said anything if you hadn't caught me off guard.'

Still shielding her eyes with the handkerchief in her left hand, Marged patted his arm reassuringly with her right. 'You are too good, Idris, too good. Don't think it's passed unnoticed. But I'm dedicated . . . dedicated to his memory . . . and I can't just follow my heart. You do understand?'

'Yes, of course. Still, if ever . . . No, I mustn't think like that. I shan't raise the matter again, Marged, and I apologise if I've caused you pain now. Perhaps we should go back to discussing your Henry.'

'Thank you. You're always such a gentleman.' Inwardly she sighed with relief.

It was now more than a month since Henry had moved in behind the shop. Siân Beynon was almost back to her full strength and George was resuming more and more of his former duties. He had already suggested to Marged that her son might like to return to live at Menai View, only to have his employer shower him with sympathy and concern and refuse to consider the change so soon. In fact she was terrified that Myfanwy might pay another midnight visit and catch Henry at home.

After supper on Saturday, she asked Henry how he felt he was progressing.

'It's odd after such a short time, but I can't remember what it was like not to work at the shop,' he said. 'I know I still have a lot to learn, but I feel as if I've picked up a great deal already.'

'George Beynon seems to share your view. Only the other day he was telling me he'd never have believed it possible for someone to learn so much so quickly. I told him that a fancy education had to have some benefits!'

'George is marvellous – so patient and not at all patronising when I make mistakes. And he always makes sure I get credit if I do anything well. In fact I like him so much that sometimes I worry about what will happen when I've learned everything.'

'Why?'

'I know the shop is busy, Mother, but there's not room for two people trained to manage it. You need someone else lower down the ladder to take on extra work, but when I'm fully trained, you'll not need two managers. It worries me sometimes. I couldn't bear to push George out of a job.'

'That won't be necessary. It's time to move on to the next stage.'

'Next stage? I didn't think there was going to be one, unless you persuaded Uncle Idris to start a combined venture.'

'Sometimes it's necessary to go along an indirect road. I need to make Idris feel he owes us something – goodness knows we owe him enough for all the help he's been over the years. I want him to feel we've contributed something to his business that he couldn't put in himself.'

'Come on, Mother, out with it. You've worked out something or you wouldn't have raised the subject.'

'I have, but perhaps I was a bit premature. Maybe you're not ready yet . . .'

His face darkened. 'Just try me!'

'Well, I don't know whether you're aware of this poky little shop Idris has got in Manchester.'

'I vaguely remember him mentioning it once. But it's nothing much, is it? I don't think he goes there more than once in a blue moon.'

'That's just the point. It's the exact opposite of our place in Bangor. The manager is finishing – in fact he's already gone – and Idris is talking of selling up.'

'I'd say that makes a lot of sense.'

'Yes, but he's salving his pride by saying that it could never have been a success. Up to a point, he's right. It will never make anyone's fortune. But if you were able to turn it round and make it at least show a profit, I think that would be the last straw in pushing him over to joining forces with us.'

'Me? Go to Manchester on my own? You'd trust me to run a business?'

'That's why I was a bit uneasy. It's a very big responsibility for such a young, inexperienced man, very big. No one would blame you if you didn't feel equal to it yet, Henry. In fact, I'm almost sorry I mentioned it. It's not really fair.'

'What d'you mean, not fair?'

'After all, you've only been in the trade for a couple of months. Just because you're such a fast learner, I got carried away . . . No, better forget all about it. I was letting my ambition get the better of me. I must stop expecting too much of people . . .'

'Nonsense! I'm willing to try. When do I start?'

'Oh, no, Henry. You were right to have such doubts. Better forget all about it and concentrate on Richmond's here in Bangor – much better. Forgive me for mentioning it.'

'I repeat, Mother, I'm willing to put all I've got into it. Even if I fail, at least Uncle Idris will see I mean business. And anyway, I've no intention of failing! I said, when do I start?'

Marged concealed her elation with difficulty. 'Idris is going up to Lancashire for most of next week. If you're sure you want to give it a try, you could travel up to Manchester with him on Monday, then he could show you the ropes and you could spend the rest of the week preparing to open for business. How would that suit you?'

'A bit sudden, isn't it? How will George manage without the extra help?'

'Well, I've been thinking over that suggestion of yours about a woman to pack the delivery orders. It's a very good idea. I thought if George knew of someone living close to the High Street who might be suitable, he could engage her to start this coming Thursday. What with that and his Siân being just about recovered, it should be all right.'

As Henry considered the prospect ahead of him, his enthusiasm grew, visibly. He beamed at his mother. 'Right, then! I'm sure you'll be well primed to break the news to Uncle Idris. I'll go for a walk after church tomorrow morning and you can deal with him before luncheon.'

'Sometimes, Henry, I think you have the makings of a schemer.'

His smile broadened. 'Fancy! I wonder where I acquired the talent?'

# Chapter Four

Beyond the brightness of the central commercial district, Manchester looked like a grey mass to Henry. All the mean streets in the neighbourhood had a false air of modernity because the ground landlord, in a fit of patriotic fervour, had re-christened them to commemorate England's recent war in the Crimea. Alma Road, Inkerman Street and Balaclava Terrace might sound like new developments, but beneath the fresh nameplates the old crumbling near-slum buildings continued to decay. The Rochdale Road area was conveniently close to the city centre, but its location upwind of the gasworks had ensured it would house an impoverished population. It was a sunny day, but somehow the brightness only accentuated the dusty shabbiness of this very ordinary street. So this was how the poor lived, thought Henry, as Idris led him into the darkened sales area of the shuttered shop in Sebastopol Terrace which was to provide Henry's home and working premises for more than a year.

His uncle seemed anxious to be gone – almost guilty at the prospect of leaving Henry alone in such an unpromising place. 'I don't know, boy, I really don't. I'm not at all sure your mother was thinking straight when she decided you should work here. You can always change your mind and come back with me.' Privately he marvelled at his own courage in saying this. Marged would murder him if she could hear him tempting her precious son back within range of Myfanwy Owen. But he was convinced that the harshness of this depressed place would prove too much for Henry.

Henry was less pessimistic, superficially at least. He made much of lighting the small wood-burning kitchen range in the back room and boiling a kettle for tea. 'Come on, Uncle, cheer up. Mother's got a point, you know. I've had it very easy until now.'

'But that's no reason to drop you in a midden,' replied Idris in funereal tones.

Eventually, still grumbling about the whole scheme, he departed for the station, leaving Henry to make a second tour of the shop and living accommodation. It was not reassuring. After eating the cold food his mother had packed for his supper, he dusted and swept the shop in readiness for next day, then went to bed.

He might have heeded Idris's advice and fled back home had it not been for Dolours Kenny. Henry met her on his second day as a Manchester shopkeeper.

Monday had been almost as depressing as Sunday. Only two or three customers came to the shop. They made tiny purchases, treated Henry with the gravest suspicion and left without giving the slightest indication that he was welcome in the neighbourhood. Determined to make the best of things, Henry spent the evening checking his stock inventory and attempting to make his wares more attractive. It was an impossible goal.

Of the shop's two adjoining front windows, one had been permanently shuttered. 'Give 'em too much glass and the temptation to break in is irresistible,' Idris had explained. 'Old Smith boarded up that window years ago, and we don't carry enough stock to need the display space.'

The remaining window was only slightly less drab. Four rows of shelves backed the twenty small panes. At the bottom were a few pounds of potatoes and other root vegetables. Above them, a couple of primitively-tinted advertisements for soap and blacking made an apparently doomed appeal for cleanliness. The other two shelves contained bottled and canned goods, largely sauces, spices and preserved vegetables. The stucco wall beneath the window had been scuffed and kicked for so long that much of it had fallen away to reveal the cheap brickwork beneath. The wooden shop door and window frames, painted black, were scarred and gouged as severely as the plasterwork. Surveying it, Henry sighed. At first he had planned to engage someone to wash and scrub outside, but now he began to wonder whether it was worth the effort.

'Monday got yer down, did it? Does the same to me, I must admit – and I get out and about an' all!'

He turned to inspect the speaker. She had just come round the corner, pushing a small handcart packed with some unidentified merchandise. Before he had time to reply to her, she was introducing herself. 'If I'd known yer'd be here I might have come in to help yer feel at home. Me name's Dolours – means tears, but don't worry, I don't blab too often – and I suppose I'm yer partner, in a manner of speaking.'

She extended a rough but spotless hand and Henry took it, puzzled by her remark but unaccountably glad to see her. 'Partner?'

The girl laughed. 'Don't worry, me boy, I've not come to steal your goods! It's more of a mutual aid society than a partnership, and it won't cost yer nothing. It's just that I have to put me little cart somewhere and old Smithy was happy enough for it to be here. I don't sell nothing that you do, and it suits the locals to get all their stuff from both of us in one go, that's all.'

'What do you sell?'

'Oh, the sort of stuff that'd go stale in your place – butter, eggs, cheese. Sometimes I gets a little milk, but that's difficult 'cos it goes off if I can't sell it the same day. Only do that in winter, really. Would it be cheeky to ask yer who yer was and where yer was from? Smithy never said nothing about somebody else coming in when he went.'

There was nothing offensive in her curiosity. On the contrary, Henry was so relieved to hear a friendly voice that he was happy to talk. 'Look, Miss, er . . .'

'Dolours, I told yer. Dolours Kenny, but ferget the Miss. I'd be looking over me shoulder all the time wondering who you was addressing. Just Dolours is fine.'

'Well, Dolours, I'm Henry, Henry Richmond. I don't think either of us is going to be fighting off customers for a bit, so come on in and have some tea in the back before you set up. You must need a bit of refreshment after pushing that load.'

She let out a shrill hoot of mirth. 'Leave me stuff out here? I'd be destitute thirty seconds after me eyes left it! No, if I'm having tea, I'll have to get the old cart inside, somehow.'

'Easy – we'll stick it in the yard for half an hour.' Henry went round and unlocked the high side gates which led to the rear of the corner premises and had presumably been installed by an optimist who thought he might need to have goods delivered. 'Does that suit you?'

'There's a gentleman for yer! Best proposition I've had all week and it's Tuesday already.' Still smiling, she wheeled her little barrow into the yard, Henry locked up again and they went inside.

Dolours would have added a dash of brightness and colour to any surroundings. In the gloom of Sebastopol Terrace she glowed like a star. What was more, she managed it with what was inside her. It was nothing to do with outward show. She was small – under five feet tall – and at first Harry thought she must be on the edge of middle age. But when he looked more closely, he could see she was probably no older than he. Experience and deprivation had given her the look of a hardened veteran normally associated with older people.

She was no beauty. Her body was thin to the point of scrawniness. Her work-toughened hands were small and knobby, the nails cut very short and straight across. Nondescript mousy hair was parted at the centre and scraped back into a small plaited bun which left the impression of being braided to give it a little more substance. Her skin was deathly pale, although a scattering of freckles hinted that this might owe as much to natural fairness as to delicate health.

Her features were good – a small, retroussé nose and well-shaped mouth – and although her eyes were rather small, they were bright blue and sparkled unquenchably.

Overall the face had a pinched, patient look, perhaps of secret suffering borne without a second thought and with no bitterness. Henry trusted her on sight.

Not that he was completely naive about letting in this stranger. She clearly had sufficient substance to finance a little market barrow. Her physical cleanliness was remarkable in an area where most people looked as if their last wash had been forcibly administered at birth. Her cotton dress was drab brown and devoid of decoration, but was as clean as her body and face. Altogether she appeared both intelligent and respectable.

Over tea, Henry explained his presence in the shop. '. . . So here I am, wondering what could ever have made me arrogant enough to think I'd make a go of this place when others couldn't,' he concluded. 'Three customers in a day aren't going to keep me in tea and sugar.'

She grinned. 'Don't fret yet awhile, me boy. Your first callers'll be all over the district by now, spreading the word there's someone new at Smithy's, and come this afternoon you'll be smothered in motherless children, widows and abandoned wives, all telling hard luck stories and asking for a little bit of credit. By the time yer close tonight, yer'll wish yer'd never laid eyes on a customer!'

He gave an exaggerated groan. 'That bad, eh? You'll have to keep an eye on me for my own good, I can see that!'

'Telling me I will! Sweet Christ, but ye're a trusting one, aren't yer? I could be the biggest thief in Rochdale Road for all yer know!'

'Not you. I'll risk that much. But in return for trusting you, I expect you to tip me off when the toughest

84

characters arrive. Now, it's time for us both to get ready for business, but first tell me why you sell your goods here.'

'It's a good spot, that's all – oh, don't get me wrong, not for a proper shop. Lousy pickings there. But I get by. I'm cheap and they know me goods are fresh. I come to them, so they needn't spend all day dragging around the town. They get my goods at same as market prices, on the days when they can't get to market.'

'So how on earth d'you do it?'

She was suddenly solemn. 'Don't laugh at this, because I feel daft enough doing it as it is. I been dirt poor all me life. With my name and the accent, yer'll already know I'm Irish. Irish Town, Manchester, that is. Never did see the Emerald Isle in me life, and I'm nineteen. If ye're lucky, *you've* never seen Irish Town. It's the worst in the world. I managed to get just enough to stake meself with the little dairy cart, and this was the closest half-way respectable area to walk to each day from where I live now. I don't raise me prices because I know what it's like to have nothing. I take just enough to stay alive. These poor sods are welcome to share in the rest.

'I chose this exact spot in the beginning because old Smithy always stuck up for me if there was trouble – any case, I'm tough enough to handle a couple of big bruisers on a good day – and in return, like I said, having my goods and his sold in the same place helped us both.'

'But it's terribly hard for a little girl like you! You must be alone in the world to be doing it all by yourself.'

Her laugh was mirthless. 'Heaven help us, sometimes I wish I was! No chance. Half me brothers and sisters cashed in their chips with anything from cholera to consumption, but there's plenty left. Don't know about me old man . . . Sometimes I suspect he was a cross between an Irishman who could swim and a Welsh mountain goat, but Ma swears he was a Liverpudlian. I've never had the pleasure of his acquaintance. I wish I'd never had the pleasure of Ma's, come to that, but yer know what they say about the poor being always with us. She keeps a flea-bitten doss house in Irish Town that the worst dregs go to when they must.

'Nah, I stay out of Irish Town as much as possible. I've got a bitty little room in a decent house run by an old widow woman. She's got a yard for me cart and I take me produce inside at night. I stay away from the family. Help me? That's a joke. They'd help themselves to all I got, the buggers, food and money, and drink it all away. It's not their fault; they don't know any other way. Yer don't blame a fox for killing chickens. Yer just give him a wide berth.'

She paused and appeared to consider his remark again, then shook her head wonderingly. 'Now I know yer not from these parts, if yer still think families are put on earth to help each other!'

He shrugged. 'Well, I'm learning. But tell me one more thing, Dolours. Where were you yesterday?'

'Oh, this place is dead Mondays. They're all either sleeping off their gin or still got a little bit of food left from Saturday. So I use Mondays to go off and buy me produce. Yer'll find yer own business a bit brisker today, just wait and see.'

Henry watched, fascinated, as she set up her pitch. The hand cart had legs at one end which turned it into a table when she set down the handles. The top closed up in

86

a sort of ark arrangement. Now she unfastened this and the hinged panel swung down to hang in front of the barrow like a shopfront sign. It was painted with the legend

'THE COW'
OUR SIXPENNY LUMP IS EQUAL IN FLAVOUR
TO THE BEST IRISH BUTTER

'And is it?' he asked her.

'I'll have yer know I don't tell lies, and I don't allow lies ter be painted on me cart.' She lowered her voice. 'As a matter'r fact, it *is* good Irish butter. I got a friend down in Liverpool who buys in quantity for the Co-operative, and he lets me have a little bit off his order at the same price. Only does it because he knows I'm straight and want to help the poor as much as he does.'

The top section of the barrow contained the promised butter, a strong basket with a few dozen eggs, a truckle of Cheddar cheese and a box of apples. Pointing at the fruit, she said, 'I never saw such fruit here at this time o' year. They're early crop all the way from America. He give me them for nothing and said to sell 'em where they'd do most good! Wasted on this lot, of course, but I'm soft.'

Over the following week, Henry quickly realised that she really was soft. Dolours' little sales operation was practically an errand of mercy. He was starting to understand why she seemed pale and prematurely aged. For one thing, she was half starved. She varied her prices according to what she perceived as the needs of her customers.

In general they respected her gesture. The more prosperous residents, with their stout clogs, woollen shawls and a regular wage coming in, were charged the market rate. A laid-off workman, with only the uppers of his boots left and a cap of folded paper on his head, could buy a single egg at half price, a pennyworth of cheese and might even receive a free apple.

In the shop, trade staggered up on to its knees on Tuesday and was reasonably brisk until Friday morning, when it tailed off again. 'No more money, me lad, that's the trouble. Friday's when yer sort out yer regular paying customers,' Dolours told him.

Sure enough, about five women brought in shopping lists and paid a reasonable sum for his spartan stocks. They were the same ones who could afford Dolours' top prices. Those who had come in earlier that week for one slice of corned beef or two of bacon were now down to a couple of pounds of potatoes, two pennyworth of tea and a pound of sugar.

'Shut the shop Saturday morning and come down the market with me,' said Dolours. 'If you've got the spending power, yer can rescue yer whole week's trade on Saturday night, but Saturday morning yer might as well be shut for all the business yer'll do.'

The reason was simple. Everyone in the surrounding streets who had a job was paid at the end of the working day on Saturday. So while the white collar workers from the suburbs were free to enjoy the low prices and fresh produce of the covered markets on Saturday morning with the money they received on Friday evening, the labourers and mill hands worked on, their wives penniless until the best goods were sold and many stalls had closed down. Everything was closed on Sunday, so if the workman's family was fobbed off with stale goods late on Saturday, the remaining food had to last through the sabbath and had usually gone off by Monday.

Dolours explained all this. 'So if I buy up good stocks of fresh food at a discount for bulk purchase,' Henry commented, 'I can stay open till midnight Saturday and flog it all at market rates. I make a profit and they get a decent Sunday dinner. Now that's what I call ethical self-interest!' It was a pompous term he had picked up at school.

Dolours stared at him for a moment, round-eyed and impressed, then said, 'I don't know about that last bit, but yer right about the rest of it!'

She put the word about Sebastopol Terrace on Saturday morning before dragging him off to the great covered markets, and within an hour of their return, a number of housewives had come along to see if the rumour was true. By seven that evening, when their men began to trickle home with the wages, Henry knew he stood to triple or even quadruple the best takings of Smith's era. He had insisted on staking Dolours to extra cheese, fresh milk and eggs which she sold from behind his counter. At the end of the evening she was able to repay his investment and still pocket more than she had taken all week out on the pavement.

'Jesus love yer for the gentleman you are!'

He had just closed the front door at ten minutes to midnight, and Dolours was radiant at their combination of success and philanthropy. She threw her arms round Henry's neck and planted a smacking kiss on his mouth. Momentarily he drew back in shock, then they shouted with laughter and he hugged her stick-thin waist.

'Dolours Kenny, you'll die rich if I can teach you to be selfish!' He was childishly delighted that the girl had proved so shrewd. Then a thought crossed his mind which effectively killed his pleasure. 'Oh, God, what an ass I am! I was so bound up with all this selling that I forgot about your getting home. You can't go back to Ancoats alone after midnight, 'specially with your cart!'

'What, an old hand like me? 'Course I can!' But her voice was shaky and he knew she was frightened. 'Stupid bitch that I am, I should have realised the time was going on. I'll admit I try to avoid the streets at this time o' night, Saturdays in particular.'

'Damn, damn, damn! If only we were chaperoned you could stay in the spare room here!'

Dolours gave him a long, level look, then let out a laugh that could have been heard in the next street. 'Chaperone? Chaperone, yer say! Henry, I grew up sharing a room with every ragtag who had the price of a bed. Ma used to cram them all in and they was no respecters of persons, I can tell yer. I thought a gent like you wouldn't give me house room, and I wouldn't blame yer. That's why I never asked yer! If yer don't mind me staying, I can take care of me maidenly virtue meself, thanks very much!'

Henry hugged her again. 'If only the world was full of women like you, it would be a better place. Let's have a cup of tea and some supper.'

As he turned away towards the fire, Dolours looked longingly after him. Chaperone? If only he would do something to make her feel she needed one. Then she shook herself back to reality and offered to cook the supper.

The trip to market became a weekly fixture. Every Saturday morning, Henry would open the shop for an hour or so, then close it and take Dolours on a buying foray. At first they toured the lot: the central Market Place for fruit and vegetables, the fish market in Old Shambles, and the covered Victoria Market for meat. Dolours was born to bargain and she taught Henry how to look behind the first grade goods beloved of the carriage trade, to seek out the spotted but otherwise sound turnips; the too-large or awkwardly shaped potatoes; the decent cheese which had only a week's ripeness left before it began to deteriorate.

'If the stuff's perfect, yer customers aren't going to be able to afford it, so yer might as well push yer advantage with the battered stuff here and give 'em what they can afford back home,' she told him in an undertone. Then 'Hey, mister, yer not expecting to sell this poor stuff, are yer? I got a gentleman here who'll take it off yer hands for horse feed.'

They gave her plenty of backchat but recognised the truth of what she was saying. This early in the day, the sort of produce she and Henry wanted was totally unsaleable. If they were able to shift it at the same time as the good stuff, it meant they had a chance of closing on time, instead of hanging around to await the evening arrival of the poor with their meagre wages.

Henry occasionally shuddered at the thought of what Marged or Idris would have said about him buying such rubbish, but they did not know and when he put it into

91

the shop, the good sense of Dolours' advice was instantly backed by a stream of customers. After the first week, he even bought small quantities of poultry and fish. He knew that anything left over on Saturday night would be wasted, but after a couple of false starts which left him eating large helpings of fried herrings or boiled chicken on Sunday, he found a proper balance. And as he learned about shop-soiled goods, he learned more about choosing the best, too.

On their rounds, he began to see a Manchester whose existence he had never suspected. In the foreground were the familiar sights: Market Street with its imposing new buildings, granite kerbs and sturdy paving setts gave the smart passers-by a chance to remain clean. But even here there was enough filth to necessitate wooden gaiters around the gas street lamps to preserve the metal from corrosion.

Behind this modern grandeur lurked an older, in parts medieval city. His favourite spot was the Old Shambles, where they went for fish, rabbits and dairy produce. Here the ancient black-and-white-timbered buildings still stood, tottering against each other like old men seeking support, their top-heavy upper storeys overhanging the narrow street.

Here and there an enterprising shopkeeper had adopted the advertising craze of the new age: in one case the upper storey of the Wellington Inn had donned a pair of giant spectacles whose frames proclaimed that a Mr Bowen offered a comprehensive range of optical and mathematical instruments. Some of the streets here were paved, too, but the warren of lanes and foul courts leading off them still raised themselves from unsurfaced mud with an overlay of rubbish and ordure.

Inevitably the filth was spread by the passage of thousands of feet, and the open stalls of the Shambles market wallowed in a stench of ripe rottenness. But along with the bad smells came the vividness of street life. Henry did not have to go back into the rookeries with these chirpy common people. He could observe them at their best and then depart before the contact became uncomfortable. He loved it all, and the shopping trip rapidly became the high point of his week. When they had finished their buying, he would leave Dolours with the loads of produce while he went to hail a horse-drawn cab to take them back to Sebastopol Terrace.

At first she tried to dissuade him – 'A cab? Never been in one in me life! It'll cost a fortune!'

'And what d'you propose to do with all this stuff – run back and get The Cow to push it all home?'

'Jesus, I should 'a thought to bring it, shouldn't I? Maybe next week, then.'

'No, Dolours, we go home in style. A shilling or so won't make that much difference.'

He committed a final extravagance in buying a huge bunch of flowers for Dolours from Victoria Market, where they had made their last purchases. He thrust them at her as she turned to put her modest extra parcels of cheese and eggs with his goods. She was so overcome that he resolved to repeat the gesture every week.

Henry often wondered afterwards what would have become of him in Manchester had it not been for Dolours Kenny. No one could have made a brilliant success of the Sebastopol Terrace provision shop, but the lesson she taught him that first week at least assured him of modest profitability.

For a while it seemed to promise more. After she stayed that first Saturday night, it seemed sensible to offer her the use of the back yard for her cart and the protection of the shop for her stock of produce.

'You did me an enormous favour,' Henry told her. 'The least I can do to thank you is to lighten your load with that damned barrow.' So now Dolours was able to go home untrammelled by the barrow, except when she took it off to re-stock on Mondays.

Then it occurred to him that as she avoided her family, there could be little to keep her at the widow's lodging house in Ancoats. After that first Saturday night, he had dismissed his misgivings about her staying unchaperoned. As that was no problem, would it not be easier for her to live here, behind her sales pitch, than in Ancoats? She already shared his mid-day meal each day – often cooked it, too – so why not take advantage of his extra room?

At first Dolours was dubious about the idea. 'This Uncle Idris of yours – what'll he say when he finds out yer've taken a female lodger? Won't he be off telling yer ma straight away, and won't they both be down on yer like vultures?'

Henry laughed, confident of his ability to handle Idris. 'My uncle will be more than pleased at the way takings are rising here. And when I tell him it's mainly thanks to you, he won't object. He's scared stiff of Mother, so he's not going to tell her anything that might throw her into a rage. Come on, Dolours, you know it would make life easier for you, and that I'm a frightful housekeeper. I need a civilising feminine touch!'

In fact nothing could have been further from the truth. Henry was naturally fastidious and he kept the living quarters spotless. He had quickly discovered that the skills George Beynon taught him in the Bangor shop were good for running a home as well as a store. Now he swept and dusted automatically, and if he was an uninspired cook, at least he was able to produce reliable bacon and eggs or chop and potatoes. The real reason for his invitation was friendly concern for Dolours and a desire to do something for her.

She adored him and often sighed hopelessly at the knowledge that he never even thought about her as a potential lover. Had he proposed she come to Sebastopol Terrace as his mistress, she would have leapt at the chance. As it was, he looked on her as just a friend, and she doubted her ability to go on concealing her feelings for him.

Nevertheless she came. Such an arrangement barely caused a ripple in the life of the neighbourhood. Within weeks, Henry was assimilated as part of the community around Rochdale Road. The residents were far more interested in his success at bringing them good market produce on Saturday nights than in any liaison he might have with the dairy stall girl.

The shop would never occupy Henry's whole attention. He soon realised that however hard he tried, he could not improve trade beyond a relatively low level. Whatever he did was limited by the poverty of his customers. Some of them survived mainly on bread, dripping and tea – and even the tea was bought in one-ounce screws of paper and re-used throughout the week.

He could buy good market produce, stock fresh vegetables and make sure his bacon was sweet and tempting. But he could never put money in people's pockets, and most of them had none.

Once he had come to terms with his position, he started seeking other outlets for his energy and inevitably consulted Dolours.

He still knew little about her. She was never at Sebastopol Terrace on Sunday, returning only to spend the night, and went off early on Monday with her cart to buy her stock. She also went out two or three evenings a week and often arrived back after midnight. Discreet probing by Henry failed to solve the mystery of how she spent her time. Her low opinion of her family made it unlikely she would be visiting them.

One Tuesday evening about three weeks after she moved in to Sebastopol Terrace, she ate a hurried supper as usual and was obviously preparing to go out. Henry's curiosity finally proved too much for him. 'Going courting, Dolours?'

She stared at him, as though suspecting him of teasing her. Apparently satisfied that the question was genuine, she said: 'Yer don't find much romantic love where I'm off to.'

'Well, what's the attraction then?'

She scowled, reluctant to commit herself. 'You'd think I was half daft if I told yer. Maybe I am.'

'Go on. You've made me curious.'

'Oh, all right . . . I told yer I've been on the bottom a lot of me life. Not for the last few years, though. Since I got me barrow, there's plenty worse off than me. I go to try and help them.'

He waited for her to continue but she fell silent. 'There must be more to it than that. Help? In what way? You don't strike me as a religious do-gooder – for one thing you blaspheme like a recruiting sergeant!'

That eased her solemn mood. 'Yer right there, Henry. But religion's got a bit to do with it, all the same. I got very sick a few years ago – me ma never did look after us, and them that grew up at all was the ones who learned to look after themselves or them who was so healthy only a gun would kill 'em. I was a bit on the weak side, so when I picked up the sniffs it was pneumonia within a few days. Ma'd shoved me out into the court to sleep by the covered passage, because even with her crowding, she couldn't fit all the lodgers in the space she had. Just as well she chucked me out, 'cos that's where this bunch of Holy Joes found me and took me off to nurse me.

'I was a long time pulling through, I can tell yer. It was November and although the cold wasn't so bad, it was that wet! Another night out in the passage and I'd 'a drowned. As it was I nearly drowned inside anyway, 'cos me lungs was so full of water. I don't remember that much of it. It turned out that one of the ones as found me was the vicar of that parish. It was his wife that nursed me. They found out that Ma wouldn't be no help and kept me theirselves for nearly two months.

'By the time I got well again, Mrs Simpson the vicar's wife said that if she couldn't save all the other lost children, at least she could save me. She had a few pounds put by and . . .' here the tears filled her eyes . . . 'she – she asked me if there was anything I could do with it that would set me up able to make me own living. I'd seen enough o' the streets to know it wasn't all as bad as

97

Irish Town and I came up with the idea of the little barrow. She laughed fit to bust – said I couldn't push a kid's toy horse on wheels, weak as I was. But I told her I was stronger than I looked and in the end she believed me. They had people all over the parish owing them favours. They was the best people I ever knew, I can tell yer. Anyway, they looked through the names of the people who owed them and they come up with a joiner to knock together me little cart and a drunken old sign painter who stayed sober long enough to do me sign board.' She paused dramatically – 'Me own wording, mind. I saw it one time on a shopfront down in Liverpool when I cadged a lift there and back on a carrier's cart!'

Henry was deeply impressed by the idea of the Simpsons. 'So you go and see them to help their street mission – is that it? I think I might like to come and meet them.'

Her expression clouded. 'No chance. Good things don't last that long with me, I'm afraid. I'd been set up about six months – they found me my first respectable lodgings in Ancoats, too, by the way – when Mr Simpson got called by the Bishop. Seems his grace didn't like all this helping the common man and decided to move the vicar somewhere out in the country where he'd do less damage. Said something about a man of the cloth setting a bad example of sedition. I think the vicar had spoken at a political rally in the Free Trade Hall and upset some important Manchester men. Anyhow, that was the last I saw of them. It nearly broke my heart when they went, and that was when I decided I owed it to them to go on the way they'd started.

'Trouble is, I can't go along with their religion. I got

no time fer God. He may be there and He may not, but all I can say is if He is, He's been asleep for a bloody long time! I s'pose really that's why I didn't try to stay in touch with the Simpsons after they'd left. They were all for it. But it bothered them that I wouldn't bend me knee to God and I know it would have caused trouble.'

'You can't be working alone, though, surely?'

'Oh, no. I split up me time between God and the Devil. Sundays I go with a bunch of Socialists – they're as bad in their way as the Christians, they just worship something else, that's all – and in the week I go with one of the Missions to the poor. They all know me well enough now not to try converting me to their crazy ideas, and they're all good at heart, or they wouldn't be out there helping. Who knows? With so many of us all working away, some day things may be better for everyone.'

She was trying to took tough and amused as she spoke, but Henry could see how deeply she was affected by her confession. The cynical slum kid in her loathed the thought of being ridiculed as a do-gooder; the saved victim wanted to devote her life to saving others. In a way it was a shame she was so bright. A less objective soul would have fitted in completely with the Mission or the political group because she was fired by an abstract cause. Poor Dolours was a misfit even among the do-gooders, because all she believed in was the need to relieve human wretchedness.

Henry let her go alone that evening, but his thoughts kept returning to what she had said. He mulled over his own privileged background. He'd grown up without a father, too, but there any resemblance to Dolours ended. Here he was, coming up to nineteen years old, the product of a rich man's school and a comfortable woman's home, healthy, well fed and expensively dressed. He even had time on his hands at the end of his working day . . . So what better way to repay his much bigger debt to Providence than to help Dolours at paying hers? He firmly pushed aside the sneaking suspicion that his real motives were boredom and a base curiosity about the seedier parts of the city. Could it really be as bad as Uncle Idris and others had hinted? Here was a way of finding out. He went off to bed that night having resolved to accompany Dolours on her next expedition into the Manchester underworld.

After considerable argument, Dolours grudgingly agreed to his joining her now and then. 'I think ye're mad meself, but I can see I'll get no peace till yer come. But I'm to decide when, all right?'

He nodded, at a loss to understand this condition. He was still too naive to realise that Dolours was vetting the areas to which she took him, showing him only the less appalling places. Even so, what he saw shocked him beyond anything he had experienced to date. The areas they ventured to made Sebastopol Terrace look like a desirable garden suburb.

Dolours also tried to keep him away from the more extreme companions who accompanied her on her forays into the underworld. The worst of these were the type of hellfire Christians who somehow felt the poor deserved all they got, and were more interested in amassing personal credit in heaven than in helping the distressed with their slum philanthropy. At the other extreme were wild-eyed politicos, who in turn saw the poor as a weapon with which one day they would pull down the edifice of the privileged society which oppressed them. The centre ground was held by more normal people – committed Christians appalled by the suffering of fellow human beings, moderate reformers who attempted to educate the children of the slums, and well-meaning young women who turned to charity work as a way of filling under-occupied days. These calmer mortals in the not-too-shocking locations were the companions Dolours weeded out for Henry's good works. The moderate reformers and the nice young women were no more capable of coping with Irish Town or Salford than Henry would have been.

The first sortie was on a Sunday in late October. 'Good thing about Sundays is you don't get the God-botherers that day,' said Dolours. 'They're all down on their knees confessing sins they never committed and ignoring their real faults. If yer come across any rum ones today it'll be the brainy anarchists!'

In fact his first new acquaintance was a gentle, elderly former schoolmaster, who was driving the horse-drawn charabanc they boarded along Rochdale Road on Sunday morning. Mr Treadgold ran the ragged school where they were to spend the day, and acted as coachman on the free transport provided for the pupils.

'A lot of 'em live close enough to get there under their own steam,' said Dolours, 'but if we don't pick 'em up, either they're given jobs to do at home or they lose interest and trail off somewhere else where they'll get into trouble as like as not. This way, a couple of us goes into the streets to chivvy them aboard, then we've got 'em for the rest of the day.'

Old Treadgold gave Henry a vague smile. 'It's quite a

change to meet children who regard education as a privilege,' he said. 'For years, in the preparatory school, it was my lot to convince more privileged pupils that learning was good for them, but once we have these rough children in the schoolroom, they seem almost desperate to acquire knowledge. Heartening – most heartening.' He whipped up the two horses and they were off at a shambling walk.

'I wouldn't have thought the old boy was strong enough to manage a governess cart, let alone something as big as this,' Henry murmured to Dolours.

She smiled. 'Don't go too much by appearances, Henry me boy, it's yer worst weakness. He's as strong as a steel cable under all that trembling humility – and that goes for his spirit as well as his thin little arms. The kids love him.'

For the next hour they followed a winding route around the working-class streets of the inner city. At each stopping point, Dolours would jump down and go into a court or along a rough street of red brick houses and return with a clutch of dirty children. Along the way a few young adults were collected, too.

'Some of them seem a bit old to start their ABCs,' said Henry.

'Never too old to learn. Poor devils never had the chance when they was babies. As long as they want to come and are too poor to pay for an education, we take them and bugger age limits,' said Dolours.

Finally, with some fifteen children and five youths aboard, they arrived at their destination, the former schoolroom of a Baptist chapel, vacated when the congregation moved on to a new building. Another eleven youngsters were already gathered. They had made their own way to the school. Also on hand were Gilbert Smith, the second volunteer teacher, an intense-looking, thin young man of about Henry's age; and James Treadgold's sister May, who would feed the children at mid-day and who tried to clean them up a little in the intervals between lessons.

'Watch yerself with her,' whispered Dolours. 'She can be a right old cow at times. Gilbert's all right, though, even if he's a bit cantankerous with strangers.'

He decided almost at once that Dolours was doing Gilbert a favour. Five minutes' acquaintance convinced Henry that the other man was a bit cantankerous in the same way as William the Conqueror was a bit assertive. He was tall, dark and very thin. Everything about him seemed spiky. He reminded Henry of a caricature of Byron in the grip of a bout of revolutionary fervour. Dolours might see him as a dashing compassionate man. To Henry, he was a loud-mouthed trouble-maker with a chip on his shoulder.

Henry was helping May Treadgold to set up a tea urn and a soup pot when Smith started baiting him. 'Lord Muck come to see the slums, eh? I thought it was only a matter of time when Dolours told us she'd found a saviour in Sebastopol Terrace.'

'At least I don't pretend I live only for my fellow man.' Henry's civilised tone enhanced the insulting flavour of his rejoinder. He was surprised at his own immediate resentment of Smith. But since I feel like this, why fight it? he thought, and continued: 'It looks to me as though you're the one who wants to be the new Messiah.'

Smith turned even paler and made a small explosive noise as he lunged towards Henry. May Treadgold, until now silent as a trappist monk, turned on him.

'Don't be such a fool, Gilbert! It's about time someone let you know you're not the only humane young fellow in Manchester. Mr Richmond's motives are unlikely to be any less noble than your own. Now pull yourself together and remember why you're here – assuming you knew that in the first place, of course.'

Without pausing to see whether her words had struck home, she turned back to her pots and pans. With visible effort, Smith controlled his temper and silently returned to the schoolroom. Moments later, Dolours came out to the scullery.

'What have you done to Gilbert? He's like a penned tiger in there – poor Mr Treadgold can't do a thing with him!'

May sniffed contemptuously. 'My brother could never do a thing with anybody, that's his trouble. One of your young men gave the other one a well-deserved talking-to, that's all.'

A deep flush stained Dolours' pale face. 'I – I'm sure I don't know what yer mean, Miss Treadgold! One of me young men? Wish I had one to call me own, leave alone two!' She flashed Henry an apologetic, agonised look, but he merely grinned at her.

May Treadgold shrugged. 'Please yourself. But let's get one thing straight. We're supposed to be here educating and cleaning up those poor little wretches in the next room, not playing out the latest romantic novel. So I'd appreciate it if you'd tell them to stop locking antlers over you and get on with the job.' She made it plain that these were to be her last words on the matter.

Somehow, Dolours managed to keep Henry and Gilbert Smith apart for most of the day. It was easier once the teaching sessions had started, because all of them had their hands full. Dolours was teaching the youngest children their alphabets and numbers. James Treadgold concentrated on penmanship with the middle ability group and Gilbert Smith was conducting a reading session with the most advanced children. May Treadgold kept Henry busy, first as her assistant in preparing the mid-day dinner, then as errand-runner.

'The curate of St Joseph's church has collected some decent clothes for us to distribute today,' she said. 'Morning service will be over by now and he asked us to send someone along then to collect them. You'll have to go, Mr Richmond. Everyone else has their hands full.'

At the back of St Joseph's Sunday schoolroom, Henry found Albert Gregg, the curate. The clothes he had to offer were quite lightly-worn and clean. 'I think our parishioners have been a little more generous than usual because winter is coming on,' Gregg explained. 'From what I've seen of Mr Treadgold's pupils, they'll appreciate a little extra warmth.'

Back at the Baptist chapel, Henry helped Miss Treadgold to sort the garments. His errand had made him look more closely than before at the children when he came back into the building. 'I didn't realise before just how badly-clothed some of them are,' he remarked to May. 'Most of them just seem to be draped in worn-out rags.'

Miss Treadgold pursed her lips. 'For years I told

myself the poor could improve their lot if they really put their shoulders to the wheel,' she told him. 'Then I started helping James with these mites, and I realised such thoughts were almost sinful. How can a child who's never been warm or dry or had a full stomach, be a good Christian member of society? I don't hold much with church any longer –' she said this in hushed tones, as though afraid of being overheard – 'so I come here of a Sunday instead. I think there's more of the Lord's work in saving the little children's bodies than our own souls.'

Fearful that she might momentarily have been mawkish, she glared at Henry and moved away from him, saying as an afterthought: 'The worst-dressed can be given full rigs from that lot when they've eaten. The others can all have something, a warm coat and scarf at least. It's a good haul this time. That curate's got a golden voice when he starts preaching about the deserving poor, I'll give him that!'

The curate was not the only one, it seemed. Henry was abashed to find that Gilbert Smith was a different character when he was with the children. He was a natural charmer, making them laugh, drawing them out, recognising which passages of a book were beyond the slower pupils and which would make the quickest stretch themselves. His young charges clearly adored him and in turn he mellowed under their affection.

Henry noticed the transformation as he stood in the scullery doorway, waiting for a break in the teaching to tell everyone their dinner was ready. Perplexed, he turned back to May Treadgold.

'Forgive me if I appear to be gossipping, Miss Treadgold, but why is Gilbert Smith so strange? One minute he reacts to me as though I were his lifelong enemy; the next he's charming those children. It can't be that he seriously thinks I have designs on Dolours.'

She shook her head. 'No one can rightly fathom that one. He's a tragedy in a way, because I'm sure he'll come to a bad end. He's from a prosperous family and he had a first-rate education. Took a degree at Cambridge University, too. You know what they say about a fallen woman – that if she reforms she's more proper than the bishop's wife? Well, I think it's the same sort of thing with young Gilbert. He came home from the university, chock full of these noble ideals, and went to work in his father's cotton mill. They say that on the first day there was a terrible accident – one of the little ones fell into a piece of unprotected machinery.

'Gilbert saw it all, and offered to help take the child home. When he went into the filthy hovel where she lived, and heard what the mother had to say about the way his own firm worked them all to death, it must have turned him a bit funny. Because from that day to this he's never set foot in his father's house or mill. He got a teaching job that earned him pennies – and he didn't keep that for long, because he was always spouting revolutionary politics. The truth is he hates himself, though he'll never admit it, and when he sees his own old life reflected in people like you, he hates them too. Can't help it. He has a dreadful temper and some day I think he'll do somebody real damage. But his love for the children is the one straight thing about him – he worships them, and not in that goody-goody way that gets nothing done. He wades in and helps. His readers learn ten times faster than James's, and James was a teacher

107

for more than forty years. Whatever becomes of him, he'll save some of the next generation, so good luck to him.'

'How does he make ends meet, if he's cut off from the family and didn't keep his teaching job?'

'Oh, that makes him even worse. He found a place at a dreadful crammer's, and now he earns wretched wages for trying to improve spoiled stupid rich children in time to get them into good schools. He sees the worst of his old world every day, and that makes him more bitter than ever . . . Anyway, Mr Richmond, this won't get our lot fed, will it? Come on, enough talk. They've finished for the present. We'd better start dishing up the soup.'

After the children had consumed vast quantities of thick meat and vegetable soup with chunks of bread, they were given boiled pudding with syrup, then large mugs of tea.

'Not a banquet, maybe, but it puts in a bit o' ballast to see them through the week,' said Dolours. 'Now for the clothes bazaar.'

The day passed in a continuing buzz of activity and was over when Henry still felt it had hardly begun. He avoided Gilbert Smith, both for Dolours' sake and because he felt sorry for the man now, while still disliking him. Their only other brush that day occurred after the pupils had left, when they were dismantling Miss Treadgold's temporary kitchen and stowing away the books and writing materials from the schoolroom.

Henry packed away the last earthenware soup plate and turned to Dolours. 'Right, methinks it's time for Sebastopol Terrace and supper. Are you ready?'

Before she could reply, Gilbert Smith, who had been

behind her, came into the scullery. Henry could feel his fury like a physical force.

'Getting you ready to pay your week's rent, is he? Well, Dolours, don't trouble yourself if you haven't the cash this week. I'm sure the landlord's willing to take it in kind.'

Before Henry could reach him, Dolours had turned on Smith, her face livid. 'How dare you! No man treats me like that. No man! D'yer hear me? I'm poor, but me pride's intact and I'll thank yer to remember it. At least Henry treats me like a lady, which is more than I can say for some here as calls 'emselves gentlemen! Come on, Henry. Let's leave this pig to wallow in his own swill!' And she wheeled like a guardsman and swept past Smith back through the schoolroom, heading for the street.

Henry's second philanthropic venture was almost as eventful as his first. This time, Dolours took him to an evening session, to help a Christian group called the Lamplighters, who ran a night shelter for destitute men and a soup run around the nearby streets for those who applied after the shelter was full. The society was well-funded and had been in existence for many years, so the night shelter was a substantial place.

The entrance hall bore a disturbing resemblance to a theatre foyer, except for its drab brown and green decor. There was a ticket desk built like a box office, and applicants had to line up there to obtain admission slips. When the shelter was full for the night, the ticket desk shutter was closed and the remaining applicants were regretfully turned away, but usually with the reminder that volunteers would be around the streets later with hot soup, bread and cheese.

Beyond the travesty of a box office, double doors led into the sleeping quarters. This was one large hall, with skylight windows. Odd coffin-like structures lined both walls, their lids now raised to reveal narrow mattresses, each supplied with a rough grey blanket and a pillow. The mattresses had removable covers but no bed linen was provided.

'These folk would never miss it, and fer the cost of laundry the society can finance a few more beds,' said Dolours.

Thanks to the narrowness of the beds and the lack of any surrounding space, the Lamplighters had managed to cram in sixty of the odd units. The wooden lids of the bed-boxes were varnished pitch pine and the walls were painted a matching brown up to head height. There, the colour changed to cream, to highlight the religious homilies painted there in huge letters. Each had a theme, rather like a holy newspaper headline, underlined. Beneath was the appropriate biblical quotation to back the homily. 'In God Have I Put My Trust' announced one, and then, below: 'Yea, though I walk through the Valley of the Shadow of Death, I shall fear No Evil, for Thou art with Me.' Beneath that was the biblical text reference. As if, thought Henry, the poor devils were itching to riffle through their pocket Bibles to check the accuracy of the inscription . . . Already he was beginning to think he preferred the Ragged School.

The vast expanses of cream wall apparently gave the Lamplighters insufficient space for holy writ, for it continued on the pitch-pine hammer beams that supported the arched ceiling. They stretched off down the huge room, five of them enumerating the virtues of godhead:

110

'God Is Truth; God Is Good; God Is Holy; God Is Just; God Is Love', they announced respectively. Henry sighed. 'I hope they can't read, poor fellows, otherwise I should think they find it hard to reconcile themselves to the idea that God is just!'

Tonight Henry was going to help out with supper run. Most helpers without special skills started off there. Later, if they proved sympathetic – and suitably Christian – they were moved indoors to supervise the preparations for bed and settling the men down for the night. One Lamplighter, invariably a clergyman, finally read them off to sleep with suitable extracts from the Gospels. Female helpers were confined to the kitchen and the foyer while the homeless men were in residence. It would have been deemed improper to expose them to male strangers in bed.

After showing Henry round, Dolours took him back to the entrance. As they came through the door, a young woman was entering the ticket office. She was very pretty and instantly attracted Henry's undivided attention.

'Now that's not the sort of girl I'd naturally associate with charity work!' he said to Dolours, with all the tactlessness of his youth.

'No – looks better suited to a piano stool in the parlour after tea, doesn't she?' Dolours' voice had a bitter edge, but Henry failed to notice. He was far too interested in the newcomer.

'You must introduce me,' he said. 'After all, we shall probably see a lot of each other if I'm to go on working here!'

And you will be, I can see that, Dolours told herself.

Then, aloud, 'As yer like – come on. Miss Bingley! Have yer got a minute to spare?'

Alison Bingley was eighteen, the well-polished product of a successful Manchester family. Her dark hair was piled high in luxuriant curls under a smart bonnet. Her eyes were lustrous brown, her skin glowed warmly and her body was all lush curves beneath a modest but fashionable gown. In short, thought Dolours, she's everything I'm not. She felt sick.

As Dolours introduced Henry, Alison Bingley looked as interested as he did. 'What a surprise to find such a young man with a social conscience,' she said, her voice all honey. 'Normally it takes longer for gentlemen to come to this work than ladies, doesn't it, Dolours?'

'I don't know as I'd say that. What about Mr Fenner and Mr Pratt?' As the words left her lips she could have kicked herself. She knew exactly what would come next.

Miss Bingley gave a tuneful little laugh. 'Oh, them! One only has to look at either of them to know why they come here. Why, Mr Fenner has that . . . uh . . . unfortunate nose and chin; and Mr Pratt, apart from being so small, wears quite the thickest spectacles I've ever seen. Neither of them is likely to have anywhere else to go, but you could hardly say that about Mr Richmond, could you? Where did you find him, Dolours?'

'I live with him.' Again, she wished the words unsaid. But then, why? This creature already thought she was Irish trash. She might as well rub it in if it put the girl off Henry.

Of course, it did nothing of the kind. It merely gave Alison a chance to blush becomingly and stammer in confusion, whereupon Henry – God damn his eyes,

112

thought Dolours – rushed to reassure her that innocent little Miss Kenny had not meant that; what she had meant was that he was her landlord . . .

After that, Dolours knew she might as well give up. She made a few remarks about getting on with the work, which were practically ignored by both her companions. They were now intent on each other and only vaguely aware of their surroundings. Trying not to cry, Dolours headed for the kitchen.

Alison Bingley was far too respectable a young lady to attend a place like the Lamplit Shelter unchaperoned. Her mother was in the kitchen, supervising the humbler female volunteers as they prepared the supper which was to be taken round the streets. Though God knows who gave her the authority, thought Dolours, seeing that most of this lot were cooking and serving cheap food before Her Ladyship ever heard of charity.

Mrs Bingley was as offhand with Dolours as her daughter. This attitude usually irritated the Irish girl, but for once she was relieved to be ignored. She found a quiet corner and started cutting wedges of bread off a quartern loaf while she brooded miserably about having lost Henry without ever winning him.

For Henry it was the start of his first socially correct romantic relationship. No one, least of all his mother, could have questioned the suitability of Alison Bingley as a companion. Nobody could chide her, either, for being seen with him. Years later, he sometimes wondered whether it was her very lushness which entranced him, contrasting so sharply with all the dirty, underfed paupers he had been mixing with during the week. Whatever the cause, he began taking an interest in the trivial girlish chatter which seemed to comprise Alison's whole consciousness when she was not actively flirting.

Henry's choice of charitable activity underwent a swift adjustment, too. During the course of that evening, he convinced himself that after all, the Lamplit Shelter was far more his sort of activity than the Ragged School. Later, he justified himself to Dolours by saying he felt he would only harm a good working partnership at the school if he continued to aggravate Gilbert Smith by his presence.

'Anyway, I'm really no teacher, Dolours, and I feel more useful helping them take the food round the streets and seeing the poor men are settled in all right at the shelter. I'd never have been more than an occasional errand boy at the school.'

'Suit yerself,' said Dolours. 'But I'd a thought if I could learn to read and then go on to teach others, it wouldn't be beyond yer own ability to teach, since yer've such a fine education and all.'

He pounced on her words, glad to change the subject. 'You mean you taught yourself to read and write? That's quite marvellous – how did you manage it?'

'Yer worst enemy had a lot to do with it. I was one of his first pupils when he came to the school. That's why the poor sod makes such a fool of himself over me. It's not so much he's keen on me that way – more that he sees me as something he . . . well . . . made up, in a way.'

'Nonsense! Perhaps he really believes it's just that, but it's obvious to everyone else that he's potty about you. He guards you like a hen with one chick!'

But she was not to be drawn into his forced

114

camaraderie. 'I've told him, and I'll repeat it for yer: I don't belong to any man. I'm me own woman and intend to go on like that. I've seen too many poverty-stricken marriages ending in blows and tears, with too many babies and not enough food. I can do better on me own!'

And she flounced off to bed. Henry was still young and foolish enough to believe her. Anyway, it was what he wanted to hear. He couldn't really believe Dolours was stuck on him. If she was, it would be embarrassing, feeling as he did about Alison Bingley. Much better they just remained good friends. Why, Dolours was like a sister to him!

Over the next six months, she needed to be just that, for Henry now took her completely for granted. They worked, dined and shopped together. Dolours went on explaining the life of the streets and factories, but she avoided the Lamplit Shelter now, and no longer went on a couple of the other all-female charitable missions which Alison Bingley patronised. Meanwhile, Henry was wooed by the whole Bingley family.

He had written to Marged about his new friendship and in turn she had asked Idris to make tactful enquiries about the girl. Everything she heard was reassuring, although Marged would have preferred the girl to worship as a member of the Anglican Church rather than with the Methodists.

'I don't really care for religious reasons,' she confided in Idris, 'but if they become serious, non-conformist religion is such a social drawback. If Henry marries her and still means to get to the top, he'll have to win her over to the Church of England the minute they're engaged.'

Idris secretly wondered how Marged would have felt if

she knew about Dolours Kenny. He had found out only a couple of weeks before, when he paid an unexpected visit to the shop, but having seen the girl he was convinced there was no romantic entanglement – at least, not on his nephew's side.

As Dolours watched Henry daily sinking more comfortably into a morass of upper middle-class tea parties, impromptu concerts around the Bingley piano, and carol singing with the Manchester Sunday School Union as Christmas approached, then the promise of involvement in the round of parties and socials that Alison constantly mentioned, she grew sadder and her jealousy of the nubile Miss Bingley increased.

In her more rational moments, Dolours knew it would be much better for her if she found another pitch for her trading, sought new lodgings and cut off all contact with Henry. But such spells seldom lasted long enough for her even to begin taking action. She did try to avoid him in the evenings when he returned from meetings with the girl. She did not trust herself to respond sanely if he started praising Alison Bingley to her.

Christmas came and went and Dolours spent the holiday alone in the Sebastopol Terrace house. Christmas Eve was a Sunday, which enabled Henry to close the shop after serving his customers late on Saturday evening and travel home to Bangor next day to celebrate the festival with his mother and uncle. Dolours even volunteered to run her own business in tandem with his between Christmas and New Year, looking after the shop so that he could prolong his stay. Her motives were largely selfish. She knew if he came back he would go to the Bingley household for their big annual New Year party. But in any case, Henry had other ideas.

'It's very kind of you, Dolours, but as long as you keep things ticking over until the twenty-ninth, that will be fine. I'll come back and do the market run for the Saturday evening stint on the thirtieth – can't let you do that, the work's too heavy. Anyway, I have some invitations for New Year's Eve and I might want to accept one.'

And we all know which, she thought, bitterly.

So Dolours held her peace and Henry continued to develop his drawing room social life in Manchester. Even early on, though, he experienced moments of uncertainty. The Bingleys were so virtuous he found it hard to be interested in them, even with the inducement of becoming better acquainted with Alison's lustrous curls and alluring figure. They were all Temperance. Their pretended ignorance of Henry's liking for the odd glass of wine was a measure of their high esteem for him. But even with this concession, their overpowering religious enthusiasm could be hard to take. It extended to disapproval of any secular activity on Sundays, along with rejection of anyone who was not either a Nonconformist or very low church, evangelical Anglican. They were isolated, too, by their intense sense of social respectability. They fraternised with the poor only as objects of charity. They regarded anyone with cultural interests as snobbish, fast or superior. Although their social life was busy, it revolved around church, philanthropy, business and the families who occupied the other solid villas, carbon copies of their own, in a desirable south-western suburb of the city.

The New Year's party was a horribly jolly affair

featuring fruit punch, a fork supper and the sort of games Henry had given up before he reached the age of sixteen. Here, though, they were played enthusiastically by adults, who seemed to think themselves adventurous in merely acting charades with members of the opposite sex. After the charades came songs, inevitably in the same league as 'Lips that touch Liquor shall never touch Mine'.

But each time he grew bored, each time, even, that he thought of Anglesey and Myfanwy Owen, Henry had only to hear Alison's soft, acquiescent voice and see her winning smile to be ensnared again. He continued to shower attention on her. As winter turned to spring he began to consider inviting Alison and her parents to stay in Bangor with his mother. As soon as Dolours got wind of the plan, she knew she was about to lose him forever. Such a visit could only be the prelude to engagement and once that happened there would be no question of Henry continuing to live under the same roof as an unmarried female Irish street trader.

In late March she decided it was time for decisive action. Nothing could be worse than her present purgatory. Maybe if she altered her appearance it would make a difference . . .

Henry had been paying her minimal attention lately, but that evening, when she walked into the small living room at Sebastopol Terrace, he turned and stared at her.

'Why, Dolours, what's happened to you? What have you done to yourself?'

The change was certainly dramatic. She had teased and tortured her hair with heated curling tongs and had achieved an approximation of Alison Bingley's hairstyle with the aid of extra padding beneath her own tresses. Face powder concealed her freckles and the resulting intensification of her natural pallor was enlivened by rouge. Her lips, too, were redder and fuller than normal, but the primitive nature of her cosmetics made her look more like a French porcelain doll than a living girl. She had exchanged her simple cotton dress for a bright green gown of sprigged silk. It had cost every penny of her spare cash, but even so it was the cheapest silk available and therefore hung limply – particularly as it lacked the support of the four or even six flounced petticoats customarily worn by more prosperous girls.

Dolours' lively spirit and natural dignity shone through and prevented her from looking ridiculous, but could not stop her appearing pathetic. Along with petticoats, silk required a full bosom and well-rounded hips – or good whalebone simulations – to maximise its appeal. Dolours' stick-thin body seemed to shelter inside her gown rather than filling it. Saddest of all, she knew the whole thing was a mistake and it made her truculent.

'Done? That's very complimentary, I'm sure! I've smartened meself up, of course. Don't yer like it?'

'Well . . . er . . . that is . . . it's not quite you, somehow!'

'And who're you to know what's me and what isn't? Yer don't know the tiniest bit about me apart from how I earn me living. Since yer so curious, I'll tell yer. Some people seem to have forgotten I'm a girl at all. This is just to remind 'em!'

Instantly he was as aggressive as she. 'Has that damned Gilbert Smith been objectionable again? I'll break his neck if he's bothering you!'

She flared back. 'Hold yer horses! Gilbert treats me like a lady. It just so happens, *Mister* Richmond, he's been at me the past month to marry him, so there!'

'Oh no, Dolours. Don't throw yourself away on that man. He's born for trouble, and anyway, you're worth ten of him. Save yourself for someone worthy of your love . . .'

'I have – oh, Henry, believe me, boy, I have. But he can't seem ter see beyond me skimpy hair and freckles . . .'

And suddenly, he knew. Worse, he was too inexperienced either to conceal his belated discovery or to act as if her passion were welcome. She stood for long moments, gazing straight into his face and reading in his eyes the hopelessness of her dream.

Dolours brushed a single tear from her cheek and turned away from him, speaking high and fast. 'Ah well, Henry me boy, I'm already late.' As she finished she was already at the door. ' 'Bye, then.' And she was gone.

He cursed himself all that evening for his crassness. If it could have helped, he would gladly have pretended to find her attractive. More sensibly, given time he began realising he could have found a gentler way of letting her down. In any case, he was deeply ashamed and sat up half the night rehearsing an appropriately sympathetic confrontation with Dolours. He was wasting his time. She did not return.

Next day he waited in vain for her to come into the shop. During the dinner hour he had to see a trader in Rochdale Road who had some cheap fruit coming in. When he returned, he found a scribbled note on the kitchen table. It merely said: 'Henry, I think I'd better move on. Have taken the Cow and my things. Good luck. Dolours.'

'She can only just have gone,' he said aloud. 'Must have been waiting until I went out.' But the street outside was silent and empty. It was as though Dolours Kenny had never shared his shop and his life.

Often in the days that followed, Henry suppressed guilt at his failure to seek out Dolours. Of course she had made her own decision. But he had forced it on her to some extent, and she was his dearest friend. He wanted to see her secure and happy. But he was still enthralled by Alison Bingley and that week was a busy one, with all sorts of extra charity jobs for the Lamplighters. Then there was the letter to his mother, finalising arrangements for Alison's Easter visit which was now little more than a fortnight ahead. Almost before he realised, it was Saturday and he was doing the market run alone for the first time. He missed Dolours dreadfully, but he managed pretty well alone. The traders were all used to him now and knew the sort of produce he wanted and the price he was likely to pay. So Dolours was pushed into the background, not forgotten, exactly, but certainly not very often in his mind. Let her cool down, let the wound heal a little, he told himself. Then I'll find her somehow. Shouldn't be too hard. After the Easter holiday perhaps . . .

The visit to Bangor went well. Alison's mother accompanied her, but Mr Bingley, the owner of a modest-sized cotton mill, was kept in Manchester by business. Marged Richmond was less well off than her guests, but her confidence and self-possession impressed them deeply. Over the years of widowhood, as she built up Richmond's Quality Provisions, Marged had acquired an air of polish and assurance which neither Bingley female could quite match. Mrs Bingley was first generation money. Her father had been a small-town butcher. She had picked up the trimmings of her new social position, but they were not inbred, as she believed them to be with Marged. It was also obvious to Mrs Bingley that Henry Richmond was bound for better things. He might have only a modest inheritance now, but of all the young men who had shown serious interest in Alison, she knew instinctively that this was the one with the biggest future.

So Henry spent the holiday in comfortable surroundings, among refined people who enjoyed his company. It made the grim environment of Sebastopol Terrace seem even more drab and unattractive. Perhaps the time had come to discuss the next phase in his mother's strategy, to persuade her to win Idris over to a joint operation, and to recall Henry himself to Bangor to get things going. Now that his relationship with Alison was progressing so well, there seemed no point in hanging around Manchester. After all, it would be only a matter of weeks before he proposed to her.

His return to the city was every bit as bad as he had anticipated. Henry escorted Mrs Bingley and Alison back by train on Easter Sunday, and accompanied them home from the station in their carriage. It was a showery, blustery day and the streets were silent because of the holiday. It was pleasant enough, though, as they bowled along the quiet main streets out to the leafy suburbs. Depression only descended after tea when he returned by

122

omnibus to Rochdale Road then walked the few hundred yards to Sebastopol Terrace. As the suffocating drabness descended on him, he found himself cheered by the thought that Dolours would soon put a smile back on his face. Then he remembered – how could he have forgotten, even momentarily? – that she wouldn't be there. Perhaps she would . . . perhaps she'd had time to recover from the misery he'd caused her and she'd be waiting there for him to come back. He found himself increasing his pace in eagerness to see whether she had returned in spite of everything.

Only that sudden burst of speed got him back to the shop in time to catch a very different caller, who was on the point of going off in the opposite direction. Gilbert Smith had just dropped his hand from the door knocker and was turning away with an expression of despair on his gaunt face.

'Smith – what brings you here? What can I do for you?' A desire to treat him as well as Dolours might have wished made Henry's tone almost placating.

Resentment leaped into the other man's eyes, but for some reason he, too, managed to be courteous. 'Oh, hullo Richmond . . . I came on – on the off chance that you might have seen Dolours. Have you?'

'Me? No – she moved away from here weeks ago and I haven't heard from her since. She hasn't gone missing, has she?' As he spoke, Henry had been taking out his keys. 'Would you like to come inside?'

In the back living room, Smith explained. As he told his story, the courtesy slipped away rapidly. 'I won't ask what the row was about, I can guess. I do know she came to me a while ago, looking like some poor washed-out trollop, with her face all painted and wearing some cheap fancy gown. A fine girl like that deserves better, but she was in such a state I didn't go into that with her. She wouldn't tell me what had happened. Just sobbed and sobbed for nearly an hour and then said she'd left this damned place. She didn't need to ask for shelter . . . I'd been begging her to be my wife for months. She knew I wouldn't try anything –' here he glared at Henry, the stored-up hatred sparking in his eyes – 'and said she'd tell me what had happened, but not just yet. She made me promise not to ask questions. Of course I agreed. I'd do anything for her.'

'Well, at least she went to someone who cared for her,' replied Henry. 'Even I can see she's in safe hands with you, and as I've heard nothing from her since she left . . .'

Smith turned on him in rage. 'You unfeeling swine! I was dreading her being here, but at least she'd have been all right. If she's not with you, Christ knows where she's gone. I haven't seen her for nearly two weeks.'

Two weeks! Henry felt dread knotting up his stomach. 'What can we do? I'll help in any way I can. If necessary I'll close the shop and cancel all my other arrangements until she turns up.'

Gilbert made a visible effort and spoke civilly, despite his fury. 'A-all right. I suppose you mean her no harm. Trouble is, I'm not sure where we start.' He sat brooding for a moment, then said, 'I've got a few strange acquaintances around the city. I'll go and talk to them. Dolours isn't the sort of girl you can hide for long. As soon as I get any word, I'll contact you and we'll go after her.'

'Then take this money. Oh, come on, you stubborn

fool. Forget your precious dignity for a moment. And the minute you have word, get a cab and either send it for me or come in it yourself.'

'Very well,' Smith agreed. 'We'll have to bury our differences for now, just till we find her. I'll be back as soon as I can.'

Even with his network of contacts in the underworld of Manchester, it took Gilbert Smith nearly two days to make any progress. Late on Tuesday afternoon, a shabby hackney carriage clattered around the corner into Sebastopol Terrace. 'You a party named Richmond?' asked the driver, when a couple of street children had fetched Henry from the shop.

'Yes, yes – you're from Mr Smith, I take it. What message?'

'Says you're to close up and come along o' me into town. And don't expect to be back here till very late.'

'Five minutes – just wait. I'll close up and be with you then.'

Henry went back inside, hastily stripped off his brown shopman's overall and put on his jacket. From the strongbox in the back room he took ten gold sovereigns – emergency money given him by Marged when he first came to Manchester. He hung a 'Closed' sign on the shop door, unfolded and barred the shutters, then left, locking the main door behind him.

The cabbie headed into the city centre at a fast pace. After a while, Henry called out to him: 'Where are you taking me?'

'Edge of Irish Town.' The driver's distaste for the journey was almost tangible. 'The other gent wanted me to drop you right inside there, but I wasn't having none o' that. Taking you too close as it is!'

The official name of Irish Town was New Town, but the reality so belied this that the nickname had been universally adopted. It was not very far from the Rochdale Road area and Henry assumed that Gilbert Smith had used a hackney only because he thought they might need it to transport Dolours out of the place. The cab drew up at the junction of Shudehill and Miller's Street, where Smith was waiting.

Henry leaned out and called to him. 'Well, Smith, do I keep the cab or are we going on foot? D'you have her yet?'

The other man eyed him scornfully. 'If she was safe with me, d'you think I'd have wasted time and money sending for you? No, of course I don't have her here, but we've a chance of finding her. We'll need to keep the cab – I think we could be travelling further before we're done.'

Henry got down and paid the driver, giving him a handsome tip. 'Take a break on the strength of that,' he said. 'If you rest at the cabbies' shelter over there for the next hour, I'll see you get another tip as big as that on top of the fare for our next journey. Will you do it?'

'It's your money, sir.' The cab driver was too greedy to reject the retainer, but clearly had scant enthusiasm for the venture. He headed his rig towards the shelter. 'No more 'n an hour, mind. I'll be gone if you leave it after that.'

Henry turned to Smith. 'Well, what have you found out?'

Smith's expression was grimmer than ever. 'Nothing I

wanted to hear. Oh, God, why did the poor girl ever set eyes on you?'

Henry could see the man was near tears. He waited until Gilbert spoke again. 'Of all people, old May Treadgold ran into her the other day. May didn't know why Dolours hadn't been at the Ragged School for two Sundays running. She started lecturing Dolours, then noticed she looked worn out and softened up a little.

'It turned out that Dolours had disappeared because she was destitute herself.'

'What? But that's impossible! She was a clever buyer; she had The Cow and enough stock to keep herself afloat, even with the silly prices she charges.'

'You're wrong. Dolours can't exist in isolation. She pretends to be self-reliant and in some ways she is – more so than either of us. But she has that odd weakness you find with so many children of large families – she can't bear solitude. She has to have someone, however unsatisfactory. That's why she clung to that namby-pamby clergyman and his wife; come to that, it's why she persisted in being nice to me, even when I treated her boorishly at the beginning. And it's certainly why she fell in with you.

'I think she left my lodgings because she felt she was there under false pretences – she could be stupidly honourable over things like that – but she couldn't bear going into lodgings alone once more and starting from scratch without friends. So she did what only desperation would make her do – she went home to her mother!'

Henry shuddered. 'Oh, God, no! Surely . . .'

'Yes, surely, and now we're going right into the witch's den. And I can tell you, Mr high-and-mighty

Richmond, you'll see sights and smell smells you never knew existed. Come on, and when you feel an impulse to puke, just remember how much you owe Dolours.'

With that, Gilbert turned away and started striding into the warren of back streets off Shudehill. Stronger than he looked, he set a punishing pace. Struggling to keep up, Henry panted: 'But you still haven't explained . . . that is . . . what about her barrow and stocks and cash?'

'My God, you're even more stupid than you look! How long d'you think she'd hold on to any of that among such a bunch of thieves? When May Treadgold saw her, she'd already parted with the cash and produce, but she still had The Cow. I'd bet a cotton merchant's fortune they've found some use for that by now, even if only as firewood. You wait and see, by the time we find her she'll be lucky to have the clothes she was wearing when she talked to May!'

Irish Town stretched up a clay mound between the filthy River Irk and St George's Road. It looked nothing like part of an inner city. The single streets and small clusters of cheap houses rose out of the bare earth like so many separate villages, wretched on the grassless soil. The dwellings had been built as slums and had been neglected from the start. Most buildings had foul damp cellars, dug out by the landlords to enable them to pack in the maximum number of families. Lack of sewers and paved road surfaces made conditions bad enough, but the filth was rendered infinitely worse by the colonies of pigs kept by the residents. Some were penned up, but many roved free through the foul streets, feeding on rubbish and adding their droppings to the fetid piles of refuse. Behind Miller's Street the dwellings crowded into a series of square courts, entered by covered passages. Henry was already fighting nausea at the stench and the sight of the sort of people who were reduced to living in such surroundings. But there was worse to come.

Suddenly Gilbert Smith nudged him. 'In there – Samuel Court – that's where Ma Kenny lives.'

Henry recoiled. 'Smith – I – I don't think I can. The smell . . .'

'Come on, you bastard – if she's in there it's because of you!' And he shoved Henry roughly into the foul passageway.

Both passage and court were at least six inches lower than street level. It had not rained for a few days but stagnant pools still spread across the area, black and scummy and burdened with everything from human excrement to rotting rabbit and chicken guts. As they made their way out of the passage into the square court, a woman came out of one of the buildings and tipped a bucket of ashes into a huge puddle. She hawked and spat, then turned back into her foul home.

'I think,' said Smith with a certain grim relish, 'that the lady yonder is Mother Kenny. You'd better brace yourself – we're going in after her. One thing – how much money have you got?'

Even in this extremity, Henry's natural thrift asserted itself. 'How much do you need?'

Smith's contempt was mortifying. 'Oh, they come cheap around here. A couple of shillings will buy you a child, so Dolours shouldn't cost more than half a guinea!'

Biting back an indignant retort, Henry handed over

two half sovereigns from his pocket and one of the sovereigns from a pouch inside his belt.

'No need to knock.' Gilbert pushed open the buckled wooden door. 'No one would hear if we did.'

The chaos inside was indescribable. There was no artificial floor; the kitchen-living room rested on bare earth. Although this was obviously both the entrance hall and main living space, Mrs Kenny had still crammed in two beds at the back. To the side was a fireplace with a tiny coal range, covered with soot and grease to an extent where cooking would seem impossible. The staircase that rose beyond the beds was little better than a ladder with a handrail. The rickety table a couple of feet inside the door was scattered with scraps of bread, a few mutton bones and a battered tin cup. An equally battered-looking man was sitting at the table, drinking from a bottle of stout. The woman they had seen in the courtyard was standing near him, swigging at her own bottle.

'And who may you be when yer at home?' Her shrillness was heightened by the sudden appearance of two such respectable men. Without apparent effort, Smith fell into a manner which disarmed Mrs Kenny without patronising her. He rested a hand momentarily on the table and one of Henry's half-sovereigns appeared there as if by magic. The woman leaned over and picked it up before the ragged man had time to reach for it.

'Mrs Kenny? We're friends of your daughter Dolours,' said Gilbert. 'When she came back to live here, she said if we should ever want to look her up . . .'

It was the last thing on earth Dolours would have said and both men knew it. She would have fought like a wildcat to prevent her friends from seeing this squalid misery. But at least the friendly words, the placating tone, and above all the money soothed Mrs Kenny.

'Ach, it's a pity she don't stay in one place long enough to say hullo ter yer, then. Ungrateful slut's been gone since yesterday.'

Henry looked at the woman in disgust. Dolours was one of the older children, so her mother was probably no older than his own. She looked at least sixty. Her bare feet and her hands were caked with filth. Her hair might once have been blond, but now it was a tow-coloured mop, more like rags than natural growth. The top of her stained dress was open, partially baring slack, shrivelled breasts. Most of her teeth were gone and those that remained appeared rotten. Henry could not conceive how the fastidious Dolours could remain in the same room as this creature for more than five minutes. It seemed she had not stayed much longer . . . Through his shifting thoughts he became aware that Gilbert was cross-examining Ma Kenny with increasing urgency.

'But what made her go just then, Mrs Kenny? Please, we need to see her – you must tell us.'

'Well, it was the money, wasn't it?' The woman was indignant but defensive. 'She ran out o' the bunce fer her room.'

'But surely, your own daughter . . .' Henry was bewildered.

'Ah, don't give me that!' said Mrs Kenny. 'She was quick enough ter clear out when she got some fancy church friends. Didn't give a tinker's fer her family then. Well, when she come whining back here I told her, "Dolours, me girl, there ain't no freeloading here.

131

Yer've got ter pay yer keep.'' At first she was all right.
She give me good butter and eggs and such – fer me
boarders, y'know.'

Henry eyed the cooking range and made up his own
mind about that. The old crone had probably sold
Dolours' precious stocks.

'And after that it turned out the sly tart had some
money too. Well, that lasted a while and then she was
skint. Kept saying she'd make it up if she could just stock
up that stupid barrow of hers. Treated it like some treasure trove, until Fergus got hold of it.'

Gilbert Smith went paler than ever. 'What d'you
mean, got hold of it?'

'The boy meant no harm. He was making a fire out in
the court down the road –' she assumed a stage whisper – 'wanting to get rid of some bits and pieces before
the Peelers talked to him, yer know. Chopped it up fer
kindling 'cos he couldn't find nothing better. He left her
the sign board, mind. Well, when Dolours went out to
the pig shed ter see to it, he told her he'd took it and she
went crazy like. Started raving and ranting and screaming that now she'd never get another chance. Yer'd think
she owned the bliddy place, the way she went on. Any
road I told her. I said, "If yer causing this sort of
trouble, yer can go as soon as yer like. Yer not paying
nothing now and I'm buggered if I'll harbour a viper in
me bosom fer nothing!" ' She crossed her arms over her
scrawny chest and shrugged in righteous indignation.

Henry took over the interrogation. Clearly Gilbert
was on the point of hitting the woman. 'And what happened then?'

'Ach, the silly cow come over all funny. Puked all over

the yard and said she felt bad. I said there was no use her putting it on because I'd have none of it without payment for her board. When she pulled herself together she shoved her few bits and pieces into her bag, strapped that bliddy stupid signboard on the outside of it and went. And that's all I know.'

But Henry had caught the way she glanced again at the bright coin in her hand. There was something else . . . something that might lead them to Dolours.

He had palmed a couple more sovereigns from the belt pouch when he gave money to Smith. Now he dipped into his trousers pocket and produced one, holding it out between himself and the woman as he talked, apparently to himself. 'Now I wonder if anyone here would know where she went . . . I really will have to find her and it would be worth money to me if I could.' He raised his eyes and stared hard at Mrs Kenny.

She was gazing at the sovereign, almost slobbering with her lust for it. 'I – I did seem ter remember hearing something about where she'd be . . .' She reached towards the gold coin.

'Not yet, Mrs Kenny. I need to know more than that. Where, and who with?' He closed his fist around the money.

She was almost panting now. 'All right, all right – I'll tell yer, though I'll get no thanks fer it! Me eldest boy Dermot was here. Don't get on well with his ma, don't ask me why, but he always had a soft spot fer Dolours when she was home. He half killed me when she got took off by them holy joes, and he didn't stay here long himself after that. He reckoned Dolours wasn't putting it on. Said she really was sick and he'd take her back with him.

Daft bugger! Said there was three more cholera cases down by Ducie Bridge a couple of days ago.'

'Cholera!' Gilbert Smith was beside himself. 'Christ almighty, you stinking thieving bitch, if that girl dies I'll have your tripes! Where is she, dammit? Tell me before I kill you!'

He grabbed her filthy bodice and shook her like a terrier finishing off a rat. Neither Henry nor Mrs Kenny doubted that he meant what he said. She sobbed in terror but held fast to her half sovereign.

'No, let me go, don't touch me, sir! Honest, I didn't mean no harm! She's no more got cholera than you or me, sir! Look, let me go and let yer nice friend give me that gold sovereign and I'll tell yer.'

Gilbert let her go, but reluctantly.

'Right, now I'll tell yer. Me son's Dermot Kenny and he lives at Medlock Terrace. Now give me that sovereign, please, sir.' Her voice rose to whine.

But Henry was getting the hang of handling her. 'A little more information first, Mrs Kenny. Where exactly is Medlock Terrace?'

'Don't bother any more, Richmond.' Gilbert Smith's voice was leaden with despair. 'Medlock Terrace is in Little Ireland. It's a death trap. If Dolours was sick before she got there, she's likely dead by now.'

Bewildered, Henry handed Ma Kenny her money. 'Little Ireland? But isn't this . . .?'

'Irish *Town*, man! And wait till you see the difference.'

'You mean Little Ireland is worse than this?'

'If possible, yes. Every bit as foul and with twice as much disease. Come on. Let's see if it's too late.'

134

They were forced to bribe the cab-driver with a sum that equalled about four days' takings. Even then he would not guarantee to take them inside Little Ireland. 'What use is a lot of money if they've took me horse or worse?' he asked. 'Them ruffians don't know the difference between mine and your'n, and they've no intention of learning!' As he whipped up the horse and they cantered off south-westward, they could hear him muttering to himself through the hatch at the top of the hackney.

Little Ireland was scarcely more than a deep hole south-west of the Oxford Road, trapped in a curve of the River Medlock. Tall factories and other high-built industrial structures surrounded two hundred wretched back-to-back cottages which somehow managed to house more than four thousand people, mainly poor Irish immigrants. Again, the lack of drains and paving added to the squalor, with the usual standing pools choked with all sorts of refuse. The rank atmosphere was even worse than in Irish Town, thanks to the poisoned smoke from innumerable factory chimneys. The ruinous cottages were often without window frames, let alone glass. Old oilskins and scrap wood had been used to patch them against some of the weather. People filthier than the pigs which swarmed here too lurked in these terrible hovels. The standard building comprising two rooms, a garret and a cellar was home to around twenty people. Only one privy was provided for each six to eight houses, often inaccessible, generally blocked up and always foul. Human waste inevitably seeped through the ground and corrupted the already vulnerable water supply. Some people even used the Medlock for their water, which looked more like black oil than anything fit to drink.

Although the last officially-designated epidemic had occurred ten years before, households were frequently wiped out and twenty or thirty deaths in one street disturbed the authorities not at all. Little Ireland was hell on earth.

'Oh, God, Smith – it's inconceivable. How could she survive here? How can any man or woman survive here?'

'They have a choice, of course!' Even Smith's anguish about Dolours could not suppress his contempt for Henry's naivety. 'Like that Bingley family you see so much of. Their delightful residence is just a mile south of this spot. I'll suggest that all this lot move down there tomorrow, shall I?' Then, tired of baiting Henry, he asked a passer-by for directions.

'Kenny . . . Kenny, yer say? Sure, Dermot Kenny's got the cellar at number three. Don't knock his door too hard – ye'll bring the roof down on him!' The woman he'd accosted, unrecognisable as male or female until she spoke, cackled at her own drollery and gestured at a house a few yards away.

No door barred their passage. The foul room inside was nothing more than a succession of dreadful beds, two of them occupied by people who seemed too sick to hope for recovery. Clasping handkerchiefs over their noses and mouths, Henry and Gilbert struggled through the fetid place and located the rickety staircase which led down into the cellar. There, two flickering tallow candles cast flaring shadows against a dirt floor and damp-streaked walls – and against the ghastly face of Dolours Kenny.

Oblivious to his own safety, Gilbert Smith flung himself on his knees beside the straw mattress on which she lay, and clasped her hand. 'Oh Dolours, Dolours my love – what have they done to you?'

There was no response. She was alive, but unconscious. Her grey-white face was coated with a slick of sweat and she seemed to have shed every ounce of her meagre flesh. What remained was stretched skin, brittle bone and suffering. Her eyelids were closed but the eyes themselves thrust against the barrier of the gaunt, exposed skull, starting from their sockets. Her skin was covered with hideous blue-black blotches, where blood vessels had ruptured. The trembling hands which tugged fitfully at the sacking that covered her were like little claws.

'I – I did me best . . . there was nowhere else I could take her.' The soft, gentle voice came out of the gloom beyond the palliasse. Both men started at the sound. They had thought Dolours was alone. The figure that loomed at them hovered apologetically at the edge of the candles' light.

'Dermot . . . are you Dermot?' said Henry.

The young man murmured assent. 'Ma's a terrible cow. I couldn't let me one sister who mattered ter me stay in that thieves' kitchen.' He raised a huge hand. 'No, sir, don't say it, I know. What's so much better about this here thieves' kitchen? Not a lot, it's true. But at least I'm here ter look after her, and I found a bit of a decent sheet to stick under the sacking. And – and I bought some clean water from the carrier out by Oxford Road.' He gestured at the cracked jug and cup on the plywood box beside the mattress. 'And candles – and – and I haven't left her alone no more than five minutes.'

Henry patted the young man's shoulder. 'How long has she been like this?'

'Happened almost as soon as we got here and I reckon she only held on while we was travelling out through sheer willpower. Soon as I got her to the end of the street up there, she sort of folded up in me arms and I had ter carry her down. Y-yer know what it is?'

Henry had his fears, but dreaded naming them. Seeing his horror-sticken expression, Dermot nodded. 'Won't go away if yer don't say the word, sir. Cholera. It's took a dozen in Irish Town and Old Town this last few days and three down here since Monday. She had it when she come here, so don't yer go worrying this place will make her worse. It's in God's hands now whether she lives or dies.'

Filled with horror, Henry had to force himself not to scream out the advice Job's wife had dispensed in her husband's hour of extremity: Curse God, and die! Instead he patted Dermot again and turned to Gilbert. 'Any way to tell how she's doing?'

Smith raised a tear-streaked face. 'None. It can take them within eight hours, or a couple of days, or they can recover. But look at her, Richmond. How can we hope?'

Henry was forced to agree. The three men hovered around her for half an hour or so, then she stirred. The hideously altered eyelids flickered, then opened. She looked past Dermot and Gilbert, apparently not seeing them, gave Henry a radiant smile and whispered, 'Me dear, dear boy! Fancy seeing you . . .' Then the smile froze. 'Oh, Christ, but here! No, not here, it's horrible. Yer don't want to be here, a gentleman like you. Please, go – go quick, before yer come ter harm!'

Vainly she tried to struggle up. Gilbert took her gently by the shoulders and pressed her back into the stinking mattress. 'Now, lovey, now rest, please . . .' His voice was soft as a loving mother's, showing none of the pain her denial of his presence must have caused.

Murmuring feverishly, she slumped back, her tiny store of strength gone. Smith glanced up despairingly at Henry. 'What are our chances of moving her, Richmond? Are you game to try?'

Stifling his horror and disgust, Henry nodded, then asked: 'But how, and where? Is there a fever hospital that will take her? She's going to need better nursing than either you or I can provide.'

'Sorry, yes, you're right. I'm not so sure now that we can even risk moving her. But God knows, Richmond, she'd gladly suffer more if she could just die out of this foul place. What d'you think?' The simplicity of the other man's plea disarmed any practical, negative argument Henry might have produced. He knew his own horror of this filthy plague and these awful surroundings were what kept him from rushing to help Dolours. She would never last long enough for them to complete the formalities of signing her into a fever hospital, even if they could transport her there. Better give her comfort now.

He moved forward and knelt at the girl's side. 'Dolours. Dolours, my dearest, can you hear me?'

The grotesque eyelids fluttered again. She opened her eyes and managed the travesty of a smile. 'H-have yer come ter take me home, home ter Sebastopol Terrace?'

'I have. But you'll have to be brave and try to stay awake for a while. Gilbert is here with me, and your brother Dermot. We'll carry you upstairs between us and get you to a cab. Can you bear it?'

'Course I can, if yer with me.' The smile slipped. 'Only go out a minute. Please, Henry, go. Dermot knows what ter do! Please, I beg yer!'

Her brother nodded and gestured them towards the staircase. 'I'll call yer, don't worry.' He picked up a large chamber pot, covered with sacking, and bent to ease Dolours up into his arms so that she could crawl on to it.

When Dermot called them back to the cellar, Dolours was lying as still as a corpse. Smith glanced at her, then turned desperately to Dermot. 'Is she gone?'

The girl's brother smiled wearily and shook his head. 'Not yet sir, but each bout tires her a bit more. They says it's the runs what kills them. Dries them right up till they blow away like dead leaves . . . If yer can get more water in without making the runs worse, they stands a chance. Otherwise . . . That's why I been making her drink so much clean water, sir.'

'Quite right, Kenny, that was quite right. Look, we have a horse cab nearby, but the driver will never knowingly take a cholera victim. Is there anything I can wrap her in, anything respectable, that will stop him seeing her true condition and keep her warm at the same time?'

'Well, there's me one good blanket. I didn't put it on her because I knew it'd get soiled and I needed ter keep something ter put on her when she was getting better. Maybe now . . .'

'Splendid, man. Get it, please.' Henry took the thick brown wool blanket from Dermot. It was ideal – dark enough not to show any marks, neutral enough not to be an obvious wrapper for an invalid. They might just manage to hoodwink the cabbie.

They wrapped Dolours carefully in the blanket, first

140

putting the scrap of clean sheet around her shoulders and neck to prevent the blanket chafing her skin. Then Henry picked her up and headed for the stairs. It was easier than taking a bag of vegetables from the shop cellar. The girl's body was so wasted by sickness that she weighed next to nothing now. Gilbert walked ahead of him and Dermot was behind, both intent on assuring him a clear passage. When they reached the doorless doorway, Dolours opened her eyes briefly and moaned. Henry spontaneously kissed her forehead. She smiled and shut her eyes again. It was her last movement until they were inside the hackney carriage.

The cab driver proved less of an obstacle than they had expected. He had lurked around at one of the turnings off Oxford Road, half afraid they would try to cajole him inside the rookeries of Little Ireland with so much money that he would be forced to agree. When they approached without such a request, he was so relieved that his interest in Henry's burden was minimal.

Smith had assumed a familiar air and now engaged the cabby in murmured conversation. 'Be as tactful as you can, there's a good chap. My friend's sister went missing a few days back and . . . well, let's say that at least he's got her back. Time to forgive and forget, now, eh?' And he slipped another of Henry's half sovereigns to the driver, who nodded with a look that mixed sympathy with salaciousness. Meanwhile, Dermot Kenny was helping Henry get Dolours into the hackney without letting the blanket slip to reveal her condition. Once inside, Henry gave him the address of the shop, then they were away.

Half way back to Sebastopol Terrace, Dolours stirred

restlessly. Suddenly her eyes snapped open and she looked up at Henry, completely rational again. 'We're travelling! Where are we going, Henry? And Gilbert, too . . . I don't follow . . .'

'Hush, now, darling. We're taking you home to bed. Home to your nice little room in Sebastopol Terrace. Then you can relax in a clean bed and get well and strong again. How about that?'

'Ah, thanks, Henry . . . I knew I could rely on you ter look after me in the end . . .' Suddenly she was anxious. 'But wait – me Cow. I can't go without it – it's all I've got now until I get started again! Oh, please, where is it?'

Once again, it was the unthanked, unnoticed Gilbert Smith who provided comfort. Dermot Kenny had handed him a little panel of painted wood as he followed Henry into the cab. 'She seems ter think it's her good luck charm, sir,' said Dermot. 'Kept it by her in bed all the time she was ill. Don't keep it from her, will yer?'

Now he slipped the board into Dolours' fragile arms and she hugged it like a baby. 'I'll be all right, now, Henry. Once I'm well, we'll stock up The Cow again and I'll make both our fortunes, you'll see!'

She closed her eyes once more and the cab jogged on. By the time they reached Sebastopol Terrace she was still and quiet again. As the hackney jingled to a halt, Smith began to open the door.

'I'll pay the driver and go and get that Findlay woman from number thirty-nine. I know her from the charity hospital. She used to be a sick nurse. Meanwhile, get her in and up to bed. Hurry, man, for God's sake!'

The cabby drove off and Gilbert knocked at Mrs Findlay's front door. Henry carried Dolours into the darkened shop, then through to the back staircase. As they reached the top landing outside her old room, the Cow sign slipped from her blanket wrapping and clattered to the floor. Henry glanced at her, words of reassurance springing to his lips. They were unnecessary. Smiling, Dolours Kenny had died in the arms of her one true love.

Henry paid for her funeral. She was laid out in her old bedroom at Sebastopol Terrace, and it was from there that they took her to the burial ground three days later. From the night of her death until the funeral and long after, Henry was swamped by guilt. It was not simply the knowledge that if he had been perceptive enough to guess she loved him, or even to have reacted more tactfully when he finally realised it, he might have prevented the tragedy; he had a blacker secret. Once he had laid her on the narrow bed and given her a farewell kiss, he fell to wondering whether there might be some way he could have caught the dreadful disease. He tried to push aside the thought but it kept surfacing, first nagging quietly, then insisting on a confrontation and finally tormenting him with a certainty that he, too, was doomed.

Life was still black and white for Henry. He had yet to learn that most people's consciences and actions originate in a grey area where there is neither great virtue nor great evil. Even as the terror gripped him, he despised himself for his cowardice, but it did not make the terror go away. He managed to control himself until Mrs Findlay arrived with Gilbert Smith. When Gilbert heard the news, he uttered an animal wail and rushed up the stairs. They heard a thud as he flung himself down beside the bed that was now a bier. For a long time they heard him begging Dolours to be alive, and moving about desperately to try and contain his grief. When they followed him upstairs, he was sitting on the edge of the bed, holding her in his arms.

'She can't be dead, not my Dolours! She wouldn't give up this easily, not just . . . slip away . . .' His voice tailed off and his eyes became almost vacant as he turned back to his lost love.

Mrs Findlay was an old hand at such encounters. She eased Henry aside and moved into the cramped room, where she bent over the gruesome tableau and began talking, soft and slow, to the weeping man. After a few minutes, she managed to get the girl's body out of his arms and to make him stand. Carefully laying Dolours back on the pillow, she turned her attention to the living again.

'Come on, now, Mr Smith. I think you and Mr Richmond will be better off going downstairs and having a good big tot of brandy or whisky. Then one of you had better go and tell the Sanitary. I've seen enough cholera deaths in me time to know another one. They'll have to be notified – it's the law. If one of you will do that, I'll see to this poor child.'

Henry took Gilbert down to the living room. After he had poured each of them a big drink, he said: 'You don't look as if you'd get two hundred yards at the moment. I'll go and tell the authorities. No need for you to worry.'

Smith looked at him like a man who had just come back from a long journey – detached from his new surroundings but nevertheless aware of all that was going on. 'What are you talking about? It's after midnight. There'll be no one at the town hall until eight in the morning. You can't do a thing until then.'

Henry wished he could have gone. His terror was mounting almost unchecked now, and he was waiting for Gilbert to make matters worse by blaming him for the whole mess. He need not have worried. Smith was too far submerged in his private grief to care about Henry's part in things. He gulped his drink and Henry poured him another. Then Smith rose unsteadily.

'You're with her now – that's what she'd have wanted. I'll not cramp your style now any more than she let me then. I'll be back tomorrow, Mrs Findlay will be able to help with the nuts and bolts. They're used to sudden death in these parts.' And he walked off, out through the darkened shop and into the night.

It took Mrs Findlay an hour or more to lay out Dolours' corpse. Periodically she came and asked Henry for clean linen, water, soap and other things. Finally she came to the top of the staircase and called down, 'You can come up and see her now, Mr Richmond. It's all right, nothing to worry you.'

Oh no, thought Henry just a life-long reminder that a girl died because of her love for me. I can't go up there can't . . . On the point of rushing headlong out of the building, he managed to control himself. At least he could do this one last thing for her, go to her and take a loving farewell. He turned and mounted the staircase to the little room.

He took no comfort from the sight that awaited him. There was still a smile on the familiar, pinched face, now so ravaged by disease. Mrs Findlay had bound Dolours' jaw with a handkerchief to prevent it from sagging, and had put a clean white nightgown on her. A white sheet covered her from breast to feet, and the large flap left at the top was obviously to be pulled up over her face once Henry had visited the bedroom. Strange, he thought. An hour ago I was carrying her and kissing her. Now I'm in a funk at even being in this room with her. I can't touch her again – can't, God help me. Instead he stood mutely over the tiny shrunken figure for a few minutes, then turned away and went downstairs again.

The sights Henry saw on the night of Dolours' death would have turned some young men into red-hot reformers who spent all their spare time trying to improve the lives of the urban poor. But Henry Richmond was not some young men. Waking and sleeping, he was haunted by the images of filth, disease and deprivation. When he was finally alone that night, he had stripped, burned all his clothes and scrubbed himself from top to toe in the tin bath which was kept outside in the small wash-house. Even his stout leather boots were consigned to the flames. The locals will think I'm making a funeral pyre in the yard, he thought grimly as he watched the thick smoke curl up from the pile of clothing.

Once the funeral was past, he lit another fire and burned everything that had been in Dolours' room, feeling wretched as he did so. Then he went to see Alison Bingley for the first time in a week. He cooked up a story about having been unwell and having to catch up with a backlog of work at the shop. Finally, he announced that, much to his regret, it would be impossible for him to devote any time to charitable work in the foreseeable future.

The Bingleys responded surprisingly well. Instead of moralising as he had expected, Mr Bingley made some sententious remarks about the desirability of setting one's personal finances in order before casting one's bread on the waters. Alison and Mrs Bingley apparently agreed wholeheartedly with him.

'I told you the evening we met, very few young men of your calibre come on charitable ventures,' said Alison. 'That's why I was so surprised to meet you there. It's all very well for people like that half-baked Mr Pratt, who have no ambition, but for someone with everything to gain . . .' Her tone made it quite clear that she admired Henry's new single-mindedness rather than Pratt's altruism.

Back at the shop, Henry struggled to understand himself. He should have been pleased that the young woman he admired agreed fully with his enlightened self-interest. Why, then, should he feel faint contempt for both her and himself? Less than a month ago, he had regarded Alison Bingley as all that was desirable in virtuous womanhood. Suddenly he found the prospect of a future with her almost repellent.

Then the nightmares started. They were all variations on the same theme. He was back in Irish Town or Little Ireland, hurrying alone through dark, stinking alleyways where grotesquely deformed, diseased figures occasionally lurched at him from the foul blackness. He was not searching for something; he was trying to escape. But he had no idea what he was running from. By the time he woke, sweating and crying, the creatures from the darkness had started reaching out to touch him, to pull him back into their terrible world. He never saw anyone he knew in these nightmares, but often the anonymous faces were hideously blotched with the black cholera spots which had disfigured Dolours at the end.

The dreams became so bad and so frequent, Henry wished for sleepless nights. But he was working hard to keep the shabby store and house bright and clean, and at the end of each day he dozed off all too easily. He attempted to banish the night-time images by spending more and more time at the Bingley household. That merely bored him and added to his growing conviction that he must free himself from Alison. But he was so weighed down with weariness and anxiety about the dreams, as well as guilty grief for Dolours, that he lacked the vitality to extricate himself.

The shop had been exploited as far as possible. It was profitable now, but would never be worth maintaining as a real business interest. Had he been less depressed, Henry would have developed ideas which had been taking root in his first months, about running a group of such places to take advantage of cheap market prices. But his state of mind eliminated any initiative beyond keeping up the daily round. His black mood lasted through the summer, increasingly turning him away from social activity. In August, Idris insisted on relieving him for a week so that Henry could spend a few days with his mother in Bangor. He had alerted Marged to the boy's depressed state, although he had no idea of its cause. He had noted that Dolours was no longer around, but Henry had already said back at Easter that the girl had left Sebastopol Terrace, so Idris attached no importance to the matter.

When Marged saw Henry, for the first time in four

months, she was horrified. He had lost over a stone in weight, there were shadows under his eyes, and his former air of quiet self-sufficiency had vanished. Instead he was nervous and uneasy, starting at every unexpected sound and unable to concentrate for more than a few minutes at a time. Never one to act on impulse, Marged merely saw to it that he got plenty of attention while he was at home, and bided her time until Idris returned the following Saturday. He would be in Bangor for the last day of Henry's visit, leaving the shop closed for forty-eight hours. As soon as she got him alone, Marged pounced.

'What in the name of faith has happened to my son?' Her tone was so ferocious that Idris had to fight an impulse to hide behind the piano.

'Wh-why, nothing that I know of . . . what seems to be wrong?'

'Haven't you got eyes, Idris? He looks like a sick dog! All the fizz has gone out of him and I don't think he'll ever laugh again. I know the shop was my idea, but if it's doing this to him, the sooner he's out of it, the better!'

'But boys of that age go through those sort of ups and downs, surely?' Idris replied.

'Not unless they've got consumption, they don't. He's coming back, but we'd better think up a way of doing it that doesn't make him feel obliged to stay there and prove what a great success he is!'

'That should be easy enough. I know it'll never be a gold mine, but this last ten months that shop's showed a steady profit, and it's the first time that's ever happened.'

'Right, then: I'll say we only ever saw it as a one-year

job, and tell him to start organising himself to leave at the end of September. Pity we couldn't give him a stronger reason for moving on so soon.'

Idris turned thoughtful. 'Well, there is one possibility . . . There's a woman, a Mrs Findlay, lives a few doors on from the shop. Very reliable type, she is – used to be a sort of midwife cum sick nurse. Her husband's always had steady jobs in the cotton mills. He was lucky enough to be given a bit of compensation a couple of months back when his arm was smashed up in a mill accident . . .'

Marged's impatience was showing. 'Get to it, then, Idris. Surely you don't think a woman can manage that shop for you to make up her man's lost wages, and look after him in her spare time?'

'No, it's not like that. He's up and about again – very brave, tough chap. She wants to use the money to get them some sort of income, because he can work, but not in a mill or factory. At the beginning of July she asked me if I would be interested in taking the money as a deposit on the shop and stock.'

'There now,' Marged was suddenly a different woman, 'I think that could be very promising. You wouldn't lose much, and Henry could be told it was as much a charitable act as a useful way of ending his spell there. When can you see her?'

'Steady, girl. I haven't thought it through yet.'

'Seems to me there's nothing to think about. If Henry hadn't gone to run it, you'd probably have been forced to board up the shop and rent off the house for pennies to some impoverished family. At least now it's a going concern.'

And before Idris could come up with any objections, the matter was settled. Almost as though it were just a postscript, Marged even managed to insinuate her son into his main business.

'Of course, if we're bringing him back here, we'll have to give him a man's work to do. Can't just put him back in the High Street with George Beynon. I've been thinking for some time, Idris, wouldn't it strengthen both our interests if we merged your wholesale and my retail business into one?'

He was thunderstruck. He had always vaguely assumed he would one day leave the wholesale concern to Henry on his own retirement or death; but now, when he was still a vigorous middle-aged man? He quickly forgot his misgivings, though. Marged exercised every ounce of her charm to convince him that such a change would enrich them both. By the end of the evening he had agreed that they would get a legal partnership drawn up and that Henry should join him on quitting Manchester six weeks hence. It only remained to tell the boy that his exile in the city's back streets was coming to an end.

As Idris departed for his own house, another thought struck him. 'Marged, I'm sorry to raise such a distasteful matter, but you haven't forgotten, have you, why you really sent Henry to Manchester in the first place?'

'I couldn't forget that in fifty years, as you should be well aware.'

'Yes, but how d'you think Henry will react? Have you told him anything?'

Anxiety made Marged sharper than ever. 'No – and it's not necessary. When Henry decided that he'd made a mistake with that Owen girl, he made me a promise. If I saw to it that she didn't suffer by his behaviour, he would never ask about her or try to contact her again. I have no reason to doubt his word.'

'But this isn't London! How long d'you think it will be before they bump into each other?'

'It's a condition of her annuity that she doesn't go anywhere near him – she loses her income if she does.'

'And what if – what if he sees the baby?'

She flushed. 'As far as I'm aware, five-month-old boys don't look much like anyone. We'll just have to see their paths don't cross, that's all. Maybe I should express greater enthusiasm about his interest in this Bingley girl. That would take his mind off old flames . . .'

# Chapter Five

Marged's about-turn over the shop made Henry more confused than ever. He knew he wanted to leave Manchester, but he was unsure whether North Wales was the right place for him either, and above all he was dubious about his mother's sudden enthusiasm for his relationship with Alison. For the moment, though, there was no fight left in him. Bangor was a haven compared with Sebastopol Terrace, and if the price of his release was an attempt to re-capture his former closeness to Alison, he was willing at least to try it. After all, he told himself glumly, I haven't asked her to marry me yet, so I still have a chance to escape . . .

Within a week of his visit to Bangor, he began to feel better. The dreams still ravaged him, but he had a feeling they would disappear once he left the scene of all his misery. He continued to see Alison once or twice a week, attending concerts or improving lectures with her and Mrs Bingley, and going to tea with the family on Sundays. As Henry's mental health improved, he even managed to re-kindle his enthusiasm for Alison. After all, she was still deliciously pretty, and if she were a little boring now, that could be changed when she was separated from her stuffy parents. This was his frame of mind when he eventually packed his few belongings at Sebastopol Terrace, locked up for the last time and delivered the keys to Mrs Findlay, shortly to become proud owner of the business. Now he was off to Bangor for good, first for a short rest, then to start setting up the new partnership with Uncle Idris. In October, Alison Bingley would visit for a week and it was assumed by her mother and his own that he would propose during her stay.

The annual autumn horse fair at Menai Bridge had been a high point of Henry's childhood, along with Christmas and birthdays. It was years since he had been to one. The event was more like one of the great medieval fairs than the glorified modern market that such terms nowadays suggested. Farmers from all over the Isle of Anglesey and from mainland areas as far away as Lleyn and St Asaph, brought their best and worst animals to sell there. Such profitable business inevitably attracted colourful hangers-on, anxious to separate the horse dealers from some of their recently-acquired cash. The fringe attractions ranged from ordinary fruit and vegetable stalls, cheesemongers and butchers, through all the normal and exotic household wares, to such desirable fripperies as toffee apples, velvet hair ribbons, Staffordshire dogs, straw bonnets and leather clogs. Hellfire preachers threatened dire consequences to those tempted by small scale gambling games or by the gimcrack travelling theatre with its garish scenery and bedraggled players. Badly-sighted rifles cracked as farmers took their turn at the handful of shooting galleries and consistently failed to hit the mechanical ducks. For one glorious week the streets were closed to traffic in the little village at the foot of Telford's suspension bridge, and the bright fairground booths took the place of vehicles.

Every year until he departed for boarding school, Marged had taken Henry to the fair. He was nonplussed, therefore, when she responded coldly to his suggestion that they take the Bingley womenfolk this year.

'I hardly think either Mrs Bingley or Alison would find that load of ruffians an edifying sight,' she said with a contemptuous sniff.

'Oh, surely not?' Alison was audibly disappointed. 'Henry's been telling us all about it and it sounds quite wonderful. After all, it's not as if these country people are really rough, like in Manchester.'

'Of course not!' Henry's tone was particularly forceful because forty-eight hours of undiluted small-talk from Mrs Bingley had proved wearing. He was desperate for some new topic, and the fair had seemed a golden opportunity to create one. 'Come along, Mother, if you could take an eight-year-old boy there, I'm sure it's fit for two grown-up ladies.'

'Your Uncle Idris always came with us. Otherwise I wouldn't have dreamed of it.' Seeing the weakness of that argument, she fell silent, but Henry pounced.

'And now I shall be with you – and I'm taller than Uncle Idris, and at least as strong, so where does that leave you?'

Beaten, it seems, thought Marged. Anyhow, I'm probably being silly. Just because he hasn't set foot on Anglesey since I prised him away from that girl, doesn't mean there's any chance of him bumping into her the first time he goes there. He'll have to cross that bridge sooner or later when he works with Idris. She's probably got her hands full down at Llanddona with that brat of hers. Realising she had been wool-gathering, she managed a smile. 'Very well, Henry. If you feel confident of escorting us safely, I suppose we have to bow to your wishes. Perhaps Friday? How would that suit you? It should provide a good finale to our guests' visit.'

'Splendid. I look forward to it.' Inwardly, though, Henry was exasperated. Friday was three days away. The week stretched ahead, full of sterile chats about chapel socials and improving books. He'd be dead of boredom by then.

Unexpectedly, Alison saved the day. Although it was rather unorthodox to allow a young lady out unchaperoned with a single man, Mrs Bingley was sufficiently confident of Henry's intentions to relax restrictions a little. So it was that they took a stroll together next morning, along the Holyhead Road just beyond the house at Menai View.

Alison sighed as they looked down on the glorious seaside panorama below. 'Ah, it's so lovely – and the fair is so picturesque! Look, you can see the colours of all the striped awnings from here.'

Sure enough, a scattering of booths spilled over from the high street down a patch of open ground towards the narrow channel of the straits. The sparkling morning sunshine caught the candy colours of their canvas. Somewhere beyond, the wheezing of a steam organ could be heard, and it was hard not to imagine a mingled smell of burnt sugar, fried herring and new ale wafting across the water.

She turned to Henry, eyes sparkling. Instantly he saw

again what had first attracted him to her. 'Couldn't we just take a peep at it this afternoon? I'm sure it wouldn't be too outrageous if they know you're escorting me, and we could have a sort of foretaste of everything before the proper visit.'

It was exactly what Henry wanted, although the thought quite escaped him that possibly Alison had made her suggestion with the idea of being alone with him and encouraging a proposal. Rose-decked arbours were not the only romantic locations which would turn a young man's fancy to thoughts of holy matrimony.

Hence the lack of opposition from Mrs Bingley. Marged might have reacted differently, but she was down at the shop checking up on how well a new type of coffee bean was selling. Henry had driven her down in the trap that morning, bringing it straight back in case the guests wished to be taken out. Idris was away all day on a buying trip.

The fair really started getting into its stride after two o'clock. The mornings were the time for real business – buying and selling of horses. After deals had been made, the traders and farmers sold on a handshake, then went off to one of the numerous public houses to seal the transaction over a drink. By the time they emerged, they were ready to watch the primitive variety sketches, shoot at the tin ducks or buy ribbons for their sweethearts. Henry and Alison arrived at three. She was thrilled at the sights, smells and sounds, giggling as the steam organ puffed its accompaniment to a roundabout ride for children, throwing refinement to the winds as she bit messily into a huge toffee apple. Henry flung wooden balls at coconuts in wobbly cups, and received a pair of china dogs when he unexpectedly knocked down three. As they walked away with their booty, the stallholder was irritably manipulating the snapped screw which had been intended to prevent the third nut from ever being dislodged.

They had been at the fair a good hour when they came to a narrow lane of tents and stalls, one selling Bristol glass, another some disgusting quack cure-all elixir, a third cheap paste jewellery. 'Nothing interesting down there – look, I think they've got a fire-eater up this way!' But before Henry could head back up to the square, Alison plucked at his sleeve.

'Oh, do wait a minute – I must go to that one at the far end – look! Please, Henry – Mama would never let me do something like that and I've always wanted to!'

Surprised at her intense animation, Henry turned back and looked at the booth which excited her so. The canvas was striped in dark red and black and the structure looked almost like the little pavilions in pictures of medieval tournaments. Above the closed door flap hung an ornate painted banner, with the signs of the zodiac weaving in and out of the legend

MADAM M, THE ALL-SEEING
LEARN THE MYSTERIES OF YOUR PAST
AND FUTURE
TAROT PALMISTRY CRYSTAL GAZING

'What, no chicken's entrails?' Henry was scathing. Fancy caring what some draggle-tail fairground trollop would make up if you crossed her dirty palm with silver! Beneath his hostile response, unease was stirring. What

158

was it about the feel of the place? Where had he smelled that combination of spice and formaldehyde before? Whatever it was, he didn't like it. 'Come on, Alison. Your mother would be furious with me if I let you go off on a thing like that.'

'But not if she never knew! Oh, go on, Henry, don't be stuffy! Me first, then you. Please!'

It was the accusation of stuffiness that did it. Good God, talk about the pot calling the kettle black! How about her own kith and kin if she was thinking along those lines? But it stung him into granting her wish. He'd show her who was stuffy and who wasn't. 'Very well. See for yourself what sort of fraud she is. Probably a tooth-less harridan with a gypsy head scarf and some amber beads, but have it your own way.'

They approached the booth. Alison, now free to embark on her adventure, was suddenly nervous. 'Ooh, what if she tells me lots of frightening things? What if –'

'Listen, you're the one who wants to go in. Now make up your mind. Fortune or fire eater?'

'All right, but you have to promise you'll go in straight after me.'

'Anything to get us back up to the square before every-one goes home!' And he held back the tent flap for Alison to enter alone.

It was a sort of ante-room, only a couple of feet across, occupied by a skinny old woman in a shapeless, vaguely eastern robe, seated on a thoroughly ordinary kitchen chair.

'Madam M?' said Alison, disappointment hovering around the question.

The woman's face was inscrutable. 'Her handmaid,'

she said in a sonorous tone. 'I introduce the seekers to her presence –' she glanced at Henry – 'but only one at a time, see?'

Alison stifled a giggle at the old girl's decidedly un-eastern accent, and Henry backed out into the fairway. 'All right, you have her all to yourself. I'll look at the glass stall for a few minutes.' He left as the woman ushered Alison into the inner sanctum.

She was gone longer than he expected. The golden autumn sunlight was fading as he turned back towards the tent from the top of the little alley. As he got to the outer flap, Alison emerged.

'Well, satisfied? Has she told you how many mysteri-ous voyages and tall dark strangers your future holds?' Then he saw her expression and stopped his banter. 'Alison – are you all right?'

She seemed to return from some remote place, with a sudden start. 'Oh, Henry! You startled me. It . . . it was so strange, not at all what I expected . . . I don't think I liked it. She's odd, somehow.'

He laughed, determined not to take the matter seri-ously. 'Oh, really, surely you're not taken in by all that hocus-pocus? Look at the place! Look at her assistant. They're charlatans!'

'Sshh – they might hear you! No, it's not that. I-it's her. Don't take any notice of the old woman. *She's* the one.'

'What on earth did she say to you?'

'I'd rather not say just now. Maybe some time, but it's private, just for me, at the moment.'

'Very well, then – I'll go and take my turn there and we shall see what nonsense she tells me. Then perhaps you'll realise that such patter shouldn't be taken seriously. Will you be all right here alone?'

'I know this is silly, but I think I shall go up to the end. I can see the fire-eater from there without getting mixed up with the crowd. I know I'm being a bit much, but I have this awful feeling that if I stand too close out here she'll . . . draw me back somehow.'

'All right, off you go, you goose. No wonder your mother warns you off this sort of thing if you take it so seriously!' She retreated and he twitched aside the tent flap irritably, ready to tick off this stupid crone for frightening his young lady.

The little stuffed crocodile should have given away her identity. There could hardly have been two of them on this provincial island. Perhaps Henry did not remember because he was afraid to. But as he confronted Madam M across the crystal ball, he had no choice. She wore loose robes like her attendant outside, but on her they seemed appropriate. The lower part of her face was covered by a sequinned muslin yashmak, but even Henry's personal defence mechanism could not rid him of the memory of those eyes. Pale, translucent and deadly, they gazed levelly at him across the tiny space inside the tent.

'Myfanwy! What are you doing here?' It was an inane question, but his brain seemed beyond anything better.

'D'you think the world ends when Mr Richmond turns the other way?' It was a sibilant whisper, laden with emotion, but whether that emotion was malice, elation or fury was impossible to tell. He took refuge in bluster.

'Why did you frighten the young lady who was just in here? What did you say to her?'

161

The yashmak prevented him from seeing whether she smiled. 'Nothing intended to concern you. After all, I didn't know you was with her, or that you even knew her, did I?'

'I don't believe you! She's scared stiff. It must have been something beyond the usual fortune teller's clap-trap.'

'I never tell anything but what I see when I'm doing this. Of course, you wouldn't know that, because you never hung around long enough to find out. I did tell you I could see the future.'

'Oh, please, Myfanwy, not that nonsense again. I tried to be polite about it before, but you must know yourself there's nothing in it.'

That seemed to touch a chord. The sibilant voice became bitter. 'Yes, I suppose from that one time, no one should know better . . . but the purpose of it all is often hidden and that thread isn't spun out yet, by any means . . .' the voice became lighter '. . . no, not by any means.'

'Enough of this! Look, I've told that poor girl I shall make you predict my future and tell her the gist of what you say, just to prove she needn't worry about whatever it was you told her. So the least you can do is give me some of the standard patter to help me calm her down. Quick, let's get on with it!'

Now there was open contempt in the fine eyes. 'How long is it – nearly sixteen months – since you disappeared without a word? Is this the best you can ask when you see me again, after all that tender talk when you was after your own way? Some man!'

He was slightly shame-faced, but ready to defend

himself. 'I – I made a promise in exchange for a promise, to someone who could have been badly hurt. I knew you'd not have to suffer because of me.'

She laughed, but there was no warmth in the sound. 'Depends what you mean by suffering, man. I didn't starve, no. But it was all up with me after you deserted me. Nothing will matter again, not like that.'

'But you must have realised there couldn't really be a future for us together?'

Finally her coolness deserted her. 'That's why it hurt me so, you fool! There *was* a future together, there was! My Sight told me, and it's never been wrong, never!'

'Well it is now, Myfanwy, and the sooner you accept it, the better. Look, are you going to come up with some mumbo-jumbo for me to give to Alison, or should I just leave and try making it up myself?'

As he spoke, she retreated again into her Madam M role. By the time he fell silent, she was quite impersonal. 'Cards, or palm, or crystal?' She said tonelessly.

'I really don't know – does it matter? Oh, crystal. It sounds as if the cards could take hours.'

The lambent pale blue eyes left his for the first time and she looked down into the little solid glass sphere sitting before her on its ebony stand. Her gaze was so concentrated she might have been alone. The silence grew longer and Henry was on the point of breaking it when she began to speak, high but softly and as if she were far away.

'Different . . . so different . . . but still true . . . You'll clutch for the world, but the part you want will evade you. Always one jump away . . . always beyond your grasp. Poor Henry. Plenty of money. Not much love, though. Oh, no, not much . . . And plenty of children. But what a mess! Our children will found a fortune over the seas. They will, you know, just as I told you, but not the way I thought at first . . . Your dream will always elude you. Second best is all you'll get, and not for very long . . .'

The disjointed soliloquy ended, and Myfanwy appeared to emerge from a trance. She raised her hand and removed the yashmak. Her smile was almost demonic. She leaned forward across the little table. 'You ruined me, Henry, but at least I've the comfort of knowing it'll do you no good! Every time you get what you want, remember, it will never be quite what you imagine. And that tribe of children you should never have fathered . . . they're doomed, too; doomed by your treachery to me! If you'd only cleaved to me, all would have been well, but I'll be avenged . . .'

Henry stood up. The warm air inside the tent was stifling. The ancient odours that had teased his memory were overpowering in here. Myfanwy seemed remote, sneering at him beyond a fog of tragedy. Thrusting wildly at the table, he lunged away, almost knocking over the old woman outside. Beyond the entrance, he stood for long moments, head back, gulping down crisp autumnal air.

God, was it still only afternoon? Inside it had felt like midnight, and as though he had been locked in for hours with that vampire of a girl. Only partially recovered, he started to stride away. When Alison snatched at his arm as he strode out of the alley of tents, he was taken by surprise.

'Henry, what on earth is wrong? You look quite ill!'

He forced himself to stop and collect his wits. 'Alison, ah, I'm not too good, actually.' He managed a horribly high-pitched laugh. 'Didn't you find that odour inside frightful? It quite fogged up my brain!'

She shook her head. 'I didn't notice any smell. Are you sure she didn't disturb you, too?'

He laughed again, this time, he hoped, dismissively. 'Oh, that was a waste of time, I'm afraid! She turned out to be a dreadful female I vaguely knew. She gave my mother a lot of trouble last year – some petty grudge or other – I expect she saw you arriving with me and decided to frighten you as a revenge. It – it might be better if you don't mention it to Mama. It would worry her frightfully if she knew you'd been upset because of a private matter of her own.'

Alison sniffed. 'As for that – you know I can't tell, because my own mama would be livid if she knew what I'd done. But really, Henry, I can't believe she was making it up. Why, she said things I've never mentioned . . .' Now it was her turn to show confusion. She realised she could not possibly tell Henry any of the things Madam M had said about her own hopes and fears, because it all made her sound like some predatory animal, stalking the forest looking for likely mates. Not even Mama knew some of those thoughts.

They stood facing each other, each embarrassed by different thoughts, neither able to confess what bothered them. After a full minute or more of silence, Henry forced himself to break the near-trance. 'Come on, young woman!' His tone was all forced heartiness. 'It looks as if the fire-eater's about to do a second performance. Let's get to the centre of things and see if we can spot how he does it!'

In the little tent down the remote alley, the old woman stuck her head through the flap to the inner compartment. 'Myfanwy, love, that man went off without paying. Tried to stop him, but he nearly pushed me over. I'm awful sorry!'

The girl gestured listlessly. 'Don't worry, Auntie, I didn't think he would have done . . . too much bad news.'

At that, her companion came right inside and hovered around her, as though steeling herself to say something unwelcome. 'Look, I know you do take them prophecies serious, but if you're going to make a bit of money out of it, couldn't you . . . er . . . soften them, like, so's the customers wouldn't rush off like that? You could starve.'

That raised a small smile from Myfanwy. 'It's all right, Auntie Meg, I shan't starve. I've always got that Judas money coming in regular from Her, haven't I? Anyway, even if I did go short, I'd have to tell them all the truth. Couldn't pretend I saw things I didn't, could I?'

'If it's such bad news, perhaps you should – well – water it down a bit, without actually lying.'

Myfanwy got up and started to change out of her robes. 'Let's just leave it. I'm tired, tired of being a freak and tired of not belonging. But most of all I'm tired of this bloody old tent. Come on, we'll close up and go. We can't leave Beuno with your kitchen girl forever.'

A few minutes later, she laced the front flap of the booth and attached a big 'Closed' notice. Nondescript in their ordinary clothes, the two women walked down to the harbour and put their small boat out into the straits, taking advantage of the fast-rising tide to hurry their journey back to Llanddona.

Myfanwy spent a restless night. A lot had happened in the year and more since she had last seen Henry Richmond. She had been savagely hurt, but with so much going on she had managed to stifle the ache of losing him. The sight of him at Menai Bridge that afternoon, particularly in the few carefree seconds before he realised who she was, had driven home the pain like a hammer blow.

She had suspected she was pregnant within a couple of weeks of their rendezvous at Llanddona beach. At first she put down his lengthening absence from Llangefni to pressure of business. Then it grew too long for such an excuse – and she became even surer that she was carrying his child. That was when she took to sailing down the straits late at night and standing below his windows on the Holyhead Road, willing him to look out, see her and come to her. She had been back there at least five times before someone did join her from the house. But it was not Henry; it was Marged Richmond.

Seeing the tall, determined figure crossing the moonlit road to join her, Myfanwy had been tempted to run. She knew instinctively there would be little sympathy here. But she stood her ground, and when the woman reached her, she merely said: 'I think perhaps you should come into the house and have a talk, Miss Owen.' Then, without even waiting to see whether Myfanwy would follow, she had turned back towards the tall terraced house.

Once inside, she had led the way to the kitchen, had seated the girl by the fire and brought brandy from the dining room. 'I think we might both need this before tonight is out,' she said.

When Myfanwy heard what followed, she certainly drank her fill. Marged did not waste words when flattery was unnecessary. 'Just tell me one thing – are you pregnant?'

The girl reddened and glanced down instinctively at her still flat belly. 'I . . . er . . . well . . . I think . . .'

'Enough. If you're sufficiently worried to be hanging around this house in the middle of the night, you must be virtually certain. Now I don't want you to interrupt. This is as hard for me as it is for you. Save anything you want to say until I finish. All right?'

Myfanwy nodded mutely. 'You and my son have been lovers – I know that. I shan't go into the appropriateness of such a situation. Even if everything else were in order, Henry isn't nineteen years old yet. He's just starting out in life and far too young to be saddled with a wife and child. Don't think I blame you entirely. He is just as responsible for his actions as you are for yours, and I'm sure he'll suffer for them sooner or later. But not now, not yet. I'm not a rich woman, but I can find the money necessary to support you and your child. It's up to you how you use it. You might want to pay someone to look after it while you seek work, or you may prefer to stay at home. That's entirely your business. I'll see you're reasonably comfortable. The money will be sent to you each month care of Beaumaris Post Office, unless you wish it to go elsewhere. It will continue indefinitely unless you make any attempt to contact my son, or to tell him about the child. There, I think that's all. What do you say?'

The girl stared at her for long moments, dumb-founded by Marged's coolness. She had expected sermons, accusations, hysterical ranting, but not a straightforward financial proposition devoid of all traces of human emotion. She had even referred to the unborn child as 'it', in a denial of the baby's human identity. Finally Myfanwy found her voice. 'And what if I say no? What if I say I'm telling Henry and damn the consequences?'

Marged even denied her the reassurance of an anxious look. She merely smiled and shrugged. 'First you'd have to find him. He's no longer in North Wales. And when you did, how sure are you that he wouldn't disown you? After all, I haven't noticed him rushing to Llanddona to see whether you're all right. And going right away from the area for an indefinite period hardly seems the action of a love-struck young man, does it?'

Myfanwy muttered something indistinctly into her brandy glass, then drained it in an attempt to cauterise the pain. Finally she raised her head in a last attempt to challenge this rock-hard adversary. 'And what do I tell my child when he's growing up? How do I explain there's no Dad, only Mam? Have you thought about that?'

'No – why should I? After tonight I have no intention of ever seeing you or yours again. This baby won't be the first bastard born on Anglesey by a long chalk, nor the last. It'll be a nine days' wonder, then everyone will forget. Alternatively, of course, you could move right away and pretend you were a young widow. If you are so worried about the stigma of illegitimacy, that might be a better plan.'

Myfanwy thought she detected a chink in the armour.

She assumed a more defiant expression. 'Never! This is the only home I have – and I think you're trying to get rid of me in case Henry comes back and searches for me. You're keeping him from me, aren't you?' As she said the words, hope flared momentarily in her heart.

Marged's cold laugh damped it instantly. 'Hardly, my dear. I didn't want to embarrass you by spelling it out, but the reverse is the case. He came to me, begging me to get him out of the whole entanglement, and, most reluctantly, I sent him away, at his own request. Forgive me for making it worse, but you did insist on knowing.'

That knocked the fight out of Myfanwy. She stood up, struggling not to cry in front of this heartless woman. 'All right, then. Beaumaris Post Office it is. When?'

'That's better, Miss Owen. I had a feeling you might be a sensible girl if you could control your emotions sufficiently. First of every month. Perhaps I had better start it immediately, so you'll have a little put by when the child arrives.' She left the room again and returned with a cloth purse. 'There – that's for this month. The October payment will be waiting for you after the first in Beaumaris. And now, it's very late, and we have no more to discuss. I'll show you out.'

And that was that. She closed and bolted the front door behind Myfanwy without a word of farewell. The voyage back to Llanddona seemed long and cold that night.

The sickness started in October. She was afraid to take any of her own herbal potions, having listened to too many old wives' tales of deformed infants. Auntie Meg, her long-dead father's younger sister, was censorious but kind to her, and kept an eye on her throughout the pregnancy. In late March, attended by her aunt and the kitchen servant at the Llanddona farm, she went through a fairly easy labour and produced a beautiful, healthy son, who was duly named Beuno.

Until now, Myfanwy had told herself the boy would be enough for her. She loved him dearly, and when she looked at him she seemed to see an echo of the young lover she had now turned into a fantasy figure. But the encounter with Henry at the fair had demonstrated beyond all doubt that fantasy and her son were not enough. The glimpses she had of the future had finally revealed the error she had made last year when she saw a cloudy vision of their descendants reaping riches. Now she understood that prophecy, and was devastated because her further involvement was not necessary for its fulfilment.

She had stayed at her aunt's farm that night, rather than disturb the baby who had been put to bed before they got back. As dawn crept out of the sea, she lay and watched the familiar room take shape around her, and knew what she must do.

She had lain down the previous night without removing her clothes or uncoiling her hair. Now she rose, did not bother to put on her shoes, and went out of the house, across the silent dewy orchard whose wall rose directly from the beach. Myfanwy sat on the top of the drystone structure, swung her legs over, and jumped lightly down the six-foot drop on to the sand. It was silver-white, freshened by the last high tide, unmarked by the feet of man or beast. As she walked across the beach, a freshening dawn breeze tugged her black hair. Without a second thought she reached up and began removing the pins from her plaited chignon. The thick braid fell across her shoulder and her fingers worked through the glossy mass, separating the hairs and undoing the plait.

The tide was half way out. By the time her hair was loose and free, she was almost at the water's edge. Barefoot at the tideline, Myfanwy slowly began to unbutton her dress, finally tugging it down from her shoulders, over her breasts and as far as her hips, whence it slipped down and lay damply about her ankles. She stepped out of the sodden mass, now unfastening the drawstring of her petticoats and letting them fall beside the dress. She was moving almost rhythmically now, like some dreamy dancer, following the receding water. Her shift came next, leaving her body naked save for white cotton drawers. Then, freeing herself from the last garment she began her long walk out into the water.

Now she began to sing, a little, crooning, almost crazy tune. The words came from no true song. They were a few phrases, meaningful to Myfanwy alone: 'Swim to the moon, swim to the moon. Come on, Henry, let's swim to the moon . . .'

The orange-gold early morning sun swung clear of the horizon and burned away the opalescent pinks and blues into full, brazen day. Myfanwy raised her head and gazed into the savage radiance. All the strength was gone from her arms. She stopped swimming, giving herself wholeheartedly to the sea, and soon there was no break in the boundless waste of golden water.

Friday came all too quickly for Henry. The last place he wanted to visit now was the fair. He had forced himself to act normally with Alison after the fortune-telling interlude, but it was a struggle which absorbed all his social energy. For a long time Alison, too, remained shaken by whatever it was she had been told. By the next day, the memory of the odd young woman in her striped tent would have begun fading had Alison not been aware of the fundamental change in Henry. Its most tangible result was that nothing she did or said for the rest of the week could turn his thoughts to talk of an engagement.

Marged was becoming exasperated with herself. Unaware that the two young people had been anywhere but out driving on Tuesday afternoon, she assumed they had quarrelled, hence Henry's oddness ever since. From the moment the Bingleys arrived, she had been questioning her own wisdom in encouraging the relationship simply to keep the boy from Myfanwy Owen. Suddenly she could see that Alison might offer no more than a different kind of servitude; more socially acceptable than Myfanwy, perhaps, but no fit life companion all the same. She had silenced her nagging conscience by telling herself she would insist on a long engagement when Henry brought the inevitable news of his proposal. Two years at least, maybe three. That had seemed so impossibly far ahead that she had stopped considering the matter any further. Now, seeing their new unease with one another, she privately decided she would support him if he tried to back out of this commitment which already seemed half made.

Alison's mother was equally disturbed, but for the opposite reason. She had expected the young man to speak long before now – in fact she had been rehearsing how she would tell him that of course, nothing official

173

could be agreed until he had spoken to Mr Bingley in Manchester, but that until then, they could regard themselves as unofficially engaged. Instead, she now found herself wondering how she could properly explain things to her Manchester women friends if she and Alison were forced to return home on Saturday without Henry having spoken. Unable to force him, Mrs Bingley awaited the trip to the fair with mounting impatience. At least the atmosphere and the gaiety of the crowds there would put the young pair in an appropriately giddy mood. She would see that she and Mrs Richmond stayed well out of their way.

Henry drove them over to Menai Bridge as twilight fell on Friday. As the trap crossed the suspension bridge, they could see the bright lights and hear the boisterous noise of the fair percolating up from the village below. Henry was determinedly jolly, but when he was not making jokes or drawing things to their attention, he rapidly grew morose. Marged watched him and worried.

His forced good cheer continued when they reached the fair. At the coconut shy, he paid for two sets of balls and was just shaping up to throw when the stallholder recognised him and laughed. 'Fancy your chances a second time, do you? Won't be so easy this time, boy, you'll see!' And the coconuts duly refused to fall. As they turned away, Marged was watching her son with the first stirrings of suspicion. When had he been here before to have met that man?

As they walked down the main fairway, Henry unaccountably started encouraging them to go a little faster. Eventually, irritated at his fussing, Marged snapped: 'Will you please let me make my own pace? We're enjoying ourselves, surely, not taking military exercise? Look down there – I love those glass stalls and I don't think I've seen one since we came when you were a boy.'

Before Henry could stop her, she had left the fairway and started down the narrow alley with its glass stall, its quack medicines and its fortune teller's tent.

Henry was debating simply leaving his mother alone to glance over the glassware and then come away when she had finished, but suddenly Mrs Bingley was interested too. 'I used to collect that glass when I was a girl. I must see!' And she too was away.

This was getting out of hand. Henry hurried behind them, Alison trailing after him, only too aware of what was at the end of the alley.

As they went over the ranks of little glass ornaments, Mrs Bingley glanced further along the lane. 'That's a funny-looking banner on that tent,' she said. 'Wait a minute, I want to take a look.' Marged followed her almost automatically.

Mrs Bingley sniffed disapprovingly. 'Oh, dear – it's one of those awful fortune tellers! I always tell Alison to avoid them, and here I am leading her right to it. Good thing it's closed. Come along, let's go back.' They returned to the glassware and Henry sighed silently with relief.

But the man at the stall had noticed their interest and was itching to gossip. 'Disappointed to have missed the fortune-teller, eh, ladies?' He gave them no time to deny his assumption. 'Well, plenty more will be, an' all. Seems she wasn't able to predict her own end!'

Henry turned cold. 'Wh-what's that you say?'

The man was no local: a local would have been reluctant

to gossip with strangers whereas he revelled in the opportunity. Now he laughed, relishing the edge he had on his audience. 'Haven't seen her here since Tuesday – Madam M, that is – and she closed early that day, too. Now we know why. Two fisherman pulled her ashore off Gallows Point this morning. Seems she got washed up with the tide.'

The Bingley women were round-eyed and horrified. 'Ooh, how dreadful! Was it a boating accident?' asked Alison.

'Hardly, miss.' He was watching her avidly as he uttered the next words. 'Not be likely to go boating with nothing on, would she now? No, either she did away with herself or she was done away with, if you know what I mean!' He winked salaciously at Henry, who stood gazing slackly into space. The public mention of nudity in mixed company had thrown both Bingleys into semi-hysterics. They were already hastening back towards the fairway before the man had finished speaking.

Marged was made of sterner stuff. First glancing at Henry, she turned back to the stallholder. 'Surely she couldn't have been local with a name like that? Must have been one of the travelling fair people.'

'Oh, no, missus, that's the interesting bit – she's from around these parts, right enough. Madam M was a professional name, that's all. Now what was the name again? One of the fishermen did tell me . . . I'm that bad with Welsh names. . . Wait a minute, yeah, that's it: Owen. Myfanwy Owen. They say she's got a little son not a year old yet, an' all . . . Hey, hang on, young sir, wait your hurry! The lady and I was talking!' But Henry, with a horrified gasp, had turned and was hurrying away from the stall.

'Henry – Henry, please wait! I must talk to you!' Marged rushed after him, their passage making the Bingleys stare in astonishment as they were left behind on the fairway.

She caught him as he headed out of Menai Bridge on the Beaumaris road. 'Henry, please! You can't just leave the Bingleys there alone! What will they think?'

He stopped and turned to her, speaking with difficulty. 'You know where the trap is. You know how to drive. You'd better take them home.' He raised a hand to stem her protests. 'I really couldn't care less if they think it isn't done for three ladies to travel unescorted. Now, are you going back to them or are they going to follow me all the way to Llanddona?'

'B-but you can't go there!'

'If I'd gone there a long time ago, none of this would have happened – and there'd be a happy girl alive today in Manchester better for never having known me. Now, get out of my way. I'm going to see my son.'

'My God, Henry, I know it's a shock, but have some sense! It's all of ten miles to Llanddona and the last mile is practically a cliff! I beg you, come back to Menai Bridge and let's hire a carriage to send the Bingleys back. I'll think up some excuse for you and me. Then I want you to give me a little while to talk about this, before you do something you'll regret.'

He laughed bitterly. 'I've already done it. What could you possibly say that would make it right? No, I know what you're doing. It's practically dark now. You're hoping if you hang on to me for long enough, it'll be too late even for me to go off to Llanddona. Well, you'll have to do better. You've hoodwinked me once too often, Mother!'

'I swear that's not what I want to do! I only want to help you. I love you, Henry.'

'So did she . . . so did someone else who's dead because of me – because of all this. If ever I needed proof that two wrongs don't make a right, I've got it now!'

'I promise, as God is my judge, that if you still feel you must go to Llanddona after we talk, I shall see you go tonight – you'd probably be faster hiring a boat and going up by sea, anyway. At least you'd miss that terrible hill.'

He shuddered. 'I don't think I could face the sea route yet. What if . . . if . . .'

Quite suddenly, all Henry's drive was gone. The enormity of Myfanwy's death combined with the shock of the news of the hitherto unsuspected existence of his son, and with the deeper-rooted guilt surrounding the tragedy of Dolours. He began to collapse under the strain. He sagged back against the low stone parapet of the little bridge which carried the road over the Cadnant River, covered his face with his hands and began to sob. 'If I should see her – her ghost – there in the water. What would I do?' His voice rose to a thin wail. 'Oh, Mother, I must be cursed! Everyone who loves me seems to be doomed.'

His disintegration hardened Marged's resolve. She grasped him by the shoulders. 'Henry – Henry, look at me. Put your hands down, come on, look me in the eyes . . . There, that's better. Now – I'm certainly not doomed, am I? And who loves you better than I do? All this can be sorted out, but not if you're in such a state. I can't let you go to Llanddona like this. Good God, even I have more concern for the orphaned child than to permit such a thing! Come back to the inn the other side of the bridge. There'll be hardly anyone in there yet, all too busy at the fair. Sit there over a mug of ale for a few minutes. Try to clear your mind. Just concentrate on thinking it's all past now, if you have to think anything at all. I'll see to everything back there, then I'll bring the trap and we'll take a little ride before we go back to Menai View. All right? You know you can trust me, whatever you may have been thinking a few minutes ago. Now stay there, mind. No wandering off.'

She kept up an unbroken stream of similar chatter while she guided him gently back to the inn. The back bar was empty and she steered him in, before going to find the landlord. 'My son's become unwell. I've taken the liberty of putting him in there –' she gestured over her shoulder – 'can you help me by keeping an eye on him and seeing he gets a drink and some peace and quiet? It's just strain and overwork – he'll be no trouble, and I'll be back almost at once.'

The publican was not used to such well-dressed, obviously respectable women entering his establishment, and he practically offered Marged the run of the place. 'My pleasure, ma'am. Don't you worry, I'll see the poor boy's all right for a while. You take your time.' As he spoke he glanced into the back bar. The young man appeared to be in a trance; certainly in no state to cause problems. He saw Marged off the premises.

Marged rushed towards Menai Bridge, dreading what she would find there. So far, neither Bingley female had shown signs of fortitude under stress. She had visions of them ranting hysterically at the crowd, shrieking for help and bringing down ridicule on the Richmond family. But she need not have worried. They were so agitated they had retreated to the outer edge of the crowd, sitting on an ornamental bench like two frightened little sparrows on a fence. Had Marged been less worried, she would have laughed at the sight. When they saw her they nearly fell at her feet with gratitude.

'Oh, Mrs Richmond, what on earth has happened?' cried Alison's mother. 'We were terrified, seeing you both rush off like that, and after such terrible news, and being left alone in this strange place . . . we didn't know where to turn!'

Marged managed a calm smile, in spite of a churning stomach and racing heart. 'How can I apologise, Mrs Bingley? An unpardonable lapse, I know, but I'm afraid the young woman was someone I'd – er – had dealings with, and Henry was quite overcome with concern in case I should become involved.' Inadvertently she had chosen an excuse which fitted perfectly with the vague picture Henry had given Alison on Tuesday. All might not be lost.

'Henry's not at all well,' she continued. 'The shock, you know, and he's been working too hard for more than a year. I think it best if I arrange a carriage to take you home, then take Henry in the trap to see a medical friend of ours. Mrs Davies is staying on tonight to make us a late supper, so if you'd like to go back now, I'm sure you'll feel better after a meal. Just let her know we're likely to be very late – and don't wait up for us yourselves. I'm sure you'll need a rest after such a harrowing evening.'

She led them up the hill at the other side of the village, to

180

the carrier's yard near the Victoria Hotel. Within a few minutes a stable boy had found someone to drive the two ladies back to Menai View. Marged paid in advance, saw them both settled in comfortable seats with a rug over their knees, then squared her shoulders and turned towards the rear of the livery stables where her own trap had been left.

Twenty minutes later she was back at the inn. The landlord met her at the door. 'Hasn't moved an inch, ma'am, except to sup his ale. I expect whatever it is will wear off soon and he'll be right as rain in the morning. Glad to have been of service.' He helped her steer the apparently catatonic Henry out to the trap, and handed her up into the driving seat. 'You sure you can manage that rig? I can always find someone to take you across to the mainland if you prefer.'

'No, I can handle it now, thank you. Don't concern yourself further. You've been very kind.' She slipped him a half-sovereign and he glanced up at her in surprised gratitude.

'No need for that, ma'am – no need at all. Glad to do it.'

'Nonsense. You keep it. I couldn't have arranged matters without you.'

And, incredibly, they finally seemed to be free of other people. Coming back into Menai Bridge, she drove around the back road near the pier. The last ferry-load of incoming visitors had already arrived and the departing revellers were not ready for home yet, so there were very few people about. They re-joined the main road just before the bridge, and she heaved a huge sigh of relief as they passed across it, away from that accursed island.

Now she was faced with the problem of what to do with Henry. It was clear that he would be in no state tonight for any serious talk. Really he should be home in bed. But if she took him to Menai View she must expose him to the Bingleys. They would hardly have finished supper yet, let alone retired. And what if Henry started fretting and roaming about during the night?

Then she thought, Idris – thank God for Idris! He had refused to join them that evening, pleading pressure of work. She knew it was because Mrs Bingley bored him to stupefaction, but at least it gave her somewhere safe to take her son. She steered the trap off down the coast road towards Bangor harbour, leaving the Holyhead road just where it ran past her house. Idris lived in an attractive small villa a couple of hundred yards away, just right for her to settle Henry and get back in time to bid Mrs Bingley and her daughter goodnight.

'Who is it, Mrs Llewelyn?' Marged heard Idris ask from his study off the hall, as his housekeeper opened the front door.

'Mrs Richmond and Mr Henry, sir,' she called.

'Show them in, show them in!' Idris hurried towards the door, then, as they stepped into the lighted hall, saw Henry and said, 'Jesus Christ in heaven, what has happened?'

By the time Marged had finished her story, Idris was grim-faced. 'By the look of the boy, we'll get nothing out of him tonight. Go home now, tell the Bingleys the doctor has sent him here to me, and for goodness' sake pack them off home on time tomorrow morning. Tell them the boy can't be disturbed – it'll be no more than the truth – and once they're gone, get back down here to me. I'll get Doctor Lloyd to come and look at him if he's no better in the morning. Go on, no more talk tonight. You and I can go over it all before we bring Henry into it, and try to make some sense of the whole mess.'

'Thank you, Idris. I really don't know if I could have managed without you.' For once she meant what she said, and was not simply flattering him in the interests of better manipulating him. Then, as she turned to leave, a thought struck her. 'Did you know of any involvement Henry might have had in Manchester, apart from this Bingley girl? Something that ended badly?'

At a loss, Idris thought over his nephew's stint in the city. 'Nothing of any importance . . . oh, hang on, there was a girl he befriended, had her own little street barrow. She helped him when he started up. But I haven't seen her about Sebastopol Terrace for ages now, and honestly, Marged, if you'd seen her you wouldn't give her a second thought. Good-natured little thing, and bright as a button, but she was all skin and bone and plain as a pikestaff. No, for all the romance there, she could have been his sister.'

'It sounds unlikely, it's true,' Marged replied. 'But from what he said, I'm sure there was someone . . . I'll have to sort it out with him.'

By the next morning, the Bingleys had recovered their composure sufficiently to feel curious, and were openly eager to learn the details of their hostess's relationship with the dead girl. Marged managed to hold them off. She had become an expert in stonewall tactics during her first year as a businesswoman and treated the Bingleys as no more than a minor irritation. She finally got them on to the noon train, assuring them that Henry would write as soon as he was sufficiently recovered. Short of accusing him of shamming sickness, there was little they could do. They left, sullen and humiliated.

Now, she thought, all I have to do is stop my son breaking down permanently, and we might all be able to live a normal life again. At least there'll be no more plagues of Bingleys!

It was almost a week before Henry showed any sign of recovery, and then it was no more than an awakening from his trance. He moved about independently now, instead of sitting or lying where he was guided. He answered when Idris or Marged spoke to him and appeared to understand what they said, but both of them felt he was still out of reach. He made no further mention of going to Llanddona to see his son, but nor did he refer to the proposed partnership with Idris, to the incident at the fair, or even to the departure of Alison and her mother.

The doctor was no help. 'We're still children when it comes to dealing with this sort of illness,' he told Idris. 'Until recently they used to call it brain fever. I suppose it was as good a term as any, but hardly helpful. I've heard it used to cover everything from states like your nephew's to raving homicidal mania. I've seen some people snap out of it as if they were never sick at all, and I've seen others become incurable wrecks. There's certainly no accepted treatment.'

'Then what can we do? It'll destroy his mother if he stays like this.'

'I'm inclined to be optimistic. The cases of recovery I've seen have been of people with either a very strong will to survive, or with family who can give them the same sort of strength. I think your sister-in-law has more than enough determination to make up for any possible lack in Henry. Encourage her to spend as much time with him as she can, and tell her not to be too tender with his feelings. I suspect that's often half the trouble. People are so anxious not to refer to the shock that started it all that the sufferers never receive enough impetus to pull themselves out of their inertia. Tell her to discuss whatever brought this on, even if the boy doesn't seem to hear a word she says. Let her go over it with him. It may well be that he'll get so angry at hearing one point of view all the time that he'll be stung into recovering.'

'Not much to go on, is it?' said Idris.

Dr Lloyd shook his head. 'I've known you too long to try false optimism, Idris, on you or Marged. If anybody can help the boy, I'm sure she can. Just see she's prepared for him to be very ungentlemanly on the road to recovery!'

With that, he left them to it.

# Chapter Six

It took nearly two months for Marged to draw Henry back from his melancholy. The techniques she used immeasurably strengthened the bond between mother and son. First she confessed every move she had made in fending off Myfanwy and diverting him to Manchester. She told him how she had manipulated Idris and how she had managed to convince Myfanwy that Henry himself wished to be free of her. She was unsparing of herself, and of him, reminding him that he really had said he wanted to end the association and had washed his hands of the girl at the first prospect of escape.

The exchanges were hard on both of them. At first she thought he was not even listening, but after she had spent three successive afternoons repeating her account of the past year or so, he seemed to draw himself back to her with a great effort.

'All right, Mother, I suppose I understand . . . I don't know whether I can live with it, though.'

Marged's heart leaped. 'Of course you can – I do! Stop feeling sorry for yourself!'

A stroke of pure luck eventually gave her the spur she needed to complete the first stage of his recovery. While still groping back to the real world, he started trying to assuage his conscience by insisting on going to see his son. Marged's response was one of fury. After all their suffering, Henry was now proposing to defeat all her good work. She seized the first threat that occurred to her.

'All right, my son, go ahead! That is, if you want to hang at Beaumaris Gaol!'

'Mother – what are you talking about?

She stabbed back at him: 'Don't tell me you can't remember every instant of that terrible evening at the fair, because I won't believe you. Think of what the glass seller said . . . "Either she did away with herself, *or she was done away with* . . ." How long d'you think it would be before they came to ask questions of you if her family knew you were the father of her child? They'd hang you, Henry. They'd never believe you hadn't drowned her yourself, particularly when they heard you'd been to see her at the fair.'

'How d'you know I'd seen her?'

She gave him a pitying smile. 'I thought I might have to extricate you from the coils of Miss Bingley along with trying to cure your illness, but it turned out to be unnecessary. It seems she was deeply troubled at what the stars foretold, particularly as Madam M had come to a bad end so soon afterwards. She confessed all to her mother, and Mrs Bingley wrote to me in turn, saying she didn't know what was going on, but she thought it best that all contact between the two of you should be severed. I think her mama was less concerned about the fortune telling than about marrying off her ewe lamb to a possible madman, but that's irrelevant now.

'And then, dear Henry, I realised that Alison could

188

not have gone to the fair alone. I worked out that the only time you were together unchaperoned for long enough was the day I went to the shop: Tuesday, the last time the girl was seen alive, the day she closed early. Now if she did that, she must have been upset . . . I understand her old aunt acted as a sort of sorceress's apprentice to her. She would probably have seen you that day, and if you turned up now to acknowledge the boy, I'm sure she'd remember you. They'd lock you up and throw away the key, Henry!'

And indeed, if anyone ever *did* make the connection, what his mother had described might well come to pass. Marged shuddered. Even her payments to Myfanwy, which she had now diverted to the aunt in the baby's name, would prove the link. Their only hope lay in the fact that unless the aunt saw Henry, she would never connect him with the unknown man who arrived at the fortune teller's tent that October afternoon. And without that link, Henry was safe.

It was at this point that his own survival instinct surfaced. He reached out and grasped Marged's hands. 'Tell me what to do, Mother, and I'll do it. What an utter, utter fool I've been!'

'Welcome back to the real world, my boy,' she said.

By late November, Henry was much better. He had started going on buying trips with Idris – though not to Anglesey yet – and worked at the High Street shop one day a week. But he was still deeply depressed, and Marged knew there was another festering spiritual wound she must cleanse before he could recover fully.

It took her some days, and a great deal of bitter heart-searching, to decide on the right course, but on December the first she breezed into the breakfast room and pushed aside the newspaper her son was listlessly reading. 'How long is it since you went to London, Henry?'

He was taken aback. 'You know as well as I do. I've only ever been there twice, and I've never stayed there overnight at all.'

'Well, it's time you did. Idris, too. We can go on Wednesday, stay in an hotel, do some Christmas shopping and come back this time next week. How would that suit you?'

She could see immediately that the idea appealed to him a great deal, though he had enough pride to pretend coolness. 'If you'd like to, Mother, of course. Does Uncle Idris know yet?'

'Oh, that's a mere formality – you know he'd go to Constantinople to keep me company!'

Henry even managed to smile at her little joke.

Marged had chosen the right medicine. Paris, Rome and Vienna might have more exotic claims, but they could not have worked the proper magic. For it was commerce that finally rescued Henry, not culture or light entertainment. They stayed at the Cavendish Hotel in Jermyn Street, so the first things Henry saw when he went for a stroll were luxury shops which made anything he had seen elsewhere look paltry. He would disappear for an hour without warning, and when Marged anxiously sent Idris to look for him, he would find Henry only yards away, gazing entranced at the way a length of shirting or a selection of hand-made chocolates had been displayed in the windows. Within a couple of days he was almost the self-assured young man they had known before the breakdown. He accompanied Marged on her shopping trips to Bond Street and Regent Street. While she fingered silks and chose handkerchiefs, he looked at the cash registers, studied the way the assistants dressed, guessed at the amounts of money taken each day and once or twice even cornered a floorwalker with questions about the number of employees and the size of warehouse facilities. Marged was delighted and congratulated herself that her cure-all seemed to have worked.

And yet, and yet . . . occasionally she caught a listless expression on his face as his thoughts turned inwards to some secret place where she could not follow. She sighed. Would she ever manage to relieve him of that agonising secret?

He finally told her everything on the penultimate night of their stay. Idris had remained at the hotel while Marged and Henry went to see *Rigoletto* at the Italian Opera house in Covent Garden. It was a glittering occasion, and as they left the great theatre Henry felt and looked better than he had for many months. Marged was almost able to forget there was still something unsaid. Outside, in Bow Street, the crush of people was so great that they despaired of getting a cab.

'It's such a wonderful evening, why don't we walk down to the Strand?' said Henry. 'We'll get a hackney immediately down there.' They strolled southward, happily discussing the opera and the beauty of the building. It was a little early for the main rush of carters and porters to the central fruit and vegetable market, but the first few carts and barrows were rolling up. As they crossed Tavistock Street, they glanced to their right, watching a huge wain full of cabbages groaning over the cobbles. Something stirred in a darkened shop doorway and Marged let out a little gasp of shock.

'Oh, no, look! Poor little mites, at this time of year, too!'

The doorway harboured a small group of boys – about six of them – ragged and barefoot and rendered grotesque by the measures they had taken to keep warm. Their hands, arms and legs were swathed in the hollow conical straw sleeves used by wine merchants to protect champagne bottles in transit. Henry started back in horror.

'Come on, Mother, please, before they . . . they touch us!'

But Marged stood her ground. 'Where's your humanity, boy? You saw just the same in Manchester. What we've spent tonight would put a roof over these children's heads and food in their bellies for months. The least we can do is give them enough to eat supper and sleep in the warm tonight!' She started moving towards the urchins, fumbling in her reticule for money.

But Henry forestalled her. Stepping in front of her, he dipped into his pocket and drew out a huge handful of loose change, threw it as far as he could beyond the boys, and as they scrambled after it yelled, 'Take it – take it all and go, for God's sake!' Then, almost in an extension of the throwing motion, he swept Marged away in the opposite direction just as an unoccupied hackney clattered around the corner. They were in it and en route for Jermyn Street almost before she could draw breath.

Furious at the crassness of the gesture, she turned to demand an explanation, but when she saw his face her anger shrivelled. He was sweating and trembling and looked almost as bad as when he had first become ill. Overcome with compassion, she gathered him into her arms.

'Henry, my love, you must tell me the rest, or it will destroy you. Come on, now, it can't be worse than anything we've gone over already. It was something in Manchester, wasn't it? Something in those awful poor streets?'

He nodded dumbly, barely managing to choke back a sob. 'I-I've tried to forget it, Mother, really I have. But the sight of that sort of thing brings it back like yesterday. I don't think I'll ever rid myself of the stink and the misery . . .'

'Hush, hush . . . we'll sort it out. Here, dry your eyes! Don't want the cabby to see you in tears, do we? We'll go up to the suite as soon as we get back and if you can, you'll tell me everything.'

She thought he would cry again, but he managed not to, and when they got to their suite he recited the whole story of Dolours Kenny, dry-eyed, looking straight ahead and speaking in a monotone.

'Well, there it is,' he said finally, with a huge sigh. 'That was why I looked so terrible when I came home for those few days. I hadn't spent a peaceful night for months. And then for the other business to happen straight after it . . . I began wondering whether I was jinxed or just wicked.'

Now it was Marged's turn to feel tearful. 'Believe me, you are neither. The trouble is you look so self-contained and mature that girls like those two will always idolise you, because you seem to have the strength they need. They don't know that inside you're still a little boy.'

'But what can I do? If this sort of thing ever happens again, I really shan't get over it.'

'No, I believe you wouldn't. But I think there's a way out. As usual, though, it needs your consent.'

'Anything – just tell me!'

'I'm a great believer in arranged marriages, Henry. If you just fall in love and follow your instincts, you've seen the worst that can happen. Even at best, love changes and dies sometimes. But if the match is made on good, sensible foundations, it's different. It gets better all the time. My father and Rhys's mother arranged our marriage, you know. We'd never met before they introduced us after discussing the whole thing. And we got on so well together, it could have been planned by God himself. Only, of course, he died so young.' She paused a moment, lost in the past, then went on: 'Anyway, I think you should promise yourself that there'll be no romantic involvements for you for the next three or four years. You're still well short of twenty, remember.'

He nodded, beginning to look hopeful.

She went on: 'Concentrate on making a real success of business. I've been thinking, what if we came south and started here, just shook off our old ties? It would be a new start.' She gave an excited little laugh. 'With a name like Richmond, we could even go to Richmond in Surrey and be Richmond's of Richmond! You could throw yourself into it wholeheartedly, then when you've made your way, I could, shall we say, make a few arrangements, and I think you'd find yourself well along the road to success and happiness. What do you think?'

He clasped her in a bear hug, planting big kisses on her cheeks and then one on her mouth. His lips lingered there a moment too long. They gazed into each other's eyes almost longingly for a moment, then she gave a slightly forced, playful laugh and pushed him away. 'Go along, now! I'm too old for such flattery. Just trust me, that's all I ask.'

He stood up, took her small hand and bowed over it, kissing it gently. 'Always, my darling, always,' he said, and went off to his room.

Marged closed her eyes and shuddered at the welter of emotions released by his kiss. Not like a son's mouth on hers at all . . . She shook her head, struggling vainly to clear it of the evil fantasy that had reared up so monstrously out of her maternal feelings.

# Chapter Seven

It was Elizabeth Rose's great misfortune to fall in love with Henry Richmond and to receive his mother's unqualified approval. After that, her fate was sealed.

When Henry promised his mother that he would postpone all thoughts of romance, he meant it. His restricted but intense experience had taught him the bitterness that came in the wake of a liaison with an unsuitable lover and he wanted no more of such disruption. He devoted his entire energy to developing the business that he and Marged planned together. In the three years following Henry's return from Manchester, the Richmonds opened a string of small grocery shops in the London suburbs and around the Lancashire cotton towns. They gave George Beynon a share of the Bangor shop early on, and that was Henry's inspiration for a retail franchising scheme which permitted shop managers to share the overall profitability of Richmond's while taking on the day-to-day management which would inevitably have slowed Henry's progress. With Idris, he concentrated on setting up an enormous wholesale supply operation which ensured that Richmond's shops offered an unbeatable range of goods at low prices. By 1863 they owned twenty-five shops, two foreign shipment depots, and were poised for an expansion programme that would make Richmond's a household name throughout the country.

That was enough for Idris. He had always assumed financial prosperity was the entire object of their venture. Marged and Henry knew better. They wanted permanence, commercial immortality. For too long, they had been insignificant outsiders, isolated from their community by Marged's early widowhood and her driving ambition for the boy. Marged was beginning to realise that Henry himself wanted something more – something which even her considerable talents might fail to achieve for him. He showed a growing interest in the doings of the rich and powerful. Suddenly, Putney was not enough. He aspired to a country estate and a house or apartment in the West End of London. These were easy to attain, Marged reflected, but the social acceptance without which such things were meaningless vanities was another matter. Sadly, she realised it and Henry seemed not to. She had never liked disappointing her son. Now the financial foundations of their empire were laid, she went hunting for a wife who could help him up the ladder. Her quarry was Elizabeth Rose.

Elizabeth was Baron Clitheroe's granddaughter; but Henry would never have won her had her closer antecedents been equally exalted. The Clitheroes had run out of money a generation ago and had married off their daughter to Albert Rose, a self-made pie and sausage magnate. At the time when Marged engineered a meeting between Henry and Elizabeth, Mr Rose's pork pies were noted chiefly for his misappropriation of English song and verse to advertise them on posters.

'Only a Rose I give you . . .' was a popular favourite, appearing in a bubble from a handsome suitor's lips as he handed a pie on a silver platter to his lady-love. 'A Rose by any other name . . .' was equally well known, this time delivered by an over-decorated lady who beamed at an equally florid packet of sausages as they nestled among long-stemmed prize blooms.

Such slogans, and such products, had made Albert Rose a very rich man, and as his only child Elizabeth would get it all. Unfortunately all her suitors seemed to be either tradesmen as vulgar as Mr Rose, or penniless aristocrats on the make. Elizabeth recoiled from the prospect of the former, and her father was set against the latter. Henry proved a perfect compromise candidate. By the time Marged introduced them, he was obviously on the way up, with his ten branches around south-west London, fifteen in the North-west, a revolutionary approach to marketing, an attractive house in Putney and the two supply depots abroad. Albert Rose could see the young man was able to make his own way. He was also cultivated, good-looking and apparently a gentleman.

At first, Elizabeth was cool and withdrawn because she was embarrassed by the thought that the meeting resembled a commercial transaction. A couple of hours in Henry's company changed all that, for she quickly found herself falling irresistibly in love with him. They were engaged within three months and the wedding date set for the spring of 1864. But even before the marriage, Marged realised she should have held out longer before marrying off Henry. She could have done better than Elizabeth eventually. After all, many men in Henry's position were thirty, or even forty, before they married. Marged had acted precipitately because she felt the time had come for him to have a family of his own. Elizabeth was a delightful girl and – almost as important to Marged – sufficiently passive never to threaten her own pre-eminent position with her son. But to her dismay, Marged soon began to understand the truth in the assertion that when women married beneath themselves, they descended into the husband's social class unless they were cast iron nobility. Elizabeth brought a large dowry, but far less social prestige than her mother-in-law had hoped.

Marged realised her error at a Mayfair ball to which she had managed to obtain invitations through a member of the Clitheroe clan. Watching Henry and Elizabeth dancing together, she blushed to hear a shrill dowager suggest to a companion that Elizabeth's crest might be the Clitheroe shield resting on crossed black puddings. They all knew that Baron Clitheroe's ancient coat of arms did not tell the whole story of Elizabeth's ancestry.

It was all nonsense, anyway! There would never have been such snubs if Henry hadn't become obsessed with getting to the top too quickly. Her own thoughts ran more towards continuity. Without heirs to carry on your work, you had nothing. But if you had them, and a successful enterprise to pass on, as far as Marged was concerned let social preferment take its time. Unfortunately Henry seemed incapable of understanding that it would take a couple of generations. A few months later, at the picture-book wedding ceremony in the ancient parish church on the Clitheroe estate, Marged glanced around the congregation and realised afresh that it would take far longer than Henry anticipated. She sighed, exasperated in spite of her overall satisfaction in the event. Their side of the church was sparsely occupied, but the Rose-Clitheroe side was packed, and it was woefully easy to separate the tradesmen from the nobility. The Clitheroe contingent were slightly shabby but totally relaxed. The prosperous Roses glittered with expensive broadcloth and inappropriate diamonds, and their very tenseness branded them as parvenues. We may look less vulgar, Marged thought, but socially we resemble the Roses far more than we do the Clitheroes. If Henry thought he could leap from here to the top in one attempt, he was in for disillusion beyond anything he had known so far . . .

The creation of a family of his own temporarily sidetracked Henry from his social aspirations. Fatherhood transformed him, but only in relation to his firstborn. He understood only one sort of familial love – singular, exclusive, a bond forged over all the years of his youth between mother and son. It survived his marriage, although it was questionable whether the marriage remained intact. Something had broken inside Henry years before when his mother promised to banish the rest of the world in order to protect him. It had never occurred to him then to question her wisdom. It never occurred to him now to doubt her assertion that a son and heir would set the seal on his plans. The reserves of tenderness within him were dammed. When Elizabeth bore their first child, a boy, the dam burst and was unleashed upon the tiny, red-faced scrap who was Henry's immortality. After that, it seemed he had nothing left for the offspring that followed.

Henry was a courteous man with a sense of propriety. As Elizabeth produced more children – a girl, then another boy, then a second girl, he paid lip service to the emotions he should have felt. But she looked into his eyes and knew instinctively that their firstborn son was his one and only hostage to fortune. Even his name, Arthur, seemed to have an almost mystical significance. Henry always said it was merely the anglicized version of Idris, chosen in deference to his uncle, who was dying when Arthur was born. Elizabeth knew it was more than that. In the secret places which had been locked since his boyhood, Henry still carried some romantic dream about founding a modern Camelot. She tried not to resent his private fantasy and dismissed as unworthy her reflection that the original Arthurian idyll had lasted barely one generation.

# Chapter Eight

## Harry, 1875

'*For man that is born of woman hath but a short time to live and is full of misery . . .*'

The yews were drip, drip, dripping against the sodden ground, in mournful counterpoint to the words of the priest who stood beside the pathetically small open grave. It was a boy, this time, so Papa had insisted that Arthur and I must be brought to the funeral. John was the second son to die as a baby, but Mama and Papa had lost five children altogether. The three daughters apparently had been so insignificant that their presence was unnecessary. Papa always did believe that women were for marrying off, not cherishing.

Tears were running down my cheeks as freely as the rain that dribbled through the trees. If only Johnny had stayed a bit longer . . . perhaps I wouldn't have been so lonely then. Johnny was my first, my only friend. He was to me what Arthur was to Papa. I didn't know then that death was involuntary. All I could think of was that he'd abandoned me. Fancy leaving me now, with Christmas coming . . . fancy preferring to lie there alone in the cold, wet ground, where I couldn't hold his hand or tell him secrets . . . I let out a sob as I imagined the immense chill loneliness of wherever Johnny had gone. Nanny *gave my hand a brusque shake. I peered up at her, hoping she would comfort me, but she only pursed her lips, then murmured, 'Brave boys don't cry – hush.'*

*They told me that Johnny had gone to play with Baby Jesus. Why, I had asked, didn't he want me any more? But no one had bothered to answer. They were all too busy telling Papa how great his loss must be.*

*I glanced across the grave, to where Mother stood beside Arthur and Father. Perhaps she would comfort me? She usually understood how terrible it was always to be shut out . . . But the heavy veil obscured her face and she appeared impossibly remote. I clutched tighter at Nanny's hand and concentrated on not crying.*

Miss Fillimore, the nursery governess, sat at the desk in her bedroom at Mapledurham, in the Thames Valley. It was her afternoon off and she was writing to her sister Parthenope. She sighed, contemplating her young charges, and went on with the letter:

Master Harry, the younger son, is an uncommon mixture. One feels he has seeds of angel and devil in him, and sadly for him, his Papa always manages to bring out the devil!

I believe the secret is that Harry dotes on his father, who can manage perfectly well without such worship, as long as he has the regard of Arthur, the elder boy, who greatly resembles Richmond *père*. Harry, of course, is quite different. Yesterday, in the schoolroom, he had been behaving perfectly. He is bright and quick, and already reads and reckons far better than Arthur, although he is four years younger. He had been working quietly all morning, unsupervised, while I attempted to improve Master Arthur's penmanship. Then his father paid us a surprise visit. What a commotion! Suddenly, all Harry's lovely mildness of expression and calmness of temper were gone. He was passionate and determined enough for any autocrat, striking the table and demanding my attention.

His father was furiously angry, saying that Arthur never behaves thus, and why should Harry think he could do so unchecked? That merely made the child worse. Within moments he was in a passion, red-faced, screaming, quite beyond control. I was mortified! Naturally, his papa said there was no justification for such evil humour, and ordered that Harry be punished by being shut in his bedroom without supper that night. Imagine! Not only to be punished, but to anticipate it throughout a long day of humiliation! The child was distraught.

I attempted to explain to Mr Richmond that Harry behaves thus because he never receives any attention, as Arthur constantly does, from his father. Mr Richmond then turned his anger on me and I realised I had said too much. Oh, Parthenope! I am so sad for the boy! He only wants proper affection, and although his mama and I myself give it in full measure, daily he sees how his father looks down on womanly affections, and daily he sees such love as more worthless. I do not think I can bear his small misery much longer.

*    *    *

Miss Fillimore was not alone. Some half a dozen governesses came and went between Harry's fourth and eighth years. Each time a new feminine presence was introduced to his world, she appeared to be snatched away almost immediately. Not even his mother was always there. She bore nine children, four of whom survived, and every year she seemed to be expecting another child or recovering from the birth. The only woman who was constantly in attendance was Marged Richmond, who ran the household when Elizabeth was indisposed. As her behaviour mirrored Henry's, Harry grew to see her more as an honorary man than as one of the endlessly shifting army of females in his life.

Marged had read enough to know that all new pupils went through hell when they first went away to school. She assumed Henry knew it from personal experience since he had told her years before how miserable he was in the beginning at Warwick. Perhaps the shadow of such memories remained, because now he seemed loath to consign his firstborn to the public school system until the last minute. Instead of going away at the age of eight, Arthur remained at home, sharing a governess with Harry and the girls, until he was twelve. Then Henry decided the boy needed the contacts he would make at Eton, and off he went. Eight-year-old Harry was afforded no such privilege. He was despatched the same autumn, to a preparatory school in Shropshire.

Harry was not quite without friends. His last nanny, Mrs Young, was still at White Lodge, the Mapledurham house, to look after Mary Rose, the youngest surviving child. The night before his departure for school, she found him sitting disconsolately in the empty school-room. He appeared to have been crying.

'Now what's this?' she asked. 'You know what I always tell you – boys don't cry.'

He sniffed hard, but said, 'I'm not crying, Nanny, really – just thinking.'

'What about?'

'Well . . . about who I'll tell everything to when I'm away. The girls are too young, and Mama's still in bed . . . and . . . and –' the tears, never far away, threatened to reappear – 'and Papa says he'll only have time to answer Arthur's letters.'

That man is as blind as a mole with this boy, thought Mrs Young. She smiled at him. 'That's nothing to cry about, my duck. Write to me. I promise I'll write back straight away. I shall miss you – and I expect your mama will want me to write from her, too.'

'D'you really mean it? You won't forget?'

'Of course I shan't forget! I'll think of you every day.'

So it was that Nanny Young learned Harry was being thrashed black and blue by a sadistic schoolmaster. It was some weeks before the boy complained, apparently having believed the treatment he received was normal. Eventually, though, it became unbearable. Mrs Young held her peace at first and waited for Elizabeth to raise the matter. She could hardly do so herself when she knew the boy wrote to Madam once a week. But Harry had not told his mother, and nothing was done to rescue him.

At half term, Elizabeth travelled to Shropshire to visit her younger son. She discovered a cowed little boy with dark shadows under his eyes, almost afraid to answer the most superficial questions. When she pressed for an explanation, he broke down and whispered a confession about the beatings. Elizabeth took him back to her hotel room and removed his jacket and shirt, then insisted he lowered his trousers. The weals extended from shoulders to buttocks and there were older, whiter scars beneath them.

Harry never returned to the school. Elizabeth took him straight back to White Lodge, then wrote a formal letter withdrawing him from the establishment, which she posted before Henry could forbid her to do so. Even then, Harry might have been returned to his tormentors. Arthur inadvertently saved him.

While Harry languished in Shropshire, Arthur had been experiencing pain of a different kind at Eton. All his life, Arthur had enjoyed near princely status. Universally indulged, adored by his parents and grandmother, worshipped by his younger brother and sisters, he had no idea how it felt to be a victim. He soon learned.

Most of his contemporaries at Eton came from households where work was something only servants did. They were taught to look down on the professions and to regard any commercial occupation as barely a step above the gutter. Shopkeepers were held in particular contempt. Another new boy, aware of Arthur's origins and frightened that his own might earn him persecution, told a group of older boys that Arthur was the son of Richmond the Tea King. From that moment, he was known as Grocer Richmond, harassed at every opportunity, alternately ostracised and sneered at. Harry might have withstood such treatment; his infancy had been less gilded; but Arthur was quite out of his depth. The environment which had indulged him had also failed to teach him the meaning of fear. When his persecutors pushed him beyond reason, he lashed out. A master who caught him fighting the lordling who led the attack demanded an explanation and Arthur blurted out the nature of the insults.

That put him beyond the pale. The unwritten rules said he should have taken the baiting in silence until his fellows became used to him and accepted him. But it seemed that was not young Richmond's way. Not only was he of questionable origins, but he sneaked. The master, a stalwart of the established order, eyed him with unconcealed distaste and said: 'Really, Richmond, you'll have to get that arrogance under control. No gentleman would behave like that!'

Arthur turned on him. 'So you're on their side, too, are you? Well, I'll teach you . . .' And before anyone could stop him he charged the master like some small, demented bull, butting him in the midriff and knocking him over. He was sent home to White Lodge, disgraced, the day after Harry's own return.

Henry Richmond had already subjected his wife to the worst browbeating of their marriage, not merely for rescuing Harry from the Shropshire sadist without his father's permission, but for even considering rescue to be necessary. 'How many times must I tell you, the boy's too soft?' he raged. 'He needs a bit of rough treatment to teach him what to expect from the real world one day. I learned the hard way, in the back streets of Manchester, remember! He won't be granted the same privilege!'

Elizabeth struggled to hide her resentment. The back streets of Manchester were already overworked by her husband as the source of all sorts of lessons from the hard school of life. She often found herself wondering whether he could have gone through such very hard times in the course of a single year as a shopkeeper there. She had no time to dwell on it now, though. Henry's next pronouncement rooted her to the spot.

'The boy has to learn you can't get out of tight corners by holding onto your mother's apron strings. He's to go back to school on Sunday. In the meantime, I'd better write and explain.'

'B-but Henry, you can't! That would make you as guilty as that terrible schoolmaster . . . more so. Harry's your own flesh and blood!'

'It's a pity he doesn't show it more often, then. I'd like to see how Arthur would have behaved in such circumstances.'

With perfect timing, Arthur gave them the opportunity to do just that. The butler arrived to announce that Mr Arthur had been sent home from school, permanently, and had just been brought up from the station by Nanny, who had found him there as she drove past in the trap on her way back from the village.

Father and son were shut up together in the library for almost an hour. When the boy emerged, Henry sent for Elizabeth once more. Unable to meet her eyes, he compensated by bombastic delivery. 'It seems we'll have to overlook Harry's weakness after all . . . fortunately for him, our elder son has distinguished himself in defending the family name and was expelled for his pains.' Elizabeth attempted to ask for an explanation, but he cut her off. 'England's finest school has more than its share of barbarism, it seems. I won't stand for such nonsense. I shall write and demand an explanation, and from now on the boys will both be educated at home. I always did think that was the proper course for a gentleman, anyway.'

When she finally sorted out what had happened, Elizabeth hardly knew whether to laugh or cry. True, Arthur's boyish rebellion had earned a pardon for Harry, too, but if only it had been delivered before she had started trying to prepare the younger boy for the return to his tormentors! Now there would be no way out of letting him know that once again, Henry thought only of Arthur's welfare.

As she had feared, sorrow at his inability to move his own father swamped Harry's initial relief at his permanent escape from prep school. 'Why doesn't he love me, Mama? You'd think he only had one son.'

Yes, you would, she thought angrily, cradling Harry in her arms in a vain attempt to ease the pain of his father's rejection.

As the years passed, Henry's preference became so painfully obvious that Elizabeth took steps to play it down as much as possible. In the summer, Henry permitted Arthur to work for short periods as a temporary apprentice in suburban branches of Richmond's, playing an elaborate game of pretending the boy received no preferential treatment, then heaping on the praise as branch managers dutifully reported his talent. After the first year, Elizabeth promised herself that if it happened again, at least Harry would not be there to witness his own further eclipse. She started taking him to Italy for the summer, where he could learn both intellectually and emotionally that he was not a creature of no account.

The golden months in Florence, Venice, Ravenna, Cortona and San Gimigniano turned into the boy's happiest childhood memories, and gave him added confidence that at least he was the focus of his mother's attention, if not his father's.

# Chapter Nine

## London, May 1889

ILLUSTRATED LONDON NEWS:
MEN OF THE HOUR, NUMBER THREE

ACCOLADE FOR THE KING OF TEA

If you have a well-stocked store cupboard, it is likely that Sir Henry Richmond helped your housekeeper to fill it, for his is the most ubiquitous name in the provision trade. The knighthood granted last year by Her Majesty the Queen was seen by all who know him as the just reward for irreproachable public and private conduct, as well as for his legendary commercial acumen.

Although hardly a poor boy who made good, Henry Richmond has built an international business empire from very modest beginnings. Orphaned before birth when his father died in an epidemic, he was raised by his mother in the small North Wales town of Bangor and educated at Warwick School. At the age of eighteen, he chose to enter the family business rather than University or the Army. Having trained in family provision shops in North Wales and Manchester, he embarked upon a joint venture with his uncle, Idris Richmond, a wholesaler of fresh farm produce.

This much was given him as raw material; but young Henry Richmond had no intention of relying on the industry of his forebears to assure his own future comfort. Sir Henry has always admitted frankly that the Co-operative movement was his inspiration when he set up a chain of provision shops across the length and breadth of the kingdom, aiming to provide the working man with quality foods at modest prices. To achieve this aim, he and his uncle travelled abroad to set up supply depots for commodities as diverse as tea, coffee, cheese, meat, fruit and vegetables.

They started out by expanding their retail outlets, moving from the first Bangor provision shop in 1860 to a handful of small stores around the growing outer suburbs of London. Once a basic retail network was established, the Richmonds set out to supply their own shops as far as possible, and to this end secured exclusive contracts with food producers worldwide. Fifteen years later, they had more than one hundred shops in Britain. Abroad, their interests included a Chicago slaughterhouse with a capacity for one million pigs each year; their own tea estates in India, with a reserve stock of twelve thousand chests of tea in the main London warehouse; and general foodstuff depots in Hamburg, Copenhagen, Stockholm and Constantinople. Today, their canneries at home and abroad supply two hundred thousand cases of vegetables annually. In England, wholesale interests

include a jam factory, wine and spirits vaults, a
coffee roasting plant, fruit farms in Kent and
cheese dairies in the West Country. Once the
Richmond branches had secured adequate supplies, Sir Henry adopted the role of middleman to
other retailers, so that today his company's
choicest teas and quality preserves grace some of
the land's wealthiest tables, as well as more modest
households.

But his brilliant combination of wholesale and
retail marketing constitutes just one part of his
unique approach. The problem of finding trust-
worthy managers has dogged many others who
attempted to break into multiple selling. Sir Henry
made his managers co-owners from the start, with
a share participation scheme that assured higher
income against optimum profits. Although
Richmond's is still technically a family-owned
company, this feature of employee involvement will
guarantee its success into the twentieth century.

Sir Henry is supported in his commercial endea-
vour by an ideal family background. His mother,
Marged, is still active as business adviser to
Richmond Provisions. He met his wife, formerly
Elizabeth Rose, only granddaughter of Baron
Clitheroe, through family connections. They
married in 1864. They have four children,
Arthur, Margaret, Harry and Mary Rose. Arthur
Richmond's marriage later this month to the Ger-
man heiress Karin Cassel will be a highlight of the
London season.

Richmond's have been royal warrant holders to

the Prince of Wales for more than five years, supplying tea and coffee to Marlborough House. Sir Henry is frequently a member of the racing set which surrounds the Prince at major meetings. He is also a keen yachtsman and has been a familiar face at Cowes since 1882.

Our pictures show the Richmond family at work and at play. Above left: Sir Henry Richmond and Lady Richmond, Mrs Marged Richmond and Mr Arthur Richmond greet Mr Arthur Richmond's fiancée, Miss Karin Cassel, on her arrival at Victoria Station last week to prepare for her wedding.

Marged let out a satisfied sigh as she re-read the magazine article for the seventh time. It was nearly two weeks since its appearance, but the house was still scattered with some of the hundreds of copies Henry had ordered. There was not a single wrong note in it. They had taken the Richmond point of view from beginning to end; no hint of anything short of the closest intimacy with the Prince of Wales; and certainly no suggestion that dear Elizabeth was less than blue-blooded. Most satisfactory . . . Her smile faded slightly as she paused to wish that all was just as it seemed.

She went to pour herself a brandy, then returned to her leather armchair to muse further over the Richmond success story. 'Well, Henry,' she said aloud, 'I promised you that if you saw to the business and left the rest to me, everything would work out – and I was right, wasn't I?'

In fact she sometimes felt a pang of superstitious dread because so far it had almost been too right. Thirty years of practically undiluted success seemed too much to hope for. Still, on balance there had been sufficient disappointments to spice all that good fortune. It had been touch and go that Elizabeth might not turn out too well . . .

Marged gave a little snort of irritation as the brandy brought her personal feelings closer to the surface. She paid lip service to Henry's social climbing merely because she loved him and wished to please him. But secretly she found it idiotic. It had not been so bad when he was devoting most of his concentration to the business. But for the past ten years, with more leisure on his hands, he had been letting it get the better of him. In spite of all his achievements he was less self-assured socially now than fifteen years ago.

Arthur's marriage would do wonders for Henry's self-confidence – not that any of his associates would have agreed that it needed a boost – because his elder son's match with a Society girl showed he had finally scaled the heights.

True, she was a foreign Society girl, but no one could deny that Karin Cassel came from whatever passed for the top drawer in Germany. Marged smiled to herself at the irony which seemed set to repeat Henry and Elizabeth's match on a grander scale. Thank God the same thought hadn't occurred to Henry! Karin's mother had been the only daughter of an obscure prince; her father was a self-made man with a vast fortune in steel and coal. Her presence in the family would ensure that Henry's grandsons were on an equal footing with the finest in the land.

Well, that was the son and heir sorted out, anyway . . .

the marriage ceremony had just taken place in the ancient country church a mile down the road from the Richmonds' Thames-side mansion. Marged had slipped into the library for half an hour's rest before joining the five hundred guests at the reception in the garden. She rose and replaced her empty glass on the table. No need to let Henry see she'd already taken a little refreshment; she could hear him coming to find her.

As he entered the airy room, Marged smiled indulgently at her son. 'Very proud of yourself today, aren't you, boy?' She only ever sounded Welsh when they were alone, sharing their secret ambition.

'I don't need to tell you, Mother. Of course I am. It's the last step but one towards achieving all my – our – plans.'

'And the last step?'

'The birth of their son, as if you didn't know! Come on, let's find some champagne and drink to that.'

'Let them get out of the vestry before you start their family!' But Marged was still smiling. Henry's dynastic drive was a solid continuation of all she had dreamed about. She glanced across the lawn and saw Elizabeth watching them. I wonder if she ever resents me, she thought. In lots of ways I'm more like Henry's wife than she is . . . As always, there was something uncomfortable locked up within that thought, so Marged discarded it hurriedly and followed her son into the vast pink and white marquee on the lawn.

Elizabeth Richmond watched her mother-in-law and husband moving to the centre stage position and decided she could become less obtrusive for a while. She preferred sitting down quietly to standing lamely just

218

behind the other two, like some junior member of the firm. A glass of champagne, a comfortable chair and a shady corner . . . that would be perfect. The shady corner was easy – from where she stood she could see a white wrought iron bench beneath the paulonia just below the south terrace. The receiving line had broken up twenty minutes ago and most of the guests were still getting their luncheon. She slipped across the velvet-smooth grass and sat down.

Her own review of the last quarter-century was somewhat different from Marged's. Her father had never needed to tell her that he had deliberately arranged her first meeting with Henry Richmond, because she fell under Henry's spell immediately and was all in favour of the match when the time came. She loved Henry now even more than she had on her wedding day, but she knew she would always take second or third place in his life behind Marged, Arthur and even, possibly, the business. It had mattered a lot at first, but since the birth of her second son she had been content.

Arthur had grown up to be all his father and grandmother could wish. He was a good average at everything. Even his weight, height and looks were within suitable limits. His hair was a light golden brown and he had bright-brown eyes. It was a pleasing combination which made him attractive but not challengingly handsome. Conveniently, he stopped growing at five feet eleven, when he was just half an inch shorter than his father. It was the same with his intelligence. Quick and eager to learn, but not the gifted type who made ordinary mortals uneasy. Neither Henry nor Marged valued individuality. In Henry's youth, they had encountered such a quality, and Henry was almost destroyed as a result. Their credo was: work hard, set your sights high, adapt the good ideas of others, and don't stand out in a crowd except as a result of solid achievement. It had brought the family success, riches and public acclaim.

But none of this applied to Harry. He was everything his brother was not; everything his father and grandmother distrusted – and so he was a misfit. But not in Elizabeth's eyes. She adored and admired the very qualities in him which worried them. She loved Arthur, too, but Henry and Marged had effectively cut her off from him by drawing him into their private magic circle. They didn't mind how much affection she lavished on the second son, because he was too unconventional for their tastes.

Elizabeth was very careful not to show how much she favoured Harry. She harboured a subconscious fear that if they knew the depth of her love, they would steal him away from her. So, on the surface, she strove to treat all her children equally. Privately, though, both she and the boy understood they had a very special bond.

It was impossible not to have extreme feelings about Harry. His father swore he even cried louder and longer than any other baby, and as he grew he seemed to do everything else more intensely too. He showed prodigious intelligence from his earliest attempts at talking. He crawled and then walked months younger than Arthur had. Elizabeth tried teaching him his alphabet, almost as a personal amusement when she saw him noticing and remembering things in his picture books. He could read before he was three, and count soon afterwards.

When Arthur's expulsion from Eton had forced Henry to hand over both his sons to a private tutor, Harry's brilliance really began to show. The tutor was the best money could buy, and soon even the pedestrian Arthur was brighter and better-informed. Harry progressed so fast that his father was put off him for good.

He seemed to absorb everything the tutor laid before him, and had a particular aptitude for foreign languages. By the time he reached his teens, as well as the obligatory Latin and Greek, he spoke French, German and Italian. The tutor, a confirmed fan of the prodigy, was nerving himself to ask Richmond senior if the boy could also learn Hebrew and Spanish. Harry, fanatically interested in the great explorer Richard Burton, was keener on trying Arabic than Spanish. His physical development was equally precocious. He played the guitar and the piano and had been writing music for three or four years. But there was nothing effete about him. He was six feet tall before his fifteenth year was out and now, at almost twenty, stood at six feet four. His red-blond hair and eyes of a similar bright brown to his brother's, made him look like a fierce but friendly young lion. He loved horses and was passionate about foxhunting, riding to hounds three or four times a week. Tennis, boxing and rowing were his other sports.

Considering him now, Elizabeth found her lips curling into an unstoppable smile. Harry, my lovely golden Harry – you've made up for so many of my disappointments. Who could ever hope to be so fortunate in a son?

'And why is the bridegroom's mother alone and palely loitering? How dare you deprive us of the light of your countenance?'

221

She looked up with a start. Harry stood in front of her, a good-natured grin on his face. She gave him a flustered smile. 'Oh, no such thing, darling! It was just that as Grandmama needed a rest while we were receiving the guests, I thought I'd let her have a little time at the centre of things.'

'Hmm, yes, very kind of you, seeing that you keep the poor old thing locked up in the cellar the rest of the time!'

'Harry – you know what they say about sarcasm.'

'Come on, Mama, there's nothing low about my wit and you know it. I bet she didn't even ask you – probably slid her arm through Father's and swept off with him like a newly-wed.' He sniffed. 'I suppose he'll be in for even more of it now she won't be able to trail round like that with Arthur!'

'She's an old woman, darling. Remember her own husband was snatched away from her almost before she had time to know what it was to be a wife. It's natural she should cling to your father.'

'Of course, of course. I've no intention of spoiling your lovely day by drawing your attention to Grandmama's desire to hog the limelight. New subject: doesn't the bride look ravishing? I'm beginning to think old Arthur isn't getting such a bad deal after all. A pretty little package and the Cassel steel mills, all in one fell swoop!'

'Harry!' She was slightly scandalised but too amused by his irreverence to be really cross. 'Stop talking as if it's a business transaction.'

His face clouded. 'Well, isn't it? I must admit, Mama, I find all that a little hard to take. I'm not a child; I realise that in our position you don't just go out and marry the goose girl on the corner, but really! It reminded me of that time Papa took us to Smithfield to buy our own Christmas turkeys – which is the fattest that would cause us least trouble to get home, and do we get a free capon or a leg of pork if we take three?'

'But Arthur and Karin love each other.'

He pressed his hand against her lips. 'Enough! I know you're too clever really to believe that, and I refuse to accept you would lower yourself to join in the bargaining. So admit it was a neatly-arranged business merger and then you and I can relax with each other again.'

'Only if you promise not to go on like this when your father is within earshot. He'd have an apoplectic seizure!'

'Of course I shan't mention it to him. Anyway, when have you ever known him talk to me for long enough to hear any of my views?'

'Now now, you know he lives and breathes the business. He's pre-occupied in my company a lot of the time, too.'

Harry scowled at that. 'Yes, but never with Grandmama. And very seldom with our noble Arthur, come to that.'

'Darling, you're awfully sharp today. What is it?'

He shrugged as though impatient with himself. 'Oh, I don't know. You're the only one in this family who seems to enjoy my company. Why is it that I'm the most popular man in town with all my friends, but my father and grandmother act as though I'm a foundling and my elder brother tends to agree? Somehow it seems more obvious than ever today, that's all.'

'It's not really like that, dear. Of course they love you,

but they – they feel a little wary of you, I think, because you're so flamboyant!'

'You mean because I'm brighter than they are and I scare the living daylights out of them!'

'No, of course not. And anyway, your sisters and I are your handmaidens. Haven't you noticed?'

That brought his smile back. 'Your approval is all that matters to me in this family, Mama. It's quite flattering having two pretty misses clinging to my coat tails, too, I suppose.' There was a ripple of female laughter from a short distance away. He glanced up. ' . . . Speaking of which, I believe I'm about to be monopolised!'

There was immense pride in Elizabeth's expression as she watched her two daughters approaching. They had never looked lovelier and Margaret, the elder girl, was almost a mirror reflection of Elizabeth herself at that age. Margaret was twenty-two and about to announce her engagement to an American businessman. At sixteen, Mary Rose was the baby of the family and the one Henry hoped to match with a title.

Today's wedding had been held in England, not in the bride's native Bavaria, because her father wanted her to be launched conspicuously in her new adopted country. He had paid the bills for the reception, though, including the bridal gowns and trousseau. And what gowns! The Richmond fortune would have run to buying them easily enough, but Henry would have shied away from Cassel's choice of couturier as too ostentatious.

Ludwig Cassel was immune to English reserve. He had sent his daughter and her two future sisters-in-law to Worth for the bridal and bridesmaids' gowns. Karin's was a magnificent confection of cream Alençon lace over a cream satin underskirt striped with dull gold. Her lace veil was held back by a tiny crown of flowers and ribbons. A heavier version of the underskirt material had been used to make her attendants' gowns. These were designed around the season's most popular silhouette – narrow, smooth skirts with cinched waists, and shoulders broadened by the latest leg-o'-mutton sleeves. The necklines were slashed to the waist, then filled with fine cream chiffon, folded into countless tiny vertical tucks which ended in a high inner collar. The outer collar stood away in the manner of a Regency man's jacket, the squared shape emphasising the femininity of the girls who wore them. Their outfits were completed by small, almost plate-flat straw hats, fastened in place behind their piled-up hair by broad gold satin ribbons, and trimmed with gold and cream rosebuds.

I can almost guarantee they'll still have those dresses when they're fifty, thought Elizabeth with a smile.

'Harry, it's no use hiding behind Mother's skirts – Millicent Ogilvie is determined to catch Karin's bouquet with you standing beside her, and she's hunting you, red in tooth and claw! Nowhere is safe.' Margaret enjoyed teasing her younger brother, and his effortless success as a heart breaker was a perennial topic.

He glowered. 'If there's a grain of truth in that, I'm off for a solitary stroll. Expect me when the toasts start.' He bent and kissed his mother's cheek, then left them.

'Well, Mama, are you pleased with the way it's all going?' Mary Rose was hovering, waiting for the compliments she knew were coming.

'Delighted, and not least at the sight of my marvellous

daughters, looking quite delicious in their finery.'

'Oh, Mama, I'll be eternally grateful to Karin for the chance to wear Worth. Papa would never have let us – and maybe now he'll feel obliged to for my wedding.'

'You scheming child!' But Elizabeth was amused by Margaret's reaction. She knew it must be puzzling for the girls to understand their father's refusal to splash out on extravagant clothes, when they all knew how much he squandered on racehorses and yachts.

'Well, you know he won't let a German tradesman best him!'

'That's enough; some things aren't funny. And what about you, Mary Rose? Are you enjoying the day?'

'Bliss, pure bliss!' The girl raised her flower-like face to the sunlight and closed her eyes to luxuriate for a moment in its glow. This one was the beauty of her generation. She was small and bouncy, with her grandmother's chestnut hair and a golden tone to her skin which always made her look as if she had just stepped in from a walk in the sunshine. Her features were small and shapely and she was full of vitality.

It was the vitality which gave her a slight edge over Margaret, whose manner was much more sedate in spite of her lively sense of humour. Margaret resembled her mother and not the Richmond side of the family. Tall and slender, she had dark brown hair, dark eyes and pale skin. Her features were almost perfect and she moved gracefully. But Margaret was so self-effacing that she was often overlooked in favour of her sister. Not that it bothered her. She enjoyed her own company and shared Harry's love of books and music. In any case, she had fallen so deeply in love with Steven Royle that it would not be necessary to bring her to the attention of other eligible young men. He noticed her to the exclusion of any other woman, and he was the one who mattered to her.

The girls chattered and postured in their lovely gowns. Elizabeth humoured them, basked in their happiness, and thought about Harry. She wondered if Henry might be a little more flexible now that the eldest son was out of the nest. It was absurd to hold back someone with Harry's talent, merely on the suspicion that he might prove to be too flamboyant for the business. What on earth did Henry expect the boy to do with his life? Even if they sent him off to university, he would graduate within three years and then the problem would return . . . She resolved to discuss it yet again with Henry.

That night, when the newly-weds had driven off to the station *en route* to Switzerland and the last guests had departed on a wave of champagne, she raised the matter.

Elizabeth was sitting at her dressing table, brushing out her long, glossy hair and watching Henry covertly in one of her swing mirrors. 'I've been thinking, darling, now that Arthur is formally in charge of the buying operation in the North-west, it might be a good idea to start training Harry at the jobs Arthur's been doing in London until now.'

Henry, in the act of departing for his dressing room, stopped in his tracks. 'It doesn't sound like a good idea to me.'

'Why not? He's twenty next week, and Arthur was already in training when he reached eighteen. You could certainly do with another hand at headquarters, to judge from what you've been saying. Harry's the obvious choice.'

'Obvious to you, maybe, but not to anyone else! That's not what I had in mind at all.'

She cringed inwardly at the implication that she had no idea of what was appropriate to the business, but persisted. 'Then what *did* you have in mind? Someone has to do what Arthur's been doing.'

'Of course, of course – but not that young whippersnapper. My God, all he ever thinks of is parties and balls. That won't help the business! No, the choice is obvious. George Beynon knows more about the provision trade than I do – on the retail side, at least. I've decided to offer him a transfer to head office as general manager, retailing, and then I shall probably promote one of the really experienced junior head office departmental managers to cover the wholesale side.'

'But that will cut Harry out completely.'

'That's a very melodramatic way of putting it, Elizabeth. You can't cut someone out of a concern he's never been involved in, can you? Harry's never shown a jot of interest in Richmond's Quality Provisions.'

'That's absurd! You never listen to him long enough to know where his interests lie.'

'No need – he makes it all too obvious. Writing clever rhymes for pretty girls and translating dubious plays from French! No, my mind's made up – and Mother agrees with me – Harry's not the right man to train for the firm.'

It was unusual for Elizabeth to display anger, but now she did. 'Oh, really? Thank you for telling me. Perhaps I would have had a view on the matter if you'd bothered to ask. You seem to have forgotten that I'm your wife, Harry is our son, and my considerable fortune is now part of the Richmond empire. I'd have thought that gave me a right to be heard.'

Good Lord, I've actually managed to surprise him, she thought. Henry turned back towards her, his tone less hectoring. 'Er . . . well . . . you always seem content to let Mother and me run things. Why should you change now?'

'Because in the past you've both seemed very competent at what you were doing and I saw no reason to intervene. Now, for reasons best known to yourselves, you're going to considerable lengths to exclude our second son from his proper inheritance. I'm not prepared to let you do so.'

'Elizabeth, really darling, now *you're* being absurd! I – we – that is, it's not permanent. Harry is the sort who'd benefit from a couple of years at Oxford. Far too talented to end his education now . . . all I was doing was arranging things so that he could go off in the autumn and then think about entering Richmond's when he's had his fill of learning. He'll make very useful contacts there, you can't deny that.'

And you didn't invent that glib explanation, either, she thought mutinously. That has all the hallmarks of a Marged Richmond ploy. 'Just let Elizabeth think we're doing it all for his own sake if she starts getting awkward.' Am I ever going to have a say in how our family business uses my money?

Henry had now reached her side. He seemed genuinely worried by her anger. 'Darling, what's wrong? You've never talked like this before. Surely you don't think your inheritance is being misused?'

She felt slightly shamefaced and looked away from the mirror, down at her hands. 'No, of course not. You've always managed the finances brilliantly.'

'And you've always been at least as materially comfortable as you were before we married?'

'Yes, yes – you know that. It's just . . .' she was about to let him embarrass her out of pressing Harry's case, as he had once or twice before. She loved him dearly and wanted to please him, but this was too important to be dropped again. She looked up defiantly, facing him in the mirror. 'No. It's not "just" anything! Please listen. I have something important to say.'

He looked quite stricken as he sat down in a rosewood chair a few feet away. 'Go on.'

'Don't think I haven't been happy with you, Henry. I have. But you've hurt me a lot, along with the joy. All our life together, I've been second best; second best to your mother.' She gestured angrily as he tried to interrupt. 'No, I must finish this now. You've been a good husband – kind and generous and loving – but only up to a point. I was never in any doubt who came first, me or your mother, even before we were engaged. At the beginning I kept telling myself it would change as we grew closer, but it didn't. Then Arthur came along and I thought, ah, now we'll be a proper family. But I was wrong again. You and your mother took Arthur and you still shut me out.

'I sometimes feel quite guilty, because at times I've been pleased that neither of you had any love left for Harry – or for the girls, come to that. At least it meant I

230

had some family to love who loved me just as much in return. But I can't let it go on any longer, because now you're really going to start harming Harry. You've hurt him before, but never at the cost of his future. You mustn't go on like this, Henry. It won't destroy him – he's too strong for that. But it will cripple him eventually.'

She drew a deep breath and sat back, flushed with a mixture of embarrassment and anger. Henry was staring at her as if he had discovered a new, unknown personality who had inexplicably changed places with his wife. He got up and moved behind her chair, resting his hands on her shoulders and looking past her into the mirror.

'I do love you, Elizabeth, truly I do. I – I never thought you were at all unhappy. I've only tried to involve Mother so that she wouldn't be excluded, but it seems I've done the same thing to my own wife in trying to cosset her. You look so lonely – and so lovely.'

He bent further and kissed her neck, then took her hands, drew her to her feet and turned her to face him. 'You're so beautiful, and so good at everything you do. I really couldn't have done half of all this without you.'

He kissed her again, tenderly and then with mounting passion. She felt her resolve slipping as the old excitement of his touch ignited her passion for him. It was so long . . . so long since he'd come to her like this. They could sort it all out about Harry later . . . Henry had more or less admitted it was all mere thoughtlessness. As she responded to his caresses, a small, doubting voice insinuated momentarily, but she shook it off. She needed to be a woman again, not a loving mother or a dutiful daughter-in-law. She'd sort it out tomorrow. Tonight was for her.

In a grand hotel overlooking Lake Lugano, Karin Richmond stood alone on the balcony of the Royal Suite and gazed bleakly across the moonlit water. She did not know exactly what was wrong, but it was clearly something very important. For the third night in succession, Arthur was lying in the huge ornate bed, pretending to be asleep but really staring at the painted ceiling. Like many girls of her rarified background, she had married with no precise idea of what would happen to her when she was alone with him, but common sense and his own shame-faced attitude told her it should be more than this. Unfortunately her ignorance was such that she did not know whose fault it was, and a lifelong habit of obeying the men in her life had prepared her to assume the blame was hers. Arthur had shown no inclination to tell her what they should be doing, so she remained bewildered and was reduced to mulling over the recent past in search of an explanation.

Perhaps she was not sufficiently enthusiastic? After all, she had hardly fallen passionately in love with her bridegroom. They had been introduced a year ago and the courtship had been conducted in an atmosphere of intense formality which positively discouraged intimacy between them. So many of her friends and relatives had gone through similar rituals in preparation for marriage that she never wondered whether there was any other way. That thought had not entered her head until she first saw Arthur's brother Harry. Thinking of it now, she let out a little gasp of anxiety. Could it be that he sensed

232

it? Had he noticed that when she was near Harry, she stopped noticing anyone else? If so, perhaps it explained his coldness now.

Her speculation was cut off by an impatient movement from the bed. 'What are you doing over there, Karin? You'll catch a chill – for heaven's sake come back to bed and stop brooding. It will be all right, you'll see.'

Reluctantly she turned away from the brilliant silver light into the oppressive darkness of the room. As she climbed back into bed, she said, 'But what will be all right? I don't understand.'

He did not answer, but grabbed her awkwardly and pulled her towards him, fumbling as he did so with the folds of the ornate satin nightgown. Impatient of the ribbons and tiny buttons at the neck, after a moment he merely pulled it up, giving Karin the disagreeable impression that he was rummaging in a sack for her. As their bodies made contact, she realised for the first time that he was naked. He must have removed his nightshirt while she was at the window. She recoiled, shocked. Karin was unfamiliar even with female nudity. To find herself in this intimate position with a naked man was incomprehensible to her, its strangeness intensified by the fact that he had made only the most rudimentary approaches on the previous two nights. What was she supposed to do? Did she just lie here, pretending they were behaving quite normally? Did she try to imitate what he was doing, touching him as he was touching her? Confusion made her nervous, and Arthur's own frenetic behaviour was no help.

She fought a desire to panic, but as he clutched her left

breast in both hands and clamped his mouth around the nipple, she began to lose control. It felt as if he was eating her! Surely married people didn't do things like this? Unbidden, a vision of Harry insinuated itself. Now if he were doing it, perhaps . . . Shocked, she thrust aside the thought almost as it occurred, but guilt only increased her agitation.

'Arthur, please, what are you doing? I don't understand . . . what am I supposed to do?'

He was panting hard as he raised himself slightly and looked down at her. 'Shut up – just shut up, you understand? You're mine, now, no one else's. You – belong – to – me. I can do what I want to with you . . . nobody to tell me what to do all the time. So you'd better just keep quiet and do what you're told!'

She tried to stay calm and tell him she wanted to do as she was told, if only he would explain, but before she could say anything he threw himself on her and started kissing her neck and face. His tongue forced her lips apart and thrust into her mouth. Now he had raised her nightgown sufficiently to expose her naked body to his own. He lay half across her and held her rigid with one hand twisted viciously through her long hair. The other hand slid down over her smooth ribs and belly. She crossed her legs and gave a little moan. He did not speak but shifted his weight and started forcing one knee against her thighs to prise them apart.

Really frightened now, Karin instinctively tensed herself against his grip. With a force that made him grunt with effort, he thrust her legs apart by virtually kneeling on her. Unable to combat his strength, she relaxed suddenly, her legs opening wide under the pressure. He was quite frantic. 'Quick, quick you bitch, or it will be too late!' He lay full length on her, freeing her hair to hold her legs apart with both hands. He seemed to be gripped by a rhythmic convulsion as he pressed down on her, apparently attempting to push something right inside her body. Karin was crying now, in terror, half convinced he had lost his sanity.

Then it was over as abruptly as it had begun. His manic thrusting movements ceased and she felt wetness spreading across her legs and abdomen. Arthur let out an animal wail and then began sobbing. 'Oh no, no, please! I must do it . . .' The remaining words tailed off into an incoherent babble. Karin, still at a loss to know what he must do or even whether he had done it, remained lying rigid and terrified in the position he had forced on her.

By now, Arthur had withdrawn to the other side of the immense bed. His sobs diminished and soon ceased. Then, without a word, he slipped out on the far side and left the room. For a long while she lay still, half convinced that if he returned and she had moved, he would become violent again. But the night wore on with no sign of him, and her limbs became cramped and cold. After a while she turned over on her side and rolled herself into a tight ball, like a hedgehog. Eventually she slept a little. When she woke, the first grey pre-dawn light was streaking the windows. There was still no sign of Arthur and Karin decided she must get up and cleanse herself of her humiliation, even if the result was more inexplicable rage.

She poured scented oil into the bath as the hot water ran into it, then swiftly braided her dark-gold hair under a lace cap to protect it from the steam. Moments later she was relaxing and washing away the night's horrors. Already the whole preposterous scene seemed an impossible nightmare. Karin wondered vaguely about Arthur's whereabouts and mood, then pushed the thoughts aside. Time enough to confront that when she was face to face with him.

That encounter took place hours later as she sat down in the suite's drawing room to eat breakfast. When she rang for the footman to serve it, she had lacked the means to cancel an order for two. As it happened, Arthur and the breakfast trolley arrived almost simultaneously. He must have put on clothes in his dressing room before leaving in the middle of the night, for now he seemed his normal self: calm, friendly and well turned-out. He carried a large bunch of flowers which he gave her with a flourish, and which the footman took away for arranging.

When they were alone, he made much of pouring coffee and buttering a croissant. Karin made no attempt to follow suit; she simply sat and stared at her husband, awaiting an explanation.

He could not maintain his self-possession for long, but no proper explanation was forthcoming, then or ever. Impulsively he got up and bent over her hand, kissing it. She flinched before she could stop herself, and he blushed. 'I-I'm so very sorry about . . . all that,' he said. 'It's not you, it's me. Something I have to sort out, though God knows how. Do you forgive me?'

She looked at him, praying he would explain what she might do to help, but he was insufficiently sensitive even to recognise her ignorance. Eventually she said: 'I wish I knew what to do, that's all. I really wasn't trying to be a bad wife. I just didn't . . .'

Before she could go further, he was talking again. 'No, I know, decent women don't like that sort of thing – my behaviour was inexcusable. But if only I could – could . . .'

'Neither of us seems to be able to finish a sentence this morning!' She attempted a little laugh but it faded and died in the embarrassed silence.

After a while, Arthur merely managed to say, 'If only I didn't have such a lot to live up to!' But that explained nothing to poor Karin, who remained bewildered.

He sat brooding beside the table for a while, then Karin announced she was going for a walk and wished to do a little shopping. He arranged for a footman to accompany her, but did not offer to go along too. She was glad to escape, if only for an hour. When she returned to the hotel, Arthur once again seemed to be the smooth young man she had married. He made no further reference to the previous night, and after that he slept alone in his dressing room.

When the honeymoon ended and they returned to England, Karin was still a virgin, and although she was not fully aware of how unusual this was, Arthur's withdrawn behaviour made it obvious that all was not as it should be. But when they got back, life became easier. Henry had reorganised the firm's management structure to create Arthur's new job in the North-west. From now on, Arthur's attention was wholly on work. Karin breathed a secret sigh of relief and set about preparing for the move to Liverpool.

Marged, always sharp-eyed in matters concerning Henry and Arthur, sensed Karin's extreme nervousness. She had no idea what was causing it, but the girl's happiness was an important ingredient in her family strategy. She considered the immediate future. A house on the edge of Liverpool, however attractive, might not be enough to foster their romantic attachment. Her thoughts turned to North Wales. Where better to give them a rural retreat for intimate breaks in the business routine? Only until Karin showed signs of impending motherhood, of course. After that, better that Arthur should stay in Liverpool, close enough to watch Richmond's northern interests day and night.

She had sold the Menai View house years ago when they moved south. But Idris had kept his pretty villa on the hill above the harbour. When he died in 1868, he willed it to her. She had spent a couple of summer holidays there with the girls when they were small, but had never been comfortable so far from Henry. After that, George Beynon and his brood of half-grown children moved in. George's promotion to North Wales area manager had required a suitably impressive home. Now George's children were all grown up and married. He himself would have retired had it not been for his important new job, the long delayed crowning of his career. He and Siân had already moved to London in preparation, and the house, Tan-yr-Allt, was vacant again. Marged made it her special present to the newly-weds.

'Only an afternoon's journey from Liverpool on the train, my dear,' she told Karin, 'and you'll be in this lovely place between the mountains and the sea. Perfect for a young bride to relax with her husband when the city is too much of a strain – and ideal for children, of course.'

Karin was naively grateful. She didn't even care

whether Arthur spent his time there with her or shipped her off alone. He was so remote that she might as well not be his wife. Nobody seemed to notice the coolness between them except Harry, and Karin suffered agonies of guilt over the secret fantasies she entertained of him snatching her away from his brother and taking her to a remote spot where they could be happy together.

Harry was quite unaware of these daydreams, although he realised his sister-in-law was uncommonly taken with him. That was no unusual thing for him. He attracted women effortlessly, almost without realising the strength of his own magnetism. He was attentive to Karin because he sensed that she was excluded from the magic circle almost as ruthlessly as he was. As a result, he started paying her attention at family parties, always making sure she had a drink or someone to talk to; always introducing her to an amusing new acquaintance or suggesting an exciting diversion for her next trip to London.

He was going through a bad patch. Elizabeth's determination to make his father treat him better had been side-tracked, temporarily at least, and Henry had started to make arrangements for him to embark on an undergraduate career at Oxford in October. Elizabeth herself seemed dreamy and inaccessible, more like a young bride than a middle-aged matriarch. When the family were told why, it dealt Harry a paralysing emotional blow.

They were alone together on the south terrace one sunny afternoon in late August. Arthur and Karin would depart for Liverpool the following week. Harry's first term was still more than a month away. Elizabeth watched him quietly for a few minutes, her heart over-flowing with love for him. If only she could express how deeply she cared.

But she couldn't; dared not. No one knew better than she how such smothering love could deform a son. Instead, she said, 'I have some rather surprising news, Harry. I – that is, er, we – are having another baby. Isn't it wonderful?'

He had been moving away from her, turning to face the glorious view across the lawn to the Thames. He stopped as though frozen. She saw the small shudder pass through him. Long, silent seconds passed, then he turned in slow motion to face her. He was white, his face stiff.

'You can't be. No, not you. You're my – my mother!'

'Yes, my darling, of course – but that's all right, isn't it? You *do* have a brother and two sisters!' She tried to laugh, and failed.

'N-no. Not all right, not at all. Oh, God, Mama – how could you?' And he flung himself at her, clinging as though he were once again a little boy and she a grown woman.

She embraced him and then pushed him back gently until she could study his face. 'Harry, my Harry – don't talk as if I've betrayed you. You mean so much to me, I couldn't bear it!'

He was on the edge of tears. 'I'm thinking of you, Mama. It can't be safe, not for a woman with grown-up children. Well, can it?'

This time she managed the laugh, but it was shaky. 'Of course it is, silly! Plenty of women go on having children from the age of twenty or so well up to my age and beyond, and they're perfectly all right.'

240

'But how? Surely you couldn't have meant to?'

That made her blush. Some things were not discussed by mothers and sons, however close their bond. 'I think that's something for your father and me and for no one else, don't you?' The touch of asperity in her voice came from her guilty feeling that the pregnancy might have resulted from Henry's side-tracking her off a subject he found disagreeable. After all, their renewed physical intimacy had stemmed directly from the confrontation the night after Arthur's wedding. Elizabeth hurriedly pushed such thoughts aside.

'I thought I'd tell you first, my dearest boy. I shall let the girls know later today – and Arthur and Karin, of course.'

He was still tight-faced. 'When?'

She started to ask if that mattered before realising he meant when was the baby due, not when would she tell Arthur. 'Oh – er – the end of January, I'm fairly sure.'

He bit his lip and nodded. Somehow this announcement of a date made the whole thing real and unavoidable. He moved close to her again, but this time he was more controlled. He reached out and gripped her upper arms, looking earnestly into her face as he did so. 'Mama, please forgive me for being so unpleasant, but I'm so scared for you. You're the only family I have, in the sense that matters to me. Oh, I love the girls, but really it's up to *me* to protect *them*, isn't it? I've always seen you as a sort of – of wall of love against the enemy. I don't think I could manage without you.'

She wanted to weep. This baby was welcome, but she might have thought twice about it had she realised for a second how deeply it would hurt Harry. Then the thought of Marged's relationship with Henry recurred and she wondered whether this quite accidental pregnancy might be the best means of ensuring that such a travesty of motherhood did not recur in the second generation. She stood on tiptoe and kissed her son on his cheek. 'Come along, take me inside for tea. You know you'll always come first with me.'

'How dare she? How bloody dare she?' Alone in her elegant sitting room in the west wing, Marged slammed savagely at a fat satin cushion. While Elizabeth was breaking the news to Harry, Henry had been performing the same duty with his mother. She had received his tidings with apparent calm, only expressing concern for Elizabeth, having a child so late in life and after a seventeen-year break. Now he was gone, and she was able to give vent to her true feelings.

'Bitch, bitch, bitch!' she yelled, pummelling the cushion again. Good God, it was almost indecent! Weren't four brats enough for her? It was her daughter-in-law who should be producing by now, not Elizabeth herself. Why, most respectable women would have stopped that sort of thing with their husbands years ago. Had she no shame? Marged went to get her brandy bottle. If she were to face tonight's dinner guests with a calm exterior, she would need a little help from her old friend.

Apart from these two devastated individuals, everyone else in the family treated Elizabeth as a heroine and Henry as a lovably wicked old roué, a totally inappropriate description of the head of the family.

Arthur was less than enthusiastic, but only Karin had any idea that this was because of his own failure as a bearer of the dynastic flame. Slowly, she was beginning to learn about the sensual life of men and women. Elizabeth quietly tried to inform her, suspecting the girl had been totally ignorant when she married. As her knowledge grew, Karin was becoming increasingly perplexed. She was sufficiently well informed now to realise that they would never start a baby of their own while Arthur found it impossible to consummate their marriage. He had tried again, several times, since their honeymoon, always with disastrous results. He seemed driven by his father's expectations and was so anxious that he might disappoint Henry that he invariably failed to complete the act he started with such aggression. He remained courteous and considerate towards her by day. By night, he increasingly left her to sleep alone. Matters had now deteriorated to the point where he only came to her room if he intended to make another of his desperate attempts to penetrate her. Karin tried to co-operate with him, but once he got hold of her he became so rough that the familiar panic started inside her again and that terrible first night repeated itself.

As though to compensate for his failure, Arthur was more arrogant in his business dealings. Men who had found him modest and reasonable six months ago now avoided him if they could. No one had the courage to tell his father, who was known to dote on the boy, so Henry remained ignorant of Arthur's declining popularity. Early in September, when he moved to take up his appointment in Liverpool, the entire headquarters management staff heaved a collective sigh of relief.

The move presented a daunting prospect to Karin. She had only just accustomed herself to her new family, substituting Margaret, Mary Rose and their friends for her German social circle, and Elizabeth for her long-dead mother. Now she was expected to make a second change. She found Liverpool uninviting. The rented house which Henry had chosen for them was in a bleak suburb. The wives of the neighbouring business and professional men were parochial and resented a newcomer, suspecting they would be patronised by this rich young foreigner who was bound to be more sophisticated than they. In fact all Karin wanted was friendship, particularly as she had no real relationship with her husband. When she realised that no welcome was forthcoming in the city, she turned eagerly to their second home in Bangor.

Arthur took her down by train on a golden mid-September afternoon. The train chugged along the North Wales coast, hugging the skirts of the mountains which seemed to drop almost sheer to the sea. The carriage which awaited them at the station drove a mile or so up the Holyhead road before doubling back down the hill to Tan-yr-Allt, giving Karin her first sight of the elegant suspension bridge and the jewel-like scattering of tiny islands in the straits.

It was love at first sight. As Arthur handed her down from the carriage in the forecourt of Idris's pretty old house, she said, 'I'm going to love it here, Arthur, I just know I am!'

Arthur had not visited Bangor since a couple of holiday trips to stay with Idris as a child. Now he, too, realised its beauty. He had fully intended to leave Karin there and to see her as little as possible. Even he had begun to realise there was no hope of him fathering the much-desired heir as long as he was so dominated by fear of his father and of his grandmother's disapproval. But the beauty of the place drew him, and after that first visit he found himself coming down with increasing frequency at week-ends to join his wife. He still lacked the maturity to cope with his sexual problem, but at least he was becoming a better companion for her. Unfortunately he still needed to prove his superior talents to make up for his flagging masculinity, and excellence as a provision wholesaler seemed to him an appropriate source of pride.

He took to spending alternate Mondays on Anglesey, visiting farmers and looking at what they had to offer. By mid-November he decided he was ready to introduce premium lines of Welsh farm butter and cheese to the Merseyside and Manchester Richmond's branches.

When Henry got his son's letter, proposing the new introduction, he was furious, largely because it was less a request for permission than a statement of intent. But beneath his instinctive resentment lay a solid base of good sense. He had established worldwide depots and invested in efficient transport services in order to bring down his retail prices until they beat the competition. Such bargains were not achieved by continuing to use a small area which produced unpredictable quantities of goods of extremely variable quality. As far as Henry was concerned, the small one-man supplier had been obsolete since the 1870s.

He was reluctant to be too hard on Arthur – after all, if the boy failed at this top job, the staff would all remember it had been Henry who sent him there – so he got hold of George Beynon to find a tactful solution.

George was ten years older than Henry but looked younger. He was an excellent general manager just as he had been first rate at running a single shop. He liked people, refused to worry about the future and enjoyed his family. Every time he looked at Henry Richmond, the sight secretly reinforced his belief that he would out-live his boss by twenty years or more.

George had sons, too, and he understood Henry's dilemma. 'Don't worry – I'll treat him with kid gloves. There'll be a hundred good reasons I can find for not using the small producers, and at least half of them can be wrapped up so that he won't feel he's failed at all.'

'Thanks, George – you know, I think you're the only man in the whole organisation I'd trust for a family matter like this.'

George twinkled at him. 'Well, now, I'm the only one working here that has ever been in a position to order you to sweep the floor, aren't I? Once a man's got that over you, you can ask him anything!'

Henry chuckled. 'Good man! If you can manage to travel up by train on Monday, I'll be eternally grateful.'

Arthur treated Beynon with some suspicion, but as this was a man who had given him piggybacks and played cricket with him as a child, it faded quickly. Over dinner, fired with enthusiasm, he described his forays into the island's agricultural hinterland.

'Just a minute, boy – it do sound as if you've been exploring up the Amazon, not working out the cheese supply! How would it be if we went and had a look round tomorrow, you and me? Could you do with a bit of advice from an old hand?'

Arthur's smile took on a stubborn quality, but his

friendship for George held. 'Yes, I suppose so . . . but don't think I've forgotten any wrinkles. I think I've got it just right – slight oversupply to insure against the ones who inevitably fail to deliver; top quality stuff; guaranteed minimum price tied to high standards of production. How does that sound?'

'Admirable, Arthur, admirable. But there may be one or two things you won't have had the need to look at yet, and perhaps it would be a good idea if we both tied them up together. All right?'

By the middle of the following afternoon, George was convinced that Arthur had been ruled by his desire to pull off a coup. He had found a handful of farms which were producing superb cheeses that would sell well in any grocer's. But these could never assure sufficient quantity to justify setting up a proper supply network. Now his concern was to let Arthur down gently. Half way through their visits to the second and third-rank farms on Arthur's list, he remarked casually: 'I don't expect you'll have needed to do much with hygiene at the source of supply yet, will you, Arthur?'

The younger man was prickly straight away. 'Just as much as the next buyer of my generation. It's hardly an urgent requirement when you're buying your cheese in sterilised blocks from overseas.'

'Quite, quite. It's only we old-fashioned types who've had any call to do it. That's really why your father asked me to come up to give you a bit of backing . . . he knew with your experience of modern buying and selling and such, you didn't need any help there, but he was a bit worried because you'd never had call to look into clean production.'

247

'But these farms are clean enough to eat off the floor. Look at this dairy – it's immaculate!'

George gave him a sad smile. 'On top, yes. But it's hard to get these smaller farmers to accept they must take sick cows out of production straight away and destroy the whole batch of milk – and any cheese they still have that may have been started when the sickness was just beginning. You're not to know, but that's a major reason why we started taking the imported cheese. When they produce on the scale those foreign farmers do, their reputation is worth more to them than one lost batch. They'll throw out anything even slightly suspect, see, and your small Welsh farmer never will – can't afford it.'

'But I've seen these people at work. They're so careful –'

'Maybe, man, maybe. But you look at this. When we come in, did you notice the pigsty?'

'Yes, what of it? Lots of these suppliers run mixed farms.'

'I know, that's the trouble. Get a really virulent bug in one type of stock and unless you're very lucky, it's everywhere before you can say Jack Robinson. Worst of all, it may be one of these things as don't show in the animals who pass it on but can kill off people.'

George had fondly hoped to win with his friendly manner and choice of an objection of which Arthur could plead ignorance without shame. But Arthur had too much to prove. As George spoke, his smile had become increasingly truculent. 'That, George, is just old-fashioned nonsense! Why, farms are infinitely cleaner now than twenty years ago. There's nothing here

I wouldn't be prepared to eat or drink myself, at this very moment.'

'Well, there's plenty I wouldn't. I'm telling you, there was something wrong with one of those pigs out there. And after we come in, I saw the pig man bring something in here. He might have cleaned himself up before he did it, but if so, there wasn't much obvious improvement when I saw him going back out just now. He'd been over by the big pans over there, too. Anyone who's seen how disease can start from food in humid weather will tell you that's how to cause an epidemic.'

As soon as the words were out, he realised he had lost. That last sentence had been too close to a challenge for Arthur's pride to take it. He turned and marched over to the pans in which the milk was beginning to separate from the cream. 'Right, George Beynon. Just to prove that I have complete faith in this farmer, and in my whole new idea –' And he picked up a long-handled ladle from the slate bench, dipped it deep in the nearest pan and drank a good quarter-pint of the acidulating milk.

George winced as he watched. He had been prepared to lay on the danger-of-infection warning to the point of excess, but when they reached this dairy he had seen he would not need to. All he had said was true. There was a sick animal outside and one of the herdsmen had come into the dairy after visiting the sty. Arthur had just exposed himself not to one but to dozens of possible maladies. Unfortunately, there seemed to be nothing more to say. The boy was headstrong to the point of madness. He might well get a badly upset stomach from that little lot. And on top of it, George was going to be unable to persuade him to abandon his wholesaling idea voluntarily. The next stage would be a fight between Arthur and Henry Richmond – and George liked Henry too much to wish that on him.

'All right, Arthur: you've got my opinion, for what it's worth. I don't want to do down your ideas, but it's only fair to tell you, I think your father will feel the same as I do about it.'

'Oh, I'm sure he will by the time you've finished with him! Well, I don't care. I'm quite able to defend my point of view, and I'll go down to headquarters to do it if he doesn't back me.'

'Fair enough.' George knew when he was beaten. He had no intention of spending a miserable day until he caught the train tomorrow. 'Let's shake hands, then, and I wish you luck. You may have a point, and if you have I'm sure your father will support you.'

That seemed to mollify Arthur. They found the farmer, said goodbye and drove back to Bangor.

George left on the London train at noon the next day. He arrived in the capital too late to contact Henry Richmond, who was out of town for a meeting of his own the following day. By the time George finally got to see him at Richmond House on Friday morning it was three days since his disagreeable farm visit with Arthur. To his astonishment, Henry met him in the main vestibule. He was white-faced and agitated. 'God, George, how was the boy when you saw him last?' he asked, his voice shaking.

'In the best of spirits – a bit tired, but we'd stayed up late talking over this and that. Why, what's wrong?'

Henry fumbled in his jacket pocket and took out a crumpled piece of paper. 'See for yourself . . . telegram

250

from Karin . . . came just a few minutes ago . . . I must get the next train!' And he turned back towards reception to arrange transport.

Full of dread, George looked down at the telegram. It said: 'Arthur gravely ill diphtheria. Please come at once. Karin.'

Sweet Jesus, he thought. What a price to pay for a single reckless swig of milk.


Arthur had been taken ill on Thursday evening with a sore throat and high temperature. The sickness progressed so fast that he was almost delirious when the doctor arrived an hour after Karin had put him to bed. The symptoms were gruesomely familiar and Dr Pearce diagnosed diphtheria within moments.

'It's progressing very fast, Mrs Richmond, very fast indeed. Have you ever contracted the disease?' She shook her head, watching him anxiously. 'In that case, I urge you to leave the nursing to someone who has. It seldom strikes twice if a sufferer has been fortunate enough to recover. I know two women in Bangor who had it as children. With your permission, I'll see if either one is free to nurse your husband.'

'Yes, Doctor, but surely, if I'm going to get it, I already . . .'

He reassured her. 'Not necessarily, unless you've been in close physical contact during the past couple of days. Your husband probably picked it up from something he ate or drank. After that, though, all the signs lead us to think it's spread by touching, not just breathing a victim's contaminated air. Well – are you likely to be infected, d'you think?'

'Perhaps I shall be lucky. We sleep in separate rooms, and I have seen very little of my husband for the past two days. I was out walking this afternoon, alone, and by the time dinner was ready he felt too ill . . .'

'In that case, please leave this to me. I know you'll be anxious to remain at his side, but believe me, he's unlikely to know who is nursing him.'

Pearce stayed on for hours. He sent the coachman for one of the sick nurses and she arrived just before midnight. They packed Karin off to bed shortly afterwards, assuring her she could do nothing by staying up. In the middle of the night, she woke from uneasy sleep to hear people moving on the landing. She got up and opened her bedroom door as the nurse passed.

'Is it worse? What is happening?'

'Nothing you can do, ma'am. It's in God's hands now – and Dr Pearce's,' said the woman. 'He've just had put in a breathing tube to stop the poor boy choking, see.'

It sounded horrific. Karin recoiled at the woman's sketchy explanation. At that moment Dr Pearce himself emerged from the sickroom. 'Quickly, now, Agnes. I'll want you to sterilise all those instruments again, in case any infection stays on them. Off you go!' He turned to Karin. 'I'm sorry, Mrs Richmond, but try not to worry. I'm doing all that's humanly possible. We're in the main crisis now – probably over it, in fact.'

She was unsure whether hope or fear leaped inside her at that. Did she want this cold, unlikeable young man to survive? She covered her confusion with a question.

'So he will be all right?'

'I can't possibly say, I'm afraid. Diphtheria does so

much damage. I've known strong patients survive the infection only to be bedridden for life by heart trouble. It will be three days or more before I can say whether he'll live – a lot longer to know if he'll be a permanent invalid.'

'I must contact my father-in-law, Doctor. He will want to come immediately, I am sure.'

'If he does, and sees your husband, I'll have to quarantine him. You too, of course, and Agnes Roberts now that she's nursing him. That applies to the housekeeper and groom, as well. They both live here, so their contact with Mr Richmond is too close to risk spreading the illness. I'm the only one allowed to come and go, and even I must be circumspect in my contacts. I'll see Sir Henry is informed at once.'

'How long will the quarantine last?'

'Ten days. You're lucky. It was forty days until a few years ago. If your father-in-law decides to see his son when he arrives, he will have to stay here until the end of next week. Otherwise, he might prefer to stay at an hotel until the crisis is over.'

Karin nodded silently and moved away. If she knew anything of Henry's regard for his elder son, he would be sitting at the bedside the minute he got here.

Dr Pearce helped Karin to compose a brief telegram in the morning, then arranged to have it sent. He went off to get a few hours' rest himself after that. Agnes Roberts fussed sympathetically over Karin and repeatedly assured her it was all in the hands of God.

When Henry's train was still less than half way to North Wales, Agnes emerged from the sick room to call through the front door and send for Dr Pearce via the

253

small boy he had stationed at the end of the drive. 'Tell Doctor Mr Richmond's much worse and he'd better come at once!' she said.

Karin came out into the hall. 'How much worse, please, Mrs Roberts?'

'Oh, ma'am, I – I'm afraid we're losing him! But don't take my word. Doctor may be able to do something.'

But Dr Pearce barely arrived in time to see Arthur still breathing. As Pearce started to examine him, Arthur's heart finally gave out. Attempts to revive him were useless.

Downstairs in the hallway, Karin waited, stone-faced. All she could find to say was, 'I do not know how to tell his father.'


Harry never forgot the train journey south when they took Arthur's body home for burial. It was like a scene out of some macabre tale of fiction. Devastated by grief, his father had sat vigil beside the coffin throughout the days until the corpse was released for burial. He only left Arthur's side when Marged took his place.

Henry had sent for Marged as soon as he arrived, and Harry insisted on going to Bangor with her, in spite of her protests. Now he was relieved at having persevered. Karin would have found life impossible without him, as the two strongest characters in the family monopolised the funeral arrangements and the grief. Elizabeth, who was suffering a difficult pregnancy, stayed at home, with Margaret and Mary Rose for company. Henry decided that only a special train would do take his dead son back to the South. Eventually they started out, in what amounted to a steam-driven hearse – two luxuriously-appointed private carriages and a locomotive. The coffin lay in state in the rear carriage, resting on crepe-draped trestles and surrounded by banks of gold and white flowers. Heavy black curtains had been hung inside the window blinds, which were kept pulled down throughout the journey. At the far end of the carriage, candles burned on a small altar, complete with crucifix, which Henry had insisted be installed for family prayer on the way down. Each time Harry saw it he was swept by an impulse to laugh hysterically. Anyone less religious than either his father or brother was hard to imagine.

The front carriage was the passenger drawing room, laid out to look as much as possible like a Victorian parlour. Two curtained areas at the front corners were closed off for Karin and Marged to rest in when they needed to. When Marged was not taking her turn sitting beside the coffin, she spent most of the time on her chaise-longue behind the curtains, drinking brandy and weeping.

Neither mother nor son had anything to say to the young widow. She thought they blamed her for Arthur's death, but this was untrue. For them, she had existed only as an adjunct to him. He was no more, and they wiped her out as though she had never been. Eventually good manners would take over from the first tearing grief, and they would acknowledge her again. But now she might have been a carving for all the attention they gave her. Harry scorned their sack-cloth and ashes approach and spent the whole journey comforting Karin and trying to keep her mind occupied. She was a good-natured, pleasant young girl and he knew she deserved better treatment than these two were handing out. By the time they were shunted into a private siding at Euston, she was his willing slave.

Fortunately Henry's desire to do the right thing prevented him from making the sort of funeral arrangements for which his grief cried out. By the time they had been met at the station by a representative of London's most socially acceptable undertakers, he was content that aristocratic dignity should take the place of the orgy of black ostrich plumes and hot-house flowers which had originally come to mind. Two days after the return to London, Arthur's remains were laid to rest after a family service in St Anselm's, the tiny parish church near the Mapledurham mansion where Arthur and Karin had been married less than six months before.

When it was all over, Karin showed a surprising streak of independence. Harry had vaguely assumed she would return to Germany; the others, if they had considered the matter at all, thought her likely to stay at Mapledurham in a permanent state of mourning. Karin had other ideas. A week after the funeral, she went to see Elizabeth, who was resting in bed on the orders of her doctor. Elizabeth was the only person apart from Harry who had treated her as a central figure in the tragedy.

'I – I have come to see what you think of my plans,' she said shyly.

'I'm surprised you've managed to make any so quickly, my dear. You mustn't rush, you know. We all realise what a bad time you've had.'

'I do not fit in any more back in Germany. I was here too long at school even before I met Arthur. They are almost strangers to me now. But here, now, I do not think I belong either. Mother Elizabeth, I want to go back to North Wales.'

Elizabeth was astonished. 'But you know nobody there, and they're very insular people – not eager to befriend outsiders. You ask my mother-in-law; she'll tell you that.'

Karin's face hid what she thought of her grandmother-in-law but she made no comment. 'I have no need to. I know already. But it is such a beautiful place, and so peaceful. I need to go away for a time to think about what I shall do now. That is a perfect place for me. What do you think?'

Elizabeth pondered for a while. 'I think perhaps it will be the right thing for you, Karin. You seem to have an inner strength one seldom sees in young women of your age. Certainly my two daughters lack it. Yes, it might work . . . but only if you promise you'll come back to us the moment you begin to feel too isolated.'

Karin dimpled prettily. 'That is a kind thought. Of course I will. But for the moment I really do need to be alone.'

'What? Scuttle off to the very spot where her husband was struck down? The girl must be sick!' When Elizabeth told Henry the next day, he was livid. He seemed to take Karin's plan as a personal affront. Elizabeth wondered just why he was overreacting.

She tried to calm him. 'But surely she knows best how to recover from it all? She's not asking us to go with her, is she?'

'Not the point! Not the point at all! Everyone will think there's something peculiar about it. No, I'll not stand for it. It's ridiculous.'

257

'I don't believe she was asking your permission, Henry. She simply told me what she plans to do.'

Now Marged joined in the fray. 'Well, she can't go. I'll see to that. I agree with Henry, it's most inappropriate. If she tries to insist, I shall simply refuse to let her have the house.'

But Karin proved recalcitrant. 'I am afraid you cannot stop me, Grandmama. You do not own the house any more, remember? You made over the deeds to Arthur and me when we went to the North. Now he is dead, I inherit his share as his widow, is that not so?'

It was so. Marged swallowed an impulse to slap the innocent little face which now turned away from her with an air of finality. Karin left the room and the three elder Richmonds looked at each other in perplexity. Elizabeth spoke first. 'Really, Mother, I can't understand why you're so set against this – or Henry for that matter.'

'I wouldn't expect you to – you're not family!' The venom Marged had been forced to hold back from Karin she now spat out at Elizabeth, who was used to it after years of exposure.

'Quite,' she replied. 'That means I know better than either of you just how overwhelmed that poor child feels at this moment. Why can't you let her go with your blessings?'

'Because North Wales hasn't been a good place for us. It's as if there's a curse on the Richmonds when they go there,' Henry intervened.

'Oh, really, darling, you can't seriously believe that. This tragedy might have happened to any family, and in any place.'

'You know nothing about it. It goes back before I even

258

knew you. We should have got out and stayed out all those years ago. If we had, my son would still be alive.'

Elizabeth's face was bleak. 'Our son, Henry. Don't forget I was his mother.'

If he did not forget, he appeared not to care. Karin duly departed for North Wales and from then on, Henry's recent tenderness towards his wife evaporated. Publicly he behaved normally. In private, he used her as a spiritual punchbag for all the misery and sense of loss he was suffering.

Harry, recalled from Oxford only a month into his first term, remained at home until Christmas. He watched his mother becoming drawn and ill and he suffered endless misery because he thought that, after all, Arthur must have meant more to her than he did. For the moment, though, he could not go away to hide his own misery. They were to decide in January whether he should resume his studies or join the business. By then some of the rawness of their collective grief might have eased.

But Providence had not finished with the Richmond family. As their blackest year drew to a close Elizabeth, in the eighth month of her pregnancy, fainted on the main staircase at Mapledurham, fell down twenty stairs and went into premature labour. She gave birth to a stillborn son six hours later and on December 31st she died of septicaemia. She was just short of her forty-fifth birthday.

259

# Chapter Ten

Harry's world became a black tunnel of misery. Arthur's death had shocked rather than grieved him – initially the memory of their rivalry was too intense to leave room for all the love. But his mother . . . No one else could occupy the place Harry had set aside for Elizabeth Richmond. He suffered even more because now he was convinced she had died of grief for Arthur, and that meant she had loved Arthur most after all.

His father confirmed this impression for his own reasons. When Elizabeth died so tragically, Henry Richmond was consumed with guilt. He had known she was ill during pregnancy, but he had been too furious at her championship of Karin to help or to sympathise. Now she, too, was gone, and Henry was unable to confront his own undoubted contribution to the event. The obvious way out was to convince himself and the world that she had died of sorrow for Arthur. He accordingly spread the myth to family, friends, business associates and anyone else who cared to listen.

The obstetrician who had been attending Elizabeth turned on him in anger. 'It's no use pursuing that line with me, Sir Henry. I warned you repeatedly that your wife must be cosseted and protected from strain. I gather that instead, you continually referred to all the worst things that were happening to the family, kept her awake at night with your own grief, and in general treated her almost as an enemy. I'd be surprised if the healthiest, youngest mother stood up to such punishment – but Lady Richmond was middle-aged, her last child was born seventeen years ago, and she had suffered a terrible blow herself when Arthur died.'

'That's what I'm saying – well, the last bit, anyway.'

'No, you're not. You're disclaiming your own responsibility for her death.'

But the specialist quickly accepted that nothing he said would divert Henry. It was not his business to share his views with the rest of the family, so he departed and left them to accept or reject what they wished. As Marged backed Henry unreservedly, soon all the surviving children believed Elizabeth had died because of Arthur.

In one area, though, Harry had grounds for optimism. Elizabeth's death had a strange effect on his father – it shook him out of the lethargy which had gripped him when he lost Arthur. Now, at last, he was realising he must fill the gap in the succession vacated by his elder son; and if he wanted to prolong the Richmond connection with the business beyond his own generation, that necessarily involved Harry.

He talked the matter over with Marged from every conceivable angle. In her view, it almost went without saying that Harry must be groomed from now on as heir apparent. Henry gave in only after a struggle.

'He's wrong for it, Mother, I just know it. All the things I've distrusted in him – his showing off, his flashy

262

social life, his extravagance – they're the worst possible qualifications for a trade like ours.'

'Maybe, but remember, he's all we've got.' Marged was sceptical, anyway, about the gravity of these faults. Her private view was that Henry disliked his son because the boy was everything he himself was not. She loved Henry too much to tell him, but she loved the business sufficiently to make sure they harnessed Harry to Richmond Quality Provisions. If one were objective about it, Harry was one of the most talented young men of his generation. Until now those talents had been largely devoted to social skills, but with a little expert pressure, he could probably be moulded into a brilliantly successful commercial magnate. Marged understood better than most that success in the second generation of a great dynasty required completely different qualities than those necessary in the first. Perhaps, after all, last year's disaster was a trick in its place . . . perhaps Arthur had been too like Henry ever to take Richmond's on to the next stage. She had a hunch that Harry might prove the ideal torchbearer.

In mid-January it was agreed between them that Harry should forget university for good and spend the next year or so working for short spells in various departments at Richmond's. Starry- eyed, he embarked on his task. He missed his mother savagely, but he was young and now it seemed the future he had always yearned for was finally within reach. It gave him fresh hope and lifted his depression. He worked harder than he would have believed possible in his days as a budding playboy. He got to know George Beynon, who took to him on sight, and the firm's elder statesman taught Harry more about food retailing in six months than most shopkeepers learned in a lifetime.

It seemed Harry would never please his father, though. In spite of tackling his work head-on, in spite of volunteering for twice as much as most other trainees, his boundless energy and fitness enabled him to continue playing almost as hard as he worked. Harry's picture appeared in the newspapers more and more often, either illustrating his prominent position at sporting fixtures, or escorting Society beauties to glossy social occasions. Henry read the items and bristled, longing to catch Harry slacking. But if he even hinted at such a possibility, the departmental managers under whom his son worked dismissed the suggestion out of hand. Henry was beaten and he knew it, but he was unable to forgive his heir for possessing such an embarrassment of talents.

Henry himself was slowing down visibly. Approaching his fifty-first birthday, he already had the look of an old man. Indeed, he looked old enough to be Marged's husband rather than her son, and uninformed new acquaintances sometimes made the mistake of addressing her as Lady Richmond. Growing consciousness of his own failing powers and of his son's increasing vigour drove Henry down new roads. He began taking an unparalleled interest in pretty girls. He, too, began to get his picture in the papers. By the end of his formal year of mourning for Elizabeth, he was more than ready to start entertaining on a grand scale at White Lodge, their Mapledurham house, and at the Belgravia apartment in London. His official explanation was that he wished to launch Harry appropriately, but many of the events managed to take place without his son even putting in an appearance.

Marged watched all this with a cynical eye, and took comfort from her brandy bottle as usual. He was hers in every way that mattered. What did she care if he now chose to fend off old age by chasing after his daughters' friends? Anyway, now Harry was marked out for running Richmond's, she wanted to reinforce his sense of family. She started spending more time with her grandson, flattering, entertaining and helping him in various capacities. Harry was no fool. He retained a touch of rueful affection for the old tyrant, but he would never love her, and could not forget his lifelong resentment of the way she had always relegated Elizabeth to second place within the family circle.

Then Karin re-entered their lives.

She had kept in touch from Wales, writing regularly to Harry and both his sisters. Mary Rose had travelled up to stay with her at Tan-yr-Allt on several occasions, even taking Harry along at Christmas 1890 to get him away from the miserable memory of his mother's death a year before. The three of them spent an idyllic Christmas together, with plenty of walks through the lovely winter countryside, carriage rides over to the island and long companionable dinners beside a roaring fire. Afterwards, Harry found it difficult to believe that the time he had been dreading most had passed so pleasurably. He knew it was largely down to the charming, pliant little German girl who had so briefly been his brother's wife.

They met again at Easter. Margaret had postponed her marriage to Steven Royle when her mother died. It had been planned for Easter 1890, but she had put it off for a full year, feeling that the family had suffered too much loss already to endure her departure for America so soon. Now, at the age of twenty-four, she felt she had waited long enough. They were to be married at St Anselm's on Easter Monday and she insisted on having Karin as her matron of honour.

'That's outrageous – impossible!' snapped Marged when she heard the news. 'The girl's in mourning, possibly for life. You can hardly have her traipsing down the aisle behind you in deepest black, and anyway, it's not respectable.'

Margaret's face set stubbornly. She was no fonder of her grandmother than Harry was. 'Grandmama, Karin is only twenty-three now. She's been widowed for seventeen months and she was only married for five! That sort of custom is intended for middle-aged women with grown-up families, not young girls with their whole lives ahead of them.'

'I don't care. Forget propriety then, if you're so set on it. That still leaves you with one of your attendants dressed all in black – she'll never have the nerve to break that tradition!'

'Oh, but you're forgetting – in Germany and France, it's different. After a year, widows there are just as respectable in white, or grey, or mauve. And Karin's German, and everyone knows it, and she'll have a mauve-and-white gown and look lovely, so there!'

Marged was furious. 'You just try it, my girl. You may be twenty-four, but your father is still head of this family – and I know he'll agree with me!'

When Henry supported his daughter instead, Marged was beside herself. 'I don't believe it! It must be a conspiracy – that's it, you've all decided I've outlived my usefulness and this is your way of showing it.'

Henry sighed. 'Mother, please don't be melodramatic. It's just, well, I've been doing a lot of thinking recently, and I can't help feeling we should involve Karin more . . . draw her out, you know. After all, you'd be the first to say the sooner we winkled her out of North Wales, the better.'

Swallowing her rage, Marged thought it over. Put like that, perhaps it made sense. The sooner they ended any family connection with North Wales, the happier she would be. But that girl made her uneasy. Elizabeth had never succeeded in affecting her so strongly, but this one . . . why did she always give Marged the impression that one day she'd wind herself around all the men in the family? She gave a little snort and shook off the idea. She'd better get used to Karin. It seemed that suddenly everyone wanted to know her.

When she found out why Henry had been so sympathetic to the girl, she was almost apoplectic.

Karin had arrived for the wedding, now less than a week ahead, and had agreed to stay at White Lodge for at least a month. She had already shed full mourning, and now wore grey or white, both of which suited her admirably. Henry behaved as if his daughter-in-law were a delicate piece of porcelain, lavishing attention on her, constantly enquiring about her welfare and in general treating her far more affectionately than he ever had his own daughters.

A couple of evenings before the marriage day, he was with Marged in her sitting room, sharing their customary half-hour talk before she went to bed. This was normally the time when he brought out all his new plans and ideas, aired them to her and waited for her reaction. Tonight was no different. 'I – I've been giving a lot of thought to something recently, Mother, and I'd value your opinion. It's a big step; certainly not one I could take if you thought it unwise.'

Marged, warmed by her nightcap of brandy and hot milk, nodded graciously.

'You know I'm not really out of middle age yet – plenty of life left in me and so on.'

Again she assented. Hardly tactful to tell the boy he looked older than she did, after all.

'Well – I've been considering the possibility of remarriage.'

She nearly dropped her toddy glass. Her first impulse was to start screaming abuse. Her second was to grit her teeth, take a big pull at her drink, and wait. After a long pause she spoke, hardly moving her lips: 'Have you a partner in mind, or are you just theorising?'

'Ha-ha – that's very good, Mother, just theorising, indeed.' His nervousness was painful to contemplate. 'Yes, as a matter of fact, I have. I was thinking about Karin.'

She was so shocked her mind went momentarily blank. 'Karin? Karin who?'

'For God's sake, Mother, it's hardly a common name in England! Our Karin, of course. Karin Richmond, formerly Cassel.'

I'm going to drop dead, I know it. I shall just have a stroke or a heart attack and that will be that . . . I can feel myself going now. Her street fighter's spirit erupted against her interior panic. 'Perhaps you'd care to tell me your reasons, Henry, because so far, I'd say you need to be certified.'

268

He gave her a deeply hurt look. 'Really, Mother, you have a cruel tongue at times. So, I'm fifty –'

'Nearly fifty-one,' she broke in venomously.

'Well, all right, nearly fifty-one. There are plenty of men my age who take second wives as young as her. After all, I'm hardly too old to start a second family, am I? And think how pleased you'd be if I had another son.'

This time Marged really did come close to collapse. She couldn't be hearing right. The strain of the past couple of years had definitely unhinged him. Except that she knew it hadn't. He obviously had some carefully worked out little scheme and if she knew her son, money came into it somewhere; money and prestige, too. Yes, that was it . . . she was beginning to understand his thinking. Well, she'd manage to outwit him this time, too. She'd always done it in the past. She smiled gently. 'Forgive me, Henry. You'd better explain it to me properly. You know how irritable I can be when I'm tired.'

He agreed carefully, although he had never known her to be physically exhausted at any time except when Arthur died. 'It's quite simple, really. You know how substantial Karin's fortune is . . . after all, when we encouraged the match, it was largely with the thought of ploughing all that money into Richmond's, wasn't it? Well, now it's reverted to her. When the time comes for the big expansion, we'll need to float a public company. No more family control if we went public . . . you know what a spectre that's always been. I've been brooding about it for ages, and suddenly I thought . . .'

'. . . And suddenly you thought, "If she were married to me, it would all come back into the family." '

He nodded happily. 'I knew you'd see it my way. And

another thing: if we had a couple of children, there would be no chance of her going off with her inheritance again once my time was over, would there?'

And I believe in those being your true motives about as much as I believe in fairies, thought Marged. Aloud, she only said: 'Wouldn't there be awful complications because she was once married to your son?'

'Mmm, I gather the Church isn't always against that. And as there are no children . . .'

So he was serious enough to have checked on it, was he? Marged decided to take her own advice on the matter. She had a hunch that such clearance was likely only if Karin was prepared to swear she was still a virgin. But she might be . . . Arthur had come to Marged with a dark confession about that not long before they moved to the North. She did not feel reassured.

'Have you discussed it with Karin?'

'Oh, no, not yet. I'd never do that without speaking to you first.'

Well, that was something. At least she didn't have to fight the pair of them. Frantically, she sought a strategy – and found one. It might be difficult; it might give Karin far more than she deserved in the long term, but it would protect Marged from the humiliation of seeing her beloved son drooling over a mere child.

'It's quite a surprise, Henry. I – I'd like to give it thought before offering any opinions. Could you bear with me?'

'Of course, Mother. That's why I raised the matter now. Think it over until after the wedding. Then, if you come to any conclusions . . . say, by the end of next week?'

She smiled again, wanting to throttle him. 'I'll do that. Until then, let's just keep it as our secret, shall we? In fact, I'd be a lot happier if you didn't even hint at it to Karin.'

His face fell. 'Oh – oh, well, if it makes you feel better, I suppose . . . I had planned just to start – er – sounding her out.'

Or feeling her up, you old satyr! she thought. She reached over and squeezed his hand. 'Humour me for a week or so, dear. It's quite a big step for me to adjust to, you know.'

'Very well then. Best behaviour until next Friday. Now I'll say goodnight, Mother. Don't want to tire you too much.'

He kissed her forehead and left. Marged let out all her pent-up breath in a great rush. Could she do it? She had just over a week, with a damned great family party in the middle of it. No choice, she had to. The alternative was unthinkable.

Next morning, Harry was surprised to find a note from his grandmother beside his place at the breakfast table. He was even more surprised at the contents:

Harry, dear – You've been so busy since you joined the firm that I scarcely ever see you! If you have time for an hour's gossip with an old woman, I'd be delighted to lunch with you in my sitting room. I'll send Louisa for your answer after breakfast. Until later –

Grandmama

271

He stared at it. You scarcely ever see me as you've always scarcely ever seen me, he told himself. What's suddenly so special about me now? He had to find out why. When Marged's maid arrived twenty minutes later, Harry handed her a gracefully-penned acceptance.

'. . . It was so touching, I felt I really must risk breaking a confidence and let you know about it, dear boy. She is such a sweet child, and it must have been extremely hard for her this past year or so.'

As they finished their lunch with a bowl of fresh peaches, Marged had moved from listening, apparently enraptured, as he described his introduction to Richmond's, to announcing she had a secret to tell him. It was, she explained, not really her secret, but it was potentially so important to her grandson that she could not keep silent.

Harry struggled to stay cool. 'You can tell me, Grandmother. I promise it will go no further.'

'Good boy.' Then she had told him of a talk she had had with Karin the previous afternoon. Apparently she had run across the girl in the little walled garden below the west wing. Karin had looked so lost, she had to join her.

In the course of an emotional journey through the months of her widowhood, the girl had confessed that her feelings for Harry were growing even stronger than the regard she had felt for his dead brother. Marged had found herself reassuring the poor child that there was nothing sinful about such feelings, that they were perfectly natural in the circumstances, and that perhaps – who knew? – there might even be hope that her affection was returned.

Marged now adopted her most confidential manner. 'So you see, I simply had to tell you. I know you'll treat her gently. You've always been considerate of others' feelings – one of your best points – and I thought if there were anything on your side . . .?'

He was covered in confusion. 'I – I don't really know, Grandmama. I'm grateful that you trust me sufficiently to tell me, of course. But I have no idea of my true feelings about Karin. I've always thought of her as Arthur's wife.'

He thought he noticed a flash of malice in her face as he said that, but decided he was mistaken. After all, she'd never have told him if she disapproved. She appeared to be expecting more of a reaction. The silence lengthened, then she said, 'Is there any possibility that you might come to think of her in any other way? You're a little younger than she is, I know, but that's no real drawback. And we Richmonds always seem to benefit from early marriage. It would certainly set your father's mind at rest.'

When Harry left her, he was deep in thought. The idea of marriage had not entered his head until now. He was not quite twenty-two yet and there was a whole world of champagne and adventure and pretty women before he settled permanently. He did not share the lax attitude to marital fidelity which many of his contemporaries professed. Harry believed in commitment and loyalty, and to him an extra-marital affair seemed nothing more than a particularly shabby betrayal. No, he preferred to sow his wild oats young and get married when he had matured a little. On the other hand, he found Karin very attractive and they had become real friends last Christmas. He had not been surprised at Marged's revelation of the girl's feeling – only that Karin had chosen to confide in his grandmother.

The reality would have surprised him more. Karin had not even been inside the walled garden the previous afternoon and had made no confession. But when Marged worked out her plan, she decided it was most unlikely the young people would ever discuss the particular incident that had spurred Harry to court Karin.

Had the matter ended here, Harry would probably have thought about it all for a while then decided to continue as he was. But two factors weighed on him more heavily than any inclination to hang on to bachelor habits. First there was the memory of Arthur. Harry had adored Arthur with all the intensity of a squire following behind his knight errant. He had been hurt again and again as the older boy gradually withdrew from him to enjoy the adulation of his grandmother and father. But he had continued to love him, more if anything. Any companion of Arthur's took on some reflected glory from the hero, and Karin had occupied the closest position of all, as his wife. Perhaps it was not logical, but Harry often let emotion overrule logic. In any event, her past association with Arthur made Karin almost an object of veneration.

The other thing was that little aside of Grandmama's . . . 'It would certainly set your father's mind at rest.' That, above all else, was Harry's ambition. To earn his father's love and approval after all those years out in the dark . . . Why, it would be worth doing something far less agreeable than proposing to sweet, pretty Karin.

And so the week progressed. On Monday, Henry

escorted his tall, elegant daughter Margaret down the aisle at St Anselm's to marry her handsome American bridegroom.

Behind them, radiant for this, her first truly social public appearance since Arthur's death, came Karin, together with Mary Rose. The soft mauve and white of her gown and the dull gold sheen of her hair combined like a drift of wood crocuses and transformed her everyday prettiness to something close to beauty. Harry, acting as best man, watched her with mounting appreciation. Yes, why not? He could wait a lot longer and do a lot worse.

At the wedding reception, held in the ballroom of White Lodge to avoid re-awakening painful memories of Arthur's nuptials, Henry monopolised Karin. Watching him, Harry strove to convince himself that his father was doing no more than ensuring that she was not a wallflower. But Henry's attentiveness seemed very pronounced for someone with merely paternal intentions. As any other motive in his father was unthinkable to Harry, he told himself he must be imagining things. In next to no time, the celebration was ending and the bride and bridegroom were being seen off for a trip to France before they went to the United States. By Tuesday, Harry was back at work in Richmond House and Karin was easy prey for Henry.

Marged had been watching her son with far more attention than Harry, and she was beginning to wonder if he were falling victim to early senility. As far as she was concerned, his behaviour towards Karin verged on raging satyriasis. At this rate, she might not need to enlist Harry. The girl herself might be so repelled at such lecherous attention that she would flee in terror.

It might well have turned out thus, but Marged's scheming back-fired on her. On Wednesday afternoon, Karin was in the small ground floor music room, playing the piano and singing. She enjoyed music greatly and her skill had been one of the things that drew her closer to Harry during his Christmas visit. Now she was playing a sequence of sentimental modern ballads, pieces she normally avoided in company. Somehow, they seemed to suit her present mood and she was totally immersed in glorious bathos:

'Pale hands I love, beside the Shalimar;
Where are you now? Who lies beneath your spell?'

To her acute embarrassment, a rusty but passable tenor voice took up the verse and finished it. Abruptly she stopped playing and turned to greet the intruder.

'Oh – oh, it's you, Sir Henry! Forgive me. Such trivial little pieces!'

'Nonsense, my dear. I've a great weakness for that sort of thing. Haven't played myself for years – let me see.'

She was even more embarrassed as he crossed the room and sat down close beside her on the long piano bench. 'No need to get up, Karin – I don't bite, y'know; not pretty little girls, anyway! And what's all this "Sir Henry" nonsense? I think we've known each other long enough now to drop the "Sir", don't you?'

'Well . . . I – er – I don't really know . . .' He had succeeded in scandalising her. She called him Sir Henry because she had never been able to bring herself to address him as 'Father'. But no polite young widow would call her father-in-law by his first name. Why, it sounded quite impertinent! Unable to voice such thoughts, she merely cast down her eyes and blushed. Henry, encouraged, promptly began to batter out the next tune in the series of Indian Love Lyrics while mouthing his half-remembered version of the words. He felt on top form and was sure he was cutting a fine, boisterous figure with Karin. He might be fifty-one, but he could show these callow youngsters a thing or two!

As he vamped on, Karin sat beside him, silently wondering how to extricate herself. Eventually he finished with a flourish and turned to her. She looked so absurdly pretty that he could not resist acting on impulse. She was a woman of the world now, after all, not a virgin straight out of the nursery . . . Without another word, he put his arms around her, turned her towards him and started kissing her forehead and cheeks. Before she had chance to move or protest, his lips closed over her mouth and he was enveloping her in a very unfatherly embrace.

Karin let out a little squeak of outrage, suddenly rediscovered the use of her legs, and swung herself away from him over the piano bench to stand on the far side. 'Sir Henry – Sir Henry, what do you think you are doing? Please stop!' The slight Germanic accent sharpened along with her nervousness.

'Ah, always liked a little flirt!' he said, lunging after her into the centre of the room.

'No, please . . . you really mustn't . . . it's not right!' But he was on her again, and this time he did not stop at a couple of kisses. He crushed her to him with one hand

and started stroking her neck and breasts with the other. When she tried to escape again, he lunged, and seemed to be squeezing any part of her that offered itself. He was red-faced and panting now and Karin was becoming very frightened. Evading him would be difficult enough, but how could she ever face him again? She backed away, heading for the door, but he was barely a pace behind her and as she got there he forced her against it, barring her one means of escape.

He still seemed determined to believe this was all light-hearted flirtation. To Karin it was beginning to look like a preliminary to rape. Pinning her against the door with the weight of his body, he began trying to undo the small pearl buttons which fastened the front of her dress from neck to waist.

That gave her strength she had not thought she possessed. She reached up and yanked his hands away from her with such force that the fine sprigged muslin bodice ripped almost into two pieces. Simultaneously she heaved forward and caught Henry off balance. He staggered back into the music room and she was able to make her escape, clutching the ruined dress to her in an attempt to hide her half-naked state.

Marged saved Henry from complete self-destruction. She had been heading for the library to talk to him and had heard someone blundering about in the music room. Before she could get to the door, it was flung open and Karin dashed out, sobbing. Marged made no attempt to follow. Her intuition told her who she would find inside. She went in quickly then closed the door and locked it, turning on her son like a fury.

'You stupid fool! Do you realise you've molested your own daughter-in-law?'

Henry had managed to regain his balance and had been about to follow Karin. His mother's sudden appearance had acted like a douche of cold water and now he stood before her, flushed and trembling, seeking words to deny her accusation and knowing he could not.

As she confronted him, Marged was suddenly tormented by hopeless pity. Dear God, it hadn't been a grim private joke, this thought of hers about premature senility. It really was happening to him . . . She looked at him closely, her dread mounting. Henry's jaw was slack. He was breathing harshly through his mouth and there was a thread of dribble beginning to form at one corner. His eyes were blank, his whole face devoid of expression. Now she felt frightened as well.

'Henry – Henry, answer me! What's the matter?'

Very slowly, he seemed to drag himself back from a great distance. He brushed away the spittle with an absent-minded gesture, then peered at Marged as though from a dark room. 'Er . . . Mother, is it? Con-confounded thing. Tried to show a bit of affection to young Karin and she took offence. Seems to have got quite the wrong idea . . . quite wrong . . . silly little chit . . .'

Stifling a sob, Marged held Henry and steadied him. 'Come on, now, boy, I think you've had a bit of a shock. Come to the library and we'll sort it out.' Once she got him there she gave him a stiff brandy and poured herself a stiffer one. That seemed to steady them both, but Henry still appeared to have only the vaguest recollection of what had taken place in the music room. He looked and sounded his normal self again, but persisted in saying he had given Karin a fatherly pat and she had panicked and run away. Marged was more scared by his obvious belief in what he was saying than she would have been had he admitted the assault and asked her to cover his tracks.

Eventually she decided it was futile to try to foresee all the possible repercussions. She must wait until she saw Karin and then handle the matter by instinct. At the moment the best she could do with Henry was to persuade him not to raise the matter with his daughter-in-law. She also insisted he should see a doctor.

'Doctor? Stuff and nonsense. Nothing wrong with me! I'm just cross, that's all.'

'Yes, darling, I know you are, now, but you must believe me when I tell you that you forgot a lot of what happened just now. I don't expect it's serious, but we'd best find out soon, just in case.' He protested but eventually agreed, to prevent her from worrying. Marged was relieved. At least she had a chance of finding out whether he'd had a stroke. All this sickness and death were beginning to frighten her. She had always felt herself to be immortal, but the past eighteen months had exposed her to a taste of the horror implicit in true immortality. If all you loved were dead, what was the point?

In the meantime, Karin had rushed down the broad flight of steps outside the front door and began running along the drive. As she reached the curve where trees hid the main house from the distant gatekeeper's lodge, a driver reined in his carriage and jumped down to intercept her. Fear swept over her again and she began sobbing hysterically. 'Oh please, just take me away from here, I can't face him! Oh, what can I do, what can I do?'

'Karin – for God's sake tell me what's wrong! Who's attacked you? I'll have the blighter's life!' It was Harry, on his way home from the station after a day at Richmond House. Karin practically fell into his arms, still trying to hold her ruined bodice in place. 'Here, let me give you my coat . . . come on, wrap yourself up – that's better.' He lifted her up into the carriage. 'Come on, we'd better get you back to the house.'

That set her off again. 'No – not there, please! Anywhere else, but not back there!'

'All right, all right. How about a short drive while you tell me about it? But then we'll have to do something about you. I think you might have to see the doctor.'

'No – it will be all right now, if you will just stay with me and talk to me. I am not hurt, just very frightened.'

He set off down a pleasant track which led close to the river. 'I'm only doing this to calm you down, you know. We must get hold of the culprit and make him pay for this.'

'I don't think so. That is why I do not want to go back there.' She gestured towards the house. 'You see, it – it was your father.' After his first shocked reaction, he simply let her tell her story. By the time she had finished, she was sobbing again, but now more with relief at having told someone than from the horror of the attack. 'I don't know what to do, Harry, really I don't. I feel that Mary Rose and – and you – are the only two people who care at all for me. If I did not have you to protect me, I do not know where I should turn. I hate Germany, I never want to go back to that gloomy house and those

281

stuffy people! But now, if your father orders me out, I shall have no one at all.'

'Oh yes, you will.' Harry's tone was decisive. 'I can take care of the whole thing. Just leave it to me.'

'Mother, I cannot go down to dinner tonight. I know there are no guests, but in a way that makes it worse. I just cannot.'

'Be sensible, Henry. There are always misunderstandings within families, you know that. Think of the disagreements you've had with Harry over the years.' Marged was trying her hardest to sound firm and certain. 'If you fail to appear tonight, matters will get worse. Tomorrow will be harder still, and by the next day you'll never be able to confront the girl. Come along. We shall go down to dinner and if she doesn't refer to the matter, neither should you. By now, she's probably decided she was a silly child and wants to put the whole trifling episode behind her.' Not half as much as I want her to, though, she added silently.

Well aware of the hollowness of his mother's last words, Henry none the less allowed himself to be won over. 'Very well . . . if you're sure there won't be a terrible wrangle. I don't feel at all well and that would be too much.'

Dinner was a curiously brittle affair. Everyone was excruciatingly polite; everyone drank at least twice as much wine as usual and, with the exception of Harry, ate half as much food. His appetite was as good as ever, but in other respects he shared the general symptoms of strain. Nevertheless, they managed to keep the conversational ball rolling. Marged commented on the finery of the female wedding guests; Harry extracted every drop of interest from his first day in the despatch department at Richmond's.

Father and son had never got on well enough to preserve the custom of remaining in the dining room after the ladies withdrew, unless there were guests for dinner. They were about to end their meal when Harry gestured to the butler. 'I think you can pour that champagne now, Murringer.'

'Champagne? What champagne? Something going on I don't know about?' Henry was butting the air with his grizzled head, a bit like a mole emerging into the sunshine.

Harry gave him a cool smile which said, Don't dare to thwart me or you'll be sorry.

'I just thought it might be appropriate, Father. I have some wonderful news. You and Grandmama are the first to know, of course. This afternoon, Karin consented to be my wife.'

He glanced sideways at Marged, who gave him the biggest, most relieved smile she could muster. 'To Harry and Karin,' she said loudly. 'A long and happy life together!'

Wild-eyed and speechless, Henry too shakily raised his glass to the engaged couple.

After the neurologist had spoken to her, Marged wondered how many more tragedies she could bear. The family general practitioner had examined Henry and then suggested a visit to Harley Street. One consultation had multiplied to four, and finally the specialist asked to see Marged alone. He had already talked to Henry.

'Mrs Richmond, this is a very difficult case for me to discuss with any certainty. I thought Sir Henry might have suffered a slight stroke at first. He had not. But he was showing symptoms of confusion and uncontrolled movement which we often associate with that type of brain damage. Having eliminated that, I'm afraid it's virtually certain that he is afflicted by a sort of premature senile decay. I've seen it in a few other men of his age, although usually it doesn't strike until at least ten years later.'

'It can't be cured?'

'I've certainly never seen a case in which the effects were reversed. You see, as far as we can make out, little parts of the brain die, so there's nothing to recover. When it strikes early, it usually seems to occur in men who have led lives of great stress, men who drive themselves mercilessly. You hardly need me to tell you that your son is just such a man.'

She shook her head, despairing. Somehow, she had known. It had been that, not a stroke, which she feared when she saw his slack uncomprehending face in the music room.

The neurologist was speaking again. 'I know it must be a bitter blow to you, but something can be salvaged. He must withdraw from active participation in his business, but you should try to encourage him as much as possible in other activities, mental and physical. The more he exercises what he has left, the longer it will last. He could be reasonably fit for years, but if he runs true to form, he'll have periodic lapses. When he really begins to degenerate, those lapses will grow prolonged. It could be two years, it could be ten or fifteen.'

'But why is it so unpredictable? You must have more idea than that.'

'I'm afraid not. It's a condition we know so little about. You see, even if his intellect ceased to function altogether, theoretically he could be in perfect physical health. Sometimes that happens, and the patient remains alive for many years, sound in body but lacking virtually any coherent mental powers. Other types appear to wear out physically as quickly as they do mentally. They simply seem to give up the struggle. It's usually diagnosed as heart failure, but at times I've asked myself whether it's just loss of the will to live.'

What a prospect, she thought. I'm going to see the Henry I love gradually wasting away before my eyes, until at the end his body's left like a sort of empty box. Once his spirit is gone, the box is no use to me, either.

In a sense the hardest part of it was that Henry seemed normal most of the time. The neurologist had let him think he had suffered a stroke: somehow the idea seemed more acceptable than senile decay at fifty-one. The whiff of mortality was enough to make him relinquish day-to-day control of his business empire, but there was no question of him assigning power of attorney, or indeed any real power, to his son.

Instead he fulminated in Mapledurham or Belgravia, ranting to Marged about how unfit Harry was to take over, how he would love to hand over if he thought the boy could cope. He promoted George Beynon again, much to George's embarrassment. Beynon believed it was time to make Harry titular head of the firm, even if Henry kept his friend and senior employee as the real brains for a while. The Welshman had never shed the habit of reporting to Marged. She had, after all, given him his first job and been instrumental in his advancement to modest wealth and substantial power. A few months after Henry's illness had been diagnosed, he came down to Mapledurham for the evening. Harry was staying in the Belgravia apartment and Marged wanted a chance to discuss the future with George. First of all, Beynon had a private session with Henry, then he joined Marged for an hour before dinner.

'If only you could make your son see it clearly, Mrs Richmond, it would save us all so much! Honestly, Harry do grasp things faster than any young man I've known since Sir Henry did his own training.' He dropped his voice, although there was no one to hear them. 'He's twice as quick as young Arthur ever was. Arthur was always conscientious but he had to work hard at it to get there. Harry don't know what hard work is, and he does more of it than practically any trainee I've got.'

Marged felt tired to her bones. 'Maybe that's most of the trouble, George. I'm beginning to see now that Henry could deal with Arthur because he knew he himself was better. It's hard to admit, but perhaps that's why I put him first, too. No competition for my precious son. But Harry . . . He's not at all sure with Harry. I think he sensed before the boy was out of petticoats that this one was the cleverest the family would produce. It makes him jealous, George, and he can't let go.'

Beynon smiled at Marged. He was fond of this woman. He knew that she had plenty of good qualities but that she had grown so used to subordinating them all to her love for Henry that many people thought her an ogress. He had long ago worked out the matters she had

286

just raised, but he respected her more than ever for having grasped it herself. Love wasn't always blind, it seemed. Pity that even when it could see, it still made a mess of things!

Now she was getting irritable because there seemed to be no obvious solution to their dilemma. 'What would happen, George, if Harry went on doing the rounds of the departments without being given any senior responsibility? How do you think he'd cope when he really had to take over?'

'Not much different from what he'd do if you made him chief cook and bottle washer tomorrow! It's rotten to say it when I know he'll feel terrible if he do have to go on kicking around like he is now, but as long as he knows the business inside out, he'll take over without a ripple. And I'm making good and sure he do know the business!'

She patted his arm. 'I'm sure you are, and I'd like to believe that, but I'm coming around to thinking we may have done Harry a lot of damage earlier on by never admitting him as a fully paid-up member of the inner family circle. I feel guilty about it and I'm afraid if he has to go on much longer in this fashion, it'll turn him into some sort of monster.'

George shrugged. 'I can't give you any comfort on that, Mrs Richmond. He's a sweet-natured young man now, but I'd be lying if I pretended he's not hurt and angry at being kept waiting for his moment like some junior counter jumper. We may all be sorry in the end, but without Henry giving us the nod, there's not anything either of us can do to push the boy ahead.'

'No, I suppose not. Oh, George, they say so much

about the sins of the fathers, but they never mention the sins of the mothers! I'm beginning to feel as if the sins of this mother will be visited on the fourth and fifth generation!'

He gave her a wicked grin. 'Cheer up, *cariad* – at least you won't be here to see it!'

# Chapter Eleven

## 1895

'How am I doing, George? Should I feel flattered that you're still here years after you threatened to retire, or insulted because you only stayed in case I ruined everything?'

'I don't think you're expecting an answer to that one,' said George. 'You've taken to all this like a duck to water. I could leave tomorrow and you wouldn't even notice, but to tell you the truth I'm enjoying myself too much!'

In the four years since Harry had taken charge of Richmond's in everything but name, the firm had expanded still further. Harry completed his training in 1891, and six months later went to Henry with a host of new ideas. His father vetoed them all and insisted that Harry maintain the status quo. He even visited Richmond House and confronted George Beynon as though he were a traitor, demanding to know why he had not been informed of Harry's revolutionary plans.

'But, Henry, they're not revolutionary. They're plain good business practice. It never occurred to me that you'd disapprove! If we expand the way Harry wants, buying premises on sites just that little bit better than we had before, we can raise the whole tone of the shops.'

'You know that doesn't make sense – time and time again it's been proved to us that a back street or small town shop for prosperous working men and their families will make us twice as much profit as a prime outlet in the main street. This is the age of the cash customer and the pre-packed product, remember, not of the craftsman grocer!' Henry's voice was high and defiant.

'It's changed, though. That was ten years ago. There's a lot of people wanting something a cut above Richmond's Quality Provisions – now, now, I'm not down-grading our achievements, only moving with the times – nowadays they do want something more like that first shop in Bangor, but with all our buying skills keeping the prices within their reach. At the moment, the schoolmaster and the solicitor's clerk do feel too much above the bricklayers and factory foremen to want to buy from the same shops. That's the market your Harry do want.'

Henry was determined not to agree. 'I made a success by catering for a mass market. Permit me to know when we're in danger of moving away from that market. Good God, think of the resources we'd have to sink into buying and fitting out that sort of shop! It would eat up our working capital!'

'Not if we didn't need to use that money. What if Harry raised the funds without calling in outside backing?'

Henry managed a scornful laugh. 'Him, conjure up money from nowhere? All he can produce is a constant stream of fresh champagne and chorus girls!'

Beynon smiled and shook his head. 'Perhaps you've

forgotten something. Harry's getting married as soon as you finally give the word, isn't he? His bride-to-be is one of the richest heiresses in Europe. And I gather that she thinks her fiancé is the last word in skilled financial advice. She'll put her money behind the business at a word from him.'

'Why hasn't he come to me with this? You're not even one of the family and you know more than I!'

'He was trying to come to you, man, but you never let him get beyond the first few suggestions. Admit it, you stopped him before you got to the funding, didn't you?'

Henry did not answer. He got up and started pacing nervously about the office. His eyes were taking on the vacant look which was becoming more obvious each day. He clasped and unclasped his hands behind his back, the movement increasingly jerky each time he repeated it. Abruptly he turned back to George. 'Well, whatever you say, that's my last word on the subject! I don't think the young ass really knows what he's talking about and I'm certainly not going to jeopardise a business I've spent a lifetime building, just to find out! As for that drivel about Karin's money providing the finance – I don't even bank on them ever marrying. Why, the girl spends every waking hour up in Wales at that dreary old house of Uncle Idris's! Wouldn't surprise me if she just went home to Germany one fine day, and then where would we be?'

George restrained himself with difficulty. The failure to set a firm marriage date was at least as much Henry's fault as anyone else's. Beynon had no idea why young Mrs Richmond was always up in Bangor, but from what he'd seen of her discomfort in Sir Henry's company, it was probably something to do with him.

But there was no point in speculating, either silently or directly to Henry. He was already turning away towards the door. By the look of him, he had forgotten where he was. He had certainly lost track of their conversation. Beynon sighed and went to arrange for him to be taken home.

Days later, Harry returned from a tour of twenty branches in the North-east and came to discuss his father's objections. Beynon was ready for him.

'Don't be so disconsolate, man. I've been giving it a lot of thought since the old boy come in last week. I think there's a way, but it don't involve going to Sir Henry any more than we can help.'

Harry looked bewildered. 'But we're helpless without his approval! You know he won't give me any real power, and not even you have the muscle to authorise my expansion programme unless he says yes.'

George smiled like a man about to deliver a special present. 'Have a look at the figures on the desk over there. They might make you feel a bit better.'

Harry sat down and started glancing through the documents. His scowl faded, first to astonishment and then to growing exultation. Watching him, Beynon appreciated afresh the younger man's speed of understanding.

'George, you old rogue! Are these what I think they are?' Beynon nodded without speaking.

'But what happens when Father sees them for approval?'

'He already has. A month ago.'

'But they were the new premises we already planned –

all the same sort of second-rate locations we normally go for.'

'Haven't you forgotten? We always submit them with a price range against each, until we know exactly what the final negotiated rate for the site will be. I've just gone for the top figure and I've taken options on first class locations on seventy per cent of those new branches instead of the originals.'

'That's what I guessed. Sometimes you leave me breathless.'

'You just think up the new ideas, young man, and leave it to me to get them working.'

Harry's face clouded. 'But wait – you've forgotten something. Having acquired the premises, we've no way of paying for modernisation, have we? We could never divert the appropriate capital for re-fitting without Father noticing and stopping us.'

'I was coming to that. Lately I've been wondering when I could get away for a while and take my Siân back up to North Wales for a week's holiday. And while I'm there, surely it would be impolite not to pay my compliments to your fiancée? And if you happened to have written to her in advance with a business proposition for her to invest in Richmond's against your guarantee to honour the deal after your marriage? You'd advise her to have a good lawyer in attendance, of course.'

'George, when I take over, I'll make you honorary vice-chairman of Richmond's for that, and what's more you'll be the only non-family shareholder!'

'Let's see if it do work first, shall we? Perhaps we'll both be looking for a job before the end of the summer.'

As Harry departed for his own office, George said:

'One thing, Harry. If I was you, I'd take Marged into your confidence. Your grandmother is a wonderful friend, but she's a terrifying enemy. And if she do get wind of our plans from anywhere else, it's an enemy she'll be, make no mistake about that.'

'Tell Grandmama? She'd rend me limb from limb! You know she regards Father as a combination of a saint and the entire Rothschild family!'

'I think you'd get a pleasant surprise if you tried her. Don't you let on I ever told you, mind, but I'm sure she regrets being so off-hand with you in the past. She's just looking for some way to make it up to you. She's always singing your praises in here when she do come to see me.'

'I wouldn't know how to begin.'

'Just give her a chance to support you, Harry. She won't let you down this time.'

He was right. When Harry finally managed to broach his plans, Marged reacted exactly as Beynon had predicted. He outlined the upgrading proposals and she listened. Then she gave a great sigh, and said, 'Thank God for that! I was beginning to think nobody would ever suggest it!'

'So you're not against the idea? The only reason I've delayed was that I thought both Father and you would say it was out of the question.'

Marged's face was sad. 'You know your father is no longer the man he was, Harry. I realise it must be very hard on you, my boy, but try to be patient. I don't think you'll have to wait very much longer. He's getting weaker every day.' There was a catch in her voice and her eyes filled with tears. 'You go on and do this. He's unable to see we have to change with the times, that's all.

294

I only ask you to be gentle about it. If we're careful he need never know.'

Harry went over and kissed her on the forehead. She started back, a look of pleased gratitude replacing the misery. 'Why, Harry! Thank you for being good to me. I'm very lonely.'

'I know. Perhaps now you realise how I felt when none of you wanted to share things with me. Let's hope all that's over and done now, shall we?'

He left her to think over what he had said. Marged was privately grateful that he seemed to lack the vengeful streak which she and Henry had shared. Otherwise, he could have been less forgiving.

When Karin considered his proposal and discussed it with her lawyer, she made a counter-suggestion. After he read her letter, Harry began wondering whether his fiancée was as simple and straightforward as she seemed.

My advisers are aware that your proposal was made in good faith, but they are not very happy about the security of your guarantee. At times like this we must think about the unthinkable. What if you died prematurely, like poor Arthur? If you did, and your father were still alive, I could expect no guarantee of recompense from Richmond's. I think you will agree it is most unlikely he would wish me well if such an arrangement ever came to light.

There is one way, though, which might suit us both. Could we not set up a separate partnership to fit and refurbish the first-class shops? If this causes difficulties in that the premises would be owned by

Richmond's and refurbished by our company, we could perhaps buy the shops too, and Mr Beynon could then go ahead separately with the agreements on the second-rate premises for the main company, so your father would not question the apparent lack of expansion next year.

If you think that is a good idea, I look forward to seeing Mr Beynon next week, and will arrange for my lawyer to be here too. Perhaps Mr Beynon should hold a senior appointment in the new company?

Take care, my dear, your own,

Karin

After a while, he laughed. So she wasn't blindly in love with him after all – or at least, not enough to risk her inheritance! So much the better. He wasn't over-fond of stupid women. It was a very sensible plan, anyway. Without any Richmond's Provisions involvement, he would have much more freedom. In fact, if anything went really wrong between him and his father, he could strike out on his own with backing like this. Better not mention it to Grandmother, though. She'd have forty fits at the idea of someone else having real power in the business, instead of merely standing at the sidelines throwing in money. As far as she was concerned, Karin's involvement would be no more than Beynon had originally outlined.

It all went almost too smoothly. Suddenly, Harry became aware that with enough money, it was possible to achieve practically anything. Until now, he had never controlled cash – never controlled anything, in fact. The new partnership with Karin taught him that given the funds, he could be every bit as powerful as his father. Modestly at first, but with burgeoning confidence as his father's mental and physical condition steadily deteriorated, Harry started setting up smart food shops to cater for the middle classes. Over two years, while senility relentlessly pursued Henry, the new-look Richmond's became the firm's badge of identity for the dawning twentieth century. Marged, full of pride and relief that capable hands were taking over, still had no idea that Karin owned a half share of the new shops.

Had she known, she might never have made the move which gave Harry legal as well as day-to-day control of Richmond's. One Sunday evening, after a particularly trying day with Henry at White Lodge, she sent for Harry as he was about to depart for Eaton Place.

'D'you think you could stay tonight and go into London in the morning?' she asked.

Harry stifled his reluctance, knowing what a toll his father's illness was taking on her. 'If it's important, of course. Or . . . or if you just need someone to share the load for a while.'

Suddenly she was crying. The sight startled and moved him more than he would have expected. He hurried to her side and put a hand on her shoulder, feeling awkward as he did it. Marged was not a woman who had ever encouraged intimacy from anyone save Henry. Now, though, she clung to his hand as though she were drowning and it was her one chance of rescue. 'He can't go on like this, Harry,' she said. 'It's not fair to him – but even more, it's not fair to you, or Karin.' She added her granddaughter-in-law's name as an afterthought, to please him. 'Something must be done to put you in proper charge. That's what I wanted to discuss.'

Later, Harry decided it had been inevitable. But it still came as a vast shock to hear her admit his father was beyond hope. If Marged acknowledged it, he must be close to the end.

After her brief outburst of grief, she was calm and business-like, proposing an examination by two physicians and then a legal application to hand over power of attorney to Harry. That surprised him further.

'You're not insisting on sharing executive control, then?' he asked.

Her laugh had a dry, grim tone. 'We wouldn't go well in harness, boy! Anyway, I've always thought petticoat power should be tacit, not flaunted. Come to me for advice and I'll be glad to give it.' They both knew he would not.

Once they had talked through the details, Harry prepared to depart, but she stopped him. 'There's something else – something that's been put off too long. It's high time you and Karin were married. Once this legal business is finished, I think you should set a date straight away. The sooner we have another generation of Richmonds, the better.'

As Harry went down the broad staircase from her suite, he shook his head, wondering at her adaptability. 'Like the walls of Jericho,' he murmured, 'once they start to topple, the whole lot comes down at once!'

# Chapter Twelve

They woke to the sound of bells, and of horses' hooves clattering on ancient cobblestones. Harry had been determined to make Karin's second honeymoon quite different from her first and had succeeded admirably. Florence on a clear mild winter's morning was a far cry from the Swiss lakes in early summer.

For Karin, Harry's presence would have made anywhere romantic. She was feigning sleep and watching him now, absorbed in his grace and masculine beauty. How could any woman not love him? He was standing over by the french window. One shutter was closed, so that only lancets of the clear pale sunlight reached out on to the bedroom carpet. The other was ajar and Harry stood eagerly watching the activity in the square below. His only garment was a long dressing gown of heavy silk in a shade of deep bronze shot with gold which complemented his own sunny look. Harry was exceptionally tall and well-muscled, his body in such perfect proportion that from a distance it was easy to believe he was of average height and build. Close up, the illusion disappeared immediately. He gave off an intense sense of power and vitality. Everything about him seemed to spark. His hair was a curly mane of springy red and gold and in him the Richmond bright-brown eyes held ferocious amber glints that seemed to belong in a jungle creature rather than a civilised man.

Karin wriggled excitedly at that thought. There was a lot of the jungle in him . . . Fancy, poor Arthur had never known that soaring pleasure which Harry had taught her to enjoy so much. Poor Arthur, lucky Karin! The thought of last night made her smile. She forgot she had been pretending to sleep and stretched, catlike, closing her eyes as she did so. When she opened them, Harry had moved silently back to the bed and was now standing beside it, silhouetted by the bright sunshine, his ruffled curls forming a fiery halo around the leonine head.

'A penny for your thoughts, Mrs Richmond!'

She felt the deep blush which stained her cheeks. 'Oh – I couldn't possibly tell you . . . it's not at all ladylike!' She giggled and looked away to hide her confusion.

'You didn't seem too interested in ladylike behaviour last night.' As he spoke, he untied the sash of the dressing gown and she gasped in admiration at his beautiful body. He discarded the robe and moved into the bed. 'Karin – you've put on your nightgown!'

She giggled again. 'Only to enjoy having you take it off . . . only you must do it quickly because I want you to touch me all over!'

He smiled lazily and reached out, burying his hand in her long dull gold hair, turning her to face him. He kissed her unhurriedly, then drew back. 'Maybe I shan't take it off. More ways of skinning a bride than one, you know . . .' His other hand slid under the silk gown, moved sinuously up her inner thigh and caressed the smooth pad of flesh over her hip bone. Karin quivered and shifted under his touch, mounting tension banishing her shyness.

'Touch me . . . you know . . . where it makes me . . .'

He was in a teasing mood. 'Tut tut, Mrs Richmond, what would Society say if it could hear you? Why d'you want me to do that?'

'Please, Harry, you know I like it so much.'

'Like this, you mean?' As he moved his hand between her thighs with almost maddening slowness, she was already panting with excitement. She reached down and pressed his fingers into her body, clasping her legs tightly against the axis of his arm. Harry watched her face closely, his own excitement mounting as he did so. Karin's eyes were dreamy with pleasure. Her lips were parted and the tip of her small pink tongue flicked in and out. She reached up and pulled him down towards her.

'Do it again quickly, darling, like before. Please, quickly! I can't bear this!' Abruptly she loosened her thighs and spread her legs, the silk nightgown twisted high under her armpits, one small pink-nippled breast exposed. Harry had been planning to take her gradually this time, to build up the tension until she was half-crazy with excitement, but suddenly the sight of her eager, submissive little form triggered a stream of images of his brother and father, both pursuing this prize, both failing, and his sense of victory overwhelmed any other emotion. He caught at the neckline of the silk gown and with a sharp downward jerk tore it in two, baring her body completely. Then he straddled her, his passion mounting further as her legs twined around his, opening to receive him and drown him in a surge of pleasure.

Karin was a small woman and he might have suffocated her as he collapsed against her, a dead weight once the force went out of him. But she was so intoxicated by his potent presence that even this crushing exhaustion thrilled her. Not that it lasted more than a moment. Harry, almost always a gentleman, opened his eyes, grinned sheepishly and said: 'I'd better give you room to breathe before I cut you off in your prime!'

He slid away from her and the separation gave her a shock. When he made love to her she ceased to be an individual and became a temporary extension of his own flesh. The inevitable severance was almost physically painful. Now he cradled her loosely in his arms, so much bigger than her that he seemed like a protective father with a small child. He was already half asleep. He said, dreamily, 'We should be up and about, admiring the Baptistry doors or shopping on the Ponte Vecchio, not wallowing around like this.'

She said nothing, merely wriggling closer, the tantalising aroma of his fresh sweat tickling her nostrils.

It was still quite early and Harry's idea of lying late in bed was a fifteen minute nap before going off to bathe and dress. By nine thirty they had finished their fresh bread and great bowls of steaming milky coffee that tasted oddly of licorice, and were on their way to a morning of galleries and churches. Karin was astonished to find that Harry enjoyed paintings and architecture with the same intensity he devoted to eating or making love. He would not hear of her wandering vaguely from picture to picture in the vast galleries of the Uffizzi, but had made a list of barely half a dozen works to look at that morning.

'You can't dismiss some chap's life work with a quick glance and then go on to the next,' he explained. 'The first time Mama brought me to Florence, I spent every spare moment for a week standing in front of the Birth of Venus, just staring at her. After about the second day, some elderly English female busybody went and found Mother and told her I was a degenerate and should be locked up to preserve the decency of womanhood. Not a bad achievement at the age of ten!'

'What did your mother do?'

'Oh, she was wonderful. Just stared the woman in the eye and said she need have no fear; I was probably unaware that she and her companion were even of the same species as the girl in the painting!' He laughed, then sobered abruptly. 'When I was a child, my mother seemed more like my best friend than a parent. Pity I never realised that some sort of betrayal comes into every friendship.'

'Harry – what an awful thing to say! Your mother would never have betrayed you. She adored you!'

'I used to think that, too, until she pined away over Arthur.'

Troubled, Karin cast around for some consolation to offer Harry. But she, too, had believed the family version of Elizabeth's death and could find no comfort to give him. He stood morosely beside her for a while, then shrugged dismissively, grinned and started to move on. 'Anyway, no point in brooding now. What's past is dead. Let's look to the future.'

He did not refer to Elizabeth again, although Karin

knew this treasure-house of a city had been a favourite destination for mother and son in the days of his childhood. After a couple of days, he suggested they should change their plans and move on to Siena. 'I only went there once; no worn-out memories there. Let's start a few new ones of our own.'

Karin's unease at discovering this facet of her husband that she seemed powerless to reach soon faded. Each day there were fresh delights to charm her. At this time of year the vast golden piazza where the Sienese ran their mad August horse race was quiet, its sloping fan-shaped expanse empty save for overfed pigeons and the handful of well-heeled foreigners who preferred to enjoy Italian art without the blazing midsummer sunshine. They strolled the narrow streets together, admiring ancient buildings and eating Panforte, the almond confectionery studded with glâcé fruits which the Sienese insisted was related to English marzipan. At night they attended concerts and an opera, drank gallons of wine and made love. Karin never wanted it to end.

But their idyll was precisely timed. After a month, they were expected back in England. As their train chugged out of the railway station in Florence, Karin sighed with regret. 'Harry, some day when we are old and grey and our children are running the business, perhaps we could come back here for good.'

He had been looking out of the open window, craning for a last glimpse of the city which had charmed his childhood. Now he turned to her with a look that bordered on bewilderment. 'Live here? My dear girl, I don't mind how many holidays we spend here, but I'm an Englishman through and through and I plan to live and die in my own country. Besides, we Richmonds have a tendency not to relinquish control of the business to the next generation while we have breath in our bodies. Or had you forgotten?'

Harry had not raised his voice or shown signs of anger, but his tone was deadly. Suddenly he was someone Karin did not know. She was appalled – not by what he said so much as by his ability to become a stranger in an instant. How many other faces of Harry had she still to discover?

George Beynon sat in his office overlooking High Holborn and smiled in satisfaction at the half-yearly figures. Even he had been surprised at the zest with which Harry plunged into the business once he was in full control. Most important of all, he had shown his grandmother who was boss right from the beginning. Maybe if Henry had done that, he'd have had a better time of it. He might not even have burned himself out before he reached his mid-fifties. Once she got the right idea, Marged had behaved better than he feared, too. Anyway, none of that was relevant today. Harry was home, and he was giving George lunch at his club before starting back at work.

George was wryly amused at his own attitude to Harry. The prospect of seeing the young man after a month's absence was more intensely pleasurable than the thought of seeing one of his own children again after such a separation. In a real sense, Harry was George's son, for George had taught him all he knew about business and had then been man enough to stand aside and allow the younger man's own genius to use the experience in ways Beynon's more pedestrian intelligence would never have dreamed up. Whistling under his breath, he rose and went to fetch his hat, coat and umbrella. Yes, a luncheon with young Harry was the perfect way to warm up a chilly February day.

'Of course Florence was lovely – always is at this time of year. Listen, George, have you had a look at Piccadilly recently?'

Harry's response to his opening pleasantries caught him slightly off balance, but he rallied. 'Not much point at my age, man. The spirit is willing, but the flesh gets weaker every day!'

'Not the girls – the buildings. Have you looked at the shop premises along the south side lately?'

George shook his head and uttered a small sigh for his ignored joke. 'No, never seem to go down there these days. Why, have they started falling down?'

Harry was exasperated. 'Come on, George, I'm beginning to wonder if you've been in hibernation while I was away. There's a double unit free just west of the junction with Duke Street. Narrow frontage, but it goes back a devil of a long way. Classic provision shop shape, in fact.'

George goggled at him. 'No, Harry – for God's sake, man, slow down a minute. You only got back from Italy day before yesterday! Are you sure the sun haven't gone to your head? They charge more for a Piccadilly frontage than any twenty of our other best sites lumped together. Think of the turnover we'd need! We wouldn't survive five minutes!'

'Fortnum and Mason have been surviving very nicely for nearly two hundred years, and since they're diversifying away from an all-food shop, I think we could give them a run for their money by sticking to quality groceries. It's kept them going long enough.'

Hell, thought George, he could have a point. But the risk! Fortnum's had the advantage of six generations of top families shopping there, never dreaming of going anywhere else . . . His gloom lifted. Because there *was* nowhere else in the immediate area. Maybe the boy had done it again.

Harry was watching his mentor with mounting amusement. 'Got you going, you old devil, haven't I? I may look young and stupid, but you know better than to believe that. Just think about it for a minute. We wouldn't even need to make a profit. The prestige would be so enormous that it would push sales through the roof in our top provincial branches. Think of all those housewives in Bristol and Manchester and Edinburgh, patronising "their" branch of the provision merchants with a flagship in Piccadilly. And by royal appointment, too . . . it's about time Father's Royal Warrant started earning its keep!'

George eyed him with open pleasure. 'Harry, I was thinking of retiring this year, now you're finally in the saddle. But you make me feel so damned young I think I may just stay on to watch the fun.'

Abruptly, Harry's exuberance faded. 'I wish you would, George. I don't know if I'd have the confidence to be reckless if you weren't there to hold me back now and then.'

There was something approaching panic in the younger man's eyes. George suddenly felt immeasurably sorry for him. 'Harry, relax, man. You've got more ability in your little finger than the rest of your family

307

put together. Forget about the past. Everything's ahead of you now. They've given you a kingdom but you'll make it into an empire.'

'I wish it were that easy. Oh, not the business – that seems to pop into my head without my even trying. It's coping with this emptiness. I may look confident, but sometimes I feel as rootless as if I'd been found in a cardboard box on the doorstep as a baby.'

'But you're starting your own family now. You've got a pretty young wife, you'll have lots of lovely children.'

'I keep telling myself that. And I know Karin adores me. But sometimes – sometimes I look at her and I think: Do you love me, poor lonely Harry, or do you love this big strong clockwork man who's been wound up to run Richmond's Quality Provisions? I don't think I shall ever know the answer.'

Beynon shook his head. 'You're asking the impossible. You think too much, analyse too much. Everybody wants something from everybody else. But that doesn't mean they don't love them and need them as well. You must know by now that love and selfishness are usually so tangled up with each other that even God must have trouble separating them.'

'I wish I knew how to do it!'

'Well, you never will, and you'll destroy your own happiness if you go through life afraid everyone only wants you for what they can get. Any man in this room would envy what you've got, and there's some pretty powerful characters in here.'

Harry managed a forced laugh. 'You're right, as always. Another reason to stop you retiring. Give me six

months without you to bring me down to earth, and I'd
be doing away with myself.'

'Not you. I've met one or two of them in my time.
You're the wrong sort.'

'Glad to hear it. Mind you, the thought of what would
happen if we failed in Piccadilly is enough to make even
you suicidal!'

George's answering chuckle was uneasy. 'You're not
definite on that yet, surely?'

'Definite as I'll ever be. Took a look this morning;
seeing the agent this afternoon. If he says the right
things, I shall be getting our lawyers to draw up a tenancy
agreement.'

'God help us if this do go wrong. We could both end
up behind the counter in the Bangor shop.'

'No chance, George. You were the one who told me
there was never room anywhere for two managers,
remember?'

'In that case, I'd better take advantage of your hospi-
tality while the Richmond money's still good. I'll have a
glass of champagne.'


Beynon need not have worried. In the three months that
followed, well-heeled passers by in Piccadilly glanced
curiously at the boarded-up shop front behind which so
much work was going on. The shutters were removed
early in May in time for the Season, revealing a bandbox-
smart scarlet door with brass fittings, and a white marble
doorstep flanked by bay trees in square tubs. The double
display windows were what the Victorians fondly imagined as charming Georgian, shallow bow shapes with
the odd bottle glass pane here and there. The overall

impression was of an idealised private house in an elegant old country town about a hundred years before, not a grocer's shop in the world's greatest city on the verge of the twentieth century.

The design of the windows deliberately prevented people from examining the display in too much detail. They could see the windows were full of bright, japanned canisters and beribboned boxes – just sufficient to tempt them inside for a closer look. They were not disappointed. Harry, George and some of their most talented buyers had been scouring the Continent and receiving samples from all over the world since March in order to offer an incomparable range of exotic food and drink. In Britain, new farm produce buyers had been appointed to seek out the best sweet-cured bacon, the most delicate kippers, the true farmhouse Cheddar and Caerphilly cheeses, the mildest oak-smoked wild salmon – the very products which Richmond's high street shops had all but eliminated from national distribution half a generation ago. Now they were brought together with the best produce of five continents in a vast gastronomic symphony performed in a red, white and gold grotto on Piccadilly.

Harry insisted that George himself should engage and train the all-female counter staff. 'You're the only old-time grocer we have left,' he said. 'I want those girls to get a speeded-up version of what you taught Father back in Bangor. By the time you've finished with them, they'll know how to slice bacon, roast coffee and gauge the ripeness of cheese at a glance. I don't want any of the new customers asking a question about the goods that can't be answered at once.'

They took on two male supervisors and copied

Fortnum's idea of dressing them in red frock coats for easy identification by customers. The Provisions supervisor, Charles Pickering, was the son of a grocer very much in George's tradition, and knew almost as much about quality in food. He had been put out of business by chains like Richmond's and this was the first opportunity he had been given since then to use his expertise instead of just selling cheap pre-packed imported goods behind the counters of modern grocers' shops.

James Fenwick was another type entirely. He was recommended by one of Harry's Society friends. A gentleman fallen on hard times, he had attended the best schools and then had held a commission in a Guards regiment until his father finally exhausted the family fortune in the casinos of France and Germany. Unable to afford to subsidise his Army career any longer, he had resigned his commission and discovered he was unqualified for anything else. Apart from an inbred understanding of all the social graces and a good schoolboy's grounding in Latin, Greek and literature, his only talents were an acutely sensitive palate and an encyclopaedic knowledge of Europe's great vineyards. He was hardly the ideal applicant for a job in a grocer's shop, but Richmond's of Piccadilly was not designed as an ordinary grocer's. After half an hour with him, Beynon and Harry agreed that this one was a top manager of the firm's next generation.

Each of the new senior men brought with them a bonus of new customers. Charles Pickering was still in touch with many of the comfortable professional families from Brixton and Clapham who had comprised his parents' friends and clients. He lost no time in telling them of the new venture and a steady stream of mothers and daughters arrived at the new shop to gaze on this Aladdin's cave of food. They made purchases merely to enjoy the cachet of carrying home a Richmond's package, gaily clothed in scarlet glossy paper and gold string, with the firm's name stamped in gold and white lettering. Fenwick's friends were far more socially prominent and usually richer. They were drawn partly by curiosity about the new venture, but more by self-interest. They knew of James's legendary skill at choosing wine and now they came to buy the results of his expertise.

The new Richmond's branch was the talk of the West End when it opened in May Week 1896. The rich and well born came to look, stayed to buy exotic bits and pieces, and later sent their cooks to do some serious shopping. The middle-class housewives on shopping trips to Regent Street looked in, saw the carriage trade in full occupation and unanimously joined them, placing orders for the specialities they never saw in the northern and south-western London suburbs.

They had been open barely three weeks when Harry slammed into George Beynon's office, in his exuberance almost knocking down a clerk who was about to leave. 'We've made it, George! After this, nothing will stand in our way!'

'Calm down, man! Not even a second royal warrant can be worth that much fuss. What has happened?'

'Fortnum's – I just heard today when I was down in our place looking round the new bottled goods section – they've shelved their diversification plans indefinitely. Seems we're too big a threat for them to take on any more problems at present!'

He was glowing with satisfaction, chattering away non-stop in spite of George's attempts to get a word in. Finally he noticed the older man was less than ecstatic and his enthusiasm tailed off. 'What's the matter? Aren't you pleased?'

'D'you realise what this might mean, Harry? Not even that new chap Harrod down Knightsbridge can think in terms of competing with Fortnum and Mason yet.'

'Yes, quite! That's why I'm so pleased.'

'But it's not good news, man, it's the worst! I grant you it's a compliment to us that they're withdrawing from an expensive programme to fight us, but follow that through. They'll crush us. They'll pull every trick they know to wipe us out. We'll be back in provisions for the working classes before you can say Jack Robinson – if we've the capital left to survive, that is!'

Harry burst out laughing. 'I'd call you an old woman but it would be an insult to Grandmother's fighting spirit! George, where did we learn our huckstering sales techniques?'

'Don't know what that's got to do with anything, but from the street traders, of course. Why?'

'D'you think the descendants of either Mr Fortnum or Mr Mason even know what a street trader looks like? We could never wipe them out, but we can block their attempt to do us in, because they're gentlemen and we aren't. Or at least, they like to be *seen* as gentlemen!'

The light was dawning on George. 'I know what you're going to say . . . special offers . . . buy one, get one free . . . every twelve bottles an extra with our compliments . . . oh, you're a bad 'un! All they can do is call

313

us common as muck while they watch the gentry swarm in to get something for nothing!'

'Got it first time, George. Only, of course, we'll have to wrap it up a bit, pander to our customers' sense of self-importance as well as their greed. Not "Get your free gift", but "We cordially invite our patrons to accept a token . . ." and then the little sweetener. And we keep it up, too. Not just a rash of presents for the first three months. It will be a regular feature of Richmond's to offer complimentary bits and pieces to our most valued customers.' He paused, then snorted with mirth. 'My God, we could even issue a smartened-up version of those funny little dividend books the Co-operative shops put out and give discount for redeeming them!' They both knew that idea was too close to the wind, but the rest of it was to win them a slice of business that turned Richmond's of Piccadilly into one of London's smartest traditional shops.

Henry Richmond degenerated daily, his lucid spells continually foreshortened by encroaching periods of insensibility. When they told him about Harry's marriage to Karin, there was no sign he understood. The remissions were almost more upsetting than the black times, because he became at least partially aware of what was happening to him. Marged was sustained by her relief that Harry was steering Richmond's expertly towards the twentieth century, but she did not neglect her son, and suffered greatly to see him so debased. A team of nurses now looked after him in a special suite – ironically once the nursery wing – at White Lodge. Marged spent three or four hours a day with him, even when he failed to recognise her. When he was lucid, Henry was almost inconsolable about his fate, and then she was with him constantly.

On the evening of one such day in April they sat together in the walled west garden, savouring the last of the sunlight. It had been the first really warm day of spring. Henry was much calmer than he had been for some time, and quite his old self. 'You're much better today,' said Marged, relieved at his lack of tension.

He smiled at her and suddenly the boy of eighteen was peering out from his ruined face. 'You won't be so pleased when you know the reason,' he said.

'I'd be pleased at anything that gave you comfort.'

'Funnily enough, this did, though I can't think why. She came to me last night and now I understand about – about all this.' Henry gestured downward, at the legs grown too unsteady to carry him, at the trembling, liver-spotted hands which shook continually, then raised his eyes to his mother. There was no need to ask him who 'she' was. Marged already knew.

'I never told you about her prophecy. It seemed too outlandish then. You were so down-to-earth, such a perfect opposite to Myfanwy. Even in those awful days when I fell apart, you wouldn't have tolerated it. You'd have said it was nonsense. Maybe I should have told you. I – I always believed in you more than anything else, Mother. Maybe if you'd ridiculed it, as I know you would have, it might have broken her spell and I'd have been free. And then, maybe, this wouldn't have happened to me . . .' He broke off momentarily and stared straight ahead, tears coursing unchecked down his cheeks.

Marged reached over and clutched his limp hand. 'Hush, hush – I'm here, don't cry.'

His smile was radiant. 'I know. You always have been. My tragedy wasn't really Myfanwy, Mother. It was that you and I were born wrong. You should have been my wife, not my mother.' He laughed as her eyes widened in shock at his words. 'I can only say it now I'm a helpless wreck. Imagine how scandalised you'd have been if I'd confessed when I was a big strong healthy young man and you were still a beautiful woman hardly starting into middle age!'

Marged gave a small shiver, Now, silently, in this moment of supreme trust, she could acknowledge the truth of what he said. Tomorrow she would deny it, even to herself. She started. Henry was talking again.

'I thought I woke up, suddenly, in the early hours, just as it was getting light. I must have been dreaming, though, mustn't I, because it's impossible for a girl who died nearly forty years ago to come back?'

Marged nodded silently, but almost believed in Myfanwy's presence as she did so. He went on: 'The light was just as it was that last time I was with her as her lover, just before I came home to Menai View and you . . . took me away from her . . . Remember that Sunday breakfast, with her old mackerel wilting in the cold larder and your ham and eggs spluttering me back to life at the kitchen table? She came drifting towards me, and she seemed to be swimming to me on those first rays of light. I said, "Van, you're not changed, not changed at all," and she said, "Oh yes, Henry. A sea change, though, you don't see it this side of the moon."

'I didn't understand and I said, "But how could we be

the other side of moon?'' She laughed. ''Silly old Henry
. . . You never could understand that, could you? But
you will soon, and all those awful wrinkles will go away
and I'll wash the big brown spots off your hands with
seafoam. We'll swim down the moon path like we did all
those years ago, only this time you'll stay with me when I
get there and call you, won't you? This time you won't
turn back and shout at me to come too. This time you'll
swim with me, strong and far, and we'll swim right to the
other side of the moon and it will all be silver and we'll
always be young.'' Then she kissed me, and I thought I
was dissolving. Only she dissolved, instead. The first
rays of sunlight came into the room and she just melted,
like ice.'

Marged did not dare to speak, for he clearly had more
to say. For a while he resumed his steady, wordless,
forward stare, then said: 'The memory of the prophecy
came later. I must have been bad the past few days – it's
all terribly vague – but now I was quite clear. I remembered what she said to me that awful day before she
killed herself. She said all I'd ever get was second best,
and that's proved so true . . . a friend of the Prince of
Wales, but only because he likes rich men about him . . .
never accepted at Court or anything. And my sons . . .
my lovely Arthur, cut down before he reached his summer. Yes, I still have a son, but he's the most second best
of all!' Now a touch of bitterness entered his speech for
the first time, and she noticed he was getting wilder.

'Sh-she had this absolute belief that what she called
''our'' children would make a fortune over the sea . . .
Madness, of course, but I was so haunted by it that when
Margaret married Steven I was half convinced it was

317

that.' He was growing more strained by the second, plucking at his dressing gown, his upper lip twitching slightly, but he still seemed in command of his mind.

'When Arthur died, I was completely convinced. I – I must make a confession, Mother. While we were in Bangor when Arthur went, I tried to placate her spirit.' He laughed mirthlessly. 'I went over to Llangefni and the herbalist's shop was still there. I went inside, and there was this funny, bright-eyed young man with my face and Myfanwy's eyes. There he was, alive and thriving, my by-blow, and there was the legitimate son, the one I worshipped, *our* son, lying dead back in Tan-yr-Allt. I was beside myself. I went and found the land agent and I bought up the four shops in the terrace there. They were all just rented. I planned to tear them down and deprive the accursed little bastard of his living.' His voice bore the ferocious intensity of the grief which must have driven him then.

'But when we got back home, I calmed down and I felt terribly ashamed. Instead of carrying out the plan, I just filed the leases of the other shops away and sent Beuno's to a lawyer in Bangor, with instructions to give him the freehold on my death. She's been back to remind me, Mother . . . She's been back to make sure he gets his inheritance . . . you must see to it . . . must see . . .' The familiar skein of spittle dribbled down from the corner of his mouth. His eyes were growing vague. The twitching in his hands was visibly worse. Marged covered them with her own and willed him into looking her full in the face.

'Henry – Henry, before you go again, listen. Try and concentrate . . . oh, God, please try! I swear to you that

318

I'll see that boy is all right. And I swear to make sure the family will know about him and try to put things right. Can you understand me? Please, my poor love, you're not to be frightened. I'll see it's all right. I promise. Do you understand?'

She thought she caught a last gleam of intelligence acknowledging what she had said, but she could never be sure. My sweet Lord Jesus, she thought, did I get through to him? Can he rest without that awful weight on him? She started for the gate set in the high garden wall, beyond which the nurse waited. Perhaps she could tell him tomorrow.

In one sense, Marged was relieved that her son finally seemed to have passed beyond the anguish of occasionally understanding his own terrible end. But she also bore a burden of anxiety and she could find no easy way of shedding it. In the end she did what she always did when she could not confide in Henry – she took the problem to George Beynon.

By now, almost a month had passed since she made her promise to Henry in that last rational moment in the walled garden. At the time it had been inconceivable that she should refuse him. But now? How could she make known the existence of a grown-up bastard son, particularly when the rest of the family might start asking questions and come up with the story of his mother's death? And yet she had made a promise. Beuno should have his inheritance and the family should be told . . . There must be some way of fulfilling that vow to the letter without going quite as far as her son had wished.

So she went to George, and told him everything. 'There it is,' she finished. 'What can I do? I can't deny

319

Henry his last rational wish, but I've no intention of landing the family with a potential scandal. Anyway, I don't want them remembering their father as someone who behaved so badly.' Or me either, come to that, she thought.

George thought it over for a while, then said: 'There's one answer that's quite easy, though you might not like what you have to do.'

'It can't be as bad as telling the family all about it.'

'It would mean making Karin your friend – and pardon me for saying it, Marged, but I get the impression you don't altogether like that girl.'

'Nonsense – though I don't see how she could possibly help.'

'Well, she's keeping on Tan-yr-Allt. You know it's not likely that Harry will want to spend much time there. Too far from the business – and from the West End! It's pretty handy for keeping an eye on a shopkeeper in Llangefni, though. If Karin plans to go up there every summer or something like that, you could make her a sort of custodian of your secret, and of Beuno's legacy. I know she's off up there this summer, because she's going to Bangor for a few days in two weeks' time to make sure everything's in apple pie order for when Harry do go with her.'

'Now I'm completely at sea!'

'Go to Karin, be the careworn grandmother with a burdensome secret vow to be fulfilled. Tell her the story but emphasise how much the truth could harm Harry's reputation – how much trouble it could lay up for the future. Then entrust her with a signed deposition about Beuno's origins, on the promise that it mustn't be shown

320

to anyone while it can still harm Harry or their children. She's a solemn little thing. Takes duty and family honour very seriously. Lay it on heavy enough and she'll be quiet as the grave. You told Henry you'd make it all right, but you didn't set a time limit. As I see it, if Beuno owns the freehold on that shop, it don't matter if he do know about it or not. If he ever fails to meet the rent, nobody will put him out on the street. After all, the rent money just goes into the holding account Henry set up for him. You trust that Karin. Confide in her and leave it to her discretion. It'll never come out in Harry's lifetime, you mark my words, but it'll help old Beuno enough to keep your promise.'

Marged had been watching him with mounting admiration. 'George, sometimes you make me think Machiavelli must have had a Welsh mam!' She laughed for the first time since Henry's latest collapse. 'I really think you've solved it for me – though you're right about Karin. I wish I didn't need to trust her.'

But trust her she did. When Karin went to Bangor a fortnight later, an out-of-town cabinet maker was engaged to build in a small cupboard behind the dining-room panelling at Tan-yr-Allt. Inside, they placed a strongbox. It contained a copy of the deed of gift on the Llangefni shop, along with the name and address of the solicitor who held the freehold, the bank account details and the explanatory letter from Henry to Beuno. Marged added her deposition about Henry's youthful love affair with Myfanwy Owen, and Karin swore that if the secret were still unrevealed on her own death, she would leave instructions in her will to ensure that someone in the family found the contents of the box.

As Marged watched the girl push the concealed door shut, she felt relieved of a vast burden. Karin turned and smiled at her. 'Don't even think about it again, Grandmother. I have every intention of growing old as Harry's wife. The whole story will be meaningless by the time anyone else knows it.'

And there seemed no reason on earth why her prophecy should prove false, thought George when Marged told him about it. His informants in Anglesey said the bright-eyed young man still went about his business at the herbalist's shop and seemed to be doing well enough without his unseen protector. Long might it continue like that.

# Chapter Thirteen

Karin enjoyed her first summer as Harry's wife more than any other. He had always been very popular outside his own family circle and since taking over Richmond's he had exploited his contacts to the full and made himself a star of the newspaper social columns. There were too many brewery barons and newspaper lords for anyone to look askance at the newness of his money as they had at his father's. He slipped through the ballrooms and salons of the rich and aristocratic as easily as a fish through water, and relished every moment. Now Karin went with him, enjoying all the attention that Arthur's grinding dedication to business had excluded from their life together.

There was none of that with Harry. He would get up at five-thirty to go over a report on which George Beynon had asked his opinion, be at Richmond House by eight-thirty and often stay until eight at night. But equally often, he finished work at noon to go racing in the afternoon, or took a morning off to catch up on his sleep after staying out until the small hours three nights in succession. He still managed to put in a fifty-five hour working week when it was necessary. It never occurred to anyone at Richmond's to suggest that the head of the firm was a slacker. They all knew he worked harder than they did.

Harry and Karin spent most of their time in the Belgravia apartment overlooking Eaton Square, going to Mapledurham only at week-ends when they were not guests at some friend's country house. Marged reigned there now in almost solitary splendour. Her only family companion was Mary Rose, whose affection for Marged had not increased with the passage of time. She could never forgive her grandmother for treating her as a tiresome little stranger for most of her childhood. Ironically, Mary Rose had inherited Marged's beauty just as her sister Margaret had taken after their mother. She was small, with a shapely, compact body toughened by hours in the saddle, for horses were her main passion apart from parties. Her hair was a light chestnut shade that looked almost delicious enough to eat, her skin rich and creamy and her eyes amber brown. At twenty-two, she had more suitors than any girl she knew, but was enjoying life far too much to wish to settle down yet. Harry was her hero and she spent a lot of time in London at the apartment. Karin was happy to have her there, because it widened their social circle still further – and none of Mary Rose's admirers was dull.

As Karin floated through her dream summer, only one small imperfection marred her contentment. There was no sign of her becoming pregnant and she knew Harry desperately wanted a son. He was far too sensitive to her feelings to raise the matter, but as the months passed and there was no sign, despite their vigorous and frequent love-making, his sexual advances took on a new urgency.

The summer season ended in July and predictably

business slackened at Harry's pride and joy, the Piccadilly shop. 'I'd have been more worried if it had stayed buoyant,' he told Karin. 'It would have meant our customers weren't the best people after all, if they were still in London, shopping, in August!'

He believed in playing hard as strongly as in working hard, so once he was satisfied he could do no more, he suggested that they too should leave London. 'I don't really want to go to the Continent at the height of summer,' he said, 'and Cowes and Scotland are out because Cowes always reminds me of Father and Scotland means deerstalking or shooting. I just want to be lazy for a while. Where shall we go?'

Karin hesitated before making her suggestion. She was not sure how happy Harry's memories were. 'How about a few weeks at Tan-yr-Allt? I haven't been there since last autumn and I'm beginning to miss it.'

'What a splendid idea! Good girl – yes, I'd like that. And if I did feel energetic after the first couple of weeks, there's swimming and fishing and boating . . . We'll go next week.'

She should have been pleased that the memory of Arthur's death and his father's grief had not ruined the place for him, and she was. But she was disappointed, too. After all, Tan-yr-Allt was where she had fallen in love with him the Christmas after she was widowed. It had been a magical time for her and she had nurtured an illusion that Harry shared her feelings. He was glad enough to be going back, but his attitude made it obvious that the place had neither good nor bad associations for him. Karin sighed. 'Don't be a silly girl,' she said aloud. 'You have almost everything. Why keep on wishing for

325

more?' But somewhere deep inside, another voice told her that she would never have Harry's whole heart or mind. At best she would have more of it than anyone else.

Harry strode eastward along Piccadilly. He delighted in taking this route to his club, because it was by doing so that he had first seen the empty shop which later became Richmond's of Piccadilly. What a different picture it made today from five months ago! He chuckled self-indulgently at his own weakness as he turned in through the cheerful scarlet front door. There was no reason why he should go there today. He had launched the place now – the regular staff were more than capable of handling the sort of business they would be doing from now until the autumn. But he allowed himself this one vanity: the pleasure of a quick look at his unique creation.

The salesgirl at the counter nearest the door instinctively bobbed him a curtsey and Harry almost laughed aloud. They really did see him as royalty! Well, he wouldn't pretend he didn't like it. He rewarded her with a broad smile and started moving leisurely from counter to counter, picking up the occasional small item; standing back to see how the decor had stood up to its first two months' heavy use; surreptitiously checking that there was no speck of dust on the chairs or counters. Everything was in perfect order.

He was having a few words with Charles Pickering beside the pâté display when a voice that sounded like a mixture of honey and barbed wire interrupted them. 'Well, if all the shopwalkers in this place are up to your standard, I shall certainly start coming here instead of Fortnum's!'

Harry turned, unsure whether he was angry or amused by such effrontery. Behind him was the most devastatingly attractive woman he had ever seen. At a loss for words, he stood gaping at her.

She seemed unsurprised. Presumably she had this sort of effect on every man she met. She merely smiled and said: 'P'raps I should open an account so I could have my things delivered. It's Standish. Nellie Standish. Care of the Gaiety Theatre, Strand. Got that? Good! Goodday, gentlemen.'

She turned and swept out of the shop in the best *grande dame* manner. Harry was still transfixed. Pickering was close to apoplexy. 'Of all the – I don't know what to say, Mr Richmond, I really don't know what to say! You were right about the best people having all left town. Now we're down to theatrical riff-raff. Shopwalker, indeed! I shall see she never . . . Mr Richmond – Mr Richmond, where are you going?'

But Harry was already out of the shop and heading eastward again, this time behind the tall figure which swayed sinuously along with surprising speed a few paces in front of him. They had travelled some twenty yards when she stopped and turned to face him. 'My God, you're not very fast at catching up, are you? Come on then, if you're coming – I'm starving!' And to his own undying amazement, Harry fell into step at her side.

She seemed disinclined to say anything more for the moment, but strode on, looking at shops, at other passers by and occasionally at Harry. Finally he managed to say: 'Where are you – that is, we – going?'

'Romano's, of course. Where else? Didn't go there for supper last night so I'll damned well have to turn up for lunch. You've never been there, I'll bet!'

'No. Not one of my haunts.'

'Well, unless you're a theatrical, you're not missing much. I don't think anybody ever went to Romano's for the food. Between you and me, I dunno how he's got the nerve to put it on the table.'

'In that case, perhaps you'd permit me . . . there are plenty of good places within –'

'Nah, told you. I got to go today because I wasn't there last night. Miss two on the trot and they start saying you're a has-been, and I haven't been round long enough for that yet. Come on, the steak's safe enough, even if it won't win him any prizes!'

He had been looking at her carefully as she spoke, trying to place her. The face was vaguely familiar, but he was at a loss to know how he could have seen such a beauty and then have forgotten her. It was no use concentrating on the name. It was vaguely familiar, but then, it was a thoroughly English name . . . or was she English? With looks like hers she could really be Italian. And that slight cockney accent? Probably an immigrant, brought up in this country in one of the Italian communities of Soho or Clerkenwell. Of course! Clerkenwell, that was it. No wonder he hadn't remembered seeing her before. It had only been a picture in the *Illustrated London News* – and it definitely didn't do her justice. Nellie Standish was a stage name. She was the rising star of the London stage, on her way to immortality beside the likes of Marie Lloyd and Lillie Langtry. And the news item said she had been born in Clerkenwell of Italian parentage.

'Is there a smut on my nose or are you just smitten?'

328

Hardly surprising that she had caught him staring. He'd been gazing at her for at least two minutes.

Harry laughed sheepishly. 'Please forgive me. I knew your face was familiar and I've just remembered you from the *Illustrated London News*.'

'Oh, that – I was thinking of suing them after I saw the picture. Not exactly a flattering likeness!'

'Hardly. That's why it put me off. It didn't begin to do you justice.'

She grinned wickedly. 'That's the way to tell 'em! Keep on like that and I might even buy you luncheon. But then again . . .'

'Permit me. A tough steak is a small price to pay for the privilege of your company.' They walked on, neither of them attempting to call a cab, flirting and teasing one another as they went. Eventually Harry surfaced for long enough to realise it would take them hours to get to Romano's at this rate, and stopped a hackney. As he handed her into the cab, he wondered what had come over him. He had responded to a blatant pick-up by some sort of actress and now he was going off to give her lunch – and he was supposed to be a contented young husband still in the first romantic year of his marriage! He could hardly back out at this stage, but once they had lunched together, he must say a final and courteous goodbye, then retreat to his own world.

Even as he contemplated the prospect, he knew it would never happen. He had caught Nellie Standish like an infectious disease and he had no notion where he might find a cure – or if he even wanted one.

At any other time Romano's would have fascinated him. Harry relished new experiences and was as curious

329

about the habits and haunts of other professions as he was about his own. But the restaurant and its colourful patrons were merely a gaudy backdrop to this ravishing creature. He compensated for the mediocre food with plenty of champagne, then sat and gazed at her. By now she knew his name and that he was one of the Richmonds, famous from tea posters and high street shop fronts. She did not know he owned the lot – or that he was married.

She had been chattering uninterrupted for some time about the show in which she was starring, the conditions backstage, her uncomfortable dressing room, when she said abruptly '. . . and if I was to say the first few lines of *Hamlet*, you'd go on nodding and smiling like a bloody puppet, wouldn't you?'

Harry collected himself with a start. 'Look, I'm sorry, Nellie, but I really can't take my eyes off you. Nothing remotely like this has ever happened to me before and I don't know how to deal with it.'

She laughed. 'Don't deal with it, then. Let it sweep over you like a great big wave. I suppose it hasn't occurred to you yet that I'm not normally in the habit of picking up strange men in grocers' shops – even posh ones – with the sort of rubbish I talked to you an hour back!'

'Well – I – er, that is – it hadn't crossed my mind.'

'Yes it had, as soon as you knew I was an artiste. I saw it in your face. Way-hey, lads, we're on to a good thing here! And you come running after me down Piccadilly like a mongrel after a pound of tripe!'

Harry blushed furiously and simultaneously tried not to laugh. She caught his amusement, but was still indignant at his low opinion of her. 'For God's sake, take a good look at me – you've been staring long enough! I'm not being vain when I say I know I'm a looker – course I do, it's what earns me a lot of my living. I'm certainly too pretty to be hard up for male attention!'

'Hear, hear!' Harry's expression was becoming dreamy again.

'Oh, Christ, don't let's go back to the star-gazing. Come on, now, have some more bubbly and perk up a bit.'

He spent most of the afternoon perking up a bit, and when they finally left Romano's they were heading for Nellie's house in Bloomsbury, 'For a little liquid refreshment,' she said, with an expression that bordered on a leer. When they arrived, the small neat house looked somnolent in the afternoon sunlight. Awnings shaded the windows of the first two floors, which were masked inside by lace curtains. It looked like a very expensive bordello. Harry began to get nervous.

'I really don't think this is wise, you know. Perhaps we'd better just have tea in a teashop somewhere, then say goodbye.'

'Rubbish! If you desert me on the doorstcp I shall be no use for tonight's performance, and it'll be all your fault. Come on in, there's no one to bite. I gave Dora the afternoon off.' And with that she took a key from her bag, opened the front door and led him into a hall that smelled of rose-based pot pourri.

Harry's disquiet was mounting to rampant panic now, but still he was unable to turn and walk away from this magnetic stranger. He stood beside her in the cool semi-darkness as the door slammed behind him like the entrance to a prison cell. Nellie stood motionless for a moment, gazing at him quizzically. Then she raised her hands, removed her hat and placed it carefully on the hall table. She glided over to Harry, stood only inches from him, and murmured, 'Don't you think you should undress me now?'

His arms went round her almost as if acting independently of him. He bent to kiss her, but she pulled away slightly and only smiled. 'No, I want you to undress me first.' Harry's fingers shook as the sexual tension mounted within him. He was a very experienced man, but he had always taken the initiative before. Now here he was, obeying orders from an enchantress who appeared to know precisely what she wanted, and had the arrogance to demand it. Still trembling slightly, he began to undo the buttons at the waist of her dress.

Nellie was wearing an expensively-cut, fashionable outfit, slightly flashy in keeping with her profession. The matte satin coat dress had a tight-fitting bodice with the huge puffed sleeves so fashionable that summer. The flared skirt split below the waist buttons to reveal a silk underdress of the same garnet shade as the coat but shot with dark blue. The very feel of the fabrics was almost as sensual as touching Nellie's skin. Harry peeled back the top layer and she slipped out of it – still almost as covered up as before. The underskirt had a matching camisole top designed to show around the edges of the coat front. She smiled at him almost mockingly and turned her back so that he could unhook the garments. He gazed entranced at her broad, white shoulders and the long neck with the huge coiled chignon of black hair, then bent to kiss the top of her spine.

She giggled and slipped free of him. 'I told you – undress me first.' Then she turned to face him again, easing the loosened underdress down over her body as she did so. It was too closely-fitting to permit the customary extra layer of underwear. The skirt had a built-in petticoat and it was now about her ankles. She was wearing an intricately-boned black satin corset, trimmed with black lace and pink ribbon, black stockings of sheer silk, and black and pink lace garters. Basking under his appreciation, she said, 'I never wear drawers in summer – unhealthy, I always say!'

'There's nothing unhealthy about you, Nellie, I can see that.' The corset was of a French cut and slightly out of date, stopping mid-way up the rib cage. There was hardly any point in her wearing the newer built-up style. Her breasts were as firm as rock and stood out without need of whalebone or cloth support. She looked indecent and utterly irresistible.

Harry began to reach for her again. She merely laughed. 'Uh-huh – now you' – and she began to undress him, slowly, systematically, putting each garment carefully on a chair. After divesting him of his jacket, waistcoat and tie, she said 'Get down – down there. Just sit on the bottom stair a minute. Now, off with the boots. Otherwise I'll never get you out of your trousers . . .'

To his own undying amazement, he found himself obeying. This couldn't really be happening. It was like something out of the dirty books he remembered from his schooldays. Except that Nellie Standish was infinitely more delectable than the badly-drawn women who capered across the pages of the books. When he stood up again, she stripped away his shirt, then ran an appreciative hand down his bare chest. Her fingers wound mesmerically in and out of his fly buttons and he felt himself stir and harden as they slid over him. He stepped out of trousers and underpants together and stood naked, almost touching her, panting to get hold of her.

'Now,' Nellie sighed dreamily, 'the corset, then the boots, then the stockings . . . and then . . .' He was already unhooking the front-fastening corset, the satin more sensual than ever against his fingers. He was not trembling now. He was fast and sure, driven forward by a need to possess her as soon as possible.

He knelt before her at the foot of the stairs, undoing the little glazed kid boots. 'I never realised how many buttons you women wore,' he growled in exasperation.

Nellie kicked the boots aside. Harry remained kneeling in front of her and wrapped his arms tightly around her waist, pressing his head hard against her silky belly. His hand slid round and down between her legs, parting the moist flesh and stealing inside. She let out a sharp gasp of excitement. 'Come on, take me upstairs, quick.'

But he was beyond that. 'No, here. Just relax.' He half rose, took her weight into his arms and lowered her on to the bottom two stairs before kneeling on the floor between her stockinged thighs. Leaning forward, he began kissing her breasts before settling back again to the centre of her excitement.

This time, as his tongue touched her, she gave a cry. 'Harry – Harry stop, I'll come if you don't!'

He raised his head and grinned at her. 'I thought that was the idea.'

'But not yet, please!'

He drew back and moved up beside her on the staircase, drawing her hand over his huge, urgent erection. 'You won't have to wait long for me, darling. Where do we go?'

She gestured upstairs and laughed shakily. 'If we get there in time, that is.'

She was a tall, powerfully-built girl, but Henry towered over her. He stood up, bent and lifted her effortlessly. As he carried her upstairs she pressed her fingers into the golden hair on his chest and crooned ecstatically at him. The first room to the left of the stairs seemed to be all bed – a vast brass structure covered with flounces of crisp white linen. Harry threw her down and said, 'Now, those stockings . . .'

He was in control again now and teased her by rolling down each long silk tube with tantalising slowness. There was no longer any question of who led whom. She was lying close to the edge of the bed, her legs dangling over towards the floor. Harry threw aside the stockings, spread her thighs wide apart, bent and pressed his face between them once more. Then he moved on to her and she clutched for him, guiding his pulsing, rigid strength deep into her body. It was as though everything were happening in exquisite slow motion, giving him a pleasure like nothing he had ever experienced. Her legs twined around his as though to squeeze every ounce of force from him. As his body pressed her into the fat mattress, her big breasts crushed deliciously against his chest. Her scent enveloped him and her mouth opened beneath his, tongue seeking tongue, making the scent become taste and the taste become part of the physical sensation of their bodies, thrusting together with an agonising intensity impossible to endure long and unthinkable to live without.

Suddenly it all speeded up and instead of floating, Harry was being carried forward on a tidal wave which would inevitably beach him somewhere, a hundred miles and a thousand years from here . . . He toppled down through a maelstrom of his own passion and heard Nellie calling out somewhere, simultaneously part of him and infinitely distant. Then it was over for them both, and for a while he was not altogether sure of where or even who he was.

Karin had travelled to North Wales three days earlier to prepare the house for their holiday. The housekeeper lived in and a gardener-handyman came every day, but she preferred to get there before Harry to ensure that all was in order for his arrival. She revelled in the perfect summer weather, taking pleasure in the smallest household activity. In London they were far too grand for her to be involved in domesticity, and in her stuffy German childhood home such interests had been condemned as unforgivably middle-class, so all this had the charm of novelty.

She had high hopes of this holiday. Recently she had seen a specialist in women's ailments and he had sounded confident that she had no cause to worry. The reason she was not yet pregnant probably had more to do with their hectic social life than infertility. 'Get away, relax, rest, eat plenty of healthy food and – er – create a sympathetic atmosphere, Mrs Richmond,' the doctor told her. 'Within the next few months you'll be wondering why you ever worried.'

So here she was, with trunks full of lovely clothes – particularly negligées and nightgowns – and a whole pile of menus incorporating Harry's favourite foods. She had done her utmost. Now it was up to him. With his vigorous appetites he would be more than ready for love-making after a week's abstinence . . .

Harry was racking his brain for a good reason to delay his departure for Wales. He hated himself as he did so, but his insatiable passion for Nellie blunted his moral sense almost beyond repair. He had gone to see her on stage at the Gaiety every evening since their wild love-making that first afternoon, and when the performance was over he hurried her back home to repeat the encounter. He had not been able to bring himself to tell Nellie about Karin and he was young enough still for her to assume he was unmarried, so as far as she was concerned, urgent business was the only thing that could tear him away from her in the next couple of weeks.

Finally, though, Harry's basic decency made him act. The day before he was due to leave for North Wales, he received a letter from Karin so full of love, longing and anticipation of his arrival that he could not bear to disappoint her. He cursed his own understanding of those who love more than they are loved, for without such sensitivity he would have stayed with Nellie and not considered any other course of action.

Now, instead, he went to see her after the Saturday matinée and told her he could no longer delay going to stay with his family. He kept their individual identities vague, though, making occasional references to his poor

337

old grandmother whose only happiness now lay in seeing him. He neglected to tell Nellie that Marged was spending July in Mapledurham and August in Switzerland.

Nellie stormed and sulked, because she was almost as besotted by Harry as he was by her. Eventually, though, she privately decided that such early separation would ultimately draw them closer. By the time he came back to town in the autumn he'd be as randy as a billy-goat. Even if he was getting a bit on the side up there, it wouldn't be in the same class as what she could give him.

So they separated after the week-end, Nellie to concentrate on the last week of her show before taking a holiday, Harry to head for Euston and his unsuspecting wife. On the train, he had leisure for the first time to consider the nature of his new affair. Until now he had thought that the easy, affectionate, but seldom exciting relationship he enjoyed with Karin was the most a man could expect from marriage. His numerous sexual experiences had been pleasurable but he had never been seriously involved with the women. Apart from a couple of brief infatuations, none of his physical relationships had lasted more than a month. When it came to girls from his own background, of course, sex had been out of the question. He had flirted light-heartedly ever since leaving Eton, but had never gone beyond that. So this sudden, devastating experience with Nellie Standish had overturned all he had known before.

He was far from prudish, but he had married Karin with a tacit vow that he would remain faithful. Now he realised he was merely fond of her, that she had seemed more desirable because of her association with Arthur,

338

and above all that he had proposed at least partly in outrage at his senescent father's lechery. He had never questioned his circumstances until now because the business had filled his life so satisfactorily that all seemed well. Nellie had made him realise it was not. Depression settled blackly on him. Still in his mid-twenties, only recently married, what a time to realise he had made a mistake! The rich green summer countryside streamed past the window and he sat brooding over an open book which he made no attempt to read.

Karin was at the station to meet him. She had driven down in the carriage, pleased at her skilful control of the horse, quivering with anticipation at the prospect of seeing Harry again. The last hour of his journey had been agonising. He was convinced she would sense his infidelity as soon as she saw him, or that guilt would make him brusque with her, or that Nellie's heady personality would make him bored by Karin's malleable nature. But he found he was really pleased to see her. She looked very pretty, it was a lovely evening, and there was no denying that a week of hectic lovemaking left a man in need of relaxation. After supper, he was surprised to find that he was even regarding his wife with mild sexual excitement. When he left London, he had been convinced Nellie had ruined him for any other woman. Admittedly it turned out to be a bit like tea and toast after the champagne and caviar of Nellie, but even tea and toast was welcome as a change.

By the next morning, Harry was already beginning to consider the possibility of continuing to see Nellie when he returned to London, without causing a ripple in his married life.

Karin, meanwhile, was in paradise. Five times! He had never made love to her five times in one night, even on their honeymoon. At this rate she would be pregnant in next to no time – and even if she were not, it was such fun trying.

# Chapter Fourteen

It was a brilliant summer and they were in the right place to enjoy it. The sea cooled the coast and the mountains of the Snowdonia range ensured enough rain to prevent the landscape from scorching. Harry and Karin basked in the afternoon sun and walked together in the deliciously long northern twilight. Often they dined on the sheltered terrace outside the drawing room windows at Tan-yr-Allt, enjoying the perfect stillness and clean air.

They were virtual recluses, knowing few people in the Bangor area. But neither of them was worried about that. Karin simply relished her temporary monopoly of Harry's company. His reasons were more mixed. He certainly needed a rest after the hurly-burly of his working year; but after a few days he realised, too, that he needed a quiet time to work out a way of dealing with his feelings for Nellie Standish. Most of all, he was as anxious as Karin to beget a child.

The renewed intensity of his sex drive was as surprising to Harry as it had been to Karin. After a while, when it did not diminish, he assumed that Nellie's cheerful depravity had enlarged his appetite for sensuality; he certainly fantasised more than once that he was making love to her and not Karin. But he would have been more honest with himself had he admitted he was driven by the need for procreation, not mere sexual gratification.

To Karin, it was miraculous. She bloomed as this new world of secret pleasure opened to her. At times she was almost beautiful, where once no one would have described her as more than ordinarily pretty. But as their holiday lengthened, the old anxiety began to creep back. They had made love at least two or three times every night since Harry's arrival, and at times had even gone to bed in the afternoon. She had already half hoped she might be pregnant when she travelled to North Wales, and had missed a period. But that had happened often before, and now, a month after their arrival, she had not experienced any other symptoms of pregnancy.

In her more rational moments, she chided herself for this premature worrying. It was early days yet . . . they had been married for well under a year. She was making too much of it. But a frightened little voice kept telling her that her lovemaking with Harry would never be this intensive again, and if she did not conceive now it was quite likely she never would.

Her fears set her off on a new course of action four weeks after their holiday began. Harry received a telegram from George Beynon about a supply problem at their Liverpool chilled meat depot. Could Harry spare the time to travel over to Liverpool and sort it out? Harry was not the sort of man who yearned for his workaday activities when he was away from the office. He enjoyed leisure as much as work, and invariably cut himself off completely from one when he pursued the other. But he was equally able to switch back when necessary, and it made sense in his mind for him to put in two days' work in Liverpool which would otherwise have needed a full week for a senior manager travelling up from London. He reserved an hotel room for two nights, planning to leave Bangor by train early on Tuesday and to return late on Thursday evening. Karin drove him to the station, then returned alone to Tan-yr-Allt.

She did not mind the short separation. With every day that passed, she was more hopeful of having conceived. A couple of days complete relaxation might be just what she needed now. After lunch she went upstairs for an hour's rest. She had been feeling lightheaded all morning. When she undressed, her underclothes were covered in blood. Karin flung herself on the bed and cried until her lungs ached.

Eventually she persuaded herself she must face the world again. If she could not stand up to this small setback, she would be an abject failure. Trying to think positively, she got up and went to take a bath. To hell with the old wives who said it was the worst thing at this time of the month. She had observed that superstition, too, and a fat lot of good it had done her!

An hour later, refreshed but still sad and listless, she went down to the drawing room. It was almost dinner time, and afterwards she had planned a quiet walk along the edge of the Straits. But now her appetite for the outdoors had vanished. There must be something she could do to fend off her depression . . . She remained preoccupied throughout her evening meal. Mrs Preece fussed over her at first but then simply assumed she was missing her husband and went on serving in silence. Karin was still playing with her dessert, looking vaguely into the middle distance, when she abruptly focused on

343

the wall panelling. Why, she had almost forgotten. That was the place where they had hidden Marged's papers. She wondered whether she still remembered how to operate the opening mechanism.

Afterwards, Karin told herself it was nothing more than a whim, a childish game on a dull night when she wanted to forget a personal sorrow. But at the time she felt almost fated to do what she did. She waited until Mrs Preece had cleared away, leaving her with coffee, and said she would need nothing further that evening. After a decent interval she got up and silently went to check the housekeeper had really gone to her own quarters. Then she locked the door and turned back to the wall panelling. Of course you haven't forgotten the mechanism, you silly, she thought. Once you know where the catch is there's nothing to forget. She pressed the bevelled inner edge of the panel and the centre swung open. Inside was the small strongbox. The sight of it made Karin smile, now. Why had they been so circumspect? As long as no one knew of the secret panel, the documents were safe. Once its presence was discovered, whoever cared enough to open it would hardly respect the security of a strongbox. Still, it was what Marged had wanted.

That made her pause for a while, for Karin knew that Marged had also wanted to leave Henry's secret inviolate. She had told Karin the gist of it, but there was something strangely intimate about that locked box with its mysterious little pile of papers, breathing of associations with long-dead love affairs and injustices. Karin had been brought up to observe a very strict Lutheran morality, but beneath her pliable exterior she had a will as indomitable as Marged's. When she wanted something sufficiently, she was equally capable of twisting the morality to fit her own inclinations. There was no reason why these circumstances should present a problem. Marged had never said that Karin must not look at the papers, but that she must keep them from the rest of the family as long as seemed sensible. Don't let any of them open the envelopes and read the papers unless you have to, Marged had said. But she hadn't said that Karin mustn't open them and read them either. Karin went to get her chatelaine, on which she kept the key to the strongbox.

The letter was sealed with red wax. Karin looked at it and smiled. Harry had inherited Henry's seal when he took over at Richmond House and had promptly given it to Karin as a trinket. For some reason he had never liked it. All she need do was to open this envelope and afterwards put the contents in a fresh one, then seal it as before. It was unlikely that Marged would ever glance at the papers again, but if she did, the presence of the seal would make her forget that Beuno's name had been written in Henry's hand on the front of the original envelope. She set aside the letter for the moment, and looked at the other papers. The legal documents held little interest, only confirming what Marged had already told her. There remained Marged's own deposition. Karin weighed it in her hand for some time before deciding it was not worth the risk of opening this one. Marged had signed her name in ink across the sealed-down envelope flap, which made substitution or steaming open impossible without immediate detection by anyone opening the strongbox. In any case, she had no reason to doubt what

Marged had told her of Henry's long-ago affair. This would merely be the written version. What interested her far more was how the sinning partner in that forgotten romance would confess to the sinned-against child. She dropped all the other documents back into the strong-box, then took the letter over to the table, slit it open and sat down to read.

November 22, 1889

My Son

I did you one great wrong, many years ago, and almost did you a greater one only yesterday. I am writing to you now to explain and to beg your forgiveness.

When I was much younger than you are now, I loved your mother. I loved her more than I ever loved another woman, save one, and I love her still. My greatest grief and shame come from having spurned her and from knowing I drove her to her death. Today I have forgotten the faces of all the women I ever loved, including my wife of twenty-five years, whom I last saw only a few days ago. But still, when I sleep, I dream of your mother, and her face is still as fresh and lovely as on that day so long ago when we swam together by the light of the moon.

Had I been left in peace to decide my own fate, I would have stayed with your mother and married her. I think we might have been happy, for Myfanwy was a woman like no other, and her enchantment was without end. But there was another love, too, then, a love that was far too strong for either of us. That love forced your mother and me apart and eventually it destroyed her. I make no attempt to avoid the blame. I should have been steadfast enough to resist the stronger sorcery, but I was not. As a result of my treachery, my beloved son lies dead – he who would never have been born had I cleaved to your mother. He died here, in this accursed enchanted land, only two days ago. When I had seen his poor body, I went out in my grief and raged off to your shop in Llangefni. Perhaps you noticed me, I must have seemed a veritable madman, standing there staring crazily into your face and then rushing out into the street without saying a word.

Perhaps I really was mad, for that was when I nearly did you the second great wrong. I took your shop, your livelihood, with the intention of razing it about your ears. Fortunately the mania did not last, and now I am myself again. I offer you a small part of your inheritance: the freehold of the shop. It would be untrue to say I offer it with love. All my love and all my hope died with my son Arthur. But I give it with a humble heart and great contrition. I could provide more material comforts, but I do not for two reasons. I have seen you at work and you seem to have all you want; and the fruits of my success came after your mother was gone. I have the strangest feeling that she would think they had no place in our private world, or in your own.

There is one last matter which might give you comfort. I have another son, a son who is alien to me. Now that Arthur is dead, he will inherit everything. I wish it were not so; I regret ever having fathered him. I never regretted having fathered you, and I never shall.

We shall not meet again. You have lived without me all your life and now I think I would take more than I could give you, for I have become an old man in less than a week. Try to live a more honorable life than your father. Perhaps your mother was a better model.

If you pray, pray for me. And if you can forgive, forgive me.

Your father,
Henry Richmond

There were tears in Karin's eyes as she dropped the letter on the table. She could never think of Henry Richmond with love, and there were parts of this letter that made her hate him. But overall she felt tenderness for this man whose life had been blighted. She knew enough of the story he left untold in the letter to realise the overpowering love he referred to was that of his mother, and for the first time she knew her father-in-law's life had been warped by Marged's own dark passion.

Karin should have been shocked. She had led a sheltered life, and a mother's incestuous obsession with her son was all but unthinkable. But then, to girls of her background, normal sexual activity between husband and wife was regarded as a disgusting duty.

Her head was spinning. For the first time she questioned her own motives in opening the panel. What had it to do with her? She was miserable at not being pregnant, frightened that she might never be pregnant, missing

Harry after only a few hours. So she had acted like an irresponsible schoolgirl in search of some temporary diversion. Pandora and her pretty little box . . . had she unleashed all the world's troubles to buzz forever about her own head? The letter was such a tragedy that she was thoroughly confused about everything. What had she been looking for?

After a while she calmed down somewhat. There were no excuses. She had acted out of burning curiosity in a dull moment. What she had read did not solve any of her problems, but it certainly took her mind off them for a while. It also made her hate Marged with vicious intensity.

It was getting late. She read the letter again, then folded it and went to get a replacement envelope, candle, sealing wax and Henry Richmond's seal. By the time she had finished, only the blank envelope front gave any indication that the papers had been disturbed. She put the envelope back in the strongbox with the other documents and locked it away. Then she went to bed.

But not to sleep. Deep in the night she lay staring into the blackness, still wondering what good it had done her to pry into the secrets of others. For some reason, she was less depressed than she had expected to be. After all, the letter was an irrelevance, wasn't it, something dead from long ago? Nothing had changed her miserable unpregnant state . . .

It was a long time before she grasped it. Him. Beuno. He was the reason. He was like her, alone, never quite belonging. She had never known her mother. Adelaide Cassel had died when Karin was the same age as Beuno when he was orphaned. True, her father was always

349

there, in a sense. But in reality he was as absent as Henry Richmond had been from Beuno. He had left her to nannies and had sent her abroad to an English boarding school before she was eight. Since then he had treated her as little more than a pawn in his financial power games, flourishing her at rich young men as a good marriage prospect. Nobody had ever really loved her until Harry married her, and maybe Harry wouldn't go on loving her for long if she was unable to give him a son.

When full realisation hit her, she was so surprised she sat up in bed. Of course! Beuno Owen was probably the one person on earth who would really understand her, even if their backgrounds were superficially poles apart. They were kindred spirits. After that, she knew exactly what she wanted to do. She settled down and slept well for the rest of the night. Next morning she drove to Bangor station and caught a train to Llangefni to embark on her own personal wild goose chase.

Myfanwy Owen might never have left the herbalist's shop. It was unchanged since the days when she had played the sophisticated siren in the dimly-lit back room. The same strange smell of spices and formaldehyde still hung in the air; the same bead curtain divided the back premises from the front; the same elegant old jars, bottles and labelled wooden drawers adorned the sales area. Karin loved it. There was no sign of life when she arrived, but a peculiarly ornate brass bell which matched the exotic door handle let out a shrill jangle as she entered. After some scuffling to the rear, someone emerged.

The bright but strangely secretive face of the youngish

man who greeted her bore a strong resemblance to Harry's, but seen through a distorting mirror. The eyes were the right distinctive colour, but they tilted upward slightly at the corners, beneath wing-like, almost satanic eyebrows. The glowing gold curls were like his, but looser. On Harry they were a lion's mane. On this man they were the locks of a faun or a satyr. Like Harry, he had a firm, well-drawn mouth, but it was wider and seemed permanently curved into a half-smile. Where Harry was a giant, this man was almost elfin. He was around five feet six inches tall and his body was slender, though not skinny. When he moved, muscles were visible, but his were the lithe movements of a dancer whose strength lay in flexibility rather than bulk. Karin was captivated on sight and inwardly scolded herself for her eagerness to like him.

She was so preoccupied in her study that she suddenly realised with some confusion that she had come in without working out any reason she could give for being there. Clearly she could not confess everything to him, however hostile she felt towards Marged. She had given her word. Now he repeated his polite enquiry about her needs, regarding her with mounting curiosity.

And then it came out – as though she had rehearsed it, as though that was why she had really come in the first place. Blushing furiously, she said: 'I – I need some help, help t-towards motherhood.'

He smiled kindly, quite unconfounded by her words. 'Don't you be confused, now, I know how embarrassing it is to come out with. Let's see, Mrs, er . . .'

'Richmond – Mrs Richmond.' Had she been confident enough to look him in the eye, she would have seen

351

the sharp momentary reaction, but her own eyes were downcast in an attempt to preserve her modesty. Beuno Owen obviously knew the name Richmond, and its significance to him. Some of the papers back at Tan-yr-Allt might have surprised him, but the identity of his father was no mystery to him. The look was gone in a moment, and he bent his attention to her problem.

'Right, then, Mrs Richmond. Why don't you come and sit down by here and answer a few little questions for me. Don't you be embarrassed. Just act like I was your doctor, see.'

In fact she found it much easier to confide in him than she had to talk to the specialist in London. It was as if she had known him all her life. A more sophisticated woman might have put such ease down to her predisposition to like this supposed soul mate, but Karin was naive and her self-analysis had stopped late last night at the point when she recognised their common experiences. Now she ascribed her happy reaction to his professional expertise.

She sat on a spindly chair beside the counter and shyly answered his questions. He managed to ask them with surprising delicacy and they were soon at the root of her problem. Beuno had also managed to elicit the exact nature of her relationship to the Richmond clan, the fact that she was in Bangor on holiday, and that she was staying at Tan-yr-Allt with her husband.

'I suppose you think I'm silly to be agitated about it so soon after my marriage,' she said with an apologetic laugh, 'but there are . . . er . . . good reasons why I'm anxious.'

'And you can be sure I understand what they are, Mrs Richmond. Don't you worry that I'll decide you're wasting my time. I'm sure I can help. Tell me, have any-body explained that there are some times when it's better to try and make a baby than others?'

She blushed so hard at this that she almost got up and left the shop, but by now she had convinced herself he would help her. She shook her head. He made a dis-approving tutting sound. 'Really, these big medical men! They do ignore the most straightforward information because they think it isn't proper. But I do always say, what's proper about the fear of being barren?'

He was not at all offensive, quite the reverse, and she relaxed as he explained that she would be most fertile about two weeks into each menstrual cycle, and that was the best time to try and conceive. She didn't even need to tell him that this should have made no difference in her case.

'Still,' he said, 'only married a few months, you prob-ably don't need to be told about special times. In the beginning it's all the time, when you're in love.'

Eyes averted once more, Karin nodded silently. He went on, 'All right, then, now we'll give you some good old country remedies. I got two of them made up, but I'll need to make a decoction for the third one. Can you get back here, say, the end of tomorrow afternoon? I can gather the herbs tonight and make them up tomorrow, then, see.'

'I-I don't think I can. My husband is away for a few days . . . business . . . and I shall be meeting him from the station on Thursday evening.'

'That's all right. I'll see it's delivered to you, or even bring it myself.'

'Oh, no! I couldn't – that is, I'd like to keep it

private.' And then she realised she was being too sensitive. Harry knew nothing of his father's old connection with the Llangefni herbalist, Marged had told her that. And as long as he didn't know, she could say quite openly that she'd gone and bought a country herbal tonic. All perfectly proper. Anyway, the chances were that Harry would never know. 'All right then, Mr . . . er . . .?'

'Owen. Beuno Owen, ma'am. You just stay by there a minute, and I'll get the other two potions.' He turned and seemed almost to melt away through the old bead curtain. Karin gave a little shiver of anticipation.

When he returned, he was carrying three bottles, not two. 'Remembered something else back there which will help. You do take baths, sitting down, not standing in a bowl, do you? Well, then, this big bottle will do you a world of good!'

'What's in it?'

'Ah, you'll be having all my secrets out of me in a minute! Nothing to worry you, *cariad*. The main thing is nep. You may know it as catmint. This is a good strong decoction with a lot of sweet herbs to give it a nice scent. Each time you do bathe, pour in about this much –' he held up three fingers against the bottle – 'and make sure the water's nice and hot. Now then, the others are for you to drink. This one here, labelled ''The Elixir'', that's a decoction of the powdered root of bistort – snakeweed, the herbal do call it, but that do put some of the ladies off. Drink it mixed in with a glass of sherry wine or madeira, because it do taste bitter. Later on, when you're with child, you'll take it to prevent miscarrying. But now it's to slow things down and get you with child in the first place.'

'What about that other one?'

'You sure you do want to know where this one do come from? It's a sovereign remedy, but I always think it's God's joke – one of his best gifts and it grows on the dung heaps!'

She made a disgusted face but he said, 'No, now wait. It's called arrach – stinking arrach – and you'll know why when you uncork the bottle. But the taste isn't too bad because it's mixed with honey and sweet herbs. It will control your courses while you still have them and stop them if they threaten once you're with child. You mind you take it.'

'What about the other one, the one you won't have till tomorrow?'

'Ah, yes, now that one is special. You won't be taking that until you're well on with child, to protect it and help you come to full term, see. That one really is a secret. I only pick it at the right phase of the moon, and tonight is the first night this month I can do that, otherwise I'd probably have some made up.' He gave her a long, sideways smile which was unaccountably chilling. 'I'll write down the instructions for that, because I expect you'll be gone back to London this long time when you need to start taking it. There we are, then, all ready for you. It's a bit expensive, I'm sorry to say. Altogether with the one I'll bring tomorrow, it will be one guinea.'

'Of course – if it works, it's worth every penny.' She fumbled in her reticule and took out the money.

'All my potions work,' he said. His expression was unreadable. Then he was all smiles again. 'Is there a shed or a summerhouse in the garden at your house?'

'Why, yes, three sheds altogether, adjoining the kitchen

355

yard. And there's a big open-fronted summerhouse on the lawn overlooking the straits.'

'Good – only I was thinking, if you want me to be discreet about it, I'll just come in last thing on my way home – it'll be very late, long after you retire, Mrs Richmond – and put the bottle inside the summerhouse. It can stay your secret, then, can't it?'

'Oh, yes, what a good idea!' She was grateful for his understanding that maybe she would, after all, prefer that her husband and servants did not know she was taking herbal remedies. She rose, suddenly anxious to be gone. This man had learned more about her most intimate self in half an hour than anyone else had throughout her short life.

She thanked Beuno Owen effusively and moved out of the shop. 'I . . . I don't suppose I shall see you again, Mr Owen.'

'Oh, I wouldn't be too sure. You'd be surprised where I do pop up. Goodbye, then, Mrs Richmond.'

She closed the door and hurried back up the high street to the station.

When she had gone, Beuno locked the shop door, drew down the blinds and went into the back rooms. In the old alchemical laboratory, he went to his bookshelves and took down a couple of battered volumes. One was a leather-bound herbal of great antiquity. The other was a buckram-covered notebook, of the type produced a hundred years earlier for use as a journal. He flipped it open. It was worn from constant use. The fly leaf bore the legend 'Myfanwy Owen, her receipt book', in an open, confident hand. But Myfanwy's was not the first name inside the cover. Four others preceded it, each of an earlier generation than the next. Myfanwy's forebears had been recording formulae and incantations in it since the 1790s. Their 'receipts' had nothing to do with cookery.

Beuno hardly needed to check the recipe he needed. He had been asked for it so often by certain clients he knew it by heart. But he wanted to be sure that he could gather the leaves, roots and seeds of the gladwyn plant that night under appropriate planetary aspects. He had never believed or disbelieved in the power of the stars and planets over his source materials: but his medicines certainly worked, so he followed the precise routine which his ancestors had developed. Maybe the herbs alone worked the cure, but if not, it was easier to follow tradition than to risk failure.

He looked at the planetary tables in the back of Myfanwy's book and cross-checked the date with a large corn merchant's calendar over his work bench. Yes, as he had thought. Perfect aspect. While he was at it, he might as well cull sufficient for half a dozen decoctions. Harvest was getting started, so there were bound to be a few needy purchasers before All Saints . . . At this time of year, the Dingle was probably the best place to find it. He could evade the gamekeepers without serious effort, but in any case there was nothing they needed to protect in the damp, dark places where gladwyn grew, so they were unlikely to run across him. And even if they did, most of them were frightened witless of him. He put together a collecting bag, a reel of twine, some jars, a pair of ordinary cutters and a couple of oddly-shaped little blades made of honed bronze, with squiggly pictograms etched on them.

Once his equipment was ready he set it aside and started on his final preparations. First he made up a small pot of ink from powdered herbal dye and a measure of precious water drawn from the cold cursing well of Llanddona. The narrow roll of paper he took from a drawer was allegedly made up from the rags of old shrouds. He cut a parsimonious strip of it – far too rare to use more than he had to. Then he dipped a bronze nib into the brownish ink and began to write in minute script:

When our Lord Jesus Christ was done on the cross, then Longius came with his spear and pierced him in the side. Blood and water came out of the wound. Longius wiped his eyes and saw a man through the holy virtue that God showed there. I conjure thee, blood, that thou come not out of this Christian woman.

Beuno sighed as he finished his laborious copying, and wondered whether there really was strength in such charms. Auntie always insisted his mother had said the sorcerer's religion did not matter, but the seeker's did; and that the name of the symbol was the most important thing. So, Jesus Christ for a Christian, a corn dolly for the pagan. And for Beuno? He wondered . . . perhaps an old Irish demon with a Welsh voice. That conceit made him smile again and he went on with his work as unconcernedly as if he were packing tea. He unlocked a cupboard and took out one of over a dozen small wax dolls, some male, some female. Then he heated another of his bronze blades in a candle flame, and pressed it momentarily against the figure's abdomen. As the wax melted, he took up the rolled slip of paper with its charm and pressed it into the soft area. The wax hardened immediately and sealed the incantation into position. From his pocket he took the lace-trimmed lawn handkerchief which Karin had carelessly dropped on the counter and which he had whisked away before she noticed. He made it into a primitive skirt for the doll, tying it in place with fine thread. He completed the task by baptising the figure as Karin Richmond, using holy water stolen from the local parish church.

The doll was not going with him tonight. That was for tomorrow. But might as well get it ready while he had the free time. Beuno glanced up at the big wall clock which ticked somnolently high above him. No point in opening up again, now. As he was unlikely to get much sleep either tonight or tomorrow night, he'd better snatch a couple of hours before starting out. He couldn't go until after dark, anyway. He locked up the cupboards in his work area and moved into the windowless back room, with its thick, dusty wallhangings and yellowing pornographic engravings. One frame on the wall stood out as more modern than the rest. It was a daguerrotype of Myfanwy at the age of nineteen, dressed in her fortune teller's disguise but without the yashmak. She appeared very young but not at all innocent.

He stood in front of the photograph for a while, smiling as though at a living person. Then he said: 'I'll show them, Mam, don't you worry. I'll show them you counted for something, all right?' He pressed his fingers to his lips, then to the long-dead face in the picture, before stretching out on the chaise-longue and composing himself for sleep.

*     *     *

It was long after midnight when he found what he was looking for. By the narrow light from his dark lantern, it looked like an ordinary iris. But ordinary irises had finished blooming long before this. The flowers of the stinking gladwyn had died only during the last few days. They hung, sinister and desiccated, from the four-foot spears of green foliage which still flourished. The stench had drawn Beuno to them, when he had begun to despair of finding any. It was as pungent as wild garlic but utterly repellent. To Beuno, at this moment, the odour was sweeter than roses.

He harvested the drying seed heads as well as the dead flowers, which he cut with his bronze blades. Then he chose two particularly large plants and dug them up, trimming away the foliage but putting the huge knotty rhizomes into his collecting bag. 'Get with child a mandrake root . . .' he said, and chuckled at the appropriateness to his purpose of the phallic root bulbs. Once he had what he had come for, he slipped away from the damp woods in the little secret valley. The gamekeepers, patrolling elsewhere on the estate, had no idea anyone had trespassed there.

Back in the shop, Beuno made himself a late supper and then got down to work. He reached out for the distilled water he normally used for such potions, hesitated and changed his mind. No, better to be sure . . . instead he turned to the precious jar of water from the cold cursing well. Yes, that was the thing! He could always replenish his supplies tomorrow night. With mortar and pestle, he bruised one of the rhizomes, then put it aside to infuse in a pint of the water. The leaves and flowers were chopped, mixed with a pound of sugar and another pint of water, and set to boil down into a syrup. Finally he ground up the seeds, stirred them into the infusion with the rhizome and boiled that, too. After an hour, he was left with half a pint of liquid in each pan. He strained them thoroughly through a double layer of flannel, then left the resulting clear amber fluids to cool. Finally he mixed them both together and poured the lot through a funnel into a wide-mouthed bottle, sealed it and went off to write the instructions for Karin.

She had just returned from a stroll down to the harbour when the telegram arrived. Harry had been delayed. He was not returning until the following day. Karin was not sorry. Since her visit to the herbalist, she had become nervous at the thought of what might happen if Harry chanced to see a stranger moving across the lawn in the middle of the night. When she told Beuno about the summerhouse, she had quite forgotten that their bedroom overlooked it.

Now there was little chance of discovery, she was all eagerness. What an adventure! It was like an old story, with the fairy godmother coming secretly at night to help the beautiful princess attain her heart's desire. Except that in this case it was a fairy godfather . . . or perhaps a wicked sorcerer, said a small anxious voice which she hastily stifled. She smiled. Fancy imagining that such a charming man would have evil in mind. Apart from anything else, he had no idea of the Richmond connection with himself. Karin had complete faith in him. What did it matter if he were just a little frightening?

She hurried off to bed early, almost as if she could

speed his arrival by doing so. Strangely enough, it worked, because she dozed off almost immediately, having spent a restless night after her visit to him the previous day.

Karin awoke abruptly at two in the morning. She lay on her back, very still, staring up at the ceiling. The events of the past couple of days came flooding back and she turned her head to look at the window. Everything was silent, but the big panes were flooded with soft white light. The moon was full. She slid out of bed and crossed to the window, looking down across the lawn to where the summerhouse made a squat silhouette against the luminous glimmer of the straits. She wondered if the herbalist had already come and gone while she slept.

But no – there he was! He must have made some small noise as he arrived, and disturbed her sleep. The small, lithe figure was unmistakably Beuno's. He was leaving the summerhouse, moving back towards the house and the main drive. For some reason she could not understand, Karin did not want him to see her. She slid back behind the heavy velvet curtains, which she always left open on summer nights. She could still see the lawn, but was concealed from view. As she watched, the dark figure stopped and seemed to sniff the air. Then the head was raised and her hand went involuntarily to her mouth as she gasped with fright. His face was deathly white in the moonlight. The angle of vision made his eyes appear even more slanted. Was it her imagination that they glittered slightly in the dark? He could not possibly have seen her, but he stared at the window for a long moment, and smiled. Then he turned away and resumed his journey towards the other side of the house.

Karin realised that she had stopped breathing. She released the air in a huge gust and scolded herself when she started to tremble. 'I know I asked you to come, but I am glad you've gone!' she said aloud, forcing herself to laugh. Now she could no longer see him, though, curiosity impelled her more strongly than nervousness. She couldn't wait until the morning. She must see what he had left.

In the summerhouse she discovered the bottle of syrup, carefully packed in a straw shield. But what was this other package? It was something lightweight, closely wrapped in a linen table napkin. A note pinned to the material said 'KEEP THIS SAFE'. Karin could just read it in the moonlight. She was about to undo the wrapper when she realised that the summerhouse was too dark to let her see much of whatever was inside. If she let something fall, she would never find it in here. There was no one indoors to see her – Mrs Preece's rooms were at the side of the house – so Karin took the bundle out on to the lawn and sat on the stone bench overlooking the straits, where the moonlight would show her what had been left for her. It was just as well that she had sat down. When she saw the grotesque little doll, she gave a squeal of terror and almost dropped it. Only the injunction to keep it safe made her catch it. But she was reluctant to hold the thing, and gingerly put it down on the bench on top of the napkin. What had she got herself into? She could not write off that mannikin as part of traditional folk medicine. That was witchcraft, and a technique as long-established in her native Germany as here in Britain.

Still trembling, Karin sat up straight and took several

deep breaths in an effort to calm herself. Her gaze wandered idly over the water below her and gradually the enchanting view restored her sense of proportion. Then, as she watched, a small boat pulled out from the unseen shore immediately below her. Someone was casting off from Tan-yr-Allt's private landing stage. The panic began to rise again, then she remembered Marged's confession. Of course! Myfanwy Owen had lived at Llanddona and even owned some sort of property there. She had assumed Beuno lived behind the shop, but it was more likely that he preferred the place where he had grown up. Myfanwy had used this means of transport to visit the Richmond household many years ago. Although the Menai View house was half a mile up the road, Marged's prospect of the departing Myfanwy must have been identical to her own of Beuno. Suddenly Karin was convinced that her moment of terror had been well founded. Of course he was practising witchcraft on her! They were a family of witches . . . who else would sail silently to a young woman's house in the small hours, to place a fertility potion and a graven image in her garden? Now she was shivering from head to toe. She could not bear to touch the vile doll again. Clutching the precious syrup to her breast, she jumped up and ran across the dark lawn to the sanctuary of the house.

Down on the Straits, sailing home on the rising tide, the dark figure turned and gazed back at the house on the bluff. Then he turned his attention on the silver water ahead and left fate to take its course.

It was different in the morning. When Karin awoke to another brilliantly sunny day, something hard was pressing against her side. She groped in the bed and found the bottle of syrup. She must have fallen asleep still holding on to it . . . Then she remembered the events of that night. The doll – dear God, she had left the doll down there on the bench! She must have been insane! Davies would be here first thing to work on the garden. What if he found it? She would have to deny everything, then Harry would be told and a general hue and cry would start. She must get there before anyone else.

By now Karin was out of bed and half way to the door. She stopped, distraught. She would cause even more talk if she rushed downstairs in her night clothes. Even if Davies had not yet arrived, Mrs Preece would certainly be up and about. What time was it, anyway? Karin turned back to her bedside table and looked at the carriage clock she kept there. Six-thirty! In her relief, she burst out laughing. Really, it wasn't fertility potions she needed, but something to cool her brain. She dressed quickly, brushed her hair and twisted it into a plain chignon, then went downstairs. It was still well before seven. She took a trug and a pair of garden scissors from their place in the hall cupboard, and strolled out across the lawn, forcing herself to dawdle. After a leisurely progress along the far edge of the grass, apparently enjoying the view but covertly studying the bench, she paused and bent to snip a couple of fat white roses and put them in the trug.

Yes, the doll was still there. How silly she had been! It was no witch's spell, just a little wax figure. What did they call it, sympathetic magic? It was nothing more than a harmless, charming custom. If it had been meant to harm her, Beuno would hardly have left it for her to see. He would have hidden it. She must stop reacting so hysterically.

Nevertheless, Karin still found it distasteful to pick up the mannikin. The wax had a texture that was unpleasantly reminiscent of dead human flesh . . . that thought brought back a hideous memory of Arthur's lifeless form laid out in the bedroom down the main landing from the room she and Harry now shared. She shuddered, bent over the doll again and thrust it inside the napkin. Then she pushed the bundle under her roses and started back towards the house.

'You're up early, Madam. Everything all right, is it?' Mrs Preece was crossing the hall to set the breakfast table as she came in.

'Perfectly in order, than you, Mrs Preece. It was such a glorious morning that I had to get up early. While you see to breakfast, I'll get a vase and put these on my windowsill upstairs.'

Satisfied, Mrs Preece went about her business. The flower arranging gave Karin an excuse to hang on to the trug. She got a vase from the garden room and rushed upstairs. But after she had put the roses in their bowl on the windowsill, it dawned on her that there was no safe hiding place here for her good luck charm. Harry was no peeping Tom, but he opened her clothes presses and chests of drawers when he was suggesting that she should wear something he particularly liked. If he ever caught a glimpse of this little monster, her secret would be out. And somehow she knew that however eager he was for children, he would disapprove violently of her experiment.

Karin paced about the room in mounting desperation. Where, oh where could she put the wretched thing? Why did she have no privacy? That was when the solution occurred to her. Of course – the very place in this house that was designed to remain secret: the panelled cupboard in the dining room. There was plenty of space for the doll behind the strongbox. Not only would it be secure, it would be permanently out of her sight, too. She had no reason to look at Marged's papers again, and if the day ever came when the secret must be revealed, she would probably be a grandmother herself by then and would be able to laugh off the doll as no more than the dim reminder of an uncertain time.

She went back down for breakfast, carrying the trug with the doll in the bottom. Mrs Preece was crossing the hall again, this time heading back towards the kitchen. She smiled at Karin. 'I've just put your coffee in the dining room, Madam. Everything else is on the sideboard or the hotplate. Unless you want anything more I'll get on with the silver, now.'

Karin dismissed her, relieved that the coast was clear for the moment. But as she moved towards the dining-room, Mrs Preece turned back towards her. 'Oh, I am sorry, Madam, I should have asked you for that old basket, shouldn't I? You don't want to be dragging that back in to breakfast, do you now?'

It was all Karin could do not to snatch the trug aside as Mrs Preece reached for it. She forced herself to sound unruffled. 'No-no, it's quite all right. I – I think I shall probably go out again after breakfast and cut a few more roses, so it would be silly to put it away now.'

To her it sounded desperately lame, but not to Mrs Preece. 'Of course, Madam. Very well, then, I'll be getting on.'

Karin pushed the dining room door shut and leaned

against it, thankful to be alone again. She poured a cup of coffee and gulped it down before she contemplated getting rid of the doll. When she felt a little more steady, she re-opened the secret cupboard and stowed the mannikin in its linen wrapping behind the strongbox. Only when the concealed panel fastening had clicked into place did she breathe easily once more. This had better work, she thought. I could never summon up the courage to go through it all again. She pushed it all to the back of her mind and ate her breakfast. Afterwards, she even remembered to go outside and fill the trug with more flowers.

# Chapter Fifteen

By the end of September, Karin was almost sure she was pregnant. But after her earlier dashed hopes, she was determined not to start building herself up for a disappointment. She did not mention it to Harry, contenting herself with getting plenty of sleep, exercise and healthy food. She moved on from taking the first of Beuno Owen's tonics to the second, as he had instructed. The third bottle was hidden away. That was not to be used for a long time yet.

She was glad of her preoccupation, because she saw far less of Harry now they had returned to London than at any time during the early months of their marriage. She did not complain; she knew he had a thousand things to do. But she missed him a lot.

So did George Beynon. The business ticked over well enough, and George understood that the younger man wanted to enjoy more time with his wife during the first year of his marriage now that Richmond's of Piccadilly was well launched. But he still missed Harry on a personal level. It did not occur to either George or Karin that Harry had never been less interested in either of them. At present all he could think of was Nellie Standish. He could not be sure when the longing had started;

probably some time after his trip to Liverpool. Until then, the peace and beauty of North Wales had seemed to seal him into a private world with Karin. But a couple of days in the great brawling, bustling seaport had reminded him forcibly of the excitement and pace of the outside world. A few weeks' rural peace was all right in its place, but the city was his true métier. When he returned to Bangor to resume his holiday, it was not the same. A hunger lurked beneath his pleasure in sea and mountains, and as the weeks passed he came to realise that only one thing could satisfy him: Nellie.

They had stayed until the first week in September. Karin had been secretly hoping that Harry would agree to spend the whole month there, but he would not hear of it. 'Six weeks is more than enough time away,' he said. 'If I get any more rest they'll think I'm falling to pieces!'

He suggested that she might care to stay longer – 'Why not invite Mary Rose up? She said something about visiting us, but never came. Perhaps she'd like to come when I've gone back to London.'

But Karin no longer wanted to be there without Harry. She could not understand why, but she had noticed that her thoughts veered back to Beuno Owen with increasing frequency. Safer to go back with Harry. No telling where it would lead if she succumbed to temptation – consciously, she called it curiosity – and went back to the herbalist's shop again.

So now she was picking up the threads of married life, making a place for herself in London Society; establishing contacts which would assure her of company no matter how busy Harry might be. Gradually Karin joined a whole range of charitable committees – mainly those associated with child welfare. She also forced herself to compensate Marged for having violated her secret, and visited Mapledurham far more frequently than before her holiday. Marged's knowing eye had noted that Karin was expecting a child long before she herself decided to consult her doctor.

When Karin shyly asked Marged to accompany her to the consultation, the old woman said: 'Of course I will, but why on earth didn't you go before? I'm sure you've suspected for a long time.'

'Y-yes, but I was afraid to tempt Providence. I have been so disappointed many times this year.'

'And that's why you've asked me to go with you now instead of Harry. You don't want him to know until you're sure.'

Karin nodded, biting her lip. Then she said: 'That's the main reason. But he is so busy all the time now, I didn't want to drag him away.'

Marged had her own ideas about the nature of Harry's business. She was the one person who knew him whose own movements spanned the family's private activities and their commercial concerns. She knew he was as much a stranger in Richmond House these days as he was at the apartment or at White Lodge. 'Hmm, I think perhaps it's about time you did start dragging him away a bit more often. He's a very attractive man.'

Karin flushed and looked away. She wouldn't let this discontented old woman sow doubts in her heart. She had seen how much havoc Marged could wreak when she set her mind to it. Resolutely she drew the conversation back to her planned visit to the specialist.

When Marged and Karin went to Harley Street it was a

crisp, bright December day. Roasted chestnuts and baked potatoes were on sale at every street corner and there were children everywhere, going on Christmas shopping expeditions with their parents. Karin looked at them longingly. Maybe, in a few years, she would be one of those lucky mothers.

The doctor made a thorough examination. When she had dressed and rejoined him at his desk, he beamed at her. 'Good news at last, Mrs Richmond! I told you, relaxation and good country air . . . as far as I can tell, you're at least four months, maybe a little more. There appear to be no problems, and you're the right age for a first child. Just follow the same régime, plenty of rest, good food, gentle exercise, no nasty shocks –' here he laughed, as though the very notion of his genteel clientèle suffering shocks of any kind was quite preposterous – 'and I'm sure I shall deliver you of a healthy child by about May. Think of it, by next summer your life will be transformed.'

She was glowing. Oh, yes! Once Harry had a son, their relationship would be even better . . . perhaps he would manage to spend more time at home. Karin half listened to the remainder of the doctor's advice. Beuno Owen had helped her to conceive this baby. His was the advice she would follow, although she would continue to consult Dr Merton at regular intervals. At times she felt almost as though this baby was as much Beuno's as Harry's. That thought made her shiver involuntarily. She bade Merton good day and went to find Marged.

When Harry heard the news, happiness bloomed inside him like a small explosion. At last! It seemed strange that they were still a little short of their first wedding anniversary and yet he should feel he had been waiting forever. His mind jumped forward five years . . . ten. By then they would have four or five sons – well, four or five children, at least three of them boys. Better not to overdo it! Suddenly the thought of Nellie snapped him out of his pleasant fantasy. My God, what would he tell her?

The day Karin told Harry she was pregnant, he broke an engagement with Nellie for the first time. His main reason was a desire to cosset Karin in his delight at her condition, but close to the surface was a reluctance to see his mistress while this news was so fresh. He had a feeling she might sense what had happened. Instead of supper and an evening in bed with Nellie – she was between shows at present – he hurried back to Belgravia for a romantic dinner with his wife. But he had to face the fact that the next day, or the day after that, he must confront Nellie.

Harry tried to console himself with the memory of her reaction to his confession that he was married. He had told her soon after returning from North Wales. By then he was getting deeply involved with her, and had begun to fear that she would see a reference to him and Karin in the newspapers. With much stammering and blushing, he had told her. When he had finished, unable to meet her eyes, he had sat staring down at her drawing room carpet.

The silence seemed interminable. Then she gave a hoot of mirth. 'Oh, for Christ's sake, Harry, stop looking like the cat that just missed the canary! D'you think I came off a Christmas tree? I'd have been a bloody sight more surprised if you'd come and confessed you were single!'

He stared at her. 'Then you knew?'

' 'Course I didn't know – how would I? It just stands to reason. You're the prettiest-looking fellow to have

373

crossed my path for as long as I can remember. It would have been a miracle if you'd still been running around loose at your age!'

'So you don't mind?'

'Well, I'd rather you were unhitched than hitched, I suppose, because I like my men to give me their undivided attention. But let's face it, dear, you wouldn't be thinking of marrying old Nellie in any case, so what's the difference? As long as I'm the one you love . . .'

'Nellie, I've never felt like this about any other woman. I can't believe I ever will again. You're the only one for me – surely you realise that.'

'Yes, that's just what I meant. I don't mind about the trimmings as long as I've got the goods.'

'Now and forever, my darling.'

That had taken care of his illusions. But it had also given him a false impression of Nellie's spirit of tolerance. He soon realised the gravity of his error.

'What d'you mean, pregnant? She can't be!'

Nellie was sitting at her dressing table and Harry sprawled across her double bed, watching her reflection in the triple mirror. Suddenly her fine eyes were black burning holes in a death-pale face. He gave a nervous laugh and tried to lighten the atmosphere. 'Of course she can! She's a normal woman, the same as anyone else. You know – two arms, two legs, a head – a womb . . .'

'Don't you get funny with me, you bastard. I'm not an idiot. You are in love with *me*, Nellie Standish, remember? I'm the only one for you – *remember*? You should, it's not three months since you were spouting about it. That means you don't get your leg over anyone else. Anyone, understand?'

374

He winced at her deliberate crudity but felt genuinely aggrieved. 'Hang on, Nellie. You remember, I was the one who felt guilty about being married . . . I was the one who came to you all miserable and ashamed, and you were the one who laughed me to scorn and as good as said you regard all men as married until proved innocent. Now, when I tell you about a perfectly natural consequence of being married, you blow up. I can't help it.'

There was a long silence like the prelude to a thunderstorm. He waited for the tempest to engulf him, but it did not. He looked up again at the mirror to discover that Nellie was gazing blindly at her own reflection, tears running unchecked down her cheeks, smearing the kohl with which she outlined her eyes. She caught his look, and said: 'Oh, you bastard. You utter, rotten, Godforsaken bastard! And I thought you were different . . .'

He got up and moved to stand behind her, clasping her around the shoulders and pressing her head back against his chest in a clumsy attempt to give her comfort. She seemed to lack the strength to throw him off, but she did not respond. She merely went on abusing him in a low monotone which was more demoralising than any shrill ranting. After a while her weeping intensified so much that she was forced to stop talking. Now she did push him aside, put her head down on her folded arms and sobbed uncontrollably.

Powerless to stop her, Harry waited until she had cried out the first intensity of her grief. Then he bent over her and gently urged her to stand, then move over to the bed. He sat down beside her, took her in his arms and started talking to her. 'Please, my love, try to calm down. I'm not a villain, and I mean every word I say about loving you so much. You're always so sure of yourself, so cynical about the world. Why does this hurt you so?'

She was quiet now, but sat rigid and unresponsive in his embrace. As he went on, he found he was repeating himself. Even in her present miserable state, Nellie finally noticed too, and managed to respond. Her bitter smile, along with the black make-up stains on her cheeks, made her look clownish. But even as a clown, she was beautiful.

'You're right – yeah, of course. Good old Nellie. Been around, you know. Amazing that someone so young should have seen it all, innit? That's the trouble, don't you see? I have seen it all, and done most of it, and enjoyed it a bloody sight better than most. But I started off with daydreams, the same as anyone else. They didn't last long, and I taught myself not to mind. But you . . . you were different. I thought you felt things. Thought you realised that I didn't care about you being married because you only loved me, not her. I knew you and me couldn't last forever, because eventually you'd want kids. But I – I thought you loved me enough to lay off it with her at least for long enough to get used to me. As it was, you were hard at it with her all along. Don't you understand, that's as good as saying all cats are grey in the dark – and that's what all men say. So I might as well start playing the field instead of thinking there's something special with you.'

She was crying again in earnest now, but still made no attempt either to disengage herself from him, or to respond to his embrace. He tried again to pull her closer. She did not even dignify the attempt with a glance his way. Staring down at her hands, twisted together in her lap, she said: 'You can stop trying to comfort me. You'll never give me any comfort again. Just get out of here and don't ever come back. I dare say there are plenty of other Harry Richmonds in the sea. There's only one Nellie Standish.'

With that her head came up again and she finally turned and gazed directly at him. The tears were gone and her look was full of contempt. He recoiled from its intensity, stared back for a moment, then stood up, defeated. 'All right, Nellie, I'll go. But don't imagine it'll end this way. We mean far too much to one another just to stop like this.' He received no reply, and after more prolonged silence he faced the indignity of putting on his clothes under her blank gaze, then walking out, his humiliation complete.

George Beynon saw more of Harry in the following week than he had in the last month. George was a solid middle-class paterfamilias, who had never so much as looked at a chorus girl's ankle, let alone taken one to bed, so it never crossed his mind that Harry was recovering from a broken love affair. He assumed that the prospect of fatherhood had released Harry from any immediate worries about Karin and freed him to devote his energies to the business once more.

Karin was equally short-sighted. She was so absorbed in her pregnancy that she assumed Harry's new atten-tiveness was caused by his delight in the prospect of parenthood. In reality, he was simply dividing the time he had spent with Nellie between business and home. Only his grandmother guessed something of what had happened. Now that Henry was virtually a vegetable, recognising no one, she had plenty of time to observe other members of her family. Since Harry's return from North Wales she had watched with growing concern as he showed symptoms very like those she had seen in his father during the affair with Myfanwy Owen. This time, though, she was powerless to alter the course of events. The bond which had existed between her and Henry was absent from her relationship with Harry. Marged knew that if she tried to separate the lovers, she would do no more than humiliate herself. That type of obsession could be broken only by a stronger preoccupation. But she still had her powers of observation, and she knew immediately when the affair was over. Even with the joyful prospect of fatherhood to cheer him, Harry was too often subdued and sad. Only a lost love could account for that, Marged decided.

She did not know whether to be glad or sorry. Try as she might, she could work up no great affection for Karin. There was something passive and complacent about the girl which was totally at variance with Marged's aggressive nature. Whoever had preoccupied Harry for the past couple of months, she must have been a lot more interesting than his wife. Marged wished she could have seen her.

Harry wished the same, but was doomed to disappointment. After a week of separation from Nellie, he was on the verge of despair. He was also aching with sexual longing and was reluctant to make love to Karin in case he harmed their unborn child. Nellie had opened in a new show at the Lyceum in the run-up to Christmas – her first at the top of the bill. She received ecstatic notices from the critics and Harry attempted to use her success to re-enter her affections. He was unable to endure the anguish of sitting in the stalls and watching her on stage. Instead, he went to the stage door and left a vast bouquet of peach roses. The card which accompanied them said he would wait for her at the stage door after the performance. He stood in the back street outside the Lyceum at eleven o'clock. It was cold and damp – the sort of weather that invariably preceded a poisonous London fog. Harry was not alone. A foreigner coming into the street would have thought that Englishmen all dressed in cloaks and silk hats. All seven of the other men outside the stage door were waiting for chorus girls or artistes. Harry hoped none of them was waiting for Nellie. They were not, but it did not help him. At eleven-fifteen, she emerged, in a flurry of scent and expensive furs. Her escort was already with her. He was a South African diamond millionaire whom Harry had met several times. Nellie did not even glance in Harry's direction. There was no sign of the roses. Harry turned away, bitterly certain of what Nellie's plans were for the night.

A week later, he was back. This time he bribed the doorman to take his gift to Nellie's dressing room. She had been particularly successful in this show with a new song called 'Hearts and Flowers'. After ten performances, the sheet music was selling like hot cakes and everyone was singing it. Harry had found a perfect souvenir of the song – a diamond and sapphire brooch fashioned into a heart surrounded by forget-me-nots. He waited half an hour. Eventually the doorman came back with a note. Harry's heart leaped. At least she hadn't sent back his present! With shaking hands, he opened the envelope, which must surely contain an invitation to meet her at the end of the performance.

Dear Harry
What a lovely gesture! Only a gentleman would send a girl such a beautiful memento after their affair was over! I shall always think of you when I wear it – especially when I leave for America after Christmas. Goodbye and good luck in the future.

Nellie Standish

The bitch – the god-damned bitch! Only Nellie would have the brass neck to accept a piece of jewellery of such value and then slam the door in a man's face! For a moment, Harry's outrage swept away his misery. She hadn't even given him the courtesy of signing it 'Your beloved Nellie' or anything like that. 'Nellie Standish', as if she were a great theatrical lady and he some desperate stage-door johnny unsuccessfully trying to meet her! His indignation carried him back out into the Strand and a good hundred yards westward towards Trafalgar Square before the note's real body blow hit him. When I leave for America . . . My God, she couldn't mean it! He turned and dashed back to the Lyceum. The doorman was locking up.

'Sorry, sir, they've all gone. Miss Standish? She went almost straight after I come back to you with that note. Gone to Romano's, I think, if you want to catch her.' He pocketed the tip which Harry handed him almost absentmindedly, then turned away.

Sick at heart, Harry went back the way he had come

and walked all the way to Belgravia through the raw night air. Go after her to Romano's? Face public humiliation in front of the latest escort and a room full of nosey theatricals? Never! He loved her, but he had too much pride for that. Maybe that bit about America was just nonsense, put in to torment him still more . . . But it was true. Next day it was in the papers. Miss Standish had been signed by an American impresario at a breathtaking fee for such a new star. It was not stated how long she would be gone, but the implication was that if she was successful, she might stay in New York for good.

That was the end as far as Harry was concerned. It was almost Christmas and they were to spend the holidays at Mapledurham. He could hardly disappear from White Lodge and come to London for the evening immediately after leaving town to celebrate the greatest family festival of the year. He agonised about it for some time, knowing that a rasher man would have gone after Nellie and damned the consequences. But under the exuberant façade, there was more of his father in Harry than he liked to admit. Henry Richmond's caution was holding Harry back now, repeatedly reminding him of what he stood to lose if he made a fool of himself. He sighed resignedly, despising himself.

If I can't consider the world well lost for Nellie Standish, he thought, I'll never do it for any woman. Maybe that's a good thing. Some day I'll get over her, and then I can settle down to being a faithful husband without any nasty secrets. But it was such wonderful fun, said the irresponsible boy within him.

# Chapter Sixteen

Christmas at Mapledurham was a Victorian fantasy that year, with a huge tree in the high-ceilinged entrance hall, the pick of the delicacies from Richmond's of Piccadilly to buttress the traditional festive foods, and extravagant presents for indoor and outdoor staff as well as for family and friends. To keep his loss at bay, at the last moment Harry invited large numbers of extra guests either to stay at Mapledurham or to attend the succession of dinner parties and receptions Marged and Karin had already planned. As a result, the big house was full of a constantly-shifting company from two days before Christmas Eve until New Year's Day.

Mary Rose had finally started to contemplate settling down. Charles Brandon was a year or two older than she, and he was handsome, rich and charming. He was the only man Karin had met who matched Harry for height and muscle, but he had a gentler look than Harry and even the unperceptive Karin could see he lacked the underlying ruthlessness so necessary in the business world. Fortunately for Mary Rose, he had no commercial ambitions and no need of them. His family had owned vast estates in Suffolk for many centuries. As long as Charles heeded the advice of his land agent and avoided rash investments, his living – and Mary Rose's – was assured. The family generally agreed it was only a matter of time before he asked Harry for permission to propose to his sister.

Only Harry himself had somehow missed this general anticipation. He had other hopes for Mary Rose and had been wondering for some time how he might tactfully bring them to her attention. However preoccupied he might be with personal matters, no male Richmond ever pushed business completely from his mind. Nellie Standish had briefly obsessed him, but in the hours he had not been with her he had still conjured up fresh commercial plans and kept an eye on how his interests were developing.

Since October he had been toying with the possibility of expanding abroad. He had tried out the idea on George, who had stared at him as though he should be physically restrained. 'You're all right, Harry, are you, man? Surely to God even you can see we've got our hands full here, without straying off somewhere else where we're complete strangers? If you're still so keen to expand, let's do it here in Britain. Done proper, we could have a Richmond's of Piccadilly in every major city in England by the turn of the century.'

Unusually impatient with his old mentor, Harry slapped the table-top in exasperation. 'No, no, no, George! How many times do I have to say that the Piccadilly shop's strength lies in its uniqueness? All the provinces will get is some of the products we sell there, and a little whiff of the place's exclusiveness. Once they have one in Birmingham and Edinburgh and Plymouth and Cardiff, who will think anything of coming to the

Piccadilly shop? But if we had some similar stores in France! Now, there's a thought to conjure with.'

'Look,' said George, 'I know I'm always the cautious one who do catch up ten minutes later with your bright ideas, I'll give you that. But this one, Harry – this one is completely foolhardy! We're all right buying good things from the French, but we could never compete with them on their own ground. I know you do speak the language like a native, but d'you know their wholesaling set-ups? D'you have any contacts in the domestic trade as opposed to the exporters? What were you planning to do, just rent a shop unit off the Champs Elysées and fill it up with food?'

'You're beginning to sound like a Little Englander, George. Do give me credit for some intelligence. I was thinking in terms of partnership with a French firm – you know, one hand washing the other. England may not have the gastronomic reputation of France, but we do have things here that the French love and would pay top price for – game, salmon, cooked specialities like raised pies or syllabub – and if we entered a co-operative partnership, the French partner could sell our stuff in France while we sell his here. We could promote each other's interests by exchanging staff for special weeks – the possibilities are endless. It would need a third level of shops in this country for us, or we could adapt the better class branches that were originally part of the subsidiary we started with Karin's backing. All we need is the right Frenchman and we could make another killing. And I think I know just the man.'

George sighed and hoped Harry's instinct was as sound as before. A man needed much more than good luck to succeed at a venture like this.

Harry's ace in the hole was Louis Lichine. Lichine was in

his mid-fifties and was that rare creature in France, a combination of commerce and aristocracy. The French were far greater sticklers even than the English for traditions which restricted tradesmen to the back door. No French prince would have gone boating or womanising with millionaire grocers and bankers as the Prince of Wales habitually did.

But Lichine was different. His grandfather had been Duc de Garonne in France's pre-Revolutionary regime. Somehow he had contrived to keep his head during the Terror, partly by voluntarily giving up vast portions of his wealth, partly by identifying himself with the republican cause from the moment he realised it would displace the *ancien régime*. Unfortunately the strenuous philanthropy which saved his life left him penniless, with an extravagant and useless family to support. To survive, he had turned to his one practical skill, a vast knowledge of the pleasures of the table. While the tumbrils were still carrying some of his oldest friends to the guillotine, the duke, now re-named Citizen Lichine, had been wrapping wind-cured ham and roasting arabica coffee beans for discerning Parisians. When Napoleon revived the idea of royalty and a new Court arose, Lichine already enjoyed an unrivalled reputation for quality and originality. The new rich flocked to buy and the old aristocrat prospered afresh. Successive generations of the family had made it a sort of inverted snobbery to eschew the old ducal title while others with far weaker claims were dredging up their dormant nobility. The Lichines had the satisfaction of knowing that anyone who was anyone in France was aware of their ancient lineage. By the 1890s, if you were ignorant of the Lichines' antecedents, you were undoubtedly a parvenue and therefore unworthy of attention.

Louis Lichine loved England and visited London often. A member of the same St James's club as Harry, he had met the younger man when a mutual friend decided they might have a lot in common. He was right. Within half an hour's acquaintance, each realised the other shared his ambition to expand abroad. From then on, everything was negotiable. But after that first burst of enthusiasm, Lichine had proved elusive. He expressed interest in Harry's plans, but made no secret of his distaste for the vulgar end of the Richmonds' business – the chain of small groceries in working-class districts on which the firm had founded its prosperity. Once or twice, Lichine had even hinted that it might be better if Harry divested himself of these cheaper stores in order to capitalise the French venture.

To Harry, that was unthinkable. He told himself it was because the bread-and-butter shops comprised too big a chunk of his wealth to be abandoned. But there was another reason, equally strong, for holding on to them. They had been Henry Richmond's first commercial venture. Harry had known for a long time that Henry Richmond was as imperfect as the next man, but nothing could destroy his childhood conditioning. He still harboured an emotional reverence for his father that verged on worship, and could not contemplate destroying his idol's creation.

It began to seem that they had reached deadlock. Harry knew there was little likelihood of another contact of this potential value, but for once he was at a loss to find something which would hold Lichine until he could persuade him to accept the continued survival of the Richmond's Quality Provisions chain. Then, by accident, he found the key. He invited Lichine to dinner in Belgravia and introduced him to Mary Rose. After that, Lichine's enthusiasm rekindled miraculously and there seemed no limit to their potential collaboration. But Lichine left him in no doubt that Mary Rose's attitude was crucial.

Harry realised he had known Lichine for a couple of months without learning anything of his domestic life. Now he discovered that the man was a widower of some twenty-five years standing. His young wife had caught infantile paralysis at the end of their Italian honeymoon and was dead within two days. Romantic gossip said Lichine had adored her so much that he found it impossible to contemplate a second marriage. Having seen him do business, Harry was more cynical. He suspected the Frenchman had found he enjoyed his freedom too much to surrender again to matrimony.

But it seemed that the prospect of a childless old age was beginning to preoccupy Lichine. He had dynastic ambitions as strong as Harry's own, and in his case they were backed by the desire to preserve an ancient name and family tradition. Harry's guess had been right about him enjoying his freedom, but in a sense, the romantic gossip also had an element of truth. After her tragically sudden death, his bride had become an icon in his memory. In retrospect she was all that was perfect in young womanhood, and if she had been less than responsive sexually, why dwell upon such a trifling detail? When he saw Richmond's sister for the first time, it was as if Madeleine had never died. The chestnut hair, creamy skin and small, shapely body were all just as he remembered. But this girl was still in her prime, and he was now a mature man, experienced in ways that would overcome any sexual reticence . . . His mouth watered at the thought.

Harry had lunch with him early in December and was surprised to learn that Lichine planned to be back in England immediately after Christmas. 'But I thought you French made a big thing of New Year! Surely you'd prefer to be at home, not in a foreign country.'

'Sometimes there are greater attractions than a noisy *reveillon*. I was invited by some friends who have a house at Whitchurch. That is very close to your house at Mapledurham, is it not?' There was a meaningful pause.

You cunning old devil, thought Harry, you're really hot for her, aren't you? Keeping his face expressionless, he said: 'We'll be down for the holidays, of course. Having lots of parties. You're welcome if you'd care to join us.'

'Delighted, *mon vieux*. Thank you for your invitation. There is something . . . er . . . of a delicate nature, which I would normally raise later. But perhaps this is an appropriate time. I think you are less accustomed to arranged marriages in England than we in France, are you not? We have a much more practical attitude. Marriage is far too serious an undertaking for the destiny of families of substance to be entrusted to the fleeting infatuations of two young people. That is something separate. Matrimony is best approached with a cool head. I have been wondering, Harry, how would you regard an approach from me for your sister's hand?'

'Well, that would rather be up to her. As you said, we

handle such things rather differently in England.'

'But not that differently. Your great families are as concerned as our own to ensure a good match. Only the middle classes are naive enough to think such matters arrange themselves.'

He had read Harry better than the younger man realised. His expression of contempt for such parvenue attitudes touched every submerged shred of insecurity within Harry, who now wanted nothing more than to prove his membership of the élite of ancient families. The Lichines had been fleecing peasants when Harry's forebears were still scratching their living as rural shepherds, but Harry would have died rather than admit it.

'I wouldn't dream of letting Mary Rose just fall in love and marry the first man to take her fancy,' he said. 'Naturally, we're more relaxed in letting our young unmarried women come and go as they please. But when it comes to marriage, it's a different matter. I shall expect a deciding voice in her choice of husband.'

The Frenchman smiled, suddenly wolfish. 'Good, good. I always feel that business is so much more successful inside families, no? If we are able to persuade Mary Rose to look favourably on a proposal from me, I am sure our own negotiations will proceed more smoothly, too.' There was no need to say more. Harry knew what he had to do; or rather, what he had to persuade Mary Rose to do.

Considering his high intellect, superb education and natural kindness, Harry could be remarkably insensitive at times. He not only failed to notice Mary Rose's strengthening attachment to Charles Brandon, he found nothing indelicate about confronting her head-on with the possibility of a match with Louis Lichine. Mary Rose found Lichine attractive in spite of his age. He was good-looking, cultivated and attentive. But she was in love with Charles Brandon and Harry's blundering approach, although well-intentioned, met with hostility at first.

'Harry, you must be mad! This is England. Brothers don't just come along and announce to their sisters – their financially-independent sisters, I might add – that they want to marry them off to some old Frenchman. In this country, girls choose for themselves.'

'Not girls from the best families . . . or anyway, only within certain limits.' Harry was intensely embarrassed and it made him bluster.

'Really? Since when have you been an expert on girls from the best families?' He looked up sharply, wondering if she had heard some rumour about him and Nellie, but he saw only righteous indignation.

'Since always, Mary Rose. You know the family always comes first. How d'you think Karin and Arthur met and became engaged? It was tactfully arranged by our parents and her father. We carry a great responsibility, and emotional considerations are often all wrong when it comes to choosing a partner for life.'

'Poppycock! Charlie Brandon comes from a family that makes us look like a bunch of upstart coster-mongers. And I know it's vulgar to say so, but if you want to compare our fortunes, he could match yours pound for pound any day. Furthermore, his is in land and property, far better than trade, if you're silly enough to think that way!' She stopped, slightly ashamed, for Harry was very dear to her. But she was genuinely outraged at the idea that anyone might think the Richmonds were more exalted than the Brandons.

Harry made a temporary tactical withdrawal. This was the first time he had realised she was serious about Brandon. Better not acknowledge it yet, though. It might crowd him if he were trying to persevere with the match with Louis. 'Persuasive young men are not always what they seem, Mary Rose.' That sounded good. Vague enough to avoid directly slandering Brandon, appropriate enough to make her wonder if he knew something of Brandon that she did not. He pursued his advantage. 'All I ask you now is to treat Louis as a decent human being. He is, you know, and he's terribly taken with you . . . goes on about you all the time.'

Mary Rose's vanity was kindled. Besides, she liked to please him. 'He is? What does he say?'

'Oh, you know, the perfect English rose at the peak of her beauty . . . should be cherished and put in a setting worthy to display her.' Lichine had said no such thing but Harry was a natural improviser. He wrote all Richmond's advertising copy.

His sister was glowing. 'Well, if it's that important to you, Harry. I can't promise anything, but I don't mind being nice to him if it helps. You must remember, though, that I've practically made up my mind who I want to marry.'

'I only want you to get to know him. That's all I ask.'

'Then I shall. I never could say no to you, Harry darling.' She came over to his chair, bent and kissed him lightly on the forehead. 'You're really my hero, you know. That's one of the reasons I love Charlie so much – he's like you, but different.'

Watching Lichine in action over the holidays, Harry realised the man had needed nothing more than an introduction. He was a seducer in the grand manner, and when such techniques were switched to legitimate courtship, they were doubly potent. Within minutes of his arrival for his first party at Mapledurham, he had Mary Rose eating out of his hand. He enjoyed a further advantage because Charles Brandon was not among the guests that evening.

At breakfast next morning, Harry was surprised to find only his grandmother present. They were *en famille* that day because their post-Christmas house guests did not start arriving until the afternoon. 'Where's Mary Rose? It's unusual for her to stay in bed late when there are horses to be ridden.'

Marged's smile was sphinx-like. 'Quite. I believe she's out riding – with your friend Monsieur Lichine. He hacked all the way over from Whitchurch at the crack of dawn.'

Harry grinned like a boy with a new train set. 'Well, well. So some people listen to me after all.' He went to serve himself with devilled kidneys from the hotplate.

Marged became solemn. 'Is there anything you want to confide in me, Harry? If you need any help, you – you only have to say the word.'

He turned and looked at her thoughtfully for a moment. 'Now you mention it, perhaps there is. Does Mary Rose ever talk to you – you know, about her hopes, what she wants from life and so on?'

Marged snorted. 'That girl wouldn't tell me what's on her shopping list! No, Karin's the one she talks to.'

'Really? Well, Karin talks to you, doesn't she?'

'You know she does. Why?'

'If you could steer the subject round to my little sister and her feelings about marriage, perhaps Karin would tell you a little.'

'Oh, she already has. You don't think I'd let anything go on here and not know about it, do you?'

He smiled at her. Now that her ruthlessness was no longer directed at him, he was getting quite fond of her. 'Listen, Grandmama. Mary Rose really must marry soon, mustn't she? A couple more seasons, and everyone will be saying she's on the shelf, even if she insists it's her own choice.' Marged nodded. 'Now, I've got a marvellous proposal for her, but I'm afraid she might throw it all away because of some girlish infatuation. I'm thinking of her happiness, you understand – well, her happiness and the interests of the family. In this case I think the two things coincide.'

'If you mean Lichine, I couldn't agree more.'

He glanced at her sharply. 'You know? How?'

'Men who look at women the way he looks at Mary Rose want one of two things. The other thing would be out of the question with a girl like Mary Rose, so it has to be marriage. Simple. But what are you going to do about Charles Brandon?'

'That's just it, Grandmama. I didn't even know she was interested in him until the day before yesterday. It really is too bad.'

Marged laughed. 'You are the limit! So bound up in your own concerns you can't see what's been obvious to everyone else for months. I take it you disapprove.'

'Normally I'd have no objection. But this could mean so much to Richmond's. It's our next leap forward, and I just know he won't play unless Mary Rose is part of the arrangement.'

'Tut tut, Harry, selling off your female relatives like an Arab slave trader! Still, if it's that important, I'm sure we can arrange something. I don't think you'll achieve it by fair play, though.'

He looked away. 'I – er – I wouldn't want to do anything underhand. I'm very fond of her, you know.'

'Of course, my boy. No need for you to be anything but a perfect gentleman. You leave everything to me.'

Later that morning, Marged and Karin were alone together in Marged's small sitting room. Karin spent part of most mornings there nowadays, sewing and talking. After moving through a wilderness of harmless conversational gambits, Marged gave a heavy sigh. 'It's such a perfect Christmas this year. If only I weren't so worried about Mary Rose, everything would be wonderful.'

Karin was all innocent concern. 'But what can be wrong? I thought she was marvellously happy – you know, with Mr Brandon about to propose and everything.'

'That's just it, my dear. Mr Brandon is not all Mary Rose thinks. The poor child must be told, but it's so terrible I can scarcely bring myself.'

Karin was stricken. 'Why? Has he behaved badly?'

Marged looked more uneasy than Karin had ever seen her. She shifted uncomfortably in her chair and avoided the younger woman's gaze. 'Well, er, you could call it

395

that. But it goes deeper . . . it's rather more to do with his nature – his baser nature.'

Now it was Karin's turn to look away. 'Oh – has he a mistress?' She felt quite daring even to mention such a matter to Harry's grandmother.

Marged was almost tearful now. 'If only he had! My dear, I'm not sure that someone who's led as sheltered a life as you have will even understand it.'

Now Karin was in an agony of suspense, more embarrassed than ever but dying to know what this unspeakable sin was. She decided to sacrifice her modesty in order to comfort Marged. 'You must tell me – it will be less difficult if you share it.'

'You're so kind, my dear, so very kind. If you insist, then; it will certainly help me.' She started fingering the edging of the napkin she had been embroidering, as she apparently cast about for a delicate way of putting what she had to say. Finally she made a start. 'You know, not all men are able to love women – really love them, that is, in the full physical sense of the word.' Karin blushed furiously. 'I'm sure it must be terrible for them, but some are unable to do so because their passions are not aroused by femininity. Such men satisfy their appetites with other men – often with young boys.'

Karin was riveted. 'But what do they do to each other?' she said, then clamped a hand over lips, horrified at her own prurient curiosity.

Marged gazed straight at her for the first time since embarking on her confidence. 'I cannot possibly bring myself to tell you, Karin, and you may rest assured that the knowledge would not improve your understanding in any way. Have you never heard anyone refer to the love that dare not speak its name?'

The girl was still staring, completely absorbed. 'Oh, yes, but – but I always thought that must be a brother and sister, or perhaps a mother and son . . .'

Now it was Marged's turn to flush. She reacted sharply. 'Nothing of the kind. It's this – what I've been talking about. And it has directly to do with Charles Brandon. I expect he told Mary Rose he was expelled from Eton for boisterous behaviour or some such childish nonsense. He left abruptly, you know, at the age of sixteen. Only the family's influence got him into Charterhouse. I happen to know the real reason. He had been carrying on an illicit relationship with one of his masters. The man was dismissed and never permitted to follow his profession again, of course. Mr Brandon got off very lightly when you consider that. He merely had to change schools and endure some family disgrace. Perhaps it's a pity the punishment was not more severe, because it did not cure him. There have been a stream of – er – companions, ever since, usually rather older than himself, so-called artistic types. I believe he said goodbye to the last one only a couple of weeks before he began pursuing Mary Rose.'

'But Grandmother, that's terrible! Poor Mary Rose! What will you tell her?'

'I have no idea. You can see I must, can't you? But how, remains the question.'

'One thing I do not understand,' said Karin a moment later. 'If he has such terrible appetites, why is he courting Mary Rose?'

'That's what worries me most! It's obvious, surely? He wants to draw a cloak of respectability around himself. Once he's won her and they're married, I'm certain he'll go back to this dreadful vice and Mary Rose will be caught up in it all.'

'We can't allow that, Grandmother!'

'I know, Karin my dear, but I'm only an old woman and I sometimes doubt whether I have the strength.'

'Maybe Harry?'

'Out of the question! If Harry got to know, he would do the man some violence, I'm sure. No, we must sort it out between ourselves.'

Karin made a hard decision. 'Perhaps I can bring myself to tell her. But you must tell me how you know. Mary Rose is bound to say he is innocent, and if I cannot vouch for the truth of the accusation, she will never forgive me.'

Marged gave her a long, cool look. She must keep an eye on Karin. If ever the girl outgrew that ridiculous naivety, she might be quite formidable. A good thing she had prepared for this – although she had done it with Mary Rose's misgivings in mind, not Karin's. 'I only wish there were some room for doubt, but my source is a very reliable one – a countrywoman of yours, in fact – Countess Boehm.'

'But I used to know her quite well!'

'So I understand. She asked after you most fondly. You know her daughter married an Englishman? Well, it seems this former Eton schoolmaster applied for the post of tutor to the children, and when the countess's son-in-law took up his references, this all came out. One of the sources who told her about the schoolmaster also knew Mr Brandon and was aware that the school episode was only the beginning of a positive career of vice. The countess saw Mr Brandon with Mary Rose when they went hunting together a couple of weeks ago. When she heard how close they were, she contacted me at once and told me.'

Such detail was irrefutable. Thank God I have such a fertile imagination, thought Marged, and that old Boehm is safely off at Spa taking the cure!

Karin was utterly convinced now. She promised she would break the awful news to Mary Rose as soon as possible.

'I'm so grateful to you, my dear, but may I press you to do it very quickly – within the next day or two? I fear he will have proposed and been accepted unless you do. And one other thing: a small deception, but I think you'll agree it's necessary. When you tell Mary Rose, could you say that Countess Boehm came to you and not to me? Since you know her, it's perfectly believable. And you were in London immediately before Christmas when the countess came to me over it. You may recall that Mary Rose was staying in Yorkshire with the Whatleys at the time, so she'll never suspect. You can say you ran into the countess at one of your charity committees and that she said she'd been meaning to contact you.' Karin sighed and nodded her acquiescence, then collected her sewing and departed.

Definitely time for an early brandy, thought Marged after she had gone. If this family had the remotest idea how far I'm prepared to go to further their interests . . .

Harry never knew what Marged had done to cause Mary Rose's breach with Charles Brandon, but it worked miraculously. Brandon was coming to luncheon next day and Harry had been mentally holding his breath in case this turned out to be proposal time. Louis Lichine was to be their guest again that evening, and it would be disastrous if he were the first one to hear that his dream girl was engaged to another man.

Harry need not have worried. Mary Rose came downstairs ashen-faced at noon, walked past Marged and Harry in the hall as though they were invisible, and spoke to the butler.

'Parkin, Mr Brandon will be arriving shortly. Please ask him to come to me in the winter garden as soon as he gets here.' Then she turned away and walked out. Harry looked questioningly at his grandmother, who merely shrugged and made a bewildered face. But inside she was jubilant.

Brandon was gone less than twenty minutes after he arrived. There were four guests staying at White Lodge that week, all of whom were in for luncheon. Marged was keeping them entertained in the library just after one when Parkin arrived and asked for a word. 'Miss Mary Rose is unwell, ma'am. She asked me to present her apologies and says she has gone to her room. She thinks she might stay there for the rest of the day.'

'Very well, Parkin. What about Mr Brandon?'

The butler was faintly troubled. 'He didn't say anything, ma'am, so I wondered if he'd just gone to do something urgently before luncheon, but he hasn't come back. The last time I saw him, he was hurrying off down the drive. A hired rig brought him from the station, so if he was leaving he must be having to walk back there, and there's no train now until three-thirty.'

'Thank you, Parkin. That will be all.' Marged found it hard to conceal her triumph. She had almost forgotten how intoxicating it was to manipulate people. Perhaps after this Harry would find more use for her talents. She ate a hearty lunch and did not think about her brandy until dinner time.

Mary Rose changed her mind about coming downstairs that evening. By now Marged had spoken to Karin and knew that when her granddaughter finally accepted the story about Brandon, she had been devastated. But Karin had looked in on her later that afternoon and had found her transformed.

'I will have a tray sent up for you, Mary Rose,' she said. 'You cannot wish to see anyone.'

Mary Rose gave a high, brittle laugh. 'Why ever not? If I'm to be a victim of *le vice anglais* I might as well put a brave face on it! It's like riding again after you've taken a bad fall. If you don't get straight back in the saddle, however scared you are, you never do it again. Well, here goes. I'm about to re-mount.'

Karin was quite shocked. Mary Rose had always been slightly fast in comparison to her. Since her father's decline she had made much of her independence and although she was still essentially an inexperienced young girl, she cultivated a specious air of sophistication. She was heart-broken about Charles Brandon, but determined not to show it. All she had left was her pride, but she had plenty of that.

Throughout the evening, she was the life and soul of the party, dazzling every man in the room but paying particular attention to Louis Lichine. Two days later the Richmonds were having a big New Year's Eve party. Lichine was not only invited; he was ending his stay at

Whitchurch and joining the houseparty at White Lodge on December 30th. From the moment of his arrival he scarcely left Mary Rose's side, and concentrated on flattery, amusing conversation and gallantry. By the time he escorted her on to the floor for the first waltz in the ballroom at White Lodge on New Year's Eve, Mary Rose was captivated. In her heart she knew that this relationship lacked the depth and sincerity of what she had felt for Charles, but much good that had done her. Perhaps Harry was right, and it was best to choose the suitor one's family had approved.

There could have been few more romantic settings for a proposal of marriage. It had begun snowing late on the afternoon of New Year's Eve and now the great lawns outside the ballroom were covered in white. The cedar of Lebanon looked as if it had been iced and beyond the drive the snowy landscape threw the black tracery of bare treetrunks and branches into sharp contrast. Inside, the gorgeous silks and satins of the women's gowns swirled as they waltzed into 1897. The Christmas decorations added still more colour and the fir tree in the hall was ablaze with lighted candles. Somehow Louis Lichine had contrived to get a spray of pink and white camelias, which he gave to Mary Rose before they started to dance.

He bowed and kissed her hand. 'I hope, Mademoiselle, that tonight you will dance with me and no one else all evening.'

She smiled at him and became slightly coy. 'You know I can't do that! It couldn't be considered proper unless we were far more intimate than we are.'

'I am hoping to arrange that. After this waltz, perhaps you would come and talk to me quietly for a few minutes – somewhere private. How about the winter garden?'

'No, I hate that place! Just like a beastly jungle! Anywhere but there. How about the library?'

After the waltz ended, he got them some champagne and then escorted her from the ballroom. Harry watched approvingly from the far corner.

Sequestered with Lichine in virtual silence after the heady gaiety of the ballroom, Mary Rose became nervous. Her high spirits were very fragile and she was seldom far from tears. What could she say to this handsome stranger? He was very attractive, but she knew next to nothing of his tastes, his background or anything else. Yet it seemed that was enough.

Lichine led her over to a small Sheraton sofa at the fireside, and sat down beside her. 'You cannot be in any doubt about why I have asked you to come here,' he said. In fact she was so dazed by the events of the past few days that she had not given it any thought at all, merely following where she was led. Lichine went on: 'I did not think I should ever again meet a creature as enchanting as my wife Madeleine. She was just your age when she died, you know, and you are the only woman I have ever met who matched her beauty. I shall return to France next week – really I should have gone long before now. But once I had met you, I could not leave your side. I hardly know if I can do so now, but one thing will give me the strength. Consent to be my wife and I shall go back a happy man.'

Before Mary Rose could say a word, he produced a small jewel case from his pocket. 'I know it is not usual to offer such a token before one is ready to announce a formal engagement, but I beg you to accept this ring and my proposal. The ring has been in my family for many generations.' Still she sat silent, as he drew out the huge, flawless solitaire emerald and slipped it on her third finger. 'You see? Even your fingers are the same size. My Madeleine was the last woman to wear that. Now it is as if she lives again.'

Something in his tone gave Mary Rose a faint unpleasant frisson. It seemed vaguely obsessive . . . She shook herself. That was absurd! No more than a reflection of her own unsettled state. She looked down at the glowing stone, then at the adoring face of the aristocrat who had given it to her. He might be twice her age, but didn't that mean he was mature enough to protect and cherish her? She felt so alone now, so abandoned since she had sent Charlie away. If only she could have told him why, but it was far too foul to discuss. It had been heart-breaking, the way he kept on protesting that he had done nothing for which he could be reproached, and begging her to explain her action. How could she, though? No one had taught her the right words, or prepared her in any way for such a calamity. She shivered and pushed the whole mess out of her mind. Louis Lichine was still gazing at her, now somewhat perplexed at her inexplicable reaction. Mary Rose made her decision. The past few months had been no more than a child's fairy story. This was very agreeable reality.

'I'm honoured, Louis. Of course I accept your proposal.' And she closed her eyes and raised her face for his first kiss.

404

# Chapter Seventeen

'Grandmother, I'm so glad you asked me to help! Mary Rose is looking really happy now, and it would have been dreadful if she had been tied to that monster for the rest of her life.'

It was the last week of January. Marged and Karin were deep in their daily rendezvous in Marged's sitting room. Karin had stayed on at White Lodge after Christmas, since her pregnancy was now becoming too obvious for her to continue to accept non-family invitations in London. Harry spent the week in the Belgravia apartment and came down to Mapledurham at week-ends. Karin had become increasingly dependent on Marged for companionship and was growing very fond of her. Sometimes, when she remembered that miserable evening in North Wales when she had opened the panelled cupboard, she felt ashamed of herself. But then she thought: if I hadn't, I'd never have met Beuno Owen and now I wouldn't be carrying Harry's baby. I'm sure Marged would forgive me if she knew. Perhaps I shall tell her when our son is safely born. At the moment the baby gave a vigorous kick, then another. She gasped and pressed her hands to her belly.

Marged chuckled. 'Lively little fellow, isn't he?' Karin

liked that informality in her. None of her mother's sober-sided German kinswomen would have considered such a topic proper, even within the family circle and in all-female company. It made Karin feel warm and accepted.

She patted herself proudly. 'You think it's a boy, too?'

'Bound to be! You're carrying it high, that's an infall-ible sign.' Marged wanted it to be a boy so much that almost anything would have been an infallible sign for her.

The kick came again. Karin started to feel elated and slightly scared. 'I think I'll say goodbye for the present, and go to my room.'

Marged was all concern. 'Are you feeling all right? I'll come with you, just in case.'

'No, everything is perfect. I just think it will be better if I undress and lie down, as he's so energetic.'

Marged patted her hand. 'Very well, then, if you're sure. Off you go. I'll see you at dinner unless you decide to stay in bed.'

There was another reason for Karin's abrupt depar-ture. It was time to begin the next stage of Beuno's treat-ment. The instructions had been most specific. When the baby is kicking more than once an hour, start the third bottle.

Up in her room, Karin undressed, turned down her bed and took the bottle out of its hiding place at the back of her clothes press. A carafe of water, a glass, a spoon and her officially-prescribed tonic were in their usual place on the bedside cabinet. She placed Beuno's bottle with them. Pointless to put it back in its hiding place, as she would be taking all of it over the next twelve hours.

She knew the instructions by heart, but unrolled the

note containing them just the same, and ran through them once more. One drachm now, mixed with water. Two drachms in two hours, then another two four hours later. After that, two drachms every four hours until it was all gone. Relax in bed while you are taking it, in case you get a few cramps. After the instructions were four lines of unintelligible characters, familiar and yet strange. She had realised early on that they were ordinary letters written backwards, but even if she turned them round, they made no sense. It was obviously another of Beuno's old charms. Karin put down the instruction paper on the cabinet and took her first draught of the medicine. Even with the honey and lemon and sweet herbs as palliatives, it was more disgusting than she would have thought possible. She poured herself a glass of water and gulped it down to chase away the taste. After that, only a lingering bitterness remained in her throat. She lay back against the pillows and dozed for a while.

After two hours she was very drowsy and the bitter aftertaste had intensified. She swallowed the doubled-up dose and followed it with another glass of water. Then she must have slept for some time. Perhaps she twisted in her sleep . . . whatever it was, she awoke shortly before the next dose was due, feeling very uncomfortable. There was a deep-seated clawing pain at the base of her abdomen, and she felt chilly, although there were plenty of blankets on the bed and the fire was well banked. Karin supposed that these were the cramps referred to in the instructions. She hadn't realised they would be so severe . . . still, she was in the best place. Another dose, some more water and she'd probably sleep through it. She swallowed another two drachms.

407

After that she felt very peculiar. The pains in her abdomen intensified, but somehow they seemed to be happening to someone else. She felt as if she were sitting high on the bedstead, looking down at herself writhing and moaning amid the increasingly dishevelled bedding. There was some sort of commotion over by the door . . . the maid . . . calling her . . . couldn't be bothered to answer . . . too far away. That was better . . . leave her in peace to sleep and take her tonic. Best thing for her son . . . make him big and strong . . . if only it didn't hurt so . . . More noise by the door. Oh, this time it was Grandmother . . . No need for her to put herself out . . . pain will go soon . . . must . . . can't keep on like this . . . must be hurting my son, too . . . Grandmother was shouting . . . almost a shriek, it was, really . . . she shouldn't make so much noise in a sick room . . . sick room . . . not bedroom . . . not sick, but oh, it did hurt, and why was there so much blood . . . Where had it all come from? Why had Grandmother got those men here . . .? The pain exploded so sharply that she reeled and felt herself tipped off her strange perch high above the bed. She was falling, falling back into that blood-spattered body writhing around on the bed . . . Harry's and her marriage bed . . . the bed where their son would be born . . .

'You've got to save it – you've bloody well got to! She's been hoodwinked by some quack because she was afraid she'd be barren! She's taken something and it's put her into labour.'

'Mrs Richmond, I am aware of that. I am her physician, you know.' Dr Merton spoke kindly. He knew Marged was beside herself and he could see why. The foolish girl appeared to have taken enough abortificant to kill herself as well as her child. He couldn't tell the grandmother yet, but the idea of saving the baby was absurd. At this stage he doubted whether the mother would survive. All they could do was wait for the poison to do its worst. He couldn't even give her opium. Whatever she had taken would undoubtedly combine with it to finish her off.

Marged would have discovered Karin's condition earlier, had not another crisis diverted her attention. She had been on the point of going up to see if Karin was really all right when the butler came to tell her that Henry appeared to have suffered a stroke.

All thoughts of Karin had fled from her mind as she rushed up to the old nursery wing with Parkin. 'What are they doing about it?' she asked, fighting down her panic.

'It's all under control, ma'am. Nurse Peters has sent for Dr Merton and he'll be here in a few minutes. Shall I ring Eaton Place and tell Mr Harry?'

'Thank you Parkin – of course! I should have thought of that. I'm sure he'll want to get here as soon as possible.'

But it soon became obvious that Harry would not arrive soon enough. Henry's breath rattled in his throat, and his face already had a wooden, lifeless look. Marged did the only thing she could: sat at the bedside and clasped his cold hand until the doctor arrived.

A cursory examination was enough to tell Henry's physician all he needed to know. 'Come outside for a moment, please, Mrs Richmond,' he said. Outside the bedroom door, he added: 'It'll be all over in a couple of hours at most. I know it's hard, but you loved him too much to want to see him drag on the way he's been this last year or two.'

Marged nodded. 'It's still impossible to accept, though,' she said. 'I don't see him as he is now. He's always vigorous and bright in my mind's eye – hardly more than a boy.'

He touched her hand. 'I know. Try to go on remembering him like that. Perhaps it will comfort you. Now, I really don't think there's any point in my staying. The nurses are highly competent, and he's not going to suffer any more pain. It will look more alarming than it really is, at the end. Perhaps it would be best if you waited downstairs.'

Her chin went up at that. 'Oh, no. We shared the good times. The least I can do now is share the bad.'

But the living intervened. Ellen, Karin's maid, came hurrying along the corridor, very agitated. 'Oh, ma'am, thank goodness I've found you!' she said. 'It's Mrs Harry. I just went up to see if she needed anything before I went off duty, and there's something wrong – something awful wrong!'

Suddenly Marged remembered her earlier concern, and she tugged the doctor's sleeve. 'Quick, come with me. I've a feeling someone else here still needs you!'

After examining Karin, Dr Merton moved to the bedside cabinet and picked up the medicine bottle. 'This is the stuff, I expect. Impossible to tell what's in it without analysis, of course. No label or anything. I'll take it along with me, Mrs Richmond.'

She nodded, grim-faced. Then, as he moved away to put the bottle in his bag, she saw the scrap of paper. Instinctively she picked it up and pocketed it. On the bed, Karin was going through a series of contractions. Marged turned to Merton, who had just taken Karin's pulse and was holding her hands. Karin's fingers gripped him convulsively, white with the pressure. Her back arched and she screamed, once, before falling back, sweating copiously.

Marged found it impossible to watch, knowing she could do nothing to help. She moved away, over to the dressing table where the light was quite strong, and, to take her mind off the suffering behind her, looked at the paper she had picked up earlier. The instructions were straightforward enough, but what was this gibberish underneath? Some sort of foreign writing? She bent closer to the oil lamp. Backwards, whatever it was, but there was something else odd about it, too. Marged turned up the lamp and pushed it close to the mirror, then held the paper before the glass. As she did so, all was made plain to her. She shut her eyes, fighting a wave of nausea. Oh, God, what was that she'd once said to George Beynon about future generations? If ever the past came back for revenge on the unborn, this was it. The four lines of gibberish resolved themselves instantly:

> *A chariad Duw;*
> *A gymdeithas yr ysbryd glân;*
> *Bod gydanu, yn oes oesoedd.*
> *Amen.*

The benediction, in Welsh. 'The love of God; the fellowship of the Holy Spirit; be with you now and ever more. Amen.' Only it had been written backwards, with an intention as sure as that behind the Black Mass. A blessing become a curse because it was reversed. And even if it didn't work, it came with a surer weapon: a violent herbal abortificant prescribed in a massive dose. How many Welsh-speaking herbalists with a knowledge of witchcraft could Karin Richmond know?

Marged gazed deep into the mirror, and cursed Beuno Owen with every ounce of malice she could summon. 'I'll find you,' she said under her breath. 'Hell isn't deep enough to hide you from my vengeance, you misbegotten bastard.'

Ellen, whom she had sent to await news of any change in Henry's condition, came quietly into the room. 'Beg pardon, ma'am. I hate to bring more bad news, when things are so terrible here, but Sir Henry . . . he's sinking fast, now, ma'am.'

Before the hammer blow of grief, another terrible thought tore through her fury. Harry! Harry was on his way here because his father was dying . . . He knew nothing about this fresh horror. Her fury changed to weeping. Oh, God, how can I tell him? How can I tell him he's losing his child as well as his father? She grabbed the maid by the shoulder, shaking her in her anxiety. 'Mr Harry – has he arrived yet?'

'Y-yes, ma'am, about five minutes ago . . . I tried to tell him where you were, ma'am, but he wouldn't stop. Dashed straight up to Sir Henry's suite.'

'Then he can't know about – about this?'

Ellen shook her head. 'No one in Sir Henry's suite knows, ma'am, except that the doctor was called away to see Mrs Harry. But they wouldn't think to tell Mr Harry about that . . . not right this minute, anyhow.'

As she hurriedly crossed the wide landing at the head of the main staircase, Marged glanced out through the window. A full moon sailed in all its silver glory above the

412

tranquil river, casting a broad gleaming path across the water. Are you swimming to the moon with him now, you bitch? she thought. Make the most of it, because when I come to him there'll be no room for you there, any more than there was in this life.

Harry stood on the landing outside his father's room. A sense of liberation flooded through him, momentarily swamping the grief. No more waiting in the wings, wondering if he'd ever get a chance to prove himself. The king is dead; long live the king! He smiled involuntarily at the conceit, then suddenly remembered that his father had been equally aware of the situation. Harry tried not to feel satisfaction over that, but it was difficult.

Poor Father! He had always wanted to control those around him, had always wanted to impose his own will on everyone else. In the end, though, he had been forced to confront reality as many another powerful man had before him. Death cancels all contracts and removes all influence. He played the autocrat for too long. Now Harry intended to put on the clothes which Henry Richmond had designed for Arthur. It was an intoxicating thought.

'Enjoying your victory, Harry?' The voice was thickened by tears, but still had enough bite to stop him in his tracks. All Marged's sudden concern for Harry had evaporated as she saw him, believing himself unobserved, exulting in his father's death.

'Grandmama . . . I . . . what can I say?' He hoped no jubilation had crept into the first stammered words.

She gestured contemptuously, as though casting aside a heap of hypocrisies. 'Nothing, yet, if you've any sense,

413

boy. I'm not going to behave as you expect. I know what he did to you and that his death has released you. I'm with you, not against you – but give me time.' Her control snapped and she began to sob. 'With all his faults, I loved him more than anyone else in the world. Oh, Harry, if only I could have gone first! If only I hadn't been forced to watch my lovely boy destroyed!'

Moved in spite of his previous coolness towards Marged, Harry embraced her. The clichés sprang easily to his lips, but they were well meant. The open despair of this ironclad old woman moved him more deeply than his father's death. 'Come on, now, cry it out. He loved you, Grandmama. He wouldn't have wanted you to be so hurt. You'll be with him again one day, you know that.'

She managed a tearful smile. 'You're a good boy, Harry. Better than either your father or I deserved, the way we treated you. Forgive me for being so sharp –' she broke down again – 'but I'll be lost without him, lost!' She turned away, suddenly unable to speak the news she had brought him. In a minute . . . she needed a pause to accept that Henry's body was gone now, leaving her without even the image of her beloved son. She managed to say: 'Wait for me here, Harry. I must speak to you before . . . before . . .' But the tears took her again and she slipped into the dressing room adjoining Henry's suite to try to compose herself.

The house was strangely silent. It's mine now, mine to make quiet or raucous as I like, he thought. No more looking over my shoulder to see if he's there disapproving; no more 'Don't tell Harry, he's not ready to know'; no more Father.

That stopped his elation. No . . . more . . . Father. Suddenly tears were coursing down his own face and exultation was replaced by a vast emptiness. All his young life, Harry had sought his father's love and approval. All his life he had seen Arthur receive it while he was excluded. When Henry fell ill and he took over, he had told himself that one day his father would recover sufficiently to understand that his second son's talents were more than a match for Arthur's. Now he would never be able to do that. So what was the point of trying to prove himself? Who would care? The only figure he revered was gone forever.

Despair began to grip him. It seemed that he was destined to be eternally defeated, left isolated from the glow of love that had surrounded Arthur, his parents and grandmother. Even Mama had finally proved Harry was wrong to think he was her favourite. The loss of Arthur had snuffed out her will to live, although Harry was there, needing her. Now, no doubt, his grandmother would soon go the way of the others. She'd made it clear that Father was all she lived for.

But wait a minute! What about Karin? Karin loved him, didn't she? And Father had wanted Karin for himself after Arthur went. Now Karin was his wife, about to bear his heir . . . If he held on to Karin, in a way he'd be substituting himself for the others. And together they could produce a tribe of sons, who would revere Harry just as he'd always revered his own father. Yes, that was the way! Strong sons, sons who would immortalise his name and love him the way he'd loved Henry Richmond. Daughters were no use . . . after all, if Father had neglected him for Arthur, he'd virtually ignored the girls altogether.

You didn't get that sort of fellowship from daughters – they saved it for their own sons. Look at Grandmama. Had she ever mentioned her husband? Harry couldn't remember her saying a word about him. No, it had all been her son, her wonderful Henry.

Harry's tears had stopped. He was all right now. He had a direction, a series of objectives. His first child – that was just the beginning. It would make up for all the misery and neglect that had gone before.

And what if Henry Richmond had apparently achieved all the business success in the world? He'd never succeeded in establishing himself as a gentleman, for all his cash. The Right People still sniggered behind their hands about Grocer Richmond. Nor had he recognised that it was time for the business to move on. Whereas Harry . . . Harry was a first-class commercial brain, and he was already accepted in the best drawing rooms. For one thing he was a generation removed from the grubbiness of trade; for another, it was only his immediate family who dismissed him as graceless and unattractive. The outside world deemed him handsome, charming and graceful. He could move effortlessly into places his father would only have seen from the tradesmen's entrance. He'd show them all he was the greatest gentleman there, and after that he'd show the world he was a business genius!

Two hours later, Karin's miscarriage reached its climax, The tiny pathetic shape which Beuno's medicine had poisoned was male.

# INTERREGNUM

# Chapter Eighteen

## July, 1934

It was the slack part of Friday evening in the editorial office of the *Sunday Globe*. Jack Antony, the duty news editor, yawned, lit a cigarette and stood up. If he spent fifteen minutes more at this desk he'd take root! He wandered aimlessly over to the grimy window that looked down on Fleet Street. Nothing happening down there, either. Ten o'clock on a warm evening at the beginning of the silly season! What could be more dead? Maybe something was happening in Chicago, or Delhi, or Rio. They were all in the full flush of daytime. Perhaps he'd go and look . . .

Antony wandered out of the newsroom and headed down the corridor to the creed room, where the big machines whirred and ticked out momentous happenings from five continents. Please let something happen, he prayed silently. I'm not up to inventing yet another love-crazed vicar this week. At first it was as quiet in there as everywhere else in the building. Then a big double bell rang and the creed supervisor called out: 'Flash! Anybody interested? Domestic flash!' It was the signal that an important story was coming over.

Antony shrugged. If it was home news, it couldn't be that exciting. Everybody worth assassinating had already

419

gone away for the summer. He ambled over to the Ex-Tel machine and tore off the first strip of printed paper as it marched out of its slot. It said: 'TEA KING DIES AFTER LONG ILLNESS. HARRY RICHMOND, MULTI-MILLIONAIRE OWNER OF THE RICHMOND INTERNATIONAL GROUP, DIED AT HIS HERTFORDSHIRE HOME THIS EVENING. RICHMOND, ONE TIME SELF-STYLED RICHEST MAN IN ENGLAND, MARRIED FOUR TIMES, ONCE, ALLEGEDLY, BIGAMOUSLY. HE LEAVES A WIDOW AND TWO DAUGHTERS.'

Antony grinned and rubbed the stubble on his chin. 'Well, well,' he said. 'I know somebody who'll sleep better for that.' He glanced up at the creed supervisor. 'I'll take this one, Charlie, but see the chief sub gets a print too, won't you? Tell him we'll be splashing it.' He returned to the newsroom, humming jauntily. Who needed an assassination, when they could spread Harry Richmond's private life all over the centre pages of Sunday's paper, with all the venom that only Ted Fisher could generate?

Fisher was still out at the pub. The news editor stuck the flash under a used teacup in the centre of his desk, with a note saying 'Get cracking – it's your big moment!' then went off to the library to see if they had any good Richmond pictures in stock. By the time he returned, Fisher was back too, and almost doing a war dance of joy around his desk. 'So the bastard's gone at last! Took him long enough, I must say. He's been bedridden for at least two years. It's only that gorgeous wife of his who's been keeping him alive . . . How much space have I got, Jack? I'm really going to enjoy this!'

'As much as you need, old chum – centre spread and a teaser on page one. That do you?'

Fisher brooded for a moment. 'We could get a whole series out of this, Jack. I've acted as personal nursemaid to that file for seven years or more. Since 1926 he hasn't picked his nose in public without me getting a note of it.'

Antony winced. 'Spare me the coarse bits. We all know how much you loved the man. One thing I don't know, though – why d'you feel so strongly about him?'

The writer's jubilation died. 'Don't suppose you remember the wife before last.'

'Of course I do! It's the main reason the world and I want to know all about him. Kitt Arundell, naughtiest girl in Mayfair, among other places. Don't say you had a thing about her and you had a grudge against Richmond because he got her?'

'Credit me with a bit of sense, man, but yes, I did have a thing about her. I met her a few times around the clubs. She was quite something. I'd have gone through fire for her, but she was too rich for my blood. She was bound to marry someone like Richmond. Kids like her, all glamour and no money, always do. I could have forgiven him that and just envied him. But he killed her, Jack – he bloody killed her!'

'Hey, now wait a minute! I know it's impossible to libel the dead, but I can't let you say that in cold print!'

Fisher grinned wearily. 'Of course I won't put it in my story. I know better than you do how far I can go. You were the one who asked me what I had against the bugger, and I was telling you, that's all. Don't worry – I can make him look quite bad enough without needing to accuse him of murder. This, old buddy, will be a labour of love.'

It took him all that night. He filed his copy at nine o'clock on Saturday morning, just as the day news editor came on duty. 'If there are any queries, don't worry,' he said. 'I'm just off to a café for some breakfast, then I'll pop back before I go home. I'm almost tempted to sit it out all day and see it off the presses.'

The day news editor shook his head. 'He's dead. He can't feel what you're doing to him now, you know.'

The feature writer grimaced. 'More's the pity! Still, at least it sets the record straight.'

'How would you know? You're not him.'

'There's times I'd have changed places, but not today!' Fisher laughed sourly, put on his hat and left.

On Sunday, the *Globe* ran a front page news story about Harry Richmond, with a brief account of his life and a trailer for the centre pages. There, amid lavish illustrations of Richmond's public and private life, Ted Fisher's character assassination told all he thought there was to know about the man he had hated.

He was back in the *Globe's* Fleet Street offices on Saturday evening when the first edition came off the presses. He had to see this . . . savour it before anyone else. He knew what it would say, but the subs had said they were tinkering with his copy a bit to break it around the pictures. All he knew was that they had split the business and personal stuff and had lots of shots of Richmond's wives and lovers. Fisher laughed at himself as he noticed his own hands shaking when he opened the paper. You'd have thought his name was Richmond.

## WITHIN THE HOLLOW CROWN
## TYCOON WHO HAD
## EVERYTHING
## EXCEPT HIS LIFELONG DREAM

Harry Richmond was born with more advantages than most. He inherited one huge fortune from his father, a self-made millionaire grocer, and another from his mother. He grew up brilliant, handsome and popular. It seemed the world was at his feet.

And yet he died on Friday, alone and unmourned, leaving behind a stagnant business empire and a series of disastrous marriages and love affairs as the tarnished legacy for his two daughters. He had never achieved his one burning ambition – a son to carry on the family name. There are no plans for his daughters to take over the chain of stores, warehouses and property from which they draw their wealth. Now the commercial despot is dead, it seems inevitable that his empire will be dismembered by faceless executives. So perish all tyrants!

Many would say that Richmond brought about his own destruction. His first wife was the widow of his own elder brother, who died tragically within months of his marriage. Richmond quickly tired of her when she failed to bear him the son he wanted. Although they were married for more than twenty-five years, they lived apart for most of that time. Their daughter, Marianne, was brought up by her mother.

In 1919, Richmond scandalised London society

– and, many said, ruined his chances of a peerage – by eloping with an American girl little more than half his age. He went through the motions of a Nevada divorce and married Nancy Rochford in the same American state, hoping thereby to evade any possible charges of bigamy on his return to England.

Although the plan kept him out of jail, it ruined him socially, especially as his first wife, Karin Richmond, refused to acknowledge the new marriage or to give him a British divorce. Not that it was to make much difference, because his quest for a legitimate male heir preoccupied him more than the lady's status.

He found his dream no easier to achieve with his new bride. She gave birth to a daughter, Isabel, almost immediately after their marriage, but there were to be no more children. Some years later, Nancy Rochford Richmond died in suspicious circumstances, of alcohol and barbiturate poisoning. At the inquest it was stated she had become deeply depressed at her inability to have more children and had drifted into alcoholism. A verdict of accidental death was returned.

In the meantime, though, few members of the smart set had failed to notice that Harry Richmond was already courting another young, eligible woman, Jennet Moore-Ross, or that his deserted first wife had now died, leaving him free to re-marry legally under English law, which had never recognised his marriage to Nancy Rochford.

Perhaps his latest lady-friend thought Nancy's accident a little too timely. She ended their relationship shortly afterwards. Not without taking away a few trophies from the battlefield, though. Richmond had given both her playboy brothers top executive jobs in the family business in an effort to strengthen his claims on this aristocratic lady. It didn't work. He kept the brothers and lost the lady. Today, Edward Moore-Ross is company secretary of Richmond International and the younger brother, Tom, is marketing and sales director. Jennet Moore-Ross married a Venezuelan silver millionaire and lives with him and their two sons in South America.

After Jennet, Richmond looked abroad again. This time he kept very exotic company and for a long time there were rumours that he planned to wed Ann Kleber, American daughter of an immigrant Polish miner turned commodities millionaire and war profiteer. Miss Kleber inherited her father's postwar empire and ran it as well as any man. Perhaps Richmond was put off marriage by the fact that she was the only child of only children . . . or was he unhappy about where the lady made her investments? Whatever the reason, they remained friends and he returned to England, still seeking a bride who would bear him sons.

There was still plenty of tragedy ahead – though people were beginning to say that while Richmond did all the weeping, his wives did all the suffering. After a chance meeting in a London nightclub, followed by a whirlwind courtship, he married penniless deb of the year, Kitt Arundell, in 1926. Richmond was fifty-six years old, ill and bloated with drink and over-indulgence when they married, his bride just twenty-three.

Within months something was obviously wrong. When Richmond was on his frequent foreign buying trips, his young wife was seen around all her old London haunts, usually in the company of the same man, a senior Richmond's executive only a couple of years younger than her husband. At the height of the gossip, tragedy struck. Kitt Richmond and her boyfriend, James Fenwick, were killed when their open sports car overturned at speed and burst into flames on the Dover road late at night. Rumour was rife about the possibility of foul play, but Harry Richmond proved he had been in Copenhagen throughout the preceding week, and the inquest jury returned a verdict of accidental death. Strong evidence that the dead pair had been eloping made the jury highly sympathetic to Richmond.

There can be few public figures this century who lost two wives in circumstances warranting inquests, both of which produced accident verdicts. Many said Richmond was very unlucky to be twice cursed with such tragedy. Others insisted he was the luckiest man they knew.

In the long run, though, Richmond was a loser. By 1928 he was fifty-eight years old but looked seventy. His health was in terminal decline and even he had stopped believing he would ever father a son. By now, he seemed unable to live as a single man. In 1929, he married his final wife, Erin Parry, a Great War widow who had worked as his personal assistant since the early 1920s. For months before their engagement, it was rumoured that Mrs Parry would wed Tom Moore-Ross, who had been her regular escort and was much closer to her own age than

Richmond. But in the end, it seemed professional loyalty won out on a personal level, too, and she became Erin Richmond in time to nurse the Tea King through his final illness.

Now everyone must be asking the same question: Who inherits the Richmond empire? King Harry seemed determined it would never fall into his daughters' hands, but now they may well get it, if only by default. The elder girl, Marianne, could claim to be his only legitimate descendant, as Richmond's marriage to Nancy Rochford was never recognised as legal in England. That puts his other daughter, fourteen-year-old Isabel, in a vulnerable position. Until the will is read, the company will be in the hands of his widow, who ran it with the help of senior managers for the last two years of Richmond's illness.

Tom Moore-Ross is still her constant companion and business adviser. It would be ironical if King Harry's crumbling empire were to fall eventually to the kinsman of a girl who jilted him long ago.

The article on Harry Richmond's business career was equally damning, playing down the tycoon's triumphs and drawing attention to the set-backs which had caused a decline in his commercial fortunes in recent years.

Ted Fisher read it for the third time, then laid down the paper with a sigh of satisfaction. He felt exalted, as though he had just gone through a great religious experience. The news editor watched him narrowly.

'All passion spent, eh, Ted? Christ, Richmond must be revolving in his grave!'

'Coffin, dear boy – in his coffin. They haven't had a chance to bury the bugger yet. If I had my way, they'd sink him at the crossroads with a stake through his heart.'

'I thought that's what you'd just done.'

That same week, in the small North Wales town of Bangor, the local newspaper published a page of degree examination results, with photographs of the graduates and human interest stories about a handful of the more unusual success stories. One such item read:

### LOCAL MAN WINS MATURE DEGREE
#### Age no bar, says Anglesey herbalist

Beuno Owen, aged 74 years, a well-known Llangefni herbalist, gained an upper second-class honours degree in botany from the University College of North Wales this session. He did not give up his work as a professional gatherer of plants during his three years' study, but found he had to close down his shop as a concession to the increased academic workload he had to take on. Since 1931, he has carried on his business from his smallholding in Llanddona.

'I enjoyed every minute of my studies,' he told the *Chronicle* reporter. 'I hope my example encourages other people to realise that education is not only for the young. You are never too old to learn, and that does not apply only to academic matters.'

Mr Owen has no plans to continue his academic career. 'But I might re-open the shop,' he said, 'if it's only for the satisfaction of hanging up a brass plate outside, saying, "Beuno Owen, B.Sc"! '

# PART TWO

# Heir Apparent

# Chapter Nineteen

## Isabel: 1935

*There was a big walk-in closet in my bedroom and when he came in I was right at the back of it, looking for something I'd put away. The door had swung closed behind me and at first he didn't notice I was inside. He was calling out, 'Bel, where's my little Bel?' in a funny sort of excited whispering shout. I don't know why, but it frightened me. Instead of going straight out to him, I crept to the door and peeped out through the crack. He was wearing a lovely dressing gown in dark red velvet. As I watched he undid the sash and the robe opened. He had nothing on underneath and I could see everything.*

*He walked over to my dressing room – he must have assumed I was in there as there was no sign of me in the bedroom. He called out my name again, in the same sort of tone as before, but even more excited and also trying to make it a bit of a joke – you know, as though he'd laugh it off if someone caught him at it, pretending he didn't mean anything. But he did. You could see from his face. For some reason I was getting excited too, the way you get when you're playing hide and seek and you're afraid of being caught, but somehow you want to be found as well, so that you can go off together and scare someone else. And he was different from usual. He wasn't just cuddly Uncle Tom any more. He looked sort of dangerous, but exciting dangerous like a handsome brigand. And his body looked so beautiful all naked under that velvet that I wanted to go and stroke it.*

*He opened the dressing room door and looked very disappointed and said, 'God damn it, where is the little bitch?' under his breath in a different tone of voice. He started moving back towards the bedroom door and if I'd stayed quiet that would have been the end of it. But all of a sudden I wanted him to stay more than anything else, so I dropped a box I'd been holding and let out a squeaky giggle. He turned back towards the closet. 'Now who could we have here – burglars?' he said.*

*I giggled again, to this day I don't know why, because I really didn't want him to find me, and started backing farther into the closet. Then the door opened wide, and he was standing in front of me, with his dressing gown still open. My room was very warm, and I hadn't put on my dressing gown when I got up. I had on the white lawn nightgown which Aunt Erin had given me at Easter. The material was very thin. I hadn't plaited my hair and it was all loose down my back. Suddenly I remembered he scared me.*

*'Well, Isabel, you're up very early,' he said. 'Got time for a little game of hide and seek with your old uncle?' Then he slipped the robe off and kicked it aside before he came into the closet after me and shut the door behind him . . .*

Erin Moore-Ross shivered and drew her negligée closer around her shoulders. Tom didn't like the central heating and always turned off the radiator when he came to bed. The trouble was, he forgot to turn it on again in the morning as often as not, and she got cold if she wanted to get up before her maid came in with the tea. Now Erin got out of bed and went to turn on the heat, before hurrying into her bathroom. She might as well take her bath now instead of waiting for the maid to run it. The hot water would get rid of the chill.

At the age of thirty-seven and in the seventh month of her first pregnancy, she was forcing herself to take things easy. The gynaecologist was more cautious each time she saw him, as though it were tempting providence to embark on motherhood so late. What choice had there been? The physical side of her marriage to Oliver had lasted precisely six months, and as he was at the Front for most of that time, there was precious little chance to beget a child. And anyone who thought there could have been a physical side to her marriage with Harry Richmond must have been blind or mad. By the time he married her, Harry had needed a nurse, not a lover. This child was her first chance at motherhood, and she had no intention of letting it be her last. Whatever the specialist said, if she had come through safely once, surely there was no reason why she shouldn't have four or five children? She knew a number of women who had given birth in their early forties. Of course, their first babies had been born when they were still in their twenties, but what of it?

Erin stirred restlessly in the warm, perfumed water. If only she could stop fretting about it. She was doing what Tom – and she herself – wanted more than anything else. That was the important thing. She heard the clink of china as Betty brought the tea tray into the bedroom next door, and called out good morning. Where could Tom be? It was unlike him to miss sharing tea with her before he went off for the day. Ungainly because of her pregnancy, Erin heaved herself upright, got out of the bath and swathed herself in a turkish towelling robe. She caught a glimpse of her reflection in the full-length mirror behind the door. Goodness, what a sight! The original white elephant. She must do a lot of exercises as soon as the baby was born, or she'd never get her figure back. Tom had made it clear that he preferred lean ladies.

She went back into the bedroom, cosy again now the heating was back on, and sat on the edge of the massive old four poster bed to drink her tea. At that moment, Tom came in, still clad in his dressing gown.

'Darling, where on earth have you been? Prowling the corridors undressed? What will the staff think?'

He laughed. 'Oh, I just woke up early with a stupid line running round my brain. In the end it stopped me going back to sleep and I just had to go down to the library to look it up.'

'Really? You're not usually so interested in literature.'

'I know, that's probably why it was so infuriating. Turned out to come from *Richard II*, of all things. "For God's sake, let us sit upon the ground and tell sad stories of the death of kings." Can't think why I'd forgotten. Always did like that line.'

Without looking at Erin, he had moved round the bed, slipped out of his dressing gown and climbed back between the sheets. She caught a whiff of his body smell as he passed her. It was like when they had been making love . . . she flushed with shame. Oh, how stupid to have pestered him! She had been unable to satisfy him for

434

over a month now because of her condition. He was hot-blooded at the best of times. He must have been so frustrated he had to . . . uneasily, Erin wondered if he had ceased to find her desirable. She adored him, and would have been happy to do anything that pleased him. If he had to go off alone early in the morning and seek such solitary relief, perhaps he found her repulsive now. She stood up clumsily and moved back towards the bathroom. If only she hadn't put on this awful robe! At least the negligée was flattering and minimised her bulging abdomen. Erin hurried off to retrieve it.

When she returned, he appeared to be dozing. She stared at him in surprise. 'Tom? Are you ill? Surely you haven't forgotten what day it is?'

He opened his eyes. 'No – Tuesday. What's so special about that?'

'Nothing, except that it's not the week-end. What about the office?'

He made a face. 'What about it? They can live without me for a couple of hours. Told you, I had a bad night. I just feel like a lie-in, that's all. No need for you to come back to bed.' He closed his eyes again and turned away, pulling the eiderdown high around his shoulders as if to shut her out. Erin felt as if she had been dismissed.

In her nursery wing apartment, Isabel was lying late in bed, too. At first she had been worried about the blood on the sheet, but he had laughed at her. 'Don't be silly, Bel! At your age that's always happening to girls – come on, don't blush! I'm an old married man and father-to-be, remember? I'm allowed to know about these things!'

He knew about so many things . . . things she had never talked about to anyone else; things she had

435

enjoyed alone, in the dark. Now he had made her feel the way she did then, and it had been better because he was sharing it. Her guilt evaporated as she remembered those powerful stubby hands on her, making her excited though she knew it was wicked . . . making her own hands reach out as though they had a will of their own and clutch at him, thrilling to his pulsing strength under her fingers and knowing before he did it what he would do . . . how it would feel. Isabel gave a little moan. If only he hadn't gone away so quickly. It would have been wonderful to do it again. Just thinking about it rekindled her excitement.

She was on her way to change when her maid came in. 'Oh – Miss Isabel. I thought you'd be up and about by now! I'll come back, shall I?'

'No, Mary – it's all right. I – I'm not too well today, that's why I'm late. I'll bathe now, while you're doing my room, then I think I shall go back to bed.'

By now the maid had reached the bedside. Glancing down at the bloodstain, she thought she understood, and hastened to begin changing the linen. No wonder Miss Isabel wanted a lie-down. It sometimes made her bad, too. If she hadn't needed to be up by six each day, she'd often have stayed in bed when it was her time of the month . . . Mary busied herself about the room and was gone before Isabel had emerged from the bathroom.

She dozed until nearly eleven, then woke with a start at the sound of an engine revving in the courtyard. Of course, Erin was being driven up to London for her appointment this afternoon, then she was dining with friends . . . Isabel tried to remain calm as the Silver Ghost slid off down the drive. Stop getting so excited, silly! He'll have gone to the office hours ago! She sighed and turned away from the window. As she did so the door opened. It was Tom.

Isabel was wearing a lightweight silk dressing gown, but she had left her nightdress in the closet where he had dropped it when he eased it off her. Now he moved towards her, stealthy as a big cat, his eyes fixed on her slender body beneath the garment. She stood absolutely still, at a loss for an appropriate response, already so excited that her breathing was fast and shallow. At last he stood about a foot away from her. He reached forward and loosened the tie belt of the robe. It slid open with a sensual whisper.

Tom eyed her appreciatively and said: 'Just the way I like it, not a spare ounce of flesh anywhere.' He rested his hands lightly on her hips for a moment, then moved them slowly up, changing to a circular massaging movement when he reached her breasts. 'Just enough there to know you're a girl,' he murmured, 'just enough to get you going . . .'

His words and his caress had a hypnotic effect and she closed her eyes, swaying forward towards him. He stopped stroking her and held her off.

'Come on, now you do it for me. I'm not wearing much, either.' Her amber-brown eyes were clouded with excitement. She reached out and undid the dressing gown sash, then parted the folds of the heavy robe. He glanced down: 'There, look what I've got for you.'

'Oh, Tom, yes! When I think of how it feels, I want –'

'This?' He pulled her forward towards him, parting her thighs with his hand, and thrust himself between the smooth legs. 'Close them, now, just feel it there . . . oh, that's wonderful . . . just – let – me –' He bent and kissed her open-mouthed, his tongue teasing hers, sucking at her lips, seeming to devour her. His big hands were locked over her buttocks, pressing her forward towards him, astride his rigid shaft.

The tail-end of a memory flitted through Isabel's mind. Erin, her beloved, trusting Erin, going off to London, not knowing. She began to draw back. 'Th-this is wrong . . . I really mustn't . . .' Her face was resting against his neck as she spoke.

Tom buried one hand in her hair and pulled her away from him, then he laughed. 'Of course it's wrong, but you don't really want me to stop, do you, my little Bel? You want me to go on like this all day . . . on, and on, and on . . .' She felt as though she were falling through warm oil, insulated from everything, unable to protest, not wanting to protest.

He eased her backwards on to the bed and she gave a little sob of anticipation. 'Go right in again, oh please, like this morning, not just playing like that!'

But he only laughed again. 'Plenty of time for that, Bel, plenty of time. See if you like this, instead.' He slid to his knees beside the bed and pressed his face into the crisp cushion of red-gold hair between her legs. It was like the teasing of his lips and tongue on her mouth, but infinitely more arousing. She arched towards him, almost weeping with pleasure. Moments later he was up, rearing over her, pushing her further back on to the bed. This time there was no delay. She watched him wide-eyed as his hugely erect penis disappeared inside her, then his full weight crushed down on her deliciously and she no longer cared what was happening.

He stayed with her for almost two hours, then, abruptly glancing around as though ending a business meeting, he said, 'My God, it's almost one! That maid of yours will be bringing you an invalid's snack any minute. I'd better disappear.'

Before Isabel had time to say anything, he was gone. She burrowed down in the bed, seeking sleep to cut off reality, but it was impossible. Tom Moore-Ross was irresistible. This time, though, she had been aware of how wrong it all was. She adored Erin and knew it would destroy her stepmother to find out what had happened today. And what about Tom? He was supposed to be madly in love with Erin. That's what he'd told everyone when eyebrows were raised about him marrying her so soon after Papa died. That was less than a year ago, and now here he was, making love to a girl who could be his daughter. In a sense, she *was* his daughter.

Suddenly she no longer wanted to lie in the bed. The smell and feel of the sheets reminded her of a betrayal which was as much hers as Tom's. Her very nakedness was a memento of their wrongdoing. What was that awful old description she'd always hated – even more so when she realised what it meant – making a two-backed beast? Yes, that's just what they'd been doing . . . Her self-disgust rose and she wanted to take another bath, wash away all the corruption. She got to the bathroom, started to run the water and then, as the rising steam heated things up, she caught the aroma of him, the lingering scent of sweat and semen on her young body, and the nausea vanished as fast as it had appeared. She slumped down on the bathroom stool, gazing into the mirror in search of visible changes in her face and body.

'Oh, Tom,' she said, 'we shouldn't have . . . now what am I going to do?' And slowly, hopelessly, she began to cry.

Isabel had been happier for the past few years than ever before in her short life. She had experienced deep and terrible grief when her father died. For every moment that she had hated him, there were two when she had loved him, and she had always sought his approval. But until those last years, he was so remote from her, apparently so indifferent, that once he was dead she seemed to recover quite fast. With Erin there, finally replacing the mother she had never known, she felt safe.

She had inherited her father's intellectual brilliance and now she redoubled her efforts to excel in the classroom. Her education was entrusted to tutors. Erin felt her childhood had already been too disturbed to want to send her away again to school. So Isabel had continued to study here at Paxton, revelling in what she learned by going over it in the evenings with her clever step-mother. The first autumn and winter after her father's death seemed more a beginning than an ending. The only thing which irritated her was Erin's insistence that she was still a child. Erin tried to explain to her that no girl of her background wore grown-up clothes or attended adult social functions until she Came Out at the age of seventeen.

'It's my own fault, I suppose,' she said with a sigh after a particularly stormy session with Isabel. 'I let you dine with us when it's just family and close friends, and you've always shared so many of my interests, it's hard for me to remember you're still a child. But you are, and

I'm not giving you a bad start in life. There's been more than enough of that already.'

She compromised by choosing clothes for Isabel which were as unchildlike as possible while remaining respectable. So at least Isabel was able to wear well-cut pleated skirts from Liberty with fully fashioned jumpers in matching vivid jewel colours, instead of the ubiquitous little white blouse and grey skirt of her age and social class. Around the estate, Erin even permitted her to wear trousers.

As though to compensate for the childish clothes, Erin did something really grown-up for both Isabel and Marianne. The east wing of the house, with its nursery on the top floor and extra guest accommodation on the lower storeys, was converted to provide virtually self-contained apartments for both girls. A live-in governess was employed to supervise Isabel's education, but Erin preserved the girl's illusion of adulthood by locating Mrs Ashley's quarters in the main block of the house.

Isabel knew she was very lucky to receive such love and consideration. Her educational progress was constantly monitored, and if Erin decided she was being badly taught or had no aptitude for a particular subject, either the tutor changed or the subject was quietly dropped. It wasn't all work, either. She was regularly taken to afternoon concerts and theatre matinées in London. The children of senior Richmond's employees and of Erin's friends from her days of earlier widowhood were encouraged to go on visiting Paxton, lessening the solitude which had become too familiar to Isabel. She often wondered what she would have done if Erin had not come along and married Papa. Probably have turned out like poor Marianne, who had been too old really to benefit much from Erin's love and care.

When Uncle Tom included her in the secret plan for him to marry Erin, it made things perfect. Or did it? Even then Isabel had harboured strong feelings for him. She remembered how she had gone off alone when he had left for his honeymoon with Erin, how she had tried to imagine what it was like to be the bride, how she had touched herself to increase her excitement at the fantasy of those light eyes gazing flatly into hers, that full, temperamental mouth covering her own . . . Well, now she knew what it really felt like, and wished she did not.

At least she wouldn't have to face Erin tonight. Her stepmother disliked travelling home late, so she intended staying in the Belgravia apartment. This evening it would be just Isabel and Marianne. An awful thought struck her. What if Tom – there was something obscene, now, about calling him Uncle Tom – what if Tom changed his plans and stayed here instead of joining Erin in London? For some reason, the thought of sitting down at the dinner table in his presence, with Marianne watching them, was worse than the possibility of confronting Erin. Isabel hurriedly finished dressing. Only one way to end the suspense: go and find out exactly who was going to be where this evening.

She was wearing one of the smart jumper and skirt outfits, this time of midnight blue, with a silk scarf of blue and primrose at the neck. Her long red-gold hair was braided into a waist-length plait. Roll on the day when she was old enough to put it up, or better still, have it cut off. She looked down disdainfully at the white ankle socks and black calf shoes with their neat instep

442

straps. They were the real give-away! With her height and graceful posture, she could easily have passed for seventeen or eighteen, but anybody looking at her feet would know straight away she was a baby!

Downstairs, Isabel rang for the butler. 'Edwardes, I think everyone may have changed their plans today. Can you tell me who is in tonight and who isn't?'

'Of course, Miss Isabel. Miss Marianne is back from her visit. She arrived on the three o'clock train. Mrs Moore-Ross went off before luncheon for her London appointment and she will be staying at Eaton Place tonight. Mr Moore-Ross drove up in the Bentley at about two o'clock and he will be staying at Eaton Place too. He'll be driving Madam back down tomorrow, so the chauffeur has already come back with the Silver Cloud. It will be just you and Miss Marianne for dinner, Miss.'

Oh well, that might be dull, but at least it wouldn't be embarrassing. Isabel gratefully pushed aside further consideration of her new intimacy with Tom Moore-Ross and instead contemplated her erratic relationship with her half-sister. Even her innocent mind found it odd that although Marianne enjoyed all the tokens of adulthood which Isabel longed for, she pitied the older girl rather than envying her. She invariably thought of her as poor Marianne, as though Poor Marianne were her name. The pity did not prevent Isabel from feeling exasperated with Marianne for most of the time, but she loved her too and wished things were better for her sister.

Marianne was still unmarried at thirty-two. She was no great beauty, but she wasn't repulsive either, thought Isabel. With the Richmond money behind her there must have been a queue of eligible men before she passed twenty-one. The reason for Marianne's prolonged spinsterhood loomed splay-legged and bulky over both their lives. It was called Harry Richmond. Isabel had an almost psychic understanding of her dead father's reactions. She understood now, without ever having been told, that Harry had always found a reasonable objection to Marianne's suitors because secretly he feared that her children would try to cheat any son he might produce of his inheritance. Other men would have accepted that the opportunity for a son had passed, once they were in their fifties and in poor health, but not Harry. So Marianne had always been treated more as a dynastic threat than an asset, and her combined adoration and terror of Harry had ensured that she obeyed his smallest whim. Then, too late, Harry had accepted that Marianne and Isabel were the end of his line. Suddenly it was crucial to find Marianne a suitable husband and to pray that his new blood would beget the boys of whom Harry had been cheated. But by then, Marianne was twenty-eight and shy almost to the point of reclusiveness. It was easy enough to introduce the prospective husbands, but close to impossible to ensure they made any progress.

Erin, that most understanding of women, had helped a lot. As soon as she and Harry were married, she persuaded him to give Marianne an apartment of her own. She took great pains to welcome Marianne as a daughter who might stay within the new intimate family circle as long as she wished, but also managed to convey to the girl that freedom was available if she wanted it. Tactfully, Erin started to go with her on shopping trips, so that Marianne soon looked less like a provincial governess and more like a rich man's fashionable daughter. She insisted that Marianne should learn to drive, and made up theatre parties and house parties to ensure that her step-daughter met the right people. Isabel, still in pinafores at that stage, had looked on with wild envy at first. Then she noticed that Marianne tried hard to take advantage of all this kindness, but usually failed dismally to enjoy any of it. That was when Isabel started thinking of her as Poor Marianne.

And if she had been bad when Papa was alive, now she was a hundred times worse. The memory of Papa's preference for boys reduced Isabel to fury and stimulated a flinty determination to prove that girls could do just as well as soon as she was old enough. But Marianne had swallowed his opinions whole. She really believed that girls were worthless without men to direct them, and that the Richmond empire was in grave danger with a female at the helm. She was steeling herself to take over eventually, but was still hoping she would find a suitable husband who would make the real decisions. Now it was beginning to look as if she had found the right man at last. Isabel loathed him.

Heinrich von Burckhardt was almost a caricature of the German nobleman seen through British eyes. He was tall and lean, with slicked-down blond hair and pale blue eyes. He even had an elegantly-positioned duelling scar on his left cheek. It prompted the only joke Isabel had ever heard him make: 'The other fellow's was less decorative!' pronounced in what he seemed to think was an upper class English accent. But von Burckhardt offered advantages which Isabel was still too young to appreciate. He was as rich as Marianne, so no one could say he was a fortune-hunter. He came from the old aristocracy;

and, most important of all, he had proved his ability to father sons. A thirty-five-year-old widower, he had two daughters and a son from his first marriage.

Initially, Marianne had treated him as she did all the other men to whom she was introduced, with a mixture of paralysed shyness and faint hostility. But von Burckhardt enjoyed a challenge and he persevered for over a year. Now Marianne was on the point of announcing their engagement. She had just returned from a three-week visit to his family in Prussia, and tonight would be Isabel's first meeting with her since she got back. Isabel sighed. If only the reunion were a more interesting prospect . . . if only she could confide in Marianne about what had happened this morning . . . The very thought made her blush. Marianne's view of morality would have made an Anabaptist seem profligate. Her miserable childhood had taught her about the fruits of sexual licence, as she watched her mother destroyed by her father's philandering. Romantic peccadilloes were the one unforgivable sin to Marianne.

The real tragedy of this morning was that in other circumstances, the one person she could have told was Erin. But how do you tell your best friend that you've been seduced by her husband – particularly when she happens also to be your stepmother?

Isabel sighed. That problem would have to join all the others she had never been able to talk about. She'd got over knowing what happened to Kitt – although those screams sometimes still haunted her nightmares – and she'd been much younger then. She had never said a word, and nobody else had ever found out about it. This thing with Uncle Tom was nothing compared with that. At least she'd liked what he did while he was doing it.

Suddenly she realised she had been sitting there brooding in the dark. Edwardes came in to switch on the lights, unaware that she was still in the room. 'Oh! I do beg your pardon, Miss Isabel. Didn't realise you were still in here, miss. Do you want me to leave the lights?'

'No, Edwardes; I was just day-dreaming. Please switch them all on. I'd better go up and dress for dinner, anyway.'

She felt more childish than ever in her dinner frock. Here Erin had drawn a firmer line between girl and woman. 'I'm sorry, Isabel, but you'll just have to put up with calf-length white georgette. I've never seen girls of your age wear a longer skirt unless they're bridesmaids. Just be thankful that you're coming down to dinner at all at your age. Anyway, it's only Tom, Marianne and me who'll see you dressed like that.'

At least she was permitted to wear white silk stockings and white shoes with the awful baby clothes, but oh, for high heels, diamonds and an ankle-length creation of cream satin with a plunge back! One day . . .

Even happiness could not make Marianne pretty – but at least she looked pleasant. And Erin's fashion advice had certainly improved her overall appearance. Tonight she was wearing a dark green velvet cocktail frock that Isabel would have killed for. Marianne was fond of Isabel but her intense shyness prevented any demonstration of affection. Now she sat eyeing her half-sister suspiciously, wondering why the girl was radiating such vitality. 'You seem very pleased with yourself, young lady,' she said. Immediately wishing it had sounded less abrasive, she nevertheless continued almost automatically, 'I suppose you've been dazzling your teachers yet again.'

Isabel was an old hand at this. 'No – everything's very dull here at present and I've not done any great things. Oh – I did go and see *Design For Living* with Erin – it was divine!'

Marianne's face darkened. 'Really, she should know better! That film is quite immoral. It as good as says that three people can live together . . . er . . . just like husband and wife.'

'But it was so funny!'

'Those things aren't funny, they're sordid, and the sooner you realise it, the better.' Marianne bit her lip and stopped speaking. *There I go again – don't, mustn't, shouldn't – what an awful bore I must seem to her, especially when Erin spoils her so disgracefully. But she's really just a child, even if she is taller than me, and prettier . . .* She shrugged, 'Still, I suppose such things are none of my business. Mama saw things differently from Erin, and she brought me up accordingly. Never mind. Makes no difference now. What else have you been up to?'

'The Chinese exhibition at Burlington House. I loved that.'

That worked. Marianne was radiant now. 'Yes, wasn't it splendid? Of course, I haven't seen you since, you wouldn't know . . . Heinie gave me a wonderful present. We went there and I was sighing at the beautiful T'ang horses. Afterwards he whisked me off to a gallery he knows in Old Bond Street and bought me one. It's quite the loveliest thing I've ever owned. That was just before we went to Germany,' she added defensively, 'so I haven't had a chance to invite you to see it yet.'

Isabel knew the invitation would not be forthcoming. Marianne treated her London apartment like an ivory tower. Von Burckhardt apparently went there at times – always chaperoned, of course – and Erin had been invited once or twice when it was unavoidable, but otherwise Marianne resolutely excluded the world. Isabel cast around desperately for another topic. Her cultural life appeared to be getting them nowhere.

'Will you be staying at Paxton for long this time? It would be nice if we could spend some time together – I don't seem to have seen anything of you since the spring.'

'Oh – have you really missed me?' Marianne flushed with pleasure at the unlikely notion.

'Yes, of course. You're my sister and I like to be with you.' Isabel hoped it sounded convincing. She wanted to make Marianne happy but it was hard going.

'I had intended going back to London on Thursday – so much catching up to do, you know – but if you'd like me to stay . . .'

'I won't hear of you leaving so soon!' Isabel stood up and went around the absurdly big dinner table to embrace Marianne. 'After all, the dashing Heinrich will be sweeping you off to his magic castle in next to no time!'

Marianne actually managed to giggle. 'Yes, isn't it exciting? We finally set the date while I was in Germany.'

'When's it to be?'

'We thought, Christmas. Erin will have had her baby

449

by then, and Heinie's son will be home from the military academy . . . of course, he and the girls will come over for the wedding.'

The prospect filled Isabel with excitement. 'And may I be a bridesmaid, Marianne? Oh, please say yes – please! I never have been one, and I would so love a long dress!'

The older girl had a momentary nightmare vision of this exquisite creature gliding down the aisle behind her, her tall, slender frame and marvellous white-and-gold colouring making Marianne seem squatter and more colourless than ever, and she almost said she would have no attendants. But for once she forced herself to put her love for Isabel first. 'Of course you may. We'll get Erin to help us with the dresses – she's much better than I at that sort of thing.' She lowered her voice as though afraid of being scolded, and said: 'I was thinking of going to Paris and ordering a couture gown.'

Isabel wondered why on earth Marianne should speak as though this were the ultimate wickedness. She was probably one of the few women in England who could afford to buy all her clothes in Paris if she chose, and instead she shopped sparingly in London. But still, if Marianne had nerved herself to pay couture prices, that meant she herself would get a model gown too. Silently she started working out how far off her sixteenth birthday would be by then, and whether she might persuade Erin to make that the first event of her debut Season.

Marianne was talking again. 'How is Erin, anyway? I'm sorry I didn't give her more notice that I was coming back, but Heinie suddenly had to come to London on business and I returned with him. It was only two days earlier than I'd planned, after all.'

'Erin? Glowing, of course. Why shouldn't she be?' Isabel might be considered adult enough to discuss philosophy with her step-mother, but even in this enlightened household, no one would talk to a fifteen-year-old girl about the complications of a late first pregnancy.

'No reason. I'm concerned about her, that's all. She always insists on doing so much.'

'Yes, she still does lots with the business. Edward Moore-Ross or Freddie Sayles is down here at least twice a week with oodles of reports and things, and she goes into Richmond House fairly often, too.'

Marianne frowned. 'I do wish she wouldn't. Since she's married to Tom now, she should hand over to him. It's too much for her.'

'While she's pregnant, you mean?'

'Really, Isabel, at times you're very coarse. It's unbecoming in a young girl. I suppose I meant now in particular, but I was thinking in the long term, too. She should be completely taken up with motherhood and making a happy home for Tom, not tearing off to London on business all the time. It's unfeminine, and anyway, it's only until I take over.'

'But if it's unfeminine for her, won't it be the same for you?'

'Of course not, silly, I shan't run things. Heinie will be in charge.'

Isabel had returned to her chair while her sister was speaking, and started on her dinner. Now she put down her fork and stared at Marianne. 'What did you say?'

'Heinie will be in charge. Surely I said it clearly enough the first time?'

'Marianne, you're talking about Richmond's. Our

family company. The firm Papa so wanted to pass on to his son. The firm we inherit instead. You can't give it away to a stranger – a foreigner at that!'

'How dare you? That stranger is my fiancé. He'll be my husband by then. And what difference can it possibly make that he's German?'

'You may think I'm a child, but I'm old enough to read the newspapers. His name appears quite often.'

'Naturally. He's an important international businessman.'

'So are lots of people, but they don't get mentioned the way he does.'

'What are you trying to say?'

'Welcoming the Reichschancellor when he opens a new Burckhardt factory. Taking tea with the Reichschancellor at Berchtesgaden. Photographed at Bayreuth, where he joined Herr Hitler for this year's performance of Wagner's *Ring*. Any minute now there'll be a photograph of him lying down to let the Reichschancellor walk over him. I'm surprised Hitler wasn't invited to dinner at Schloss Adler while you were there.'

It had been no more than angry speculation, but she realised she was right. Marianne looked away, her composure shattered, and muttered, 'What's wrong with that?'

'I know what's wrong with it and I'm only fifteen. Just because the *Daily Mail* keeps saying we mustn't be beastly to that nice Mr Hitler, it doesn't mean we all believe it. He's a warmongering monster. And you intend to hand over our company to one of his biggest supporters.'

'Enough. I don't think I've ever been so insulted! If

Erin and Tom had been here you'd never have dared talk like that.'

'If Erin and Tom had been here, you'd never have dared admit you're handing over Richmond's to that – that Hun! Uncle Tom would have you locked up!'

Marianne's eyes were glittering with tears and temper. 'And we all know why your precious Uncle Tom would do that! It certainly wouldn't be because he wants to save our inheritance for us. For himself, more like!'

'Now you're the one who'd better explain what you mean.'

'Gladly. Tom Moore-Ross would sell his soul to get his hands on Richmond's and never give it back. Why on earth d'you think he married Erin? Because he loved her? Never! Because I turned him down flat and because you were too young to be in the running! Since he couldn't have either of us, he hoped that by marrying her, he could turn things around before we came into control so that he'd be permanently in charge. Well, now it's all over. He won't last ten minutes once Heinie's in the saddle!'

The table seemed to be hurtling up to hit Isabel in the face. She heard a distant clatter as her glass and silver were scattered by her falling body. Then a soft, black, comforting silence enveloped her.

When she came round, Marianne was shaking her and muttering, 'Oh, Bel, Bel, please wake up! I didn't mean it, honestly . . . please, darling . . .'

Isabel shook her head and managed a shaky laugh. 'D-don't worry. No need to fuss. You know it often happens.'

'Not for years now – not since Papa died. And I've

453

brought it on again. Oh, I'm sorry! I should have remembered you're still just a little girl for all your grown-up ways, and not talked to you about such a grim topic.'

'But that's not true, is it, Marianne? You did say it just because you were cross with me? Honestly?'

Marianne stammered and looked past her. 'Said what?'

'You know. About Uncle Tom. He didn't really ask you first?'

Marianne gave an angry little laugh. 'Is that so inconceivable?'

'Please, you know I didn't mean it that way. It's just that he married Erin so soon because they were madly in love. That was why they didn't wait any longer, wasn't it?'

'I expect so. Come on, we're getting you up to bed.'

'No, it's important. I know you think I'm still a baby, but I'm not. Wasn't that why they got married so quickly?'

Marianne's tone was resigned. 'All right, if you insist on knowing. Erin was madly in love, certainly. Tom Moore-Ross wasn't madly in love with anything except Richmond's. He persuaded Erin to say yes while she was still in a bit of a state over Papa because he was afraid she might change her mind about it once she'd got used to being a widow again. Oh, darling Bel, I'm sorry I told you like this, but you were so terribly rude that you made me angry and it just slipped out. I know you think the world of your Uncle Tom and the last thing I want to do is destroy your illusions. Heaven knows, neither of us has been allowed many of them.'

Isabel shook her head. 'It's all right, Marianne. I

should have found out for myself one day, I expect. When did he ask you?'

Marianne was obviously relieved to be able to tell someone at last. 'Oh, it was frightful! All the time Papa was in his last illness, he was trailing around after me like a big bloodhound, saying he was madly in love with me and he couldn't keep silent any more, especially as I was so upset about Papa. I tried to make him stop, but he went on and on. In the end, he was quite . . . indelicate. I know these are the enlightened Thirties, but really! I thought I was going to have to cry for help.'

'Wh-what made him stop?'

'That was the frightful thing. Dr Soames came in to tell me that Papa had just died, and interrupted us – that is, him . . . I made jolly sure he didn't get me alone after that, and then the day after the funeral I wrote him a very stiff note, saying that if he ever dared behave in that manner again, I'd see he lost his job.'

'Oh.'

'Don't you think that was strong enough? I know it sounds a bit milk-and-water now, but I really was very cut up about Papa, and of course it never occurred to me then that he'd go after Erin, otherwise I most certainly would have made sure he never set foot on company property again. Oh dear, why am I worrying you with all this? I've upset you quite enough for one night. Here's Mary – I sent Edwardes for her while you were unconscious – come on, we'll get you up to bed.'

'I'm all right now, really. You know these fainting spells go as quickly as they come.'

'Yes, and I also know that you've had three or four bouts within twenty-four hours in the past. I don't want

455

that happening again. Off with you, now. You can have supper on a tray.'

'Oh, no! I couldn't eat anything.'

'Very well, but bed. And no more nonsense about what we've been discussing. It will all look different tomorrow.'

If only I believed that, Isabel thought as they took her up to her room.

Next morning, while Tom was at Richmond House, Erin returned to her gynaecologist's consulting room. He had taken some X-rays and wished to see her when he had the results. When she emerged an hour later, she was moving like an automaton. Coming down the steps into Harley Street, she ignored the taxi which the receptionist had called for her. She turned left and moved off down the pavement, aware of nothing beyond the need to keep walking. The taxi-driver, taken by surprise, let her go on for a few moments, then pulled along behind her, leaned out of the cab window and said, 'Hey, lady, don't you want me no more?'

Momentarily roused from her stupor, she got in and gave him the Eaton Place address. Nadia Farrar was lunching with her, but Nadia was her oldest friend and probably the one person she could bear to see. She slumped back in the cab and closed her eyes. It seemed to be happening to someone else. Perhaps she could remain detached enough to keep it that way.

But her self-containment lasted only as long as she was alone. The housekeeper had been sent off for a free half-day, having made up a cold luncheon, so that the two women could talk in privacy. When Nadia arrived at

12.45, expecting a couple of hours' light-hearted gossip, Erin opened the front door and collapsed, sobbing, in her arms.

'Darling, what is it? Has something happened to Tom? What on earth is wrong?' She steered Erin back into the drawing room and sat with her on the long leather sofa. 'Pregnant or not, I think you need a big gin and tonic. Wait a tick. I'll mix them – I certainly want one!'

Erin took a swallow from the drink, then blurted out: 'They want to kill my baby!'

'Who does? Who could possibly want to do that?'

'Th-the consultant . . . he says it's the baby or me. Oh, Nadia, what on earth am I to do?' And she started crying again.

Nadia took the drink from her, then embraced her. 'Come on now, my dear, calm down a bit and tell me exactly what happened.'

'I went in this morning for my X-ray results,' she stopped again.

'And there's something wrong with the baby?' Nadia prompted.

Erin shook her head. 'In a way it would be better if there were. No, it's nothing to do with my pregnancy. There – there's a growth of some kind, behind my womb. They can't tell how bad until they open me up to look. B-but it's so big it can't wait until after the baby is born.'

'You're a long way on in your pregnancy. Surely, if they risked waiting just a couple of weeks longer, there would be a good chance of the baby surviving if they did a Caesarean and they wouldn't be leaving it too late to treat you?'

Hope leaped in Erin's eyes. 'D'you really think it might be possible?'

Possible or not, thought Nadia, I'm not letting you suffer without comfort. 'Of course, darling. Remember Jennifer Pearson? She was mid-way through her sixth month and she gave birth prematurely to her baby. He's as healthy as her other two now, and Jennifer's as right as rain. They can't be planning to do anything to you for a fortnight or so, anyway, and you'll be fully seven months by then.'

Erin gave a little shudder. 'Actually he said I should go straight on to the clinic from his consulting room, and have it done tomorrow. I practically had to break out to get away.'

'Oh, I see. Still, if they would wait the fortnight . . .'

Erin nodded. 'What would I do without you, Nadia? I'm quite prepared to do that. I want that baby so much.' She began to cry again.

Nadia squeezed her hand. 'Have your drink, poppet. I'll telephone Tom. Why on earth didn't you ring him from the consultant's office?'

'No – you mustn't! I don't want him to know!'

'Why ever not? He'll have to be told soon, and why are you worried? Tom adores you.'

'I – I don't know. I just want to get it straight in my own mind . . . decide for myself. I couldn't bear to worry him.'

'All right, but I'm staying until he gets back here to take you down to Paxton. I wish you'd tell him, though. You'll have to say something when you go into the clinic two months early.'

'I'll probably tell him before another day has passed. But I need time. Oh, it's all such a mess!'

In the end she made a firm decision to follow Nadia's

458

advice, and telephoned the consultant while her friend was still with her. He was dubious, but reluctantly accepted her proposal in face of her flat refusal to sacrifice her baby for an immediate exploratory operation.

Erin replaced the receiver and managed a smile. 'There, that's settled. I feel better now I've decided. Don't worry about me telling Tom. I'll break it to him tonight when we're safely back at Paxton. Honestly, Nadia, you can leave me alone without worrying. I shall be fine now I've sorted out what to do.'

Reluctantly Nadia took her word for it and left. Half an hour later, Tom came bouncing back into the apartment. 'All ready for the off, darling? I couldn't be bothered to stay at the office any longer. Bloody Ted throwing his weight around and asking for the most obscure information. "Now look here," I said, "you may not want to go home, and I don't blame you with what's waiting for you, but I have a beautiful, blooming bride and I'm off." And hey, presto, here I am!'

Erin managed a small giggle. She did not like Tom's brother much more than he did, and she openly loathed Eleanor Moore-Ross, who was one of the worst snobs in London. 'You really shouldn't bait him, you know. One day he'll make you suffer for it.'

'Have to catch me first, and he's never been as quick as me – that's half his trouble. What did the quack have to say?'

Now, she told herself, go on, it's your golden opportunity, tell him. But something stopped her. She looked away. 'Oh, all terribly vague. He's getting in touch with me in a few more days when they've got some blood tests back.'

'Isn't it marvellous? We pay them enough practically to fund a charity hospital and still they can't give any straight answers. It was a damn sight simpler when women just gave birth behind a bush and then got back to work! Never mind, old girl. In a couple of months you'll be wondering why you ever got so het up.'

'Yes, I'm sure I shall. Come on then, Tom, I'm ready to go home now.'

After that there always seemed to be a good reason not to tell him. With a guilty start, she realised that four days had passed. He was relaxed after two days away from the office. She'd tell him this evening before dinner.

Tom was no churchgoer and Erin usually went to Sunday Evensong alone. Today she lingered there after the service had ended and the other worshippers had departed. It was a tiny medieval parish church, an architectural jewel in a mixture of Norman and Early English styles. It sat in its pretty stone-walled churchyard, drowsing through the days, giving the local people an added sense of security and continuity. Erin had decided long ago that when she died she would be buried here. Sitting there alone in the dusk, with only the lamps and candles lighting the nave, she found tranquillity in spite of what was to happen so soon. Of course she could tell Tom. What on earth had she ever been worried about?

She already knew the answer to that. She had been afraid that when she told him, she would see in his eyes the desire to keep the child and not her. And she found it unbearable to think that he might love her less than she loved him. How absurd! She knew he adored her. She was facing the unknown alone because she did not quite trust his love. Well, it was about time she started doing so.

He was usually in the library at this time of the evening, having a quiet drink before dinner. She looked in. One lamp burned beside his favourite chair, and the fire crackled hospitably, but there was no sign of Tom. Erin checked the drawing room, then went upstairs to change. He was probably still dressing for dinner. But he was not in their suite, either. He couldn't be out – their nearest neighbours were beyond easy walking distance and his Bentley had been in the garage beside the Silver Ghost when she drove back in from church. Unless he was down in the gun room, he must be keeping Isabel company in her sitting room over in the nursery wing . . .

Erin's composure slipped slightly. And why shouldn't he be there? The girl was his stepdaughter, after all, and they were very close. Yes, very, very close, said that nagging little voice in her head that had been silent since her pregnancy started. So close that you had to join in their jolly little games and pretend you enjoyed it, just in case you left yourself time to think and got jealous of your own stepdaughter.

'This is stupid!' she said aloud, trying to be exasperated with herself and failing. The nursery wing was a bit of a walk now that she was so encumbered, but it was worth the effort just to set her mind at rest. She must cure herself of this petty obsession.

She was out of breath when she reached the top landing of the nursery wing. She stood at the stair head, holding the newel post and composing herself. Yes, Tom was here. She could hear his laugh faintly, somewhere

461

ahead. The landing was dimly-lit and the stronger light in Isabel's sitting room made a brighter splash which spilled out under the closed door. But it wasn't the sitting room . . . Erin realised as she drew level that this was the outer door of Isabel's bedroom, located there to give the maid direct access in the morning instead of the more indirect entry through the sitting room.

Of course, that explains everything, Erin told herself with forced brightness. Isabel must be out of sorts again and Tom's up here entertaining her. I expect she's not feeling well enough to come down to dinner . . . Almost of its own volition, her hand crept out and turned the door handle. Why was she moving so stealthily? There was no need to be secretive.

Then the door was open and there was no longer any room for pretence, in her own mind or in their behaviour. Isabel, her glorious hair loose, was sprawling naked across the bed. Tom, half dressed, was embracing her with a familiarity that spoke of habit. As Erin stood there, transfixed, Isabel looked up, saw her and froze. Tom turned, very slowly, and gazed at his wife, the lascivious smile still pasted crookedly on his face. Erin turned and ran.

# Chapter Twenty

Practicality had always been Erin's salvation. In the awful days after Oliver had been reported missing, believed killed, she had organised transport for isolated country people, had worked as a volunteer nurse in the local convalescent hospital for wounded officers, and had filled the blank spaces with everything from knitting baby clothes for the poor to rolling bandages for the Front. It had little to do with philanthropy and everything to do with survival. Now the same instinct served her again.

She came through the first storm of weeping in her headlong dash back down from the nursery wing. By the time she reached the library she was already in control again. In all fairness, she could not even hate Isabel. Go on, her inner self told her, you'll feel better if you do. But she suppressed the base instinct and forced herself to think constructively. Isabel was still a child. Tom Moore-Ross was a dazzlingly attractive man – she knew, she was hopelessly in love with him, even after what she had just seen. And she had behaved as though she approved their closeness in the past – all that complicity with his flirtatiousness which amounted almost to abetting a sexual assault if she considered it rationally.

No wonder poor little Isabel had succumbed in the end.

It was unbearable to contemplate keeping the child here at Paxton at present – or sending her to the London apartment, for that matter. Anyway, one couldn't cast a fifteen-year-old loose, unsupervised, in London. The important thing was to get her away, beyond Tom's reach, and then to put the whole thing behind her and concentrate on how she would deal with the matter of her own health problems.

That was when she thought of Marianne. She had stayed on for two days at Paxton after her quarrel and reconciliation with Isabel. In her undemonstrative way she was very fond of Erin, and she was the only one who had sensed something was wrong when her stepmother returned to Paxton after her visit to the consultant.

Before leaving on Saturday morning, she had said: 'I think you should be resting away from everyone except Tom, not taking on anything that will worry you. Why don't you get right away for a while?'

Erin had laughed, putting her arms around Marianne and kissing her in gratitude for the considerate suggestion. 'Out of the question, darling! Where could I go? There are so many people who want me to do little things . . . I can hardly blame them if the million little things all add up to one huge call on my time, can I?'

But Marianne refused to be mollified. 'Really, Erin, you know you're supposed to be cossetted, and you're anything but that. I know precisely where you'd go if you had the sense you were born with – and you wouldn't come back until the week the baby was due.'

'And where is this Shangri-La?'

'My mother's house in North Wales. I always had

464

plans to stay there myself but they never seemed to materialise. Mother had painful memories from her days there, so she hadn't really stayed in Bangor since the turn of the century. But it's a lovely place and I never could nerve myself to sell it. It just sits there, waiting for an occupant apart from the housekeeper. I don't think you ever went there, so there's not even any question of unhappy associations from Father's time.'

Erin was staring at her, touched to find the girl had deeper sensibilities than she had realised, and grateful that such tender feelings were directed towards her own welfare.

'You're very sweet, my darling, I almost wish I could.'

'You can. Pack a bag, get into the Bentley with Tom and go. You'll be there by this evening. It's hardly as if Richmond's would crumble without the physical presence of either of you for the next eight weeks or so.'

Erin could not tell her the awful medical secret which made the suggestion no more than an impossible dream. Instead, she made a couple of lame excuses about consulting her London physician at frequent intervals, then made a fuss of Marianne for her kind offer. In the end, Marianne departed for London, still reproachfully saying the house was at her stepmother's disposal should the need arise.

Well, it's arisen now with a vengeance, thought Erin. And oddly enough, Marianne is about the only person I know who will have a glimmer of understanding about getting Isabel away from Tom, but won't ask me lots of horrid questions. She went to telephone Marianne's London apartment.

Her stepdaughter understood without the need for

more than a minimal explanation. Had she been in better health, Erin might have paused to wonder how Marianne could have developed such infallible intuition about the problems of having Tom and Isabel together under one roof. But now she let it pass. She had far more immediate worries.

'Heinrich is away on business,' Marianne told her, 'so I have plenty of free time this week. You leave it all to me. I'll drive down tomorrow and take Isabel to Bangor myself, in your car, if you can spare the Rolls-Royce and Dawkins for a few days. I shall take her to Tan-yr-Allt, arrange for a car and driver to be available while she's up there, and come back when she's settled in.'

Erin felt the first stirrings of hope. Maybe this wasn't going to be the end of the world after all. 'Oh, Marianne, you're being so kind. Perhaps I should tell you . . .'

'No need to say anything. I think I understand the problem. Don't think about it again. You manage this evening, and after that you can concentrate on having your baby and getting over it in peace.'

She hung up and left Erin with a new problem. After what she had learned this evening, what was she to do about the caesarean operation and her own dangerous physical condition? She no longer felt certain enough of Tom to discuss it with him. 'I'll just have to wait and see . . .' she whispered. But deep inside she already knew what she would do.

It was a frosty journey. Isabel squeezed herself into the far corner of the passenger seat and Marianne sat rigidly upright on the other side. Isabel had been almost totally isolated since the previous evening. Unable to face her with equanimity, Erin had pleaded illness and stayed in her suite. Mrs Ashley, her governess, had brought the news to Isabel that she was to be sent away.

'B – but what can I do in a place like that? It's practically the end of the earth!'

'Now, Isabel, don't exaggerate. It's just a few hours from here. You'll be going up with Miss Marianne to keep you company and when she comes back, I shall be ready to join you. We'll just go on as we do down here.'

Isabel's resentment flashed out at her. 'Of course we shan't! What shall I do without Robin and George and the Knollys girls and the Beynons? And – Uncle Tom? I shall die if I don't see Uncle Tom!' She started to cry.

Kate Ashley sniffed. 'If you ask me, it's seeing so much of your Uncle Tom that's led to this trouble. And I don't blame Madam for deciding it's time you went to the country, either. Far too much monkey business there for decency's sake.'

'You've been spying on me!'

If Isabel had expected shamefaced denials, she was disappointed. Mrs Ashley burst out laughing. 'God bless us! If I'd been spying on you, dear girl, I'd have a far better idea of what's going on around here. As it is, I'm only guessing. Looking at your face now, though, I'd say I was guessing right. Perhaps Madam is regretting giving me those rooms in the main house instead of adjoining yours where they should have been.'

'If you're going to start spying on me now, Kate Ashley, I – I shall starve myself to death, that's what I'll do!'

Her governess merely laughed again. 'You're the wrong sort to fade away, Isabel. You might fling yourself off a cliff in a fit of pique, but starving would be far too slow for you. You'd lose interest and start eating again long before you reached crisis point.'

'Oh, leave me alone! I hate you!' Her charge turned away and glared mutinously out of the window. Mrs Ashley shrugged. She had seen Isabel get this annoyed about all sorts of things in the past. This mood would play itself out like all the others.

Marianne was not so sure. She had been concerned for a long time that Tom Moore-Ross might renew his pursuit of Isabel, although she had hoped her own revelations last week might make the younger girl cautious. Clearly they had not. Now she watched her sister secretly and realised that she had suffered some deep hurt since their last meeting. Marianne's own emotional balance was not sufficiently sure to permit her to volunteer as Isabel's confidante, but she could see the girl needed one. She sighed and turned to look out at the scenery. The world would be a better place without people like Tom Moore-Ross.

When they arrived at Bangor, Isabel was impressed with Tan-yr-Allt in spite of herself. On the first floor, she rushed to the big window which looked down across the lawns and the Straits from the master bedroom. 'What a view! Talk about charmed magic casements! Oh, Marianne, it's beautiful! How could your mother ever bear to leave it?'

Marianne was slightly troubled by a memory. 'I've often wondered. I know she spent lots of time here in the early days of her marriage – Papa's grandmother gave it to her, you know. It had been in the family for ages. Her first husband, Papa's elder brother, died here, but I don't think that had anything to do with it. I remember once when I was very young, Papa was trying to persuade her to come here for a few weeks one summer. At first she simply refused to discuss it with him, but he kept on about it and in the end she turned on him and said, "I detest it! Tan-yr-Allt is accursed for the Richmonds!" I can remember it so clearly because I was so young I didn't know that Tan-yr-Allt was the name of the house and I spent hours trying to work out what a Tan-yr-Allt was. Isn't that silly? I never did find out why Mama had suddenly gone off the place, though.'

Isabel was staring at her in wonder. 'You remember that and you've never been curious about why the Richmonds were accursed here? I'd have been unable to think of anything else.'

'Of course – that's so typical of you, Isabel! Always off on some imaginative wild goose chase instead of facing up to reality. I've never speculated about it because there was nothing worthy of my curiosity. The most obvious explanation is that something unpleasant probably happened to our great-grandmother here, then her elder grandson died here, and I suspect that Mother had one or more of her miscarriages here. You know she had several before I was born. That would have been enough to put her off, and a few earlier family tragedies would have given her the excuse to think the place itself was responsible. After all, no woman wants to blame herself for a string of miscarriages.'

'How dull! I don't want to live in a commonplace world like that. I want fairy princesses and handsome princes and fiery dragons, and – and . . .'

Marianne interrupted. 'Even when you day-dream, you forget that all worlds have a black side. If you have fairies and princes and dragons, you have to have wicked witches and evil wizards, too. Your magic world and my ordinary one both have fearsome things in them, only you won't admit it.'

Isabel tossed her head. 'Maybe I know better than you about that.'

'What d'you mean?'

'I know you were dreadfully unhappy because of Papa and my mother, and you and your mother being sent away, but in some ways that was better for you. There were some things you never had to see . . . or hear.'

Marianne was getting angry. The hurt of her banishment from her father as a child never diminished. 'Don't start saying he was beastly to you, because I shan't believe it.'

Isabel remained unruffled, but looked deeply sad. 'I don't mean that. He was no nastier to me than he was to you. It's just that being away at school, then at Mapledurham, you didn't hear . . .'

'Hear what?'

In a rush, Isabel said: 'He locked Kitt up, you know, for weeks.'

'Isabel, this is absurd! What are you saying?'

'Please believe me, Marianne. I've never told anyone else . . . couldn't.'

'Well, I certainly don't want to hear your wild imaginings!'

'It's not imagination, and I have to tell someone – oh, please listen! All this upset has brought it back and I can't bear it if you just leave me without anyone to tell!'

She had been growing agitated as she spoke and finally the intensity of her distress broke through Marianne's reserve. She sighed. 'Very well. If you feel you must. What was it?'

'We were living at Stoke Winyates. I was awfully young, so I suppose they thought I wouldn't notice that Kitt wasn't about any more. But I did. I liked her because she wore those wonderful clothes and she always came and did a sort of little fashion parade of them for me, and let me play with that long string of pearls Papa had bought her.'

'Flighty little creature! She never wore anything under those frocks and they were so short it was positively indecent!'

'Oh, Marianne, she looked marvellous . . . Anyway, I certainly did miss her. But no one would tell me where she'd gone.'

'Of course not. She ran off with a man. Who would tell a little girl that?'

'That's what I'm trying to tell you! She didn't. Papa had her locked up in Stoke Winyates.'

'Isabel, normally I don't mind your flights of fancy, but this one is downright wicked. I can't allow you to slander our father!'

'I'm not, honestly. I asked about Kitt one day after I hadn't seen her for a week or more. My nanny said she was away on holiday, but she made eyes at the governess as she said it. Stoke Winyates was a funny old house. In some places the walls were so thick you could have been next door to a battle and not heard it. In others, it was just wattle and daub and the sound carried perfectly from floor to floor. A day or two after they'd said Kitt was away, I woke up from my afternoon sleep and I heard her singing. I thought, Oh, good, she's back, and got up and went out into the corridor to find her. Only she wasn't there. I ran over to the window that looked down into the enclosed courtyard and there she was, walking along with a big burly man and chatting to him. I was just going down to join her when Nanny came out of the day nursery and got really cross with me and pushed me back to bed. She swore nobody was down there and said I had no business looking out when I should be asleep.'

'That doesn't make sense. Kitt would hardly have returned after she ran off. You know Papa's temper as well as I do. He would have taken her apart.'

Isabel looked quite desperate now. 'That's what I'm trying to tell you. There's more. I knew I'd really seen her and I was so puzzled it kept worrying me. Two nights later it was very mild, but the heating was up high. I woke up and I was too hot to go back to sleep. In the end I thought I'd go over to the long gallery. D'you remember it? There were huge windows down the whole length of it and it was the coolest place in the house.'

Marianne nodded silently, captivated now in spite of her previous incredulity.

'It was all flooded with moonlight and deliciously cool. I came into it from the hall end, above the main staircase. At the far end it connected with a wide corridor that ran the length of the house, with Papa's suite off to the left and the guest wing to the right. The guest wing had one odd suite with its own staircase and outer door to the central courtyard. It must have had some special use before he modernised the old manor. All of a sudden I heard a woman sobbing.'

She gave a little mirthless laugh. 'The funny thing is, if that happened to me now, I'd be convinced I was hearing a ghost and I'd run away. At that age, though, I was just curious about who was crying. It was Kitt.'

Marianne wanted to insist that Isabel was inventing the story, but there was a terrible sincerity in her sister's tone. 'A moment after I heard the first cry, she dashed into the long gallery from the guest corridor, making for the master suite corridor and calling Papa's name. Suddenly this big man – probably the one who'd been talking to her in the courtyard – came rushing after her and caught hold of her. You know she was quite small, but she fought like a mad thing. Then she started screaming, "Harry, Harry, please save me! Please don't let him take me!" and the man started dragging her away, back towards the guest suite corridor. She was still shrieking her head off and fighting like mad. And then there was a really ghastly silence. Papa was there. You remember the funny way he used to stand when his leg was first giving him trouble, a sort of straddle, as if he was bracing himself to push up a huge weight? Well, he was standing like that and wearing his silk brocade dressing gown, so he looked even bigger than usual. Kitt looked like a little child next to him. She was wearing a filmy white nightie and no dressing-gown or slippers.

'When she saw him she broke loose from the man and threw herself down in front of Papa. She actually grasped hold of his ankles . . .'

'What did he do?'

'Nothing. It was as if he were made of stone. He just went on standing there, staring down at her, and she sobbed and pleaded and pawed at his feet. Finally he raised his head and just said to the man, "I told you to get rid of her quietly." Then he kicked her hands away from his legs and turned away.'

'And then?'

'That was the worst bit. The big man just bent down and grabbed her arm and started dragging her away as if she were a sack of potatoes. She was crying and screaming for Papa still, and then the man stopped and hit her, once, very hard. Then there was no more noise. He picked her up and carried her off down the guest suite corridor. I'd pressed myself flat up against the wall between two of the windows and the heavy velvet curtains hid me from them. As soon as the man went off with Kitt, I ran on tiptoe down to the end of the gallery and looked after them.

'He was just taking her into the suite with the courtyard staircase. I didn't dare go after them, but I came back and went to the first window on the long gallery, because it looks down into the courtyard. The man got Kitt down the stairs and half carried, half walked her across the yard. She seemed to have come round enough to stagger along with him. He opened a door at the far side of the courtyard and they went through. I never saw her again.'

Marianne sought helplessly for appropriate words. All she managed to say was, 'Didn't anybody say anything?'

Isabel shook her head. 'Even with the funny acoustics in the house, Nanny and the nursemaid must have heard. Kitt was shrieking so hard I wouldn't have been surprised if they'd heard her in the servants' quarters, but they'd have been too far off to see anything. I expect Nanny had gone into my bedroom when she realised I couldn't possibly have slept through it all, and of course I wasn't there. I was still standing staring out of the window when she found me. She had a quick look out, but they'd gone by then. It was so strange: she didn't say a word, just took my hand and led me back to nursery. I was so terrified I didn't try to resist.

'When we got there, she put me to bed and got in with me – she'd always done that when I was really little and woke up crying for Mama. She put her arms around me and started stroking my hair and I started crying. I went on and on and she stroked my hair and said "There, there", until I cried myself to sleep. In the morning it was all over.'

'All over? It can't have been! They couldn't dismiss something like that!'

'I don't suppose they did, but I wasn't in on whatever happened next.'

'But what did they tell you?'

Again the mirthless little laugh. 'When I asked Nanny, she said I must have been having an awful nightmare, because she'd found me sleepwalking in the long gallery and led me back to my room. Said perhaps I should stay in bed late that morning to make up for the lost rest.'

Marianne tried to restore an everyday conversational tone and failed. 'Surely it could have been just what they said?'

'No doubt that was why they got rid of Nanny, the nursery maid and the governess.'

'They can't have!'

'Really, Marianne, not even you can believe I imagined that! One week there I was at Stoke Winyates with Nanny Murrenger, Nelly Hammond and Miss Pike. The next, we'd moved to Paxton and Kate Ashley took over as nursery governess. There never was a new nanny and they gave us a housemaid for the nursery floor instead of hiring a new nursemaid. Papa was so meticulous with household staff records that you have only to look up the lists for Stoke Winyates in 1928 and Paxton in 1929 to confirm the change.'

'No, I believe you. What happened about the other servants?'

'You don't remember Stoke at all well, do you?'

'Are you surprised? I was completely shut out. Mother had died and I was all alone in that great echoing barn at Mapledurham. It didn't help to know that Papa was up at Stoke Winyates in the bosom of his various new families, indulging you, and revelling in his pretty young wife. I never thought about it unless I had to, and the few times I came there at Christmas or for a holiday, I got away as quickly as I could.'

'I really am sorry about that. I wasn't having the wonderful time you've always imagined. He usually ignored my existence. I was too much of a reminder that he didn't have a legitimate son, for one thing, and for another he liked to think of himself as a dashing young hero, not an elderly man with a half-grown family. I was a sort of live doll for poor Kitt to play with when she was feeling bored. But that's not what I was thinking of. I meant, you probably never noticed how far off the servants were in the manor.'

'That's right; now I'm beginning to remember. They lived in some sort of outbuildings, didn't they?'

'I'd hardly call the Clock House that. It was put up as a hostel for servants a generation or so after the main house was built. Over the years it had been modernised each time the manor was done up, and by the time Papa bought Stoke Winyates, some of the senior servants has self-contained flats there. Only the younger staff had to share and even then, the accommodation was far better than most servants' quarters.'

'I'll take your word for it, but what has this got to do with that business over Kitt?'

'Isn't it obvious? The Clock House was away on its own to the south-east of the main house. The small courtyard was bounded by the north wing and the long gallery down its west side. To the east, the main bulk of the house cut it off from the Clock House. Apart from the nursery staff, only Papa's valet lived in the main house. The only other people likely to have heard or seen anything were the gamekeepers, assuming they were out that night close to the house. Usually they were miles off across the park. Even so, when we left Stoke Winyates, we left the entire staff of servants behind. Apparently the new owners employed them.'

'Including the valet and the nursery staff?'

'Marianne, I know lots of people from this country emigrate to Australia now times are so hard in England, but how easy d'you find it to believe that my nanny, nurserymaid, governess and Father's valet all went off within a few weeks of each other?'

'You're making it up!'

'Honestly, no. Nanny didn't go to Australia, but she might as well have done. She went off to join her grown-up son in Canada. The others all went to Australia. I asked Erin why Papa had changed valets and she said that Richardson had gone to New South Wales. Kate

Ashley had no idea about that, and when I asked if she knew what had happened to my old governess and nurserymaid, she said wasn't it a coincidence, they'd both gone to Australia, because the governess had told the maid what good opportunities there were for self-improvement.'

'Who else knows about this?'

'I told you, nobody. Papa knew Erin then – she'd been working for him for ages. But she didn't know anything very much about our home life until a year or so after they got married. She only knew about Richardson because she'd known how close he was to Papa. Remember, Papa never travelled anywhere without him after he started to get ill in the early twenties. He told Erin that Richardson had always wanted to go abroad and had come to him with a recommendation for his own successor, the man who ended up staying with Papa until he died. I don't expect Erin ever thought about the nursery staff.'

'Are you sure she'd never chattered to anyone about the complete change in domestic arrangements after Kitt's . . . er . . . accident?'

'Who would she tell? Who'd be interested in the little details of our private life?'

'Tom Moore-Ross for one. He always had an insatiable curiosity about everything that went on in Stoke Winyates – and Mapledurham and Paxton.'

'What are you suggesting? Tom never had anything but our family interests at heart!'

'If you believe that, Isabel, you still believe in fairy tales!'

'Why d'you think Tom would take advantage?'

'Because that's the way he is, you silly little girl! Remember what I said at Paxton the night of our quarrel? He wanted to get his hands on one of us but Erin was the closest he could get. What you've just told me frightens the life out of me. I wish I didn't believe it, but I do. All those servants going off like that . . . Papa must have bought them off. If Erin knew more than you think and accidentally let it slip to Tom, he'd use it against us for the rest of his days.'

'No, Marianne, you're wrong – you must be, he's not like that at all!'

'That's enough. I won't ask you what happened to make Erin send you here, but I have a fair idea. I've never seen her look so frightened and unhappy. I'm not blaming you. You're still a child, even if you look and sound grown up. It's that man. He's wicked. And now you've told me about Stoke Winyates, I'm terrified in case he knows something.'

Her tacit reference to the reason for Isabel's banishment momentarily turned the girl away from her spirited defence of Moore-Ross. The memory of poor Erin's stricken face swept back and Isabel blushed with shame. Marianne was speaking again and Isabel wrenched her attention back from her own guilty thoughts.

'Knowing Papa, I don't suppose there are any loose ends lying around. He was far too careful to make any mistakes.'

'He seems to have made a real beauty in marrying Kitt!'

'Stop talking like that! You should know well enough that love is blind. What worries me is that whoever was involved in it with him must still be at liberty. He can hardly have bribed *them* to go to Australia.'

'You mean the burly man?'

'And whoever lured Fenwick to join Kitt. If we accept that you really did see her being held prisoner, we also have to face the probability that Papa had her and Fenwick killed.' Isabel tried to protest but now she had accepted the story, Marianne pursued it to its logical conclusion. 'Someone must have helped Papa. Who came to the house in those days, apart from associates from the company? I can't remember when he dropped the horsey set.'

'He was seeing less of them by then, because his leg had stopped him doing so much riding. It mostly seemed to be business people . . . oh, and Ann Kleber, of course.'

'But Ann never even came to England with him. She was just one of his American crowd.'

'No. Erin said she often came to see him in England when she was over on business. It's hard to remember clearly because I was a bit young, but I think it was after he and Kitt started having rows.'

'Odd, isn't? Hardly the ideal guest for a couple with problems. You'd think that would be the very time he'd keep women friends at arm's length.'

'She came only a couple of times, as far as I know, and that was when Kitt was already flitting around up in London and making Papa so miserable. I suppose she realised how bad he felt and popped down to cheer him up.'

Suddenly Marianne wanted no more of the discussion. 'This will get us nowhere. Forget it, Isabel, it's best for everyone. If the only witnesses we know of are safely on the other side of the world, it's the end of the story. Poor Papa.'

'Poor Papa? What about poor Kitt? She was only twenty-five when she died, younger than you are now. She never really lived, and you're sorry for Papa!'

Marianne's tone was poisonous. 'Whose fault was that? She saw what she wanted and she went after it. She wasn't too young to be a little gold-digger. He adored her – all she had to do was keep her side of the bargain. She didn't even have to love him, as long as she said she did. He was far too besotted to notice her insincerity. But she was incapable even of honouring her promise. Running around with his own employees! Imagine what it did to his reputation with the staff at Richmond's. Whatever happened to her, she got what she deserved.'

'Really? Just like that! Good old innocent Papa. And what about all the other women? Your mother, and mine, and his mistresses, and poor Erin, just wanting to live her own life and instead being emotionally blackmailed into marrying him to comfort his dying days! Face it, Marianne, our father was a monster. Perhaps Kitt Arundell was exactly what he deserved. Whether she was or not, she certainly paid for her fun!'

Isabel's temper was quite beyond control now. Marianne was angry, too, but a lifetime's self-discipline had taught her to hold herself in check. She was affronted by the depth of bitterness Isabel was showing against their father, but could not find it in her heart to blame her. The outburst had taken her by surprise, but now as she reflected on what must have happened to her half-sister recently, she realised that this lashing out was merely a symptom of the girl's impotence to deal with her more immediate misery. Marianne made a great effort to stay calm, reached forward and clasped Isabel's hands.

481

'Now listen, this has gone quite far enough. I understand more than you think. All this – and your other trouble – must stay secret between the two of us. I shall certainly never mention it to anyone else. I want you to go to bed, get a good night's rest, and then tomorrow you can start afresh. In a week or two you'll wonder why you were ever in such a state.'

Isabel flung herself against Marianne and sobbed as though her heart would break. 'Oh, Marianne, I'm so afraid he's made us into monsters, too! I loved him so much, but he didn't love us at all, and it's so terrible knowing there are secret things about him . . . There can't be any more, can there?'

'No, of course not. This one was just a terrible thing he did under unbearable provocation. Try to remember the good things about him.'

'I do, but this blots it all out!'

'In the end, he realised he loved us. He'd never have left the business to us if he hadn't.' As she said it, Marianne hoped Isabel was too far gone to follow that one up. It would not bear much scrutiny.

She need not have worried. The events of the past few days had defeated Isabel. She nodded miserably. 'Yes, I suppose so. When you think how important it was to him, it must mean he thought something of us.'

Marianne kissed her gently and said goodnight. How did you tell a distressed fifteen-year-old that she was an heiress only because her father could find no other heir?


The sisters stayed together at Tan-yr-Allt for three days, then Marianne began getting restless. 'Heinie is due back in a couple of days,' she said on the fourth morning. 'As

Mrs Ashley is coming up tomorrow evening and you're already so much better, would you mind if I left in the morning?'

'No, of course not. You go. It's kind of you to have spent this much time with me.' In truth, Isabel was growing bored with Marianne. Although the older woman's intentions were good, she had a pedestrian mind and lacked any trace of humour. Once their initial stormy confidences were over, life rapidly became dull. Isabel was looking forward to the arrival of her quick-witted governess, with whom she had much more in common. A day on her own while she waited would be a welcome diversion. She might even go off alone and explore. 'Perhaps you'd prefer to leave today, Marianne. Now you've got me a car, I shan't be marooned. If you started after lunch, you'd be back in London well before midnight.'

'I couldn't leave you at such short notice . . .' But Marianne's voice betrayed her anxiety to be gone. She was no more comfortable with Isabel than Isabel was with her.

'Nonsense. You said yourself that I'm already a lot better than on that first night. There's plenty to keep me occupied until Kate arrives, and once she's here it will be work, work, work all the time.'

'If you're sure . . . It would give me the chance to do some shopping before Heinrich gets back.'

So the sisters parted, with few regrets but with the new bond of a shared secret. As the Rolls-Royce disappeared down the drive, Isabel uttered a sigh of relief and went back indoors. She suspected that Marianne never unbent even when she was completely alone. If only there had been that little extra something in their relationship, she would have been able to confide in her about Tom. Isabel had no idea what she should do, but she knew she needed some advice. Not that Marianne could have given her any. Although she was already in her thirties, she was less worldly than Isabel herself.

Isabel was standing beside the mantelshelf in the dining room, absent-mindedly looking at a painting which hung above it. Suddenly she had a mental picture of Marianne's reaction if it had been she and not poor Erin who had caught her with Tom the other night. The mere thought provoked a whoop of nervous laughter and Isabel smacked the wall with the flat of her hand. Her blow released the catch in the old panelled cupboard. It swung open, silently revealing the secret which Marianne's mother had consigned to oblivion more than thirty years before.

# Chapter Twenty-One

Tom Moore-Ross was shaving and practising arrogant expressions in his bathroom mirror. It was an up-hill task maintaining his confidence in front of Erin these days. Silly cow! Why did she have to pry into places where she had no business? If she'd just stuck to her part of the house, she'd never have walked in on him with Isabel and she'd still be as happy as a lark. It wasn't as if it had meant anything. She hadn't been so stand-offish about it before . . .

He wondered how long she could keep up her air of martyrdom. Good God, plenty of other married men had little flings, particularly when their wives were pregnant. There was nothing so terrible about it. But it seemed to have knocked the stuffing out of old Erin. She'd been looking really rough ever since that Sunday. No, wait a minute, since before then. Perhaps she really wasn't well and that's why she was taking things to heart so. But surely she'd have told him if there were complications?

Tom washed away the last of the lather and dried his face. It was nearly a month now since Erin had sent Bel away. Since then she had virtually turned into a recluse, saying it would be better if he stayed in London during the week to be near the office, and leaving her to get plenty of rest down in the country. Okay, so she had a right to make him feel shamefaced. But a whole month? The novelty of this temporary return to bachelor status had worn off quickly. He had become accustomed to Erin's uncritical adoration. She was intelligent and well-educated, too, and her conversation never failed to entertain him. Back in London, he had taken out a couple of good-looking girls with alluring bodies and empty minds and had discovered he had lost his taste for them. Unfortunately his attempts to persuade Erin that she needed him back at Paxton all the time, not merely at week-ends, were rejected coldly. He was amazed at her determination. He had no way of knowing she was keeping him at arm's length because her physical condition was now deteriorating so rapidly that he would have noticed it if he had spent any more time with her.

Tom went back into his bedroom and looked at the clock. God, it was barely eight o'clock! If he went on like this he'd get a reputation at the office. He'd been first to arrive and last to leave at least four times in the past fortnight – a circumstance which had been unknown before this separation from Erin. He was not enthusiastic about becoming a byword for industry. He liked to be thought of as the slightly louche but talented younger brother of the grey power broker who ran Richmond's on behalf of Harry's heirs. Still, even being at the office early was better than sitting here alone staring at the carpet. He put on his jacket, adjusted his plain gold cufflinks and prepared to leave. As he reached the front door the telephone rang. Mrs Jackson, the housekeeper, came out of the kitchen and answered it.

'It's for you, sir. Mrs Moore-Ross's maid.'

'Betty? Why on earth would she want talk to me at this time of the morning?'

'I've no idea, sir, but she says it's urgent.'

Tom took the receiver from her. 'Yes, Betty. What's all this about, then?'

The maid was crying. 'I-it's Madam, Mr Tom. She said not to tell you, but, oh, sir, something's got to be done. I think she's going to die . . .' Her sobs blotted out whatever else she had intended to say.

Tom stared at the telephone as if it held the solution to this new mystery. 'Dying – what d'you mean dying? Why don't I know about this?' Pull yourself together, you fool, he thought, you sound like a bloody parrot. He knew why he felt so defensive. His immediate fear had been that Erin had attempted suicide. He forced himself to calm down. 'Now, Betty, take it easy and tell me what this is all about. I wasn't aware my wife was even ill, and I saw her three days ago.'

'I know, Mr Tom. That's why she insisted on you staying in London – so you wouldn't know how bad she was. She can keep up the pretence for a day or two, but no longer.'

Pretence of what, you stupid bitch, he wanted to yell, but he managed to control the impulse. 'Why is she so bad, Betty?' He could hear the hysteria in his own voice.

'I p-promised I wouldn't let on to no one, sir, but I've got to tell you now. The doctor told her weeks ago that she mustn't have the baby because she had a growth. She was to have an operation straight away and she'd lose it, but she had a chance of being all right. She said to me, "Betty, I've thought it over and I just can't take my

487

baby's life. i'll risk it. Doctors have been wrong before.''
But they're not wrong this time, Mr Tom – she's ever so
bad, sir.'

'When was this?'

'Just now, sir. She'd been in bed ever since you went
back to –'

'No, you damned fool, how long has she known?'

'Oh, er, let me see . . . yes, I remember now. It must
have been two or three days before Miss Isabel went off
to Bangor, because she told me then she was sending her
away so she wouldn't know about it, in case it made her
scared when she was ready to become a mother. But Mr
Tom, don't ask about that now. I must get back to her.
I've called the doctor and she'll be that angry when she
knows.'

'Yes, Betty, of course . . . you go back to her. I'll
come straight down.'

'I wouldn't if I was you, Mr Tom. I think I know what
the doctor'll do. He'll whisk her straight off to London.
I was going to suggest that I might ask him to ring you
when I've told him about the situation down here.'

'Right. Good thinking. I'll wait here. You go to your
mistress now. And – er – tell her I'm thinking about her
if she comes round.'

'Yes, sir, of course . . . I must go to her now. Goodbye, Mr Tom.'

Tom Moore-Ross had been brought up by a rigidly
Calvinist father with a total belief in hellfire. Tom had
rejected the religion as soon as he was in his teens, but
beneath the cynical surface he was still convinced that
the Devil got the wicked. He knew he had more to fear on
that score than many other men. Now he shuddered as he

thought of the week-end when Erin had caught him with Isabel. Reluctantly, he recalled that Erin had made several attempts to tell him something just before that. It had been irritating, the way she kept starting and stopping, and in the end he had shouted at her to spit it out or shut up. He had been meaning to apologise for his coarseness later, but by then she had discovered him in bed with his stepdaughter.

He wandered into the drawing-room and opened the drinks cupboard. This was one early morning when coffee just wouldn't do.

Half an hour later Erin's gynaecologist rang. 'Moore-Ross? I simply can't understand why you had no notion of your wife's condition. You must have noticed something, surely?'

Tom was sulky. 'How could I? She chose not to tell me.'

'Good God, man, she shouldn't have had to! Married less than a year and you don't look at her often enough to see the obvious deterioration in her health?' Alisdair Heaton paused, allowing the silence to give his remarks the required significance.

'All right, so I'm a rotter. More to the point, what's happening now? Are you with her?'

'No, I've got her GP down there. It was quicker than making her wait until I could drive down to Paxton. He's examined her and we've discussed it. She's in an ambulance now, on her way to the London Clinic. I plan to operate as soon as she gets there, so if I were you I'd come along as soon as possible. She'll be in no state to sign the consent forms herself.'

'What about the baby?'

'You might as well forget all about that. Just pray you're not a widower by this time tomorrow.' Heaton hung up on him.

Tom swore. 'I could get you struck off for treating me like that, you arrogant bastard,' he murmured. But it was pure bluster. Heaton must find it incredible that a newly-married man had failed to notice his wife fading away before his eyes. Tom swallowed his drink and once again prepared to leave. 'Mrs Jackson, if anyone calls I'm at the London Clinic until further notice. The number and the consultant's name are on the pad. Mrs Moore-Ross is seriously ill.' He slammed the door behind him before she could respond and felt a savage satisfaction at leaving her ignorant of what was happening.

The abdominal growth had been only one of a host of secondary tumours all over Erin's body. The others had remained concealed because the routine pregnancy X-rays had concentrated on her womb. She was delirious as she lay on the trolley awaiting surgery, the pre-med sedatives making her garrulous. As Tom arrived outside he could hear her talking rapidly in a high, uncontrolled voice. 'All of them . . . they're all against me . . . all plotting! Isabel, you're the worst! What did I ever do to deserve it? Tell me – I was always good to you, wasn't I? Why you . . . Oh God, how could you?' She became incoherent. Tom felt the sweat on his forehead and was grateful she had lost consciousness. Heaven knew what she might have said next.

She died under the anaesthetic. Heaton was surprised she had lasted so long. Some people seemed to survive through sheer strength of will. Pity about the swine of a husband. From what he'd seen of Erin Moore-Ross, she had deserved a lot better.

Tom exploited to the full the dramatic possibilities of his sudden widowhood. He left the hospital early that evening, his tie loosened, his hair ruffled, and refused all offers of transport back to Paxton. He drove himself at breakneck speed in the Bentley, occasionally indulging in a fit of weeping. Back at the house he locked himself in the suite he and Erin had shared, and went through the cupboards and drawers, touching her clothes, sniffing her scent bottles and weeping again over her ornaments and jewellery.

Then he saw the letter. Erin must have been sitting in the big armchair beside the window when she read it, and had dropped it – possibly when she collapsed. It was from Isabel.

Tan-yr-Allt
May 10, 1935

Dearest Erin
I know you probably never want to hear from me again, but I feel so dreadful about the pain I have caused you that I must write.

As long as I live I shall never forget your face when you saw us together. I am sure that I shall eventually be punished for my behaviour. In a way it makes it worse that you are too gentle to do anything cruel to me, even when I so richly deserve it.

There is no justification for what I did, no excuse. I love Tom. I love him more than I value my self-respect or my loyalty and gratitude to you. I understand what a terrible thing that is, but I can't help it. There, I've said it, I loathe myself for hurting you even more by writing it down, but I must tell you I did not just betray you out of childish caprice. I knew it was wrong all the time and I could not stop myself.

I shall not ask you to forgive me. I understand that you probably never can. But I love you as much as always and I wish you nothing but happiness. I only wish I could protect you from what I did. Please try not to blame Tom too much. I know he couldn't help it, either.

Take care of yourself, and think of me kindly sometimes,

Isabel.

How many other fifteen-year-olds could have thought out a letter like that, let alone written it? thought Tom, quite forgetting momentarily that he was supposed to be incoherent with grief. His ego feasted on the girl's confession of love. Not just some star-struck child – Isabel was a beautiful, talented, rich girl, exceptional in every way. She'd really been the woman for him from the start. Such a pity she'd been just that little bit too young . . . such a pity he'd had to settle for Erin or lose touch completely with the inner circle of the Richmond family. That thought brought him back to earth. Poor Erin! His ambition had done precious little for her. If he hadn't married her she'd be alive now . . .

Nonsense, said his ego. She was riddled with cancer, you heard the surgeon. Amazing she lasted so long. The pregnancy only masked it for a while. Even if they'd known about it, they'd never have been able to treat it. She'd probably been too far gone even when he married her. Tom shuddered with revulsion. To think, she'd been rotting away when he first made love to her . . . One way and another he'd done her a good turn. At least she'd enjoyed a few months of happiness with him. If only she hadn't caught him with Isabel she'd have died content.

That gave him pause again. Obviously she'd been reading the letter when she suffered the last big collapse. Maybe the letter had caused it . . . which led him back again to the fact that he had brought misery to her last days and possibly hastened her end. No point in dwelling on that, old chap, he thought. Only make yourself morbid. Time for a drink, then arrange the funeral. That'll keep you occupied. And of course, Isabel will have to come back from that remote hole . . . That thought brightened him up. He went off to get his drink.

Isabel was torn between desolation and nervous excitement. The desolation arose from her deep love for Erin, mixed with guilt at the unhealed suffering she had caused her. The excitement returned every time she thought of the fact that Tom Moore-Ross was now unattached. The very idea filled her with a sick longing for him that nothing short of physical fulfilment could allay. As the Rolls-Royce carried her south she day-dreamed about the future that was opening before her, and close behind the daydreams slunk a monstrous guilt.

The funeral took place in the parish church at

Wingfield, the nearest village to Paxton. Erin had been popular among the local people and the church was crowded. They sang 'The Day Thou Gavest, Lord, Hath Ended', and Isabel stifled sobs as she considered how Erin's day had ended too soon. But there, in the same pew, separated from her only by Marianne, was Tom – muscular, cat-like Tom, with his predatory eyes and his sly smile. He was not crying. He was looking straight ahead, his hands clasped tightly together in front of him. Isabel shivered. He still attracted her like a magnet, but there was something repellent about him, too.

They dined together back at the manor. Heinrich von Burckhardt joined them early in the evening. He had been abroad when Erin died and was unable to return immediately. His visit was hardly one of tribute to the dead. He was here for a conference with Richmond's top executives, to represent Marianne's interest in the company in any proposed administrative changes which might be necessary now Erin was gone.

Everyone was attempting to be normal. Edward and Eleanor Moore-Ross had stayed on after the other mourners departed, apparently because they felt Tom should have at least one blood relation with him at such a bad time. The brothers' mutual dislike made nonsense of the family tie and when the couple left soon after dinner, the atmosphere lightened perceptibly. Von Burckhardt attempted to be kind to Isabel, knowing that Erin had effectively been the girl's mother for years.

'You have been brave today, Isabel. I am sure it was a great strain. Not for much longer, now, though. In the morning you can go back to your peaceful retreat in Wales.'

Isabel tried not to let her instinctive hostility show. 'Why on earth should I do that? There's no reason for me to go back there. I shall stay at home now I'm here.'

He frowned slightly. 'Please? I do not think I understand you.'

'I don't know why, it's fairly obvious. This is my home. I went to stay up there for a short while to give Erin some time alone while she had her baby. There's no longer any reason why I should return to Bangor.'

Now Marianne joined in. 'Of course there is! You can't stay down here unsupervised.'

It was Isabel's turn to frown. 'I shan't be unsupervised. Erin and Tom were my guardians. Erin is gone, but Tom's still here.'

'Not for long enough to make any difference,' said Marianne. 'You inherit Paxton. Erin never changed the will she made before marrying Tom.'

Tom had set down his drink with exaggerated care and was watching the two sisters intently. Isabel was getting angry. 'Then why are you making a fuss? Just because I own it instead of him, it doesn't mean I'll be asking him to leave. I don't think one can ask one's guardian to leave,' she finished with a triumphant smile at Tom.

'You really won't understand, will you, Isabel? Tom isn't your guardian – I am.' Marianne delivered her bombshell, then she, too, turned to look at Tom.

'Y-you can't be! He's been my stepfather since he and Erin married.'

Marianne softened a little. 'Isabel, you're very upset and this is hardly the time or place to discuss such an intimate matter. I think you and I should go over it privately together, in the morning.'

495

'No. I insist on settling it now. It's my life you're talking about.'

Marianne shrugged. 'There's nothing to settle. That was done long ago. You must see that Tom's link with you was through Erin. Once that was severed, he had no further claim on you. There is no legal or blood relationship, and it's quite improper for a young woman of your age to live with a widower who is unrelated to her.' Their old conversation about Moore-Ross's ambitions hung leaden and unmentionable over the discussion, but Isabel chose to ignore its implications.

'Once and for all, if I own Paxton, I'm staying here with Tom, just as I stayed here with him and Erin. That's all there is to it.'

'You're forgetting the rest of what I told you, Isabel. I am now your guardian.'

'So?'

'I absolutely forbid such an arrangement. Until you reach your legal majority, I have power to say where you will live, and with whom. And I assure you that the last place I choose will be Paxton and the last companion Tom Moore-Ross.'

Tom could no longer remain aloof. 'I think you're coming on a bit strong, Marianne. Isabel's had a very hard time. You can't separate her from all the familiar faces. She's never lived with you, and anyway, while you're preparing to marry and then settling down as a wife, you're going to have precious little time to play mother.'

'Erin managed it, and tried to start a family of her own,' snapped Marianne. 'Her death had nothing to do with excessive responsibilities. I've no reason to doubt I can do as well as she did.'

496

Tom began to bluster. 'Now look here, you can't just come along and fling me out of my home because of some technicality over my wife's will! What am I supposed to do?'

'That's your business. You had a home and an income of your own before you married my stepmother. You must resume what you were doing before. Anyway, I have no intention of moving to Paxton. Heinrich and I will live in White Lodge. I shall close Paxton until Isabel comes of age and decides what she wishes to do with it. In the meantime she will return to Bangor and continue her education there.' She drew a deep breath and continued speaking, raising her voice slightly to talk down the barrage of protest which erupted from both Tom and Isabel. 'You both know that it would be improper for the old situation to go on, I don't think we need discuss that in detail, even in the intimacy of present company.' She glared at them both and neither of them was in any doubt about what she meant.

Isabel blushed furiously and looked down at her hands. More than anything, she wanted to go off on her own and forget all this misery for a while, but they were discussing what amounted to permanent exile for her and she must make another attempt to avoid her fate. 'Marianne, I know Tan-yr-Allt's a lovely house and so on, but all my friends are down here. How long do you propose to keep me up there – five years? Ten?'

'It all depends on how things work out. Mrs Ashley will resume the educational plan she and Erin had devised for you. Your friends can come up and stay during the holidays – properly chaperoned, of course. Heinrich and I will come up regularly. I assure you that you won't be banished. Many young girls grow up like that – I did, and came to no harm.'

As far as Marianne was concerned, that closed the discussion. She tried to steer the talk back to less contentious matters. God save me from turning out the way you did, thought Isabel. But it was becoming clearer by the minute that not God but Marianne and Heinrich were to decree her immediate future – a future devoid of Tom Moore-Ross.

Everyone was reticent about how the company was to be run. When her father died, Isabel had been too overwhelmed by grief to take any interest in the inheritance. Shortage of money had never been a problem and her standard of living had not changed in any way. But Erin had formed a bridge between the company's past and future. Harry had trusted her absolutely and had used her as his proxy to steer Richmond's through to the day when his children might be deemed ready to take over. His prejudice against daughters had led him to postpone that date to the unforeseeable future, but now Erin's death had imposed a more rational development.

Under the terms of Harry's will, Erin would have been in overall charge until the girls either married or reached the age of forty – the age by which he had assumed they would be unmarriageable. The only way either of them would take control otherwise was if Erin predeceased them. Harry had regarded this as so unlikely that he had not bothered to nominate someone to take over from Erin should she die before his conditions were fulfilled. Now that she was dead, it appeared that Marianne inherited immediately and Isabel got her share on reaching her legal majority at twenty-one. Not that any of this was spelled out. Isabel had not seen copies of either Harry's or Erin's wills. She knew that Marianne was to be her guardian only because Harry had not thought to name a successor to Erin, and Erin herself had nominated Marianne in a will she made shortly after Harry died. If only she'd made a new one when she married Tom, thought Isabel, he and I could be together now without anyone being able to change things.

Normally her natural curiosity would have spurred her to find out more about her inheritance. But the events of the past couple of months had exhausted her, emotionally and intellectually, and now all she wanted was a little peace. She made her excuses to the grown-ups and left them to their uncomfortable conversation. As she lay in bed at Paxton that night, her virtue ensured by the presence of Kate Ashley in the room next door, she began to wonder if North Wales would not be the best place for her after all – at least for a while. Tom would find some way of getting to her . . . he felt as passionately about her as she did about him. What else could explain his betrayal of Erin, whom he loved so much?

An answer pressed blackly on her spirit, dredged from Marianne's account of Tom's earlier attempt to marry into the family. Angrily, Isabel shook it aside. Then other memories began crowding in. That awful night when Kitt had pleaded with Harry for mercy and instead she had been beaten and dragged away. An earlier, vaguer remembrance of something horribly similar . . . As the image wove through her sleepy mind, she tried to grasp it and failed. What was that? Something from a time when she was too young for conscious memory. Something that had made the awful confrontation between Harry and Kitt seem like the repetition of another fatal rejection . . . something to do with her mother . . .

Memory faded to dream and she was very small, toddling along another gallery in the same house, with Teddy for company. There was sobbing and pleading then, too, in a voice she hardly recognised but which in some strange way was dearer to her than all others. Teddy was very heavy, dragging along and tripping her. She'd leave him here to rest and get him on the way back . . . when she'd seen Mummy . . . that was it, Mummy, and that was Papa shouting at her, names Isabel didn't understand, and the Mummy-lady was crying just like Kitt . . . She pushed against the heavy door behind which they were shouting at each other. It opened, oh, so slowly, because she was too little to push very hard, and then it gave way and she was falling forward, falling into her bed at Paxton, into her fifteen-year-old body which sweated with terror at what she had so nearly seen, so nearly remembered.

Shakily, Isabel got out of bed and walked across to the window, where she stood and took great gulps of cold night air. What had she been dreaming? Some awful nightmare . . . Funny, so vivid and yet she couldn't remember any of it. If only Tom had been there to comfort her . . . No! Whatever it was she could not remember, it made her afraid to have a man near her. She shuddered. What on earth was it? Papa, Tom, the Beynon boys, Robin Lester, even Heinrich von Burckhardt whom she hardly knew – the thought of being protected by any of them filled her with fear. 'Oh, Erin, my Erin,' she whimpered, 'I do miss you – why did you leave me?' She began to realise the depth of her loss. Crying, she turned back towards the bed. As she lay down, she was still repeating, 'Erin, please come back . . . Mummy, I'm frightened . . . don't let them hurt me, please.'

Eventually she slept again. Wakefulness was no comfort. Suddenly her real world seemed more uncertain and dangerous than any dream.

They packed her off back to Bangor very soon after the funeral. Marianne tried to be kind but only sounded cold and irritable. 'I'm sorry, Isabel, but it won't make matters any easier if you mope around here until the last minute. Of course there will be people here for a couple of weeks. You know as well as I do that it takes a long time to close a house this size. But the sooner you leave, the easier you'll find it.'

'Can't I just stay a week or so?'

'Out of the question. I have to join Heinie in London tomorrow to start sorting out the company. No, I'm afraid you must go in the morning.'

'But Tom will be here.'

Marianne's patience was exhausted. 'We've already been over that, and you know the answer.' Her tone softened somewhat but she was still disapproving, 'Isabel, servants talk. Erin hinted – well, I won't go into that, but I think I know what happened – and the servants' gossip told me the rest.'

Isabel blushed but stood her ground. 'What did they tell you? I've done nothing to feel ashamed of!'

'I think you have. I think you've done something you'll regret for the rest of your life. But that isn't my problem. Your moral welfare from now on most certainly is. Mrs Ashley will travel back to North Wales with you tomorrow. By Christmas, she'll let me have a revised study plan and we shall start looking into possibilities for tutors up there. That's my last word.'

Before Isabel could delay her with further protests, she turned and left the room. Almost crying with frustration, Isabel ran out into the garden. She stood on the terrace, fighting to control her temper, knowing that a tantrum would do her even more harm with Marianne. Of all the people to be put in charge of her, it had to be that dry old stick! She seemed closer to fifty than thirty. Isabel looked around for some distraction from the disagreeable prospect of departure from Paxton.

Then she saw him, crossing the lawn deep in conversation with Heinie von Burckhardt. Tom was doing most of the talking. As usual, he was gesturing widely, his whole body in motion to emphasize whatever point he was making. Isabel thrilled at the sight of him, her misery replaced by a more urgent tension. What was absorbing them so much? Tom normally had nothing to say to Marianne's fiancé. He must be a bit worked up. She could hear his raised voice from here, although it was impossible to distinguish what they were saying. Somehow she had the feeling that was the reason they were holding the conversation outside. She started strolling ostentatiously back and forth along the terrace, confident that the minute Tom saw her, he would break off the exchange with von Burckhardt and rush to her side.

Nothing could have been further from Tom's mind. At present he was desperately trying to salvage his career from the wreckage created by Erin's death.

'What d'you mean, dispensable luxury? Everyone sings my praises on the sales side! You know nothing about the business and you come in here suggesting I'm excess baggage . . . bloody meddling! Remember, you're getting in by marriage. Some of us worked our way up.'

Von Burckhardt threw back his immaculate head and laughed. 'Oh, you English can be so amusing! Such a suggestion, from you, has a wonderful irony!'

Tom was furious with himself for having exposed his weak flank. For lack of any better weapon, he tried aggression.

'And what does that mean? If you're referring to Erin, I was already a top manager in this company when she married Harry Richmond, so let's have no nasty little hints that I got there thanks to her pull.'

Von Burckhardt stopped laughing as abruptly as he had started, and regarded Tom with a flat, hostile stare. 'I was not referring to your late wife. I have followed your early career with interest. It was not Harry Richmond's last wife who got you where you are today, so much as the not-quite-wife who happened to be your sister.'

'You bad-minded bastard! You don't know what you're talking about. A man like Harry would never have found jobs for the boys. He was far too brilliant a businessman!'

'Correction – he was exactly the sort of brilliant businessman who can afford such gestures to satisfy his own whims, because he knew only one man ran Richmond's, and the rest of you were only minions. So when he hoped to lure your sister down the aisle, what better bribe than

503

to put both her dear brothers in line for plum jobs?'

Tom sneered. 'Sorry, old man, you're just not making sense. If he only wanted yes-men who owed him favours, how come both Edward and I ended up with a real say in the business?'

'Because even the greatest business genius has blind spots. Harry Richmond's was his refusal to accept his own mortality.'

'I don't get it.'

'Really? You amaze me. It's quite straightforward. Richmond could afford to have people like you on his payroll as long as he was running the company. And he seemed to think he would live forever. Of course, he didn't. He not only died; he conveniently left a widow with a weakness for plausible young men-about-town. Make no mistake, Moore-Ross, that is the only reason you retained a senior post at Richmond's after he was gone.'

'But the Moore-Rosses are the backbone of the company! How long would the firm have prospered after Harry's death without Edward explaining the state of play to Erin, week after week?'

'We are not discussing your brother. Sometimes men of great ability get started thanks to an unfair advantage. In his case, that was true. If Richmond had not taken him on as a matrimonial inducement to your sister, some other big company would have snapped him up and I'm sure he would have been as successful with them as he has been with Richmond's. But we were talking about you. Without that initial boost from your family connection, I think you might have been hard-pressed to earn your daily bread.'

'I'm not listening to this, it's next to slanderous! Just because my side of the company is less easy to evaluate than Edward's. You can't reduce promotional flair to cold columns of figures, you know.'

'I do know – it's fortunate for you that one can't. Everyone in the company knows you were put into sales and promotions because it was Richmond's own forte. That was the one place where you would not be required to demonstrate any originality or talent, just the ability to agree with the boss.' He paused momentarily but silenced the other man with a contemptuous gesture as he attempted once more to establish his worth. 'Tom, I believe we have exhausted this subject. I am not dismissing you – I do not have the power, yet. I merely thought this was a good opportunity to . . . er . . . forewarn you that things are likely to change. As I see it, there are several options open to you.'

'Such as?'

'The most obvious is that you seek suitable employment elsewhere. I'm sure you could secure an appropriate post, if your talents are as exceptional as you say. Or you could stop work altogether, of course. Erin was hardly a poor woman, irrespective of what she inherited from Harry Richmond. You could become a gentleman farmer, perhaps, or a country squire. Alternatively, you could apply yourself to your present job and start justifying the considerable salary that Richmond's pays you. It's possible you will survive the management review I intend to carry out; but if you do, I fear you must give far better value for money than you have in the past.'

He smiled at Tom, bowed with the infuriating Teutonic

heel-click which always increased Tom's hostility, and started to turn away.

'Wait a minute, von Burckhardt! I haven't finished with you yet!'

'But I have finished with you, Moore-Ross, and you are going to have to learn I'm the one who gives the orders now.' Heinrich moved off across the lawn, heading for the house.

Isabel was aware of nothing beyond Tom's apparent dissatisfaction with the encounter. She could see him across the grass, glaring after von Burckhardt with murder in his face. She must go and find out what had upset him so . . . But von Burckhardt intercepted her. 'Ah, my lovely prospective sister-in-law! Come along inside with me and show me a few of your favourite paintings. There should be plenty of room for you to have some of your things around you in the Bangor house, and the rest can go into store.'

'Th-there's something else I have to do – something urgent.'

'Nonsense, my dear. I saw you dawdling around up here for some time before I came up. I think you're just trying to postpone your trip.'

That was the end of her attempt at defiance. Afterwards, Isabel was unsure how Heinrich had managed to steer her indoors and away from Tom so effectively. It proved to be the last time she saw her lover before they sent her back to North Wales.

Isabel raged at Kate Ashley for a while during the journey. Her governess merely smiled and nodded, refusing to commit herself to any opinion about von Burckhardt,

Marianne or Tom. When Isabel finally challenged her to respond, she grimaced and made a tiny gesture towards the chauffeur. Clearly she had no intention of risking any controversial remarks which might be repeated to her employer within hours. Isabel sighed and settled back to gaze blankly out of the window. After a while her outrage faded. Even in the grip of her infatuation for Tom, she could see he was less than a perfect knight in shining armour. Eventually she became absorbed in the grandeur of the mountain scenery along Telford's spectacular highway through the Welsh heartland. The problems of her turbulent, amoral family began to seem remote and unreal. This other world might serve her better for a while.

At Tan-yr-Allt they were greeted by a new housekeeper, Mrs Griffiths, a cheerful soul with rosy cheeks and pretty silver grey hair that escaped its stern chignon and curled in tendrils around her face. She was a friend of the Beynon family and seemed to share something of their happy-go-lucky temperament. Isabel took to her on sight.

Dawkins was to return south the next day, with the Rolls-Royce. Marianne had bought an Armstrong Siddeley saloon for Tan-yr-Allt and had engaged a driver-handyman, again on the recommendation of the Beynons. The staff was completed by a gardener, a kitchen maid and a parlourmaid. Kate Ashley, officially her governess, volunteered to double as her personal maid when Isabel flatly refused to let Marianne engage one for her. 'I know she'll spy on me, Kate. I'd rather look after myself, anyway. Most girls do nowadays. Marianne's such a stick-in-the-mud she thinks it's common not to have one.'

Privately, Mrs Ashley agreed with Isabel. She had no

desire to have some sharp-eyed young creature from London living with them, watching their every move and reporting back to Marianne. She knew Marianne would insist on appointing someone if Isabel were officially without a maid, and so she volunteered hei own services. It was unlikely that Isabel would ever want her to perform them.

The new household settled down to its self-contained existence. Isabel was not Out, and she was the only 'above-stairs' resident at Tan-yr-Allt, so the local County would not call. Kate reflected on her charge's isolation and decided it was a golden opportunity to polish an education which was already far ahead of that offered to most other girls. The sooner she finalised a programme of special subjects and proposals for tutors to teach them, the less time Isabel would have on her hands. The university college at Bangor would undoubtedly provide a good source of teachers. Plenty of the junior lecturers must be on small enough salaries to welcome extra income.

In the meantime, Isabel had a private project she wanted to pursue. She did not even tell Kate, now her substitute for a best friend, what she had in mind. She pretended she was interested in studying the geography and natural history of Anglesey and Snowdonia. Her real mission was to discover what had happened to the strange man referred to in the documents she had found in the dining room.

She had thought of little else during the month of her exile in Bangor before Erin's death. When her violent gesture opened the wall panel, she felt like the heroine in countless adventure stories, discovering the secret which saved the family fortunes. Only her family still had its fortune intact. This discovery seemed more likely to bring trouble than salvation. At first she was unaware that the papers existed. The strongbox sat at the front of the cupboard and she took it out, expecting concealed jewellery or love letters. Then she noticed something behind the box that stopped her in her tracks. Whatever was in there looked rather unpleasant . . . With a conscious effort, she pushed her arm inside and grabbed the dusty scrap of cloth and whatever it enwrapped. When she drew it out and looked closely, she gasped and almost dropped it.

What a horrid thing! Who'd want to play with a doll like that? It was hard to imagine it had ever been attractive, even when it had hair and a proper face and more clothes. The lawn skirt it wore was yellow and dusty. It had some sort of edging which had not discoloured so badly. Wait a minute, it wasn't a proper doll's petticoat – it was a handkerchief. That edging was good lace. No child could have played with it. The skirt was not sewn together, merely tied with a piece of fine red silk thread. As she touched the thread, the handkerchief fluttered free and fell. Isabel saw the paper charm pressed into the pelvic area and realised with growing horror what she must be holding. She had gone through a craze for occult adventure stories three years ago and her tutor had insisted she learn about the real tradition of doll magic when she plagued him with questions about the wildly inaccurate descriptions in a particularly bloodthirsty book. This must be the real version of the fanciful creations she had read about.

Disgusted, Isabel flung it aside. Filthy thing! Some

diseased person trying to frighten an enemy long ago, no doubt. She'd have no more to do with it . . . Then her curiosity revived. Who could it have been? The handkerchief was old, but not antique. Perhaps she knew something about its owner, even if they had never met. She bent and picked up the scrap of Swiss lawn. In the corner she found what she had been seeking, a pair of delicately-embroidered, interwoven initials: KR. Kitt? It must be. But no, she'd never had anything to do with Tan-yr-Allt, couldn't have. Father had never owned it. When Marianne's mother died it went directly to Marianne.

Marianne's mother . . . of course, KR – Karin Richmond – Karin, not Kitt. She had quite forgotten that Marianne's mother's name was Karin. What was it Marianne had said? Her mother had not been here since the turn of the century? This must be at least thirty-five years old, then, possibly older. She knew Karin and Harry had married in 1896. Such dates were imprinted on both her and Marianne's minds. Their father's subsequent behaviour had ensured that.

She had been so absorbed by the doll that she forgot the strongbox. Now she turned to it. Perhaps that would provide a clue. She had assumed it would hold jewels or a treasure map – nothing as mundane as documents. Now she prepared to find out. It was a well-made box, and securely locked. Isabel gave a little snort of exasperation. She would not be baulked now! Everything was so quiet she could do anything short of burning down Tan-yr-Allt without attracting attention. Tucking the box under her arm, she went off to find some means of breaking it open. At first she had visions of needing a mallet, chisel and all sorts of heavy implements. But although the box

510

was solid enough, the lock was fragile. It sprung as soon as she inserted a broad-bladed kitchen knife and applied sharp downward pressure.

Not for Isabel the cagey deliberation about how to open the papers so that they might be resealed later without demonstrating that they had been disturbed. She recognised her grandfather's seal on his letter to Beuno, because Karin had passed it on to Marianne, who treated it with the veneration normally accorded to religious relics. But all the papers were yellow with age and it never occurred to her that they would refer to living people. Her immediate assumption was that they would lead to buried treasure.

In a sense, they did. She read the contents of the box with growing fascination. It was like a part-finished Sherlock Holmes mystery. What fun if she could bring it to a satisfactory ending! This Marged Richmond must be Papa's grandmother, who had died, paralysed by a stroke, ten years before she was born. What a terrible woman, standing between her son and his one true love . . . She turned to Henry's letter to Beuno and some of her sensationalist curiosity subsided. Now she recognised the presence of true tragedy. This was a real man exposing himself and his poor secret. For him, and for the unknown son, she felt nothing but pity. She knew much of what that son must have felt. She had lived in the shadow of bastardy, never sure of her place in the world. She had grown up without a mother and almost without a father. This long-ago boy had been reared like an orphan, too. Isabel picked up the last set of papers, the instructions about the solicitor and the freehold of the shop. Surely, the boy must be dead now, or somewhere far off, with a new name and his own family . . . Instinct told her perhaps he was not. Well, she could soon find out. She hurried to the hall and took the North Wales telephone directory from its shelf. Yes, Llewelyn and Fonseca still practised in Bangor. They had offices in the High Street. That was a start. She could find out more from them.

That was when the telephone rang, making her jump. It was almost as if the solicitors had read her mind and were contacting her. The housekeeper came into the hall. 'Why, Miss Isabel, why didn't you answer it?' she said, too surprised for courtesy. She brushed past the girl, lifted the receiver and said, 'Tan-yr-Allt: Richmond residence . . .' Thirty seconds later, Marianne was telling Isabel that their stepmother had died on the operating table and arranging for her to return to London.

Isabel did not forget the enigma of her missing uncle. Erin's death merely pushed it to the back of her mind temporarily. Now that she was back at Tan-yr-Allt, she could think of little else. The doll and the strongbox had been bundled back into the panelled cupboard. Isabel meant to take the papers with her to Paxton. Then something stopped her. Perhaps she would mislay them, or maybe someone would go through her things. Better to leave them here where they had rested undisturbed for so long. Her last act before leaving had been to replace the papers in the strongbox and fasten the panel again. Once you knew where the catch was, it was easy enough to reopen the secret cupboard. As soon as she was alone in the dining room on her first day back, she went to the panel and took out the documents. A few days later, while Kate Ashley was at the university, discussing her education with a lecturer, Isabel went into town and visited the solicitor's office.

Neither the Llewelyn nor the Fonseca of the earlier era was still in practice. Fonseca had sold his partnership on retirement to a Mr Lewis, who ran the practice in collaboration with Rhys Llewelyn, grandson of the lawyer of Isabel's grandfather's time.

At first it looked as if Isabel was unlikely to meet either of the partners. The head clerk, Meshach Bowen, eyed her with profound distrust. In his day, little chits of her age had been confined to the nursery or the servants' hall. They certainly didn't dash around unchaperoned, wasting the time of important men. He clucked disapproval at her for some five minutes before Isabel's patience snapped. 'I came here to see one of the partners. If you haven't the courtesy to ask them if they have a few minutes to spare a young lady, perhaps you will tell them that Henry Richmond's granddaughter is here and wishes to see one of them on extremely urgent business.'

The magic name had the desired effect. Old Bowen was of her father's generation and as a boy he remembered people remarking on the fabulous fortune made by Richmond senior from a humble start in Bangor High Street. The very name spelled power and privilege to the clerk, and transformed his manner.

'Now why didn't you say so, Miss Richmond? Do have a seat. I'm so sorry to keep you waiting. I'm sure Mr Llewelyn will want to see you immediately. Just you wait by there a minute.' He hurried off to the inner sanctum of the partners' office, returning almost at once to usher Isabel in.

Rhys Llewelyn looked at Isabel with open appreciation.

What a lovely creature! Her clothes were those of a young girl, but she seemed far too mature for them. He rose and shook hands, then showed her to a chair. Isabel took out the two sheets of paper concerning the shop freehold and the rent money. 'I think it will be easier if you read these, then ask me anything you wish,' she said.

He nodded, intrigued, then turned to the papers. After reading them, he said: 'May I ask how these came into your possession, Miss Richmond?'

'Of course. I was going through the old writing desk in my room at Tan-yr-Allt, sorting out space for my own things, and these were pushed into a pigeon hole with other, private letters about the recipient of the freehold. As it seems clear that your firm would never have informed Mr Owen of his inheritance without further express instructions from my grandfather, I thought I should come to you immediately.'

'Very kind of you, Miss Richmond. I'm sure you are right about nothing further having been done. This covering note seems to suggest that someone else might inform us on Henry Richmond's behalf.'

'I know, but I can only assume that whoever was asked to do it left Tan-yr-Allt before they had a chance to comply. I have no one I can ask. My mother has been dead for many years, and my father died nearly two years ago. I know my grandfather died fairly young. Perhaps he expected to be able to leave full instructions himself. What can we do about it? I imagine that this Beuno Owen is long gone by now, too, so it would be a matter of finding his heirs. I'll be very happy to help with the search.'

He smiled at her. 'It will help if we dredge up the

original papers that we had on deposit. Shouldn't take long – we have comparatively little from so long ago and it will be in deed boxes for the year in question. That should make it simple enough.'

It took less than ten minutes to locate the dusty old box, which must have lain undisturbed for almost half a century. Beuno's inheritance was the only package inside, apart from a faded will which still awaited other untraced inheritors. Llewelyn glanced through the contents. 'Mmm, these are straightforward enough. Certainly nothing which need debar us from acting on your instructions.'

'I don't understand.'

'It's hardly an everyday occurrence for a young lady of your age to walk into a solicitor's office and start issuing orders for the disposal of her grandfather's property, Miss Richmond. Normally I would require authorisation by your legal guardian, but since this is so straightforward . . . In fact, if the housekeeper or even a family friend had come in with this information, we could have gone ahead. All the instructions are here; it's been delayed simply because your grandfather appears to have assumed there would always be someone available to tell us when to proceed. As there was not, we can go ahead now.'

'What will you do? How can you find out about him?'

'That might be a complex task in London, but it's a different matter up here. People have deep roots. They don't tend to move about. If Mr Owen is still alive, I'm sure we shall find him. If he isn't, his relatives will probably still be on the island. We'll write to the shop, and also find out from the bank whether they have any other address for him from when he used to pay rent on the premises. I might even be able to do it now. Let's see . . . it's Lloyd's in the High Street . . . wait a minute.' He picked up the telephone. 'Eleri, get me Mr Jones, the manager at Lloyd's bank, please. Yes, put him through to me in here.'

The manager agreed to trace the old rent account and pass on the relevant information. By now, Isabel was burning with curiosity. 'Can I wait in case he gets it quickly?'

Llewelyn tried not to keep smiling at her and failed dismally. This one could charm her way around every man in Caernarvonshire, he thought. 'You may have a long wait. I was lucky; it was such an old file we didn't need to look far. But this man could have stopped trading, say, ten years ago, and he might be one of a hundred old bank accounts which are technically still open. Goodness knows how long it will take.'

'I don't mind. Unless you're too busy, I can sit here and ask you to tell me all about Anglesey, if you know anything about it. I'm so new up here that no one comes to call, so there's nobody to ask.'

Entranced by the smooth pale face and the vivid bright-brown eyes, Rhys Llewelyn relaxed in his big leather chair and showed off the intimate knowledge of Anglesey which he had acquired as a member of the local antiquarian society. After about ten minutes of talk about the island's prehistoric remains and ancient Celtic churches, he remembered something about the papers in front of him. 'Ah, even if the bank can't help immediately, this will lead us to our man fast enough – this deed of gift clearly says "Beuno Owen, of the Herbalist's

516

shop, Llangefni, and the parish of Llanddona".
Llanddona is a small place. Everyone there will know the
Owens, just as they'll know all the other families. It
would only take an afternoon visit to find him or his
descendants.'

Isabel felt the elation of a hunter sighting his quarry.
She suppressed an impulse to say she would go this afternoon and track him down. No, if she appeared too eager,
this careful man would start to question her right to
make the enquiry, start remembering that really she was
still a child . . . And once they involved Marianne, or
even practical, down-to-earth Kate Ashley, she would be
forbidden to go on with her quest. With a great effort,
she merely thanked Llewelyn coolly and said: 'If they fail
to find him, I might volunteer to go over there some
time. Perhaps you should come too, just to ensure that
all is in order.'

'Delighted, Miss Richmond. You'll probably need a
local escort, anyway. A lot of the country people either
can't or won't speak English.'

'That must make your job difficult.'

He laughed. 'Good lord, no! You're the first client
with whom I've spoken English all day. Almost all my
business is conducted in Welsh.'

'Oh. I didn't realise I was such an outsider.' She felt
suitably chastened for having assumed that all professional people here spoke only the King's English.

Then the bank manager telephoned and their plan
proved unnecessary. Llewelyn thanked him, made a note
and hung up. 'Well, it seems your man may still be
around after all. He gave up the shop just three years
ago; wrote to the bank and said there wasn't sufficient

517

custom any more to justify keeping it open, but said he'd leave all his things there for the moment unless they had another tenant. They agreed – didn't tell him he owned it, of course, because they didn't know – and he left his home address with them for notification if they wished him to clear the premises.' He scribbled on a piece of paper. 'Here's the address. We'll write to him, but as he's related to you in a way, perhaps you'd like to go and see him. Don't expect too much, though. He must be a very old man now if this deed was made out before 1890. Oh, and the suggestion of using me as a guide . . . feel free to take it up whenever you like.'

Isabel gave him her most radiant smile and said she would think about it. She had no intention of dragging along a stranger to spoil her own private chase. As she rose to leave, she looked down at the address on the slip of paper. 'Ty Ffynnon Arian – what a lovely name. What does it mean?'

'House of the silver fountain. At least, that's the most poetic translation. Welsh is a much more economical language than English. Ffynnon also means well or spring. In fact, it's most likely to indicate a well in that part of the island.'

'What makes you think that? Don't deprive me of my magic fountain!'

'If it's magic you want, this is much more potent. Llanddona has a number of the old cold cursing wells where the Celts used to go to put spells on their enemies. If it is the house of the silver well, it will have more than enough magic for one curious little English kinswoman!'

She made herself join in his laugh, but suppressed a

518

shudder as she did so. That was when she guessed Beuno had probably made the witch-doll.

The sunlit street was empty except for a sleepy dog which scratched itself aimlessly before wandering off. It was Tuesday afternoon and the little town had suspended commercial activity in preparation for its Wednesday and Thursday livestock and provision markets. Isabel had told Jenkins to drive the Armstrong-Siddeley around the side streets and return for her in ten minutes. A desultory inspection of the modest terrace of shops was enough. The former herbalist's crouched in tattered glory in the centre, 'OWEN - HERBAL AND NATURAL REMEDIES' still lingering in faded gold paint across the sign board. The blinds had been left raised, and an assortment of small bottles lined the front of the window. Behind them were ranks of fine old earthenware apothecary's jars in rich dark blue, highly-glazed and with scrolled labels proclaiming the contents. Behind the half-glazed door hung a sign which said 'Closed: please apply to Ty Ffynnon Arian, Llanddona'. Isabel smiled. So all her enquiries in Bangor had been unnecessary once she knew where the shop was. His address was here for everyone to see. Between the English words and the address was a scattering of Welsh. She assumed it repeated the English translation.

She leaned close to the door, shielding her eyes against the sunlight, and peered into the dim interior. But it was too dark to discern more than the shadowy outline of a counter backed by storage shelves and a curtained archway which presumably led to the accommodation behind the shop. She turned away. Perhaps, if I get to know him, he'll bring me back and show it to me himself, she thought. She was not altogether at ease with the idea. In fact, the whole place made her feel uncomfortable. Perhaps it was a hare-brained notion ever to have come here. He wouldn't be a romantic hero at all, he'd probably be a crotchetty, half-educated old bore. He might not even understand a word she said, bearing in mind Rhys Llewelyn's remarks about the islanders' first language.

She was on the point of abandoning the whole thing when Jenkins appeared round the corner in the Armstrong-Siddeley. It was such a mundane sight that her misgivings vanished. He had scarcely pulled up before Isabel had opened the door and clambered inside. 'Right, Jenkins, this is where we test your local knowledge. Take me to Llanddona. We're looking for a cottage or maybe a farmhouse called Ty Ffynnon Arian. How long will it take to get there?'

'We'll get to Llanddona within half an hour, miss, but the roads down there are pretty rough. Could take us as long again to find the place. Maybe the car won't even get up to the house if it's really out of the way.'

'Oh, well, it's a nice day for a walk!'

The farm proved reasonably accessible. It perched beside the precipitous track which hair-pinned down to a magnificent beach. Isabel gazed at the view in wonder. If I lived here, I'd never want to go away from the house, she thought.

The track was barely wide enough for one vehicle. Outside a sagging five-bar gate a faded sign announced the name of the house. Jenkins opened the gate then drove in, to avoid blocking the lane to any other traffic.

Only a gable of the house was visible from here, because of a curve in the track and the steepness of the slope.

'Wait here, Jenkins. I'll go on alone,' said Isabel.

'You do realise that some of these country people don't speak no English, do you, miss?' he asked.

'Don't worry – I'll call you if that's the case with Mr Owen.' Somehow, giving his name to the driver added a whiff of respectability to her errand.

'Very well, miss, I'll leave the window wound down.'

She set off down the track, which quickly deteriorated into a broad path. Jenkins couldn't have got the car down here if he'd tried, she thought. It was utterly silent around the house, a single-storey building, very simple, built of hard grey stone cut into huge slabs. Small windows appeared to have been swallowed by their deep embrasures. The walls must be eighteen inches thick. But in spite of its squat strength against the ocean winds, it was cheerful enough. The little house was clean and well kept. One window was open and spotless white muslin curtains fluttered in the breeze. A geranium in a pot glowed redly on the wide window ledge behind them. Smoke trickled lazily from the chimney. But the bright blue door was firmly closed. An enormous tortoiseshell cat sat beside it, watching her with unblinking yellow eyes. He appeared to be the only living creature present apart from herself.

Isabel started feeling uneasy again. Of course the place isn't abandoned, she scolded herself. It's a perfectly normal establishment. Call at any small farm in the daytime and the owner will be out tending his fields. But what about his wife . . . children . . . grandchildren? She stood still and the silence lapped around her. And yet – not total silence. Somewhere she heard running water. She let out a huge sigh of relief. So much for Llewelyn's old wives' tale about the cold cursing well! The silver fountain was obviously the spring that provided the farm's water. She could hear it trickling from here. Isabel followed the sound around the side of the cottage, moving back into the shadow of the steep hillside. Buttressing the slope was a stone arch, like a miniature church window. Within it was a battered stone figure, so weathered that it was unidentifiable as male or female. It appeared to be seated on some sort of throne, and from the foot of the throne gushed the spring. The water poured into a semicircular stone trough, which was permanently full. A primitive pipe emptied it into a stone-lined gutter and thence to a brook which chattered down the hillside. The whole was utterly enchanting. Isabel stood gazing at it, momentarily forgetting her nervousness.

'You do look as if you'm cursing somebody good and proper.'

Isabel gave a scream, then blushed with shame. The man who had spoken might have a strange look, but he was real, not a phantom. And it was his place, not hers. She felt foolish.

'I . . . er . . . that is . . . are you Mr Owen?'

He did not speak immediately, but only nodded. Then he smiled as if he had known her a long time and was remembering past meetings. Isabel knew he must be very old, but age was somehow not relevant to him. He had an elfin quality which defied wrinkles and stiffening joints. There were silvery streaks in the curly hair, but it was still thick and golden. The eyes, cheekbones, brows, and above all, the beautifully-sculpted mouth, all followed the faun-like upward curve which had haunted Karin Richmond more than thirty years ago. He had the body of a young man, a horseman or a dancer, with small hands and feet and a slender but muscular body. His skin was golden brown from constant exposure to sun and sea spray.

I know you too, thought Isabel. You're my brother, my soul's dark brother . . . She tried to shake off the thought but it merely slipped down through the surface of her mind and settled somewhere deep inside her spirit.

Beuno had tilted his head sideways and was studying her from top to toe, motionless except for his eyes. Then he said, 'Which Richmond are you?'

She was not even surprised. Somehow it would have been odder had he not recognised their common blood. 'Harry. Harry Richmond's daughter.'

'But not with Karin.' It was a statement, not a question.

Isabel shook her head. 'No. Nancy. Nancy Rochford Richmond.'

'Dead, now though? And Karin?'

She nodded.

'No boys.' Again, not a question.

'We're a well-known family, always in the papers. You'd know he only had daughters.'

Beuno chuckled. 'Not in the *North Wales Chronicle*, you're not. That's the only paper I do ever see. Don't matter now, anyway. Never should have mattered. Never would have mattered if it hadn't been for her . . .' He seemed to be looking far away, over Isabel's shoulder.

'Her? Who was that, your mother?'

That brought his attention back. '*Iesu*, no! Poor

harmless little creature couldn't hurt no one but herself. Maybe I'll tell you one day. It's an old story. It will keep. But there's rude I am – keeping a young lady standing out here like this without so much as an introduction beyond Mr Owen! I'm Beuno, all right?'

Suddenly trusting him, Isabel smiled back. 'All right. I'm Isabel. Isabel Richmond.'

'Do they ever call you Bel?'

'No. Never. I hate it.' The nickname brought back black sinning memories which made her feel guilty. They had no place here. 'Isabel. Just call me Isabel.'

'I was just going back to the house for a cup of tea. Would you like to join me?'

'I'd love to, thank you.' The nervousness had vanished. This man might be dangerous, but not to her. She followed him into the dolls' house cottage.

# Chapter Twenty-Two

Bcuno Owen was seventy-six years old. He wore his age lightly, perhaps because he had always been an outsider, who knew no more of society's conventions for growing old than he did of their ideals of childhood or maturity. Beuno had always ploughed his own furrow and ignored convention because he did not understand it.

He had paid a high price for his freedom. He had no wife, no children – no close kin of any kind since his old aunt had died more years ago than he now remembered. Long ago, he had exchanged human company for the companionship of animals, plants, the endless sea and a wide sky. Now he looked on Isabel Richmond and understood that his life was about to change dramatically. He had been waiting for Isabel for forty years or more.

She sat with him in his small bright kitchen and told him what she had found in the secret cupboard. Then she opened the shopping bag she had brought with her, and took out the doll. 'This is yours, isn't it?' she said.

Beuno picked it up almost affectionately, like a man shaking hands with an old friend after they had been parted beyond hope of reunion.

'Well, well – so she kept it, then. I thought she'd be

too frightened.' He put the mannikin down on the table and smiled at Isabel.

'Aren't you going to say any more than that?' Her indignation was tangible.

Beuno smiled at her. 'Expected a bit more for your money, did you, love?'

'No – but I want to know about it. I've come to you with these old secrets. The least you can do is confide in me.'

'D'you think it's any of your business?'

'I think perhaps it's what made my father such an awful man. You have to tell me, Beuno.'

'Maybe, maybe not. Mostly we make ourselves, you know. Awful or good, it's up to us. P'raps I'll tell you after. But I'd like to look through these old papers first.'

She nodded. 'Go ahead. They made me cry.'

Beuno said no more until he had read them all. Then he looked up at her. 'Now why would you want to cry about it?'

Isabel was nonplussed. 'Well – it's all so tragic . . . your father and mother torn apart by that terrible woman . . . you growing up an orphan because of it. I've never heard such a tragic story.'

'Then you've never been very far, girl. You only get torn if you let someone tear you. You only fail if you listen to what other people think you should do. Them bits of paper don't make no difference to me.'

'But they must! I'd feel like a different person. Haven't you always felt . . . cut off . . . as if you belonged somewhere but you didn't know where?'

He shook his head. 'I never belonged nowhere. Papers don't change that. I come with the tide, a long time ago, and one day I'll go with the west wind. But the wind and the tides haven't got room for papers, girl.'

He poured tea for her and then studied her closely as she drank it. Isabel began to get uncomfortable. 'Why are you staring at me?'

'Because you're one of the most beautiful things I ever saw. I could look at you all day and not get tired.'

'I wish I felt beautiful! It doesn't seem to be doing me any good.'

'Why should it? It's just part of you. It's not there to do anything. You can use it if you want to. If you don't, no matter.'

She was accustomed to reading people quickly and getting what she wanted from them. But this Beuno seemed invulnerable. Then she understood that the artifice of normal conversation was a waste of time with him. It was time to hear some truths. She said: 'Please tell me about our family.'

When he finished, he said: 'I haven't paid yet for what I did to Karin. I will, no doubt. I don't believe in regrets but that do bring me close. She suffered for someone else's wrong. My mam did, too, mind, but she chose to be caught up in it. That poor soul never chose nothing. She was pushed all her life.'

Isabel sighed. 'My mother, too. Her life went wrong and ended in tragedy.'

'It had to. Your great-grandmother thought she could change the course of history. She did that all right, but she forgot about the consequences. None of you was ever meant to be, see. She did that. But once she set it in motion, she couldn't order matters the way she wanted, and it all went mad. We won't see the end of it in my lifetime.'

'In mine, perhaps?'

He gazed at her, suddenly troubled. 'Yes, I think perhaps in yours. You'll bring it back full circle in the end.'

'I don't understand, Beuno.'

'Nor me, neither, love. I do just see the broad sweep of it. I'm none too good on the details, though. You're responsible for that.'

She shuddered. 'I wish I could just make my own way.'

'But you will! That's why you can make it come full circle. Before, they've either not known what they was fighting, or they went galloping off after the wrong thing. You're like me. You know you can only answer for yourself. Mind you don't change.'

'All right, if you'll help me.'

'For a while. For the important time. Then I'll have to go – but you'll be all right on your own by then.'

'On my own? But what about a husband . . . children?'

'That's for you to decide – but I don't see them around you, and I do usually see things like that.'

His gaze was so intent that Isabel glanced over her shoulder, half convinced he could see the participants in her future in ghostly array behind her. Beuno laughed when he saw her look. 'No, you won't see anything. That's a gift of my side of the family, not yours. You'll have to take my word.'

When she finally said goodbye, Isabel was already wondering how she would persuade Kate Ashley to let the friendship with Beuno develop. 'What if they try to stop me seeing you?' she asked him. 'There must be something I can tell my governess.'

'What's the matter with the truth?'

He proved to be right. Haltingly at first, then with growing confidence, she confessed about her strange kinsman, explaining her discovery of the old documents. She considered mentioning the doll, but decided that some aspects of the truth might be less helpful than others, and kept it to herself. Mrs Ashley always instinctively took Isabel's side if she could, and she was unable to see any harm in this new relationship. After all, the girl was virtually friendless – and what harm could a seventy-six-year-old man do her?

'I don't think your sister needs to know about this Mr Owen, do you?' she said.

Isabel shook her head. 'I – I did think of something on the way back from Llanddona . . . He knows all there is to know about plants, and nature and things. If you told Marianne someone had recommended a first rate botanist to teach me, d'you think . . .?'

'I think that would be a very good idea. I'll be writing tomorrow with some suggestions that came out of my visit to the university. If I simply put his name in, too, that should make everyone happy.'

She invited Beuno over to Tan-yr-Allt to meet Kate a few days later, and the governess was only slightly less impressed than Isabel had been. 'Strange,' she said after he left, 'it's impossible to think of him as being old. You feel as though he always looked like that.'

'I'm so glad you liked him. Now I don't feel so bad about being all the way up here.'

*　　*　　*

But before Isabel had time to immerse herself in her new life, the old one intruded and temporarily excluded everything else. She returned from a walk one afternoon to find Tom Moore-Ross in the drawing room.

It was as if all her dreams had come true at once. She stood motionless in the doorway, afraid to stir in case he dissolved. Then he broke the spell.

'Hasn't my Bel got a kiss for her poor old Uncle Tom?'

Then she was across the room in a rush, flinging herself into his arms, clutching him round the neck, sliding deliciously into the kiss and touch which had haunted her ever since their parting.

'Hey, there, slow down!' But he did not try to loosen her embrace, merely held her closer. 'What if someone came in?'

'No one will come . . . Wednesday afternoon . . .' She was too incoherent with joy to explain further so for the time being he simply took her word.

'We really won't be disturbed?' he asked, moments later, when her mounting passion threatened to overwhelm him, too.

Isabel collected herself with difficulty. 'Staff afternoon off,' she said, 'and Kate Ashley has gone to Chester for the day. How did you get in?'

Moore-Ross smiled wolfishly. 'Back door. Nobody here seems to expect burglars. That makes it easier for the prince to rescue the beautiful lady.'

'Will you really rescue me, Tom?' Her one thought now was to be with him. She did not care where.

'We'll talk about that later. But now, if there's really no one here, perhaps . . .?'

'I don't know, Tom. I'd be in terrible trouble if some-one caught us.'

He did not try to argue with her, but bent and kissed her again, caressing her body as he did so, murmuring how lovely she was, how desperately he had missed touching her. He did not have long to wait. After a few minutes, Isabel said: 'All right, come on,' and led him out of the big sunny living room towards the staircase.

Once her bedroom door was closed behind them, she opened her arms and came to him again, pressing herself against him, moaning and begging him to make love to her. She was so eager that he did not even bother to undress her, instead pulling her across to the bed and lying down, fully clothed, beside her. He raised her short skirt, slid his square, powerful hand inside the gusset of the silk panties she wore, and with a brutal downward motion tore them apart.

He was breathing harshly, lips parted, sweating with his desire to possess her again. For a moment Isabel was frightened. He was more like a wild animal moving in to kill its prey than a lover. But before her fear took over, his hands were on her bare skin, stroking, seeking and exciting. The panic subsided and she pressed close again. 'Wait a minute – don't move,' he said, and paused momentarily to unfasten his trousers. Then, before she could react, he was on her, thrusting into her oblivious of any need but his own desire.

Isabel uttered a shocked gasp as he penetrated her. Not yet, she wanted to cry – don't finish it yet! He prob-ably would not have heard even if she had cried out. The need for possession had gripped him and his world began and ended with the violent rhythm of his conquest. He forced his tongue between her lips as though attempting to fill every part of her, then put his hands inside the light cotton blouse she wore and tore it apart as easily as he had destroyed her panties. His obsessive lust was finally creating an answering excitement in Isabel now. She raised her legs, locked them around his waist, and tilted her pelvis up to meet his invasion of her body.

Moore-Ross let out a guttural cry and relaxed against her. Isabel was taken by surprise, and her own responsive movement continued for a while before she realised that he was spent. Is it often like this? she thought, dismayed. There was nothing beautiful or magnificent about this; merely two half-dressed people rutting and sweating in a manner that seemed better suited to a dark winter night than a sunny afternoon. After a while, she struggled to disengage herself.

Tom stirred and said: 'What's wrong? Not ready for more so soon?'

She ignored him and managed to slide out from beneath him. He reached out and pulled her back. 'Is my lady in a mood? I can't just do it to order, you know.'

She flared at him. 'You don't seem to care, as long as it satisfies you!'

He laughed. 'So that's it! All over too quickly, eh? Well, you're to blame for that, my dear. One look and I couldn't stop myself.'

Suddenly she was crying. 'Why weren't you like you were before? You were never rough with me then – you cared about me, not just yourself!'

'I'm always the same, Bel. Maybe you've changed. Come on, where's my beautiful princess? You can't have tired of me already.'

She did not look at him. She was too upset. Instead, she surveyed her ruined clothes and shuddered. 'Don't be silly. You know that isn't true. I'm going to get rid of these things, and – and get clean.'

She went into the bathroom which adjoined the master bedroom, and soon he heard the bath filling. He sighed. Really, women! You could never keep them happy . . . He got off the bed and removed his own crumpled clothes. He had left his suitcase in the entrance hall. Better find out which room he'd be sleeping in, then go and change. Someone was bound to come in eventually, and they'd know at a glance what he'd been up to if they saw him in this state. Bel would be able to tell him. Naked, he walked into the bathroom. She was just getting out of the bath, wrapping a vast white towel around herself.

'I was just wondering, where should I –'

She started to cry again, low, despairing sobs which shook her whole body. Oh, God, he thought, not a scene! Better humour her.

Before Isabel had time to say anything, he was beside her, holding her and kissing her, telling her there was no need to be unhappy. This time he was more delicate, and within a few minutes the tears were forgotten as she clung to him, eager to have him make love to her again. Remembering why he had come to Tan-yr-Allt, this time Tom made sure he was the perfect lover. An hour later, when he went off to one of the guest rooms, Isabel was as captivated as ever.

Kate Ashley was less so when she returned that evening to find Moore-Ross ensconced at the house.

'Really, sir, I can't understand why Miss Marianne

didn't write or telephone to tell me you were coming,' she said. 'I have clear instructions that there are to be no visitors unless she authorises it.'

Moore-Ross was nonchalant. 'But that can't apply to family, surely, Kate? You know I'm more of a father to Bel than anything else.'

'No sir, I don't. I'd be much happier if I could discuss this with Miss Marianne.'

'You're wasting your time. She's been away in Scotland for a week. I think she might be back in London tomorrow, but you won't get hold of her before then.'

'In that case, I shall leave a message for her. If she has any reason to think I don't follow her instructions, she'll never trust me again.'

He shrugged and tried to look as if he did not care. He knew precisely what that Richmond bitch would say: Out with him, and don't let him near my sister. He'd have come up a few days earlier if he'd realised Kate Ashley would turn so hostile. Still, he had twenty-four hours. He could achieve a lot in a short time.

Dinner was a strained affair. Isabel devoured Tom with her eyes, making the nature of her involvement all too clear. Kate Ashley was rigid with anger. Tom wondered whether he would be allowed anywhere near Isabel that night.

He left it until after midnight, then got up, put on his dressing gown and crept along the landing to Isabel's room. Kate Ashley's quarters were below those of the housekeeper, beyond earshot on the far side of the house. Unless the old bat was on guard outside Bel's door, he was in.

But he had underestimated the governess. Isabel's

door was locked, and there was no sign of a key. He rattled the doorknob and knocked, calling her name in a low voice. After a while, she answered.

'Come on, Bel, open up! What's this supposed to be, the Castle Perilous?'

'I can't, Tom. Kate locked me in and took the key.'

'Without a by-your-leave? That's bloody insubordination!'

'Sh – she said I wouldn't need to come out until the morning, and it was for my own safety. Oh, Tom, I'm so sorry.'

Sorry! What bloody good was sorry? He had planned to leave Tan-yr-Allt with Isabel's consent to be his wife. At this rate, he wouldn't be allowed close enough to make sure she'd accept him. With a huge effort, he made himself sound civil.

'Never mind, my darling. I expect she means well. Once she's talked to Marianne, we'll see – all right?'

Isabel sighed. 'I think Marianne will be pleased that Kate locked me up, Tom. We'll get into trouble, that's all. They won't let me be with you, I know it.'

'We shall see about that.' He wished he felt as confident as he sounded. Christ, he couldn't be bested by a jumped-up servant – a woman, at that! He'd find a way to get at her. He started to move away along the landing.

Behind the locked door, he heard a tearful Isabel say: 'I do love you, Tom, really I do, in spite of everything.'

Kate Ashley had never known Marianne to be as angry as when she explained the situation on the telephone next day. She thoroughly approved of Kate's action, and wanted even greater vigilance. 'He must leave as soon as possible, Kate. If he has to stay another night, you are to sleep in the same room as my sister. That man is evil.'

'Very well, Miss Marianne. But how am I to tell him he must go? I tried yesterday, but he refuses to take any notice.'

'Get him, this minute. We shall see what he has to say to me on the matter.'

Once Tom had spoken with Marianne, there was no question of him remaining at Tan-yr-Allt. It was too late for him to catch that day's last London train, but he was forced to assure Marianne he would be on the first one the following morning.

She was about to hang up, when he snarled at her: 'I want to see you as soon as I get back. There's something we have to discuss, and it won't wait.'

Marianne seemed undaunted by his threatening tone. 'What a good idea. I needed to see you anyway, to review your position at Richmond International. You'd better come and see me on Tuesday morning at ten.'

She broke the connection without giving him a chance to respond.

In the drawing room, Isabel was railing at Kate Ashley for betraying her to Marianne. Mrs Ashley was distressed but unrepentant. 'You must understand, Isabel, what you're asking is impossible. I'd lose my job the minute Miss Marianne found out, then you'd be surrounded by your enemies. The next governess wouldn't be a friend – your sister would see to that.'

'You're not my friend! If you were, you couldn't bear to make me so unhappy. If you hadn't told Marianne, she'd never have known.'

Mrs Ashley's laugh was humourless. 'She'd know

soon enough the minute you became pregnant.'

Isabel went white. 'What did you say?'

'You heard me, child. If you want to be treated as an adult, you must be prepared to discuss adult matters.'

'B – but that won't . . . it can't . . .'

'You're not the first young woman to think it can't happen to her, and you won't be the last. But it can, Isabel.' She crossed the room, clasped the girl's trembling hands between her own, and said: 'I know what happened when your stepmother was still alive, and I'm sure it happened again yesterday while I was away. I only had to look at you. If there's anything wrong, I'll do all I can to help, but I won't see you tricked by that terrible man.'

Isabel shook free of her with an explosive little sob. 'No, he's not. I love him, I tell you! Oh, why won't anybody believe me?'

Kate Ashley sighed. 'Because he'll bring you nothing but trouble, my dear. One day you'll wonder what you ever saw in him.'

They were prevented from further argument by Tom, who swaggered in, attempting to give the impression he had got the best of Marianne Richmond. 'There – I knew I could make her see reason. I stay until the end of the week.'

As he spoke, the telephone rang again. Mrs Ashley went to answer it.

Marianne Richmond said: 'I thought I should speak to you again immediately unless there was any doubt. Mr Moore-Ross is to leave first thing in the morning. Tonight, as I said, you are to sleep with Isabel. I think he's quite capable of trying to hoodwink you even about

537

the nature of the conversation he had with me.'

'Yes, Miss Marianne. Thank you. I'll make sure your instructions are carried out. Goodbye.'

She returned to the drawing room like an avenging fury. 'That was Miss Richmond, Mr Moore-Ross. You are to leave first thing in the morning. Come along, Isabel. It's time you were in your room.' Before there was time for further objections, she chivvied her charge ahead of her out of the room and closed the door in Moore-Ross's face.

Isabel insisted on going to the station with Tom. When Mrs Ashley objected, she snapped: 'He can hardly seduce me as Jenkins drives us down the Holyhead road, can he? I'm going whatever you say. I don't know when I'll see him again.'

Never, if I have my way, thought Mrs Ashley. But she was convinced that Marianne would never let Moore-Ross within striking distance of Isabel again, so the trip to the station seemed a minor concession.

Tom gazed at her soulfully throughout the short journey. Eventually he said: 'I love you, Bel, and I'm going to marry you. Will you wait for me?' Her native good sense told her that was overdoing it. Who would spirit away a fifteen-year-old girl? Nevertheless, it was intensely flattering. 'Well, will you?' he repeated.

Isabel nodded. 'I can't imagine loving anybody else. You promise you'll come back to me?'

'Of course I will. I came to see you and risked my job, didn't I?'

Isabel had not given any thought to that. 'Oh – what will you do if they fire you?'

'Sing for my supper, I suppose. Don't worry about

538

me, I shall manage. It'll be a living well lost if you turn out to be my reward.' He neglected to tell her that Erin's £100,000 estate had come to him free and clear. Tom Moore-Ross would never starve if Richmond's dismissed him.

Jenkins made no attempt to stop Isabel going on to the station platform with Tom. Isabel had feared he would, but Kate Ashley had not wanted to disclose any information about the relationship to the other servants, so the chauffeur treated Tom as just another guest.

He leaned out of his compartment to say goodbye. Oblivious of anyone who might be watching, Isabel kissed him with desperate passion. 'You will come back for me, won't you? Promise?'

'I promise, Bel. I can't imagine a future without you, either.'

The train pulled away and she walked along the platform behind it, wondering how long she must wait.


The morning sickness started eight weeks later. For a few days, she managed to keep it secret, but at the end of the first week, she emerged from the bathroom to discover an ashen-faced Kate Ashley standing beside her bed.

'How long? How long since this started?' There was suppressed hysteria in Kate's voice.

'What d'you mean? I just don't feel very well this morning, that's all.'

'You know better than that. I know your stepmother made sure you wouldn't grow up ignorant. How long, Isabel?'

'Five days, six – oh, what's the difference? I don't know.' Her bluster turned to fear and she went to Mrs

Ashley's arms in a little rush. 'Tell me what to do, Kate – please tell me!'

'I wish I knew, my dear. We can't let your sister in on it though, I'm sure of that.'

A wild hope stirred in Isabel. 'If she knew, she'd have to let me marry Tom, wouldn't she?'

'Isabel – no! You're under age. You couldn't marry him.'

The girl's face crumpled. 'Dear God, help me! There must be some way . . .'

Kate strove to keep her own emotions under control. 'Listen, my darling. He was here in the last week of June. It's late August now. Your baby should be due at about the end of March . . .'

'. . . and by then I shall be sixteen. There, I'll marry him, you'll see, everything will be all right.' But she started to cry as she said it, and added fearfully, 'Please say it will be, Kate.'

The older woman held her close. 'I can't lie to you now, my dear. It will be even worse for you later if I do. I know you think you love him, but that will change. He's not a nice man.'

'I won't listen!'

'You must, or I think you're beyond saving. Try to remember he was just as passionate as this less than three years ago after your father died. But then his true love was Erin. Isabel, she's only been dead three months, and he was proposing marriage to you barely six weeks after she died. Does that sound like a man with deep, true feelings?'

'No. Yes – oh, stop it! I don't know what to do. Marianne will kill me.'

'Not until after she's killed me. Try to keep calm and let things take their course for the moment. I'll think of something, I promise.'

In her more rational moments, Isabel knew Tom Moore-Ross was a scoundrel and an opportunist. But at present she had very few rational moments, and by the end of each day, she was usually sufficiently keyed up to regard her seducer as the one man who could rescue her. It was in one of these fits that she came back downstairs long after her bedtime, when Mrs Ashley, too, had retired, and telephoned Tom in London.

Without pausing to identify herself, she said: 'Tom, I'm having a baby. What can we do?'

There was a long silence at the other end of the line, interrupted at one point by something that sounded like whispering. Then he replied: 'Bel? What are you saying? It can't be true!'

'It is – I'm being sick all the time and I want to eat things I never used to like. Oh, Tom, please tell me what to do!'

His voice was suddenly decisive. 'I want you to stop worrying. There's only one thing to do – what we've always planned. Let's see, we must still have quite a long time . . . March – April?'

'Yes, about then.' Somehow she found it shameful that he could calculate her term so casually.

'Right, then. Even your sister must be capable of seeing reason at this stage.'

'No – you can't go to her!'

He laughed. 'If I don't, there's no power on earth that can marry us until you're twenty-one, and that'll be a little late, I fancy!'

If only he didn't sound so casual about it. Didn't he realise what it was doing to her? 'Very well. But what shall I do if she comes and confronts me with it?'

Another chuckle. 'If you think that's a possibility, you don't know your sister. She'd be far too embarrassed. No, in the end she'll give in gracefully, then as soon as you're sixteen, I'll be up to make it all legal. We should manage it just it time.'

Just like arranging a holiday or an advertising campaign, she thought.

'Bel? Are you still there? How does that sound to you?'

'I – I don't know . . . I'm just so miserable.'

'Well, don't be. Your Uncle Tom has it all in hand.'

'Don't call yourself that. You know I hate it.'

'Please yourself. Now go on to bed, and leave this to me. Sleep tight, Bel.'

That was the last time she even considered asking him for help. Whatever the solution was, it was one she must come to herself. Tom Moore-Ross would help no one but himself. Nevertheless, she half expected him to call or write within the next couple of days. When he did not, she decided he must have had second thoughts. She did not tell Kate Ashley she had spoken to him.

In the weeks since Isabel's arrival in North Wales, Beuno Owen had become almost part of the family. Marianne had accepted his name along with the others recommended by Kate for special tuition. He visited Tan-yr-Allt twice a week and Isabel went to his farm once a fortnight to do botany fieldwork projects. After one of these visits early in September, Beuno went to see Kate Ashley.

'This may not be my business, Katie, but do you know she's with child?' he asked.

Kate winced inwardly. Was it showing already? 'Yes, I know. But I thought no one else did.'

'Only me, girl. She didn't tell me. I just always seem to know about these things. What's she going to do?'

Kate needed a confidant. She explained the whole squalid story, and Beuno listened in silence.

After she had finished, he nodded. 'Poor child. We can't leave her to him, can we?'

'I don't think her sister would permit it anyway, but no, I agree with you. The trouble is, I have no idea what we can do.'

'I could help.'

'You? But how? We can't let her have it in secret and find someone to raise it . . .' She broke off. 'Oh. Stop it being born, you mean?'

'Yes. I do know how. I haven't done it for years, mind. Not a good thing to do. It do catch up on you in the end. But I'd do it for her. Anyhow, their line has to end with her.'

Now that there was hope, Mrs Ashley was only half listening, but the last sentence gave her pause. 'Their line? What do you mean, Beuno?'

'Nothing, girl. Just an old bit of superstition. Nothing to worry you. Now, let's see. Do you want to talk to Isabel about it, or shall I?'

In the end, Isabel herself made the approach to Beuno. They were sitting outside his cottage on a patch of grass overlooking the full sweep of Red Wharf Bay. Isabel said: 'You know what you did to Marianne's mother – well, would it work for me?' As she spoke she turned away from the broad view and gazed at him. 'Will you kill my baby?'

'That's a very murderous way to put it, isn't it? Sure you want me to?'

'Yes.' The monosyllable was fierce. 'It's a traitor's baby.'

'You won't be as bad as Karin Richmond was, *cariad*, but it will be bad enough. Are you ready for that?'

'I don't think I've got a choice.'

'There's always a choice.'

'Yes – the choice that brought you into this world, and then me, to parents who wanted something else. That's no choice.'

'Would you prefer never to have been born?'

'Why are you saying this? I know it will hurt me and I'm ready for it. The sooner the better. Is that good enough?'

He moved across to the girl and laid a brown hand on her shoulder. 'It have got to be, girl. You'm making it come full circle.'

'This is nothing to do with anyone else's sins – only mine.'

'You're wrong there. "For the fathers have eaten sour grapes, and the children's teeth are set on edge." That's us, Isabel, you and me. It's their sins, too, coming back to reproach us.'

She shivered. 'Will we ever be free of it?'

'Never. But that don't mean life is worthless, do it?'

'At the moment, I feel as if it is.'

'It will pass. Everything do pass.'

She looked away across the sea again, then said: 'When will you do it?'

'Next week. No use wasting time, but I need to make up the decoction, and the moon will be right by then.'

'Do you really believe in that part of it?'

'No, but I don't disbelieve, either. It have always worked before and it's only my rational side that says it's the herbs. My dark side do say it's the old magic. I'll never know which it really is.'

A week later he came to her at Tan-yr-Allt, bringing with him a couple of bottles. He took Isabel and Kate Ashley through the dosage instructions, then said: 'It will give you bad stomach cramps. I've put in some sedative, but unless you do work with it, like if you were in labour at full term, it may do you some harm. You've got to rid yourself of all of it, see.'

She shuddered. 'And if I don't?'

'Septicaemia, probably. But no need to think about that. This is the proper strength. Kate – watch her close. Don't leave her by herself. Once the labour have ended, her temperature should be normal and there shouldn't be any shock. If there is, don't waste time on me. Send for the medical doctor. It shouldn't be anything too bad, but it will mean she's having a haemorrhage. If that do happen, hospital is the best place.'

Kate nodded, praying the need would not arise. 'What if that did happen? Wouldn't the doctor know what brought it on?'

'Not if he don't see me around here! No, once it's gone, the symptoms of abortion and miscarriage are pretty much the same if you do use herbs.'

'How long will it take?' asked Isabel. She felt cold and distant, as if she were asking questions about someone else.

'Ten to eighteen hours. A bit less if you're lucky. It starts about three hours after you do take the second dose. It's only at the end that it do get really bad.'

'All right. Let's start now. I want to get it over and done with.'

She took the second dose of the decoction at six o'clock that evening. Shortly after eleven, when the contractions were under way and she was in bed, her sister Marianne arrived like an avenging angel, demanding to know what was going on.

# Chapter Twenty-Three

## Isabel, 1938

*Looking back, I can see Papa married Erin as much to spite Tom as because he loved her . . . but it turned into something else, thanks to dear Erin. Whatever would have happened to me without her? I was too young to see it at the time, but really Erin was the first thoroughly decent woman he had ever met. He knew he could never be her great passion, but she treated him as if she loved him, and he came to believe she did. He certainly loved her.*

*Papa was so demanding, I wonder now how on earth she managed to stay cheerful, patient and interesting all the time. She even had the strength to laugh at his terrifying moods. Through it all, she was quite without complacency. She'd burned her boats, and after that she devoted herself to her marriage and to giving Marianne and me a belated taste of family life. She found me the first friends I ever knew, the only friends . . . and she found Robin . . .*

*She seemed to find people with children everywhere, and within months Paxton was full of them. She was always organising visits, parties, excursions – anything to bring the children closer to me. Soon I'd almost forgotten what it was to be lonely. The latest brood of*

Beynon children lived at Bishop's Stortford; Erin's friend Nadia Farrar had a son and a daughter aged eleven and nine. My cousins – Aunt Mary Rose's children – were only a year or two older than me. And then there was Robin Lester, my best friend.

The Lesters owned the estate which adjoined Paxton. They had twin thirteen-year-old daughters, a six-year-old son, and Robin. He was born in the same week as I. I remember the day we met, we squabbled like cat and dog when I tried to steal the best place for minnow-fishing on the bank of the lower lake at Paxton. He fought me for it and we both fell in. At first I was still so cross I just went on yelling at him, then I remembered I couldn't swim and I started screaming instead. I was terrified. Robin rescued me and brought me back to the house looking like a drowned rat.

After that we were always together. He taught me to swim; I taught him to play badminton. Both of us were mad about horses and we rode every day. After a few months, I found it impossible to remember life without Robin.

It was too good to last, though. The first cracks appeared in the summer of 1932. That was when Papa began to get really ill, and Erin had to spend so much time with him that the parties and outings tailed off rather. But somehow, I didn't realise it was the beginning of the end. He had been ill for so long . . . the next blow hit me far harder. I was out for my regular ride with Robin one day, when I realised he was acting oddly. He was very quiet, and several times he shut up completely as he began to tell me something. Finally, when we were within sight of home, he managed to get it out.

'They're sending me away, Isabel.'

'I don't understand. What for, a holiday? Where are you going?'

'Not a holiday. Nearly for ever, I think. School.'

'No, you can't leave me, Robin. You're my best friend. I can't come with you, can I?'

He shook his head. 'I knew ages ago that I'd be going when I was twelve, but it was never important before. I didn't mind until I met you. But I don't want to leave you, either.'

'Then let's run away.'

He looked dubious. 'I think they'd find us, Izz. Grown-ups always do.'

'Not if we stow away on a ship and sail away to America or Canada or India.'

'You don't really mean that. Babies talk like that.'

'Then I want to be a baby. Oh, Rob, I can't do without you – don't go. Please don't go!'

Our ponies were standing shoulder to shoulder and I leaned across, flinging my arms around his neck and knocking his riding hat askew. 'I think we'd better get down a minute,' he said.

On the ground, beneath an enormous horse chestnut, we sat down. The ponies grazed quietly, unaware of the tragedy being played out behind them. Robin took out the scout knife he carried in a flat leather sheath on his belt.

'Will it help if we swear a bloody oath?'

That made me stop crying. I said: 'Would it hurt?'

'A bit. Not much.'

'I want it to hurt a lot. We'll never forget then.'

'Come on, Izz. This will keep us true. Give me your hand.'

549

*I held out my grubby palm and he stared at it for a moment. 'Let's try our thumbs,' he said. 'I can bind them together easily.'*

*Robin held out his own left hand and pressed it against my right. 'When I say ready, we press them together like this, all right?'*

*I nodded. He dug a handkerchief out of his pocket, and folded it like a bandage before laying it across his knee. Then he said, 'Ready, now.' We pressed our hands together and Robin made two small nicks at the bases of our thumbs. As the blood began to flow, he bound the handkerchief around them and said solemnly: 'That's so that the bloods can mingle, you see.'*

*After that, we sat in silence for a couple of minutes. Then I said, 'D'you think they've mingled now?'*

*'I 'spect so. Let's see.' He unbound our thumbs and we both looked at the sticky redness. We were quite impressed. 'Looks like it, doesn't it?' he said.*

*I only said: 'Will you kiss me goodbye?'*

*'I'm not going until September.'*

*'I know, but this is our goodbye, just you and me. There'll be other people around when you really go.'*

*'All right.' Slowly, almost reverently, he leaned forward and kissed my lips. We sat like that for ages, our lips pressed together as our hands had been before. Then he drew away and said: 'You won't marry anybody else, will you Izz?'*

*'No, Robin. We're engaged to be married the minute we're old enough. Then nobody will ever split us up again.'*

*Something touched us both then, and we pressed our bloody hands together again, as if to reaffirm our vow.*

*That was the beginning of the end of all friendships,*
*because first Papa died, then, after Erin married Tom, I*
*fell in love with him before I had time to find my feet*
*again . . . and my lovely Rob had gone away and now I*
*seem to have lost him forever . . .*

The steady beat of the train wheels over the tracks had
imprinted itself subliminally on her thoughts and her
mind kept emerging from memories of less lonely times
and fitting its current obsession to the imposed rhythm:
what-will-become-of-me, what-will-become-of-me,
what-will-become-of-me, what-will-become-of-me?

She shook herself angrily. Time enough to think of
that when she confronted Marianne.

Isabel thought the train would never get to Euston.
These days, a trip to London was such a rarity for her
that she should have delighted in the journey. Instead she
gazed unseeing at the ripening cornfields and rich pas-
tures of England as they paraded past her window.

Marianne – that awful old wreck! That she should
have control over me, at my age, Isabel seethed. That she
should have control of the company, even worse . . .
(what-will-become-of-me, what-will-become-of-me?). It
couldn't go on forever and the sooner Marianne accepted
that she was a free agent, the better. There was a whole
world out there, and she was expected to spend her life
pent up in a forgotten corner of the kingdom. This time,
Marianne must listen. She wanted independence, and a
say in Richmond International. And after that? Well,
after that, anything was possible! (What-will-become-
of-me, what-will-become-of-me?)

Finally, in the late afternoon, the train chugged into

the terminus. Isabel was in the corridor, waiting to jump off the moment it stopped. She saw Dawkins beside the ticket barrier, towering over the other passers-by, his pearl grey chauffeur's uniform like something out of an American movie. That's new since last time, she thought. Bet it was slimy Heinie's idea. She loathed her brother-in-law even more than she resented Marianne.

'Dawkins – here I am!' she called, waving furiously. 'There's just the one bag, it's all right.'

'Good day, miss. The car is around the corner. Mrs von Burckhardt said I was to take you straight to Eaton Place.'

'I expected her to meet me.'

'She sends her apologies, Miss Isabel. An urgent meeting out of town – Windsor, I believe. She took one of the pool cars from Richmond House. She said to tell you she should be back shortly after we arrive.'

He drove down Gower Street, into Shaftesbury Avenue, and Isabel felt the excitement of the capital catch her and hold her. This was the place to be, not way beyond Snowdonia! Oh, to be grown up and independent and in charge of her own affairs. The billboards outside the theatres advertised at least three plays she was dying to see. Then they were past Eros and heading west along Piccadilly. First there was Fortnum's, and then there was Richmond's. She remembered the order as a childhood chant she had learned from her father in one of the periods of his favour, when he would take her past Fortnum's to Richmond's Piccadilly shop. In those days, she had never known which she preferred, the gorgeously ornate clock above Fortnum's main entrance, or the vivid red, white and gold paintwork which made

Richmond's stand out like a beacon against the grey stone façades.

They drew level with Richmond's, and swept past almost before she noticed it. 'My God, Dawkins – what's happened to the shop livery? It looks terrible!'

The chauffeur shook his head. 'I know, miss. Awful, isn't it? None of the staff like it, but Mrs von Burckhardt says the new colours are the coming thing. At least, she says Mr von Burckhardt thinks so,' he added gloomily.

'But that was what made us distinctive! It looks like a cheap imitation of Harrods, now.'

'I think Mr von Burckhardt was hoping it looked like an even more expensive version, miss.'

'Well, he's wrong. White looks dreadful against that dark green. It's all right with their gold trim – but white? It looks like a great big bottle of disinfectant!'

She was so incensed at such meddling that she hardly noticed anything during the rest of the journey. When they arrived outside the Eaton Place apartment, she bounded into the entrance foyer like a young fencer ready to engage an opponent. Dawkins smiled secretly. He wished he had an excuse to be hanging around up at the apartment when Miss Isabel had a go at Madam. It looked as though it would be worth waiting for.

Marianne had arrived home earlier than she expected, and was there to greet Isabel on her arrival. Her determined effort to be welcoming and friendly was dented by Isabel's instant attack on the Piccadilly shop decor.

'How could you? That was Papa's pride and joy, the thing that got us up out of the bottom end of the retail trade, and you've thrown it away!'

'I really don't think this is an appropriate time for such a discussion, Isabel – we haven't seen one another for almost a year. Surely you have something a little more agreeable than that to say?'

Isabel scowled ferociously. 'I don't think so. I can't imagine anything more important than that.'

'Can't you? In that case, perhaps you've wasted everyone's time in coming all the way down here. I thought you had important matters to discuss with me.'

'I have, but I'm not as rude as you seem to think. I was going to let all that wait. I can't let that horror pass without mentioning it, though.'

'You never accept reality, Isabel, that's your trouble. If Richmond's of Piccadilly were painted red, white and blue and had a grenadier guardsman on duty outside, it wouldn't be any concern of yours. I run the company, remember. Now, are you going to sit down and take tea with me like a grown-up, or must I go on treating you as a child?'

'Very well. I apologise if I behaved badly. Let's leave it for the moment.'

'Your apology is accepted. Tell me about your journey. Was it interesting?'

My God, Isabel thought. I've come nearly three hundred miles to discuss my future and my sister prefers to talk about the British landscape as seen from a railway carriage. She gritted her teeth and responded appropriately to Marianne's banality. It lasted until bedtime.

By then, Isabel was beside herself. At the best of times, she found Marianne hard going, but this was absurd. She had been in the other woman's company for almost five hours now, and after the first exchange, they had said nothing that mattered. Marianne was already preparing to depart for bed, and Isabel clutched at the first gambit she could find to hold her a few minutes longer.

'I'm surprised not to see Heinrich.'

Marianne became evasive. 'Ah – er, yes – he's in Germany. So much to do, you know. He spends quite a lot of time there now.'

'Isn't that strange? I always imagined you two as inseparable. When did he go?'

'Mmm, let me see . . . it must be a little under three months.'

'Oh. So you've been popping back and forth between Richmond House and Berlin, I imagine.'

'N – not quite. I've had a lot to do here. No, I haven't seen him since he went. Of course, we write every day.'

'When's he coming home?'

'He's at home already, Isabel. He is a German citizen, remember. I'm the one who should be going to him . . . when I have time to leave the business, that is.'

'In that case, the sooner you give me a job, the sooner you'll have a bit more free time.'

'What are you talking about?'

'I'd have thought that was obvious. I'm talking about when you propose to start training me to take my proper place in the company.'

'I can't think what put such an idea into your head.'

'And I can't think what's enabled you to ignore it. Remember Papa's will?'

'You never even saw it.'

'I know. But I also know that I get a share of the company when I reach my majority – and that's getting closer every day.'

'There are complications . . . anyway, it's still at least three years off.'

'Complications? I don't understand.'

'Must we discuss this now? I was about to go to bed.'

'And in the morning, no doubt, you'll be frightfully busy and not have time to discuss it then, either.'

'I do have to go out, yes.'

'Then it has to be now, Marianne. Tell me about the complications.'

Isabel was deeply troubled by the fact that Marianne seemed unable to face her directly. What was she ashamed of? They must be trying to cheat me, thought Isabel. I wonder how?

Marianne plunged in at the deep end. 'You know that under the original terms of Father's will, Erin was to administer everything until you and I either married or reached the age of forty?'

Isabel nodded. 'But Erin's death negated that. After the funeral, they said you were to inherit immediately and I was to come into my share when I reached my normal legal majority.'

'Yes, but Heinrich has been going over it again with specialist lawyers, and he's of the opinion that the original conditions of the will should have remained in force.'

'Now wait a minute. I know I'm supposed to be a little innocent from up in the mountains, but even I can see that means you have your share, because you married in 1935, but unless I marry, I don't get a penny until I'm forty.'

'It's hardly that terrible, Isabel. You're not short of money, are you? Your allowance is more than generous, and if you want anything special, you know I'm always prepared to listen.'

'And you know it's not the money!' Isabel was furious. 'It's the company. Our company. Yours and mine, not yours and Heinrich's.'

Marianne became evasive again. 'As I said, Heinrich and his lawyers are convinced they could make a strong case for upholding the original will.'

'But how does that leave Erin's will?'

'It doesn't raise any problem. Erin left clear directions that I should take over her role as your guardian if she died while you were still a minor. According to the lawyers, once I had fulfilled that condition of Father's will by getting married, Erin's offered no contradictions at all. I simply took over her role with regard to you. Otherwise, Father's will continued to apply.'

'That's only Heinrich's opinion. I prefer the advice of the Richmond lawyers who said I inherit at twenty-one.'

'I think you'll decide it's best to do as we suggest, Isabel.'

'If you believe that, you're mad.'

Marianne was very unhappy now. 'If you're determined to go into this, tomorrow would be better. I'll rearrange my engagements and we can talk in the morning.'

'Why not now? You've gone far enough to make sure I shan't get any sleep if we leave it.'

'This is very silly. There's no reason why I should ask you to approve what I do,' said Marianne. 'I'm your guardian and you are a minor. You have to do as I say.'

'I'm more interested in why you think I should continue to do so once I'm over twenty-one.'

'Perhaps it would be better for all of us if you simply took my word. I wish you no harm, Isabel.'

557

'That's a matter of opinion, too. Anyway, I'm still more interested in what you wish for Richmond International than any half-baked plan to keep me in my place.'

'Heinrich does not make half-baked plans.'

'Oh, so he's the brains behind this? I might have known!'

Anger banished Marianne's reticence. 'I'm not going to stand for any more of this. Whatever you think yourself capable of doing, you're still a child, and your past behaviour makes it clear that you have neither the experience nor the moral judgement to play a major part in the development of Richmond's.'

She might have been reading from a prepared text. I wonder who wrote it for her? Isabel thought. No prizes for guessing . . .

Marianne said: 'Before you make a complete fool of yourself, I want to show you something. Then perhaps you'll be persuaded to let us make the decisions.'

Before Isabel could protest, she went off to the small room she used as a study, returning moments later with a legal envelope stuffed with papers. 'I have no wish to do this,' she said, 'but you leave me no choice. I am prepared to go to court to demonstrate that you are morally unfit to control your own affairs in the foreseeable future, and that the original conditions of Father's will should stand.'

The silence was tangible. Isabel's whole attention focused on the papers in Marianne's hand. Finally she could contain herself no longer. 'What has that to do with me?' she gestured at the envelope.

'I hoped you would never need to see it. But, since you

give me no choice . . .' She removed the papers from the envelope and handed them to Isabel. After a slight hesitation, the younger girl began to open them. 'You'll need some time to read it,' Marianne said nervously. 'I'll be in my study if you wish to discuss it afterwards.'

'No – the least you can do is stay here. It's hardly likely to take me all night.' Isabel sat down and unfolded the document.

Afterwards, she was sure she had known all along what it would be. It was the only thing Marianne had against her, after all.


In September 1935, Tom Moore-Ross was convinced he finally had the weapon he needed to win part of the Richmond empire for himself. The day after Isabel telephoned from North Wales to break the news of her pregnancy, he went to see Marianne. She was surprised and irritated when he arrived. The management review Heinrich had undertaken at Richmond's was nearing its conclusion and they planned to dispense with Moore-Ross as soon as possible after that; but until then, Marianne thought they had no need to meet. Surely even someone as thick-skinned as he could see there was no place for him here?

Then he dropped his bombshell about Isabel's condition. 'The choice is yours, Marianne,' he ended gleefully. 'Either you let me make an honest woman of your little sister the day after her sixteenth birthday, or you deal with all London knowing she's tucked away in the provinces giving birth to her stepfather's bastard. Hardly the stuff of polite conversation, is it?'

Shock saved Marianne from impulsive action she

might have regretted. When she found words, it was only to ask Tom to give her time. He left, still gloating, saying he would return the next day. After that, Heinrich von Burckhardt took over and Moore-Ross never stood a chance. When Tom came back early the next evening, they were ready for him.

He had made one terrible miscalculation: in his family, the blood link was all-powerful. The brothers and sisters felt far more deeply about each other than about their spouses. Only their children meant as much to them as their siblings. His background had left him incapable of understanding rivalry like that which was building up between Marianne and Isabel Richmond. He assumed Marianne would be prepared to do anything to save her sister grief. In fact, she was prepared to do anything to see her sister did not take part of her own inheritance. Instead of permission to marry, Tom found himself receiving threats.

Von Burckhardt gave him a silky smile and said: 'I think we owe it to Society to see that men with your inclinations are not permitted to prey on innocent girls. We are prepared to go to the courts, and make Isabel a ward of the state. I think it likely we would get a hearing in camera, but even if we did not, it would be our duty to go ahead. Naturally, you would be liable to criminal prosecution.'

This was not at all what Tom expected. He attempted to bluster his way through it. 'Very funny – what would the charges be, pray?'

'In America, they would call it statutory rape. I always feel that is the appropriate designation. Somehow, the British equivalent has less impact. Just the same, I think you will find that illegal sexual intercourse with a girl below the age of consent carries appropriate penalties – particularly when that girl was under your legal guardianship.'

'You can't prove a thing!'

'But we can. Marianne is visiting North Wales now –' that was not quite true, since she planned to leave next day – 'and your behaviour has been witnessed by servants both there and at Paxton when your wife was still alive. In any case, I understand that Isabel is prepared to say almost anything to avoid being locked up until she is deemed morally fit. I think I should be right in saying your life in this country would be finished once the hearing was complete.'

Moore-Ross was trembling now. My God, could they do that? He knew the answer almost before posing the question to himself. Of course they could. This bloody Hun never made threats he couldn't carry out. They had him. Only the details remained to be discussed. He slumped in his chair. 'All right, what do you want me to do?'

Von Burckhardt gave him a chilly smile. 'That's better. You'll be surprised how easy it is. We have nothing but Isabel's welfare at heart. I want two legally witnessed, signed statements from you. One will describe, in detail, your sexual relationship with my sister-in-law, complete with dates and places. I have no objection if you feel it necessary to point out that she encouraged your advances. The other will be an undertaking to leave Britain and live abroad for at least ten years. No – don't interrupt; I have not finished. In return for the undertaking, we will guarantee to pay you a sum which matches your inheritance from your late wife. It will be paid to you, in the country of your choice, at the rate of £5,000 a year over twenty years. Even you should be able to make ends meet on such a sum to augment your capital.'

Moore-Ross considered the proposal. It had its merits. He was quite surprised that von Burckhardt was not planning to ruin him financially as well as socially. 'Why the sudden spurt of generosity?' he said.

'Ah – that was my idea. Marianne was not wholly in agreement at first. I always feel that in the end, financial inducement works better that threats. You have so much more to lose if you refuse, do you not?'

He was certainly smarter than his wife, damn him. Tom shrugged. 'All right, then. Produce your bits of paper. When do I have to go?'

'As soon as you can set your affairs in order – by the end of September at the latest. If you are still in England after that, we shall initiate proceedings to make Isabel a ward of court. Once that was under way, you could estimate your freedom in days.'

Marianne had stayed at Tan-yr-Allt only long enough to confirm that her sister would recover. After savagely cross-examining Kate Ashley, she accepted that the miscarriage was natural, particularly when Isabel's doctor said he thought so. Before she left, she browbeat Mrs Ashley into signing a statement implicating Tom Moore-Ross, and had it legally witnessed. The threat was one she would later use to effect on Isabel herself: sign, or my sister goes into an institution.

When Isabel was a little better, Kate explained as

gently as she could that Tom would not be seeing her again. At first, Isabel tried to resist, but she had already gone through too much misery over Moore-Ross for her feelings to endure against such odds. She accepted the inevitable, and settled down to life in North Wales.

Mrs Ashley's deposition, together with Tom's highly-coloured account of how his stepdaughter had seduced him, had been saved against the day when Isabel should decide to assert herself. Now Isabel sat in her sister's London drawing room and read the mass of lies and half-truths which would undoubtedly get her locked away if she tried to fight.

She did not cry. She merely promised herself that one day she would extract vengeance, from both Marianne and Tom Moore-Ross. She had finally learned no one could be trusted – no lover, friend or family. She intended to profit from the knowledge. Through it all, she made an exception for one person – Beuno Owen. Beuno knew suffering just as she did. For a little while, at least, she could cling to him.

When Marianne returned, Isabel had folded the papers and replaced them in the envelope. She said nothing, merely handing it back to Marianne and giving her a neutral look. Marianne, unable to meet her eyes for more than a second, said: 'It really is for the best, Isabel.'

'Whatever you say. Do you know the train times to Bangor? I might as well go back tomorrow.'

This was the last thing Marianne had expected. She knew her sister as a fighter. If she appeared to be giving up without a struggle, she must have some scheme in mind. 'You can't go so soon! I thought you wanted to see some plays, and I'm sure you'd like to go shopping.'

Isabel shrugged, dismissing such trivial activity. 'You know that's not why I came. Since I have to go back, I may as well go at once. I might get too keen on London again, and that wouldn't help me, would it?'

'But I thought we could do so many things together.'

Now the girl looked at her directly and Marianne found herself unable to look away. 'You don't want to do things with me, Marianne. You want to do things to me. You've won. Don't expect me to congratulate you.' She turned and went off to her bedroom.

Next morning, Isabel was up by six o'clock. If she was to face her sister today, she must get away first and calm herself. Hyde Park was only half a mile away. She dressed and went for a walk.

When she returned nearly two hours later, Marianne had already gone out. The housekeeper gave her a note.

Isabel – you can't dash back to North Wales quite yet. I have a surprise visitor for you, someone I'm sure will make you want to stay. He is calling at about eleven. Enjoy your day.

Love, Marianne

Who will it be? she thought. Probably some decrepit old type who knew Papa and wants to reminisce. She'd never trust me with anyone interesting.

But Isabel had underestimated the depth of Marianne's guilty need to propitiate her. At precisely eleven o'clock, the housekeeper showed in Robin Lester.

At first Isabel could do little but gaze at him. It was

564

four years since she had seen him – at her father's funeral – and then the enormity of the occasion had made him stiff and remote. Then, too, he had been at the worst point of his adolescence, all uncoordinated limbs and his cheeks an unhappy mix of peach-fuzz and pimples. They had parted with little regret. Now, miraculously, he was her Robin again.

'Marianne said I could take you wherever I liked, including out to dinner and a theatre this evening – so name your choice,' he said.

His smile dazzled her. 'Let's just get out of this place so that I can breathe freely,' she told him. 'D'you know, I've never been out in the streets of London in grown-up clothes? This will be what passes for my debut.'

It was almost possible to forget her present misery as they strolled down Piccadilly. Then she remembered the ghastly new façades of Richmond's, and wished to be somewhere else. 'Quick,' she ordered him, 'get a taxi. I know where we'll go – the British Museum!'

Once they were inside the cab, speeding north-eastwards, he said: 'You must be the only girl in London who'd choose a museum when she was given the freedom of the city! Talk about a bluestocking.'

Isabel merely laughed. 'It's wide, and cool, and I feel safe among the gates of ancient cities and images of dead pharaohs,' she said. 'They can't hurt me, and they'll give me a bit of peace to talk to you. Oh, Rob, I'm so glad you found me again!'

'I didn't know you were lost. I thought we were just off in different places, growing up.'

Her smile faded. 'Some growing up is harder than others. What about the blood brotherhood?'

'I'd never forget that. I can still see your little face, now, under that tree, terrified I'd maim you but determined not to let go. See? I still bear the scar.'

He held out his hand and she saw a thread of white tissue along his thumb. 'How about yours? Don't tell me it's faded.'

She shook her head. 'There, see? Fainter than yours, but it'll never go. It hurt like mad, you know.'

'Good things usually do.'

She moved closer to him and clasped his hand. 'It's still just as easy to talk to you as it was that day. I wish we could have stayed together, Robin. Maybe things would have worked out better then.'

'You're unhappy.'

Isabel managed not to blurt out the full extent of her misery. 'You could say that. I don't suppose it's that uncommon. What about you?'

'I'm fine – it's such an exciting time for me, after all.'

She was bewildered. 'Why? What's happening?'

'Didn't Marianne tell you? But that's why I wanted to see you so much. As from the beginning of next week, I'm a fully paid-up member of the Royal Air Force. I had to see you again before they send me away. It's been such a long time.'

'No, I didn't even know until this morning that you were coming.'

'That's strange. When I rang to ask her, a couple of weeks ago, she seemed to think it would be the highlight of your visit to London.'

'It will be, but I'm afraid they never tell me anything. Never mind that, though. Why the airforce? Why the military at all? I never thought you wanted that sort of career.'

'I don't. But surely you realise there's bound to be a war soon?'

'From the depths of North Wales, all that sounds very far away.'

'It isn't, you know. We'll all be in it up to our necks before long. I decided that if I joined up now, I'd have some choice, instead of being pushed where they wanted me later.'

'But flying?'

'Flying is just part of it. I've heard too many ghastly reminiscences from men who were trapped in the trenches last time ever to want to be in the army. I thought this would keep me away from all that. At least you know where you are, up in a plane.'

The logic of that escaped her, but she was far too taken up with his plans to go into it. 'So I shall lose you again as soon as I've found you?'

'Not a chance of it! I'm very hard to shake off. I thought, I could see you today and the rest of this week, then when I'm posted, you might write to me.'

'Oh, yes, please. I couldn't bear to be cut off from you again.'

It was hard for Isabel to accept that the years which had been lonely and empty for her had been filled with the business of school, new friends and the endless activity of a close family for Robin. He had no great understanding of her solitary existence. In his mind, the time had come for them to resume their old, intimate ties, which he did not consider to have been broken. The sense of happy normality which surrounded him cheered Isabel more than anything.

She watched him covertly as they explored the

museum. It was quiet on this sunny summer day, and at times it seemed they had the place to themselves. Time and again she was tempted to tell him about the dreadful things that had happened to her since last they met. Time and again she remembered the men she had trusted and who had betrayed her: Tom Moore-Ross; Harry Richmond; in a sense, even Robin Lester, because he lacked the ability to comprehend that something had gone badly wrong with her life while he was absent. Fight the temptation, she told herself. He's here now, but that might pass, and then it will be just another betrayal . . . So she held her peace.

Even so, over the next few days they recaptured that delicious childhood intimacy to which all later relationships bear poor comparison. To Isabel, it was as if one short week made up for the years of exile, the years in which she had been deprived of the things she longed to do. The interlude was not even spoiled by its inevitable termination: she enjoyed herself so intensely that it would have been unthinkable to continue in London alone once Robin had departed to the airforce. When he went, she was willing to go back to North Wales and await the time when he would come again.

Marianne looked on approvingly as the childhood friendship blossomed into a youthful romance. If she felt a little envy for her lovely sister, it was swiftly banished by the knowledge that this unlooked for improvement prevented the girl pursuing their vendetta.

Marianne was deeply lonely now that she saw so little of Heinrich. There had been no open rift between them, but he had left her with no illusions about her ability to hold him at her side in England when his main interests lay in Germany. In other circumstances, she would have hurried to join him, and counted her commercial career well lost. But it was not that easy.

Richmond International was beginning to creak at the seams. Whatever magic Harry Richmond had possessed was clearly lacking now. The prosperity had continued for a year or two after his death, but then the firm seemed to mark time for a while and now it was in a decliné of sorts. Marianne tried to take comfort from the fact that no one was doing well in the longest depression within living memory. But deep down she knew there had been other depressions and that her father's innovative genius had minimised them. She dared not leave while matters were in such a state of flux. Then, too, there was the consideration of what might happen in Germany in the near future.

Heinrich von Burckhardt had never made a secret of his admiration for Adolf Hitler. He was not one of the aristocrats who sneered and said they would put up with this shabby charlatan because Germany needed a firm hand. He was committed heart and soul to his Führer's cause. Marianne was not as intelligent as Isabel, but she was not stupid, either. She recognised the value of her father's old advisers who still worked for her. They all said there would be war; and they said that an Englishwoman in Nazi Germany once hostilities started would need more than her German husband's influential name to protect her life and liberty. Heinrich laughed at them, but much as she loved him, Marianne recognised the voice of truth in what Robert Beynon, Tim Maxwell and Edward Moore-Ross told her. So she stayed in England and grieved.

But although she could not bring herself to join Heinrich permanently in Germany, she longed for his infrequent invitations to her to stay with him there for a limited time. Now, unexpectedly, he sent for her, and asked her to come to Berlin two days before Isabel was due to travel back to North Wales. Marianne agonised for a while, but there was really no contest. She would not permit her guilty feelings of obligation to Isabel to prevent her from going to the one person she really cared for. And if the price of escape was the tiny risk of letting her sister spend a couple of days unsupervised with the Lester boy, so be it. After her recent experiences, Isabel should have sufficient sense of self-preservation to keep herself aloof from trouble.

So the sisters said a cold goodbye and Marianne departed, leaving Isabel to spend Friday and Saturday morning in Eaton Place before she returned to Bangor. Inevitably, on Friday evening, she was alone at the apartment with Robin Lester. When Marianne was away, the housekeeper only worked part time, finishing at noon and going to her sister's home in Tooting until she started again at seven in the morning. As she got ready for their last night out, Isabel wondered how the evening would end. In Tom's day, this would have been an opportunity to dream of . . . somehow, the thought did not please her.

Robin took Isabel to see Emlyn Williams in his own tear-jerker play, *The Corn is Green*, the smash hit of the year in the West End theatre. Afterwards, they had supper at Quaglino's. 'It's a last night for us both,' he said. 'Might as well push the boat out.'

Afterwards they walked back to Eaton Place. Isabel

had drunk enough champagne to let her youthful romanticism emerge once more, and she kept singing snatches from 'A Nightingale Sang in Berkeley Square'. 'I wonder if there really are angels dining at the Ritz tonight?' she said as they passed the great colonnade on Piccadilly.

'Of course not – how could they be? They were all around us in Quaglino's . . . Goodness, Isabel, what a send-off for a chap! The gods might have laid on the moonlight, and the quiet – and you.'

They paused under an ornate lamppost and he kissed her, not the way Tom had kissed her, but sweetly, innocently, asking only her presence and her friendship. He drew away from her, puzzlement on his face. 'You're crying. I wanted to make you happy, not sad.'

She started to walk again. 'You do . . . it's just that I wish it could have happened years ago. Perhaps it's too late now.'

'Too late? Don't be silly! We're only eighteen. Everything's still ahead of us.'

'Is it? I wonder. Sometimes I feel as though I've lived a dozen lives already, and they all make me sad.'

'I'll never make you sad, Isabel. That's a promise.'

'Don't make promises. It's worse if you can't keep them.'

'But I shall keep that one or die in the attempt. When we're a bit older, I'm going to marry you.'

She stopped, and turned slowly to face him. 'Don't say that unless you mean it, Robin.'

'But I do. I'm not even going to ask if you'll have me, because if you said no I'd have to abduct you, feeling the

571

way I do . . . You won't change while I'm away, will you?'

Isabel shook her head. 'I won't, Robin. But what if you do?'

He laughed. 'What if the world ended? Honestly, that's far more likely than me changing my mind about you. I can't imagine feeling like this about another girl.'

She tried to quell her sense of foreboding. 'It's a long time before we're really grown up, Rob, 'specially if we have this war you keep on about. In the meantime, though, we can go on being blood brothers, can't we?'

'Never doubt it!' He raised his hand, palm outwards, and she pressed her own against it so that their scarred thumbs met again. 'Star-crossed to the end,' he added.

'Don't say that! It's bad luck!'

'I didn't mean it that way – I meant our stars run together. After all, we were even born the same week. Come on, Isabel, don't spoil our last evening – we've got everything to look forward to. "O brave new world, that hath such people in it!" '

Isabel sighed. 'Obviously you don't know the rest of that.' Robin shook his head. She went on, ' " 'Tis new to *thee* . . ." '

'I won't have you being so sad. Look, we're nearly home. You can't send a chap off like this. I'll come round in the morning and show you my uniform before I go. Tell you what – if you catch a train before eleven, I can even take you to Euston. How will that suit you?'

'Oh, Rob, I do love you! Please don't forget me!'

'Forget you? How could I? It would be like forgetting myself. See you in the morning, beautiful girl!' And he left her outside her sister's front door.

As she let herself in, she thought, if he'd come in and tried to make love to me, I'd have let him. But he's still a boy . . . it would never occur to him to ask a nice girl like me. If only he knew . . . She said aloud, 'Thank God he doesn't!' and slammed the door behind her.

# Chapter Twenty-Four

'You'm a terrible family for writing things down, aren't you?' Beuno was sitting at the study table in Tan-yr-Allt, supposedly going over a botany assignment, but really listening to her account of the confrontation with Marianne.

'I think it's a combination of guilt and malice,' said Isabel. 'At least when my grandfather and great-grandmother did it, it led to me finding you. There doesn't seem to be any good side to this latest lot.'

'Oh, I don't know, though. It got you away from that Tom fellow, didn't it?'

'How do you come to that conclusion?'

'Stands to reason. They either bought him off or scared him off. He was far too keen on you to up and leave you flat otherwise.'

'D'you really think so, Beuno?'

He could have cut out his tongue as he saw the hope leap momentarily in her face. 'Now, *cariad*, don't get me wrong. If they did frighten him off, it was a good thing in the long run. He was a bad one through and through.'

The hope faded. 'You're right, of course. If only everyone didn't go off and leave me, though.'

'It's the way of things. Even I'll have to leave you some time.'

'No! I couldn't bear that.'

'Isabel, I'm seventy-eight. I feel fit as a fiddle, but I've had my three score years and ten this long time. You've got to get used to that.'

'You'll outlive me.'

'I don't think so. Anyhow, while I'm still here, we'd better make use of my old brain, hadn't we? There's somebody me and Katie want you to see, down in the university.'

As soon as Kate Ashley heard what had happened during Isabel's visit to London, she had discussed it with Beuno. 'She'll fade away if we don't give her something useful to do,' she said. 'Have you any ideas?'

Beuno pondered for a while. 'Well, there's the obvious thing, isn't there? She could study for a university degree.'

The thought had never crossed Kate's mind, but it certainly merited consideration. University to Kate had always been Oxford or Cambridge. But what was wrong with Bangor, as it was on the doorstep? Then doubt started creeping in. 'The trouble is, Beuno, she's been so well taught from an early age that I can't see her getting a great deal from a literature or history course. She's practically at degree standard already. It's the same with Latin.'

'Not in the sciences she isn't. She needs something more than just my teaching. Anyway, I'd like to see her have a try at chemistry or biochemistry, not just stay with botany. I was wondering . . . what if we went to see them at the College? The professor of biology do know me quite well. I got my botany degree so late on I stuck in his mind, like.'

The idea appealed to Isabel. 'Why not?' she said. 'If I'm banned from the business until I'm forty or married, I'd better find something to do with my life. When do I start?'

'Wait a minute,' said Beuno. 'We've got to find out if they'll take you first.'

Isabel started to read for a chemistry degree the following October. Along with her newly-commenced correspondence with Robin Lester, it transformed her life. The longing to be part of Richmond's had not died, but at least she was able to push it into the background now and concentrate on other things.

For a long time, she tried to ignore the growing threat of war. Robin's letters were full of it, as he chronicled his training as a pilot and passed on snippets of gossip about the deteriorating international situation. In February 1939, he got a week-end leave pass and came to stay in Chester. Isabel, respectably chaperoned by Kate Ashley, went to see him there. She was half afraid to renew their earlier contact, in case the magic had faded, but if anything, it was better than before.

When she went to see him off at the station at the end of his leave, he said: 'D'you think you could persuade Marianne to let us get married when I get my wings?'

Isabel was stunned. 'We're only just nineteen,' she said. 'Of course not!'

'But I keep telling you, the war is coming. It's different, now, we have to grab everything while we can.'

'Rob, you wouldn't convince Marianne of that in a million years. For one thing she has a German husband.

If she faced up to war being inevitable it would wreck her life, so she'll bury her head till the last minute. For another, the minute I get married she has to hand over my share of the company. And that really would be the day. I would say my prospects of matrimony are precisely nil.'

'I'll go and see her. She can't spoil your life like that!'

'Why not? She's been doing it for long enough to be something of an expert.'

He tried to persuade her to let him approach Marianne, but Isabel was adamant in her refusal. As long as Marianne could regard him as an overgrown child in the grip of his first infatuation, their friendship was safe. The moment she started taking him seriously, Isabel knew her sister would banish him from her for good.

Back at her studies, Isabel became resigned to her quiet life. In fact, she was beginning to enjoy it. In June 1939, she sailed through her Part One university examinations and was offered a place on the honours degree course. By September, England was at war and her world had changed forever.

For Marianne, the change was even more dramatic. It brought tragedy and comfort in almost equal measure. There was no longer any question that her marriage might survive after September 1939. Heinrich had been in London briefly earlier that summer, but he had been almost a stranger, tying up any remaining loose ends of his London interests without any effort to conceal from Marianne that this was his final visit. By then, she was so miserable and isolated that given a chance, she would have thrown up all her British concerns and settled permanently in Germany. She stayed because von Burckhardt never offered her an alternative. On the positive side, only the outbreak of war prevented Richmond International from sliding into irreversible decline. For years, Marianne had failed to stem the firm's problems, or to listen to the advice of those better suited than herself to the task. But September 1939 effectively froze all food retailing operations into their pre-war positions. Price controls, food rationing and swingeing cuts in manpower rationalised the business to an extent where even Marianne's lack of expertise could not damage it. She was able at least to preserve the illusion that she was doing a good job of consolidating her inheritance. All talk of success or failure could safely be postponed until the conflict ended.

In North Wales, Isabel turned to and enthusiastically dug for victory on Beuno's smallholding, while continuing her studies at the university. Beuno was getting frail now, but he seemed determined to hang on until Isabel had completed her education.

'We've still got work to do, you and me,' he told her. 'Remember, the chapter do end with us, but it's got to end tidy, not half finished.'

She was at a loss to understand what he was talking about, except that it had something to do with his mother's prophecy. These days, Beuno often seemed to spend more time talking to characters she could not see than to inhabitants of the real world. She had come to respect his shrewdness too much to write off these ramblings as senile dementia.

In August 1939 he had advised Isabel to buy a couple of horses. 'I don't suppose they'll requisition them this time, like they did before,' he said, 'and you'll find out soon enough there's no other way to get about.' Isabel silently praised his foresight for the next six years. The sturdy cobs were always available to take her or Kate Ashley about when the niggardly petrol ration was exhausted. Her small sailing boat became the other favourite means of transport, particularly to carry her out to Beuno's farm.

She saw even less of Marianne after the war started than she had before. Travel was difficult and uncomfortable; London was more dangerous every day; and the sisters had nothing to talk about even when they did meet. Friendless, childless, deserted by her husband and despised by her company executives, Marianne spent more and more time trying to persuade herself that she was not a failure. She refused to leave London. The one illusion she had left was that her presence was necessary to the survival of Richmond International.

The triumvirate of Maxwell, the company lawyer, Robert Beynon and Edward Moore-Ross, were all far beyond military age and were sufficiently committed to the company to beg Marianne to leave London. 'If only she would go,' Robert Beynon told Tim Maxwell, 'we'd have half a chance of getting Richmond's back into good health while we're still protected by rationing. God knows how we'd have survived without it.'

But Richmond's was all Marianne had left. She had every intention of going down with her sinking ship.

Had it not been for her fears for Robin Lester's safety, Isabel would have found the war quite enjoyable. No one else she cared for was involved. For the first time in her life, she had more work to do than there were hours in the day; and her relationship with Beuno Owen had become a core of security beyond anything she had known in her childhood. Her worst moment came in August 1940, when Robin's fighter was shot down over the South Coast during the Battle of Britain. But Lester parachuted to safety and ended the year by being promoted to squadron-leader.

He managed a leave at Christmas, and spent part of it at Tan-yr-Allt. It was the first Christmas Isabel ever remembered enjoying. Beuno came over from Llanddona and stayed for a few days. He arrived laden with all sorts of black market treats: a whole leg of pork from an illegally-killed pig; sausages, sausage meat and pounds of black puddings from the same source; a capon from his own yard, and sufficient dried herbs to season a year's food. By now they were keeping hens at Tan-yr-Allt, and part of the flower garden had been turned over to vegetables. The cellars had always been well stocked, and thanks to Mrs Llewelyn's hoarding instincts, there was enough dried fruit for a pudding. Robin was almost speechless with delight.

'My family are being frightfully stodgy about rationing,' he said. 'They keep making awful things like Woolton pie. I'm damned glad I escaped up here. I can't help feeling I've done my bit in shooting down Germans, without having to starve for them as well!'

He stayed for three days, and Isabel found herself feeling like a young, romantic girl for the first time. On his last day, Kate Ashley and Beuno tactfully left them alone as much as possible. Sitting by the drawing room fire that evening, Robin drew Isabel into his arms and kissed her with a hunger he had not shown before. As she began responding, his hands slid over her body, caressing her breasts and legs outside the long silk dress she wore. Suddenly, unaccountably, she began to panic, pushing him away.

Hurt flared in his eyes momentarily before he gained control of himself. 'I – I'm sorry, Isabel. I shouldn't, I know. But there isn't any tomorrow now, is there?'

If he had tried again, she would have forced herself to respond. But he did not. He assumed she was a normal, well-brought-up girl, rejecting improper advances. If she was a little old-fashioned, it could only be a good thing . . . Isabel almost saw the thoughts written in his boyish face, and wished with all her heart that she could give herself to him.

'Never mind,' he said. 'You're going to marry me, remember? We'll both be twenty-one in the New Year, and then neither the War Office nor Marianne can stop us.'

The thought seemed to cheer him, but Isabel wondered what on earth she would do when the time came. She wanted to marry him as much as ever, but what would happen if she got scared like that each time he touched her? She shook off the thought impatiently. Of course I shan't be frightened, she told herself. It's just that if I let him make love to me now, I'd be terrified of getting pregnant. She tried to forget that as he reached for her, she had a nightmare vision of Tom Moore-Ross's face, distorted by lust, and a memory of his hard fingers tearing aside her clothes to invade her body.

She was almost relieved when Robin rejoined his squadron at RAF Brize Norton. On balance she preferred to fret about his physical safety than wonder whether she could ever let him make love to her. By now the pressure was temporarily off the young fighter pilots, as the Luftwaffe withdrew across the Channel and the day of the long distance bombing raid began.

Robin was back again in July 1941, to attend the ceremony at which Isabel received a first-class honours degree in chemistry. Beuno and Kate came, too, but Marianne sent her usual excuses. Isabel was relieved. It could have been no more than an embarrassment to have her there – and Robin might have told her they were getting married.

By now it was a subject he seldom dropped. 'You can't keep me waiting any longer, Isabel. You know I'm serious – for God's sake, I've been waiting for you since we were children! We could get a special licence and be married before I went back to Brize Norton.'

'Give me a little longer, just to sort myself out,' she said. 'I promise I'll make up my mind soon.'

He managed to laugh. 'I'm not asking you to make up your mind. That was decided long ago. All I want to know is when.'

But once more, he returned to duty with no definite answer. In October, she had another visitor who had more than a passing interest in her plans for matrimony. Robert Beynon had no wish to see Richmond International disintegrate. He had given up hope of dislodging Marianne, but now the time was ripe to involve the other Richmond sister if the company were to survive.

'Tim Maxwell has told me that the von Burckhardts persuaded you there was no chance of you inheriting except under the original terms of your father's will,' he said. 'But that was only their opinion, you know. I think it might be worth testing it in the courts.'

'Marianne would fight it every step of the way,' said Isabel. 'She still sees me as the interloper whose mother toppled her own, and she'll never forgive me.'

'That's up to her. But I think you have a strong case. No modern court would regard a woman's matrimonial status as grounds for postponing her inheritance rights.'

'Believe me, Robert, she has some big guns. I'd hate to put her to the test.'

Beynon had heard enough gossip over the years to guess what Marianne's weapon might be. He tried another approach.

'Of course, if you chose to get married now you're over twenty-one, she couldn't do anything about it – and once you're married, the age qualification is cancelled out. Forgive me for prying, but I understood you were serious about Robin Lester.'

Isabel strove to play down her unease. 'Yes, but we're still so young. I hadn't planned . . .'

Beynon sighed. 'Look, Isabel, I'll tell you frankly, if things go on as they are now, I don't know whether Richmond's will survive the war. It looks as if it will be years before we find out, but it has to end eventually. If you're going to have enough experience to turn the company around, even with our help, you need to start now. If you intend to get married anyway, surely it's worth bringing forward your plans with so much at stake?'

'If you put it like that, I suppose so. But what makes you think I'd make any better job of it than Marianne?'

'You're quick, you're highly educated, and you're a chip off the old block. Marianne was penned up with that mother of hers for far too long, and she doesn't behave like a Richmond at all. In fact, she behaves more like Queen Victoria. You can't run a twentieth century company like that. Bringing you in wouldn't solve all the problems. Even if you were active on the board, she'd still need to be reckoned with, but as it is now, hers is the only voice that's ever heard.'

'Let me think about it, Robert. There's a lot you don't understand.' And how can I begin to tell you? she thought. You'd never understand that my stepfather ruined me for any other man, any more than Robin would . . .

Robert made one more attempt. 'Very well, but there's something I'd like you to do. I've brought up a whole pile of business plans, forecasts, all sorts of projections. I've also brought some financial summaries that give a good idea of what's been happening to Richmond's in the immediate pre-war period and since 1939. You're a bright girl. Go through them. See how much sense they make to you. I think you'll be so indignant about what's happening to your father's company that you'll decide to fight. At least consider it.'

'All right, you win. You're very persuasive. I only hope Marianne doesn't find out.'

'Sooner or later, she has to face the fact that she wasn't cut out to be a grocery tycoon. The trouble is, neither was her husband. He might have known all about coal and steel, but retailing was a closed book to him. We're suffering now from what he did in the thirties.'

The summaries and forecasts had been brilliantly prepared. Isabel understood most of it immediately, and the rest after a little determined application. What she saw

appalled her. It was a doleful story of individual enterprise stifled; conservative thinking applied when radical
innovation was necessary; and total lack of understanding that even small, cheap shops required consist-
ent capital investment to maintain their standards. She
itched to get hold of the company. Only two things
stopped her: her reluctance to marry yet, and a lingering
dread of what Marianne might do to her in court if ever
the matter got that far.

In the end, she did what she invariably resorted to in
times of trouble: she took it all to Beuno. He was fading
fast now, and usually spent half the day in bed. Isabel
arrived with her sheaf of papers, and he eyed them with
disfavour.

'You do know better than to push that stuff on to me,
girl. Tell me what's in it, will you? I bet you've been
through it all with a fine tooth comb.'

She summarised the papers and he watched her
unblinkingly throughout. Then he said: 'So what makes
you think you need my advice?'

'Well, I just do. I don't know whether I should involve
myself or not.'

'You've already given the answer to that. Anybody
who can talk it out the way you just did do know exactly
what they're doing. You're wasted up here digging my
vegetable patch and doing chemistry research.' Then he
looked at her more suspiciously, understanding dawning
on his face. 'Wait a minute, now. You don't need no
business advice, do you? This isn't about Richmond's.
It's about you.'

Isabel bit her lower lip. 'Yes. I'd have to get married to
get a place on the board before I'm forty, or go to court

586

to break Papa's will. You know what Marianne's got over me.'

'Excuses, excuses! You don't need me to tell you no court in the land would take them depositions seriously now. You're a grown woman. Ten years ago, they might have put young girls away for life because they made mistakes when they were too young to know better. But that may as well be a century ago now. There's a war on, girl. They'm all at it like rabbits. Nobody's going to take no notice of what you did before you was old enough to know better.'

'So you think I could win by just threatening her?'

'No, I think she'd fight it. But she wouldn't have a chance of winning and I think her lawyer would tell her that in no uncertain terms.' He grew impatient again. 'Anyway, that's a lot of damned nonsense, isn't it? All you need to do is marry Rob, and he's panting for you. So why don't you? . . . Ah, that's it. Thought so. Your wicked uncle put you off – you know – didn't he?'

Isabel burst into tears. 'What am I going to do, Beuno? I love him so much, all I want is to be his wife . . . But every time he does more than kiss me, I get hysterical. If he married me, it wouldn't last five minutes. Oh, I'm so unhappy – I'm going to lose everything, Rob, the business . . . there must be some way!'

He pondered that for a while. 'I'm not at all sure there is, Isabel. Tell you the truth, I don't think it's your Uncle Tom's fault – he was just the last straw. I think it's what your father did to all those poor wives of his.'

Momentarily, he had startled her out of her despair. 'That's ridiculous! I'm not them – why should it make a jot of difference to me?'

'From what you tell me, you was never reluctant for Tom to have his way with you.'

Isabel stopped crying and tried to think about what he was saying. 'Are you suggesting that the idea of being a wife is what's frightening me?'

Beuno's face was sombre. 'No – just that it may be. I was only saying you always seem to have been keen enough when Tom Moore-Ross wanted to mess about with you. Listen, *cariad*, how much do you really want that old business?'

'More than anything in the world, Beuno.'

'More than your Robin?'

'How can I tell until I know what it's like to have both?'

'Anybody could ask that, about every big decision they ever make. This is a bit different, isn't it? We're talking about your happiness and Robin's. You mustn't be tempted to throw them both away just because you think the business will matter more than anything else. Mind you, I think that even getting married might add up to throwing yourself away, if that's the thing that's making you so scared.'

'Did you ever know what you wanted?'

'No. Don't think I know that even now, and it's a bit late for me!'

He fell silent for a while, then said: 'They do tell me that those psychiatrists help a lot of people. Maybe you should go and talk to somebody like that.'

'I couldn't. It's hard enough telling you.'

'But you have told me, just the same. Perhaps it would help if you were saying it to a stranger.'

'No, Beuno, this is something I have to sort out for myself.'

'Well, all I'm saying is, don't do anything hasty. No old company is worth that much grief.'

'Perhaps I'll have the grief anyway, whatever I do. If I'm going to be unhappy, I want to be unhappy with something to fill my time. If it was the company, at least I wouldn't be making Rob's life a misery, too.'

'What, so no marriage and a fight with Marianne to get your share of Richmond's? It's a hard road.'

'I realise that. But perhaps it's the only one I've got.'

Then she realised that Beuno was no longer listening. His face was contorted with pain and he started clutching his throat, as if trying to open it to the air

'What's the matter, Beuno? Oh, God, don't say I've hurt you, now, as well!'

He managed to shake his head, pointed at the chest of drawers in the corner, and gasped: 'Little bottle, over there . . . forgot to put it near . . . get it . . . and spoon . . .'

The spoon had been left beside the dark brown bottle and she brought them to him. He was beyond speech now and merely raised three fingers, apparently indicating the number of spoonfuls she should pour. He swallowed the thick liquid and lay back, panting. Eventually he managed to speak again. 'Sorry, didn't want you to see that. Old age, see.'

Isabel was horrified. Of course he was old! He'd been old the day she met him. But he couldn't die. It was inconceivable.

Beuno might have read her mind. 'It's natural, you know. It do happen to all of us in the end and I've had a pretty good run. There . . . it's passing off now.'

'What is that stuff?'

589

He managed a wobbly smile. 'Bits of this and that. You know me . . . nerve tonic.'

'You're not going to start treating me as a child now – you never have before. What is it?'

'Digitalis . . . sea onion . . . They do remind my heart it's not time to stop yet.'

'But digitalis is a poison.'

'Yes, in the end. But while it's finishing you off, it do keep you going, if you see what I mean. And there's always other things to take to slow the poison down a bit.'

'Have you ever seen a medical doctor, instead of just treating yourself?'

'*Duw*, no! Why would I do that? I've always been the one they send for when the doctors give up.'

'Well, you're seeing one now. I'm paying, and I'm insisting, too, so no arguments.'

Isabel's own GP went out to Llanddona next day to see Beuno. Isabel was there to meet him. After he had examined Beuno, he joined her in the little farmhouse kitchen. 'There's not a great deal I can do, Miss Richmond,' he said. 'He's a very old man, you know, and eventually his heart will just pack up. He's had a good life. One thing, though – I wish I could get him in somewhere where they could look after him. He seems to have angina as well as the condition for which he takes the digitalis. The digitalis won't help his angina and if he lasts a few months longer, it might give him a lot of pain. I don't like the idea of him staying here all alone with that prospect.'

'I could try and persuade him to move over to Tan-yr-Allt.'

590

'That might be an ideal solution. See what you can do. Otherwise, he's going to die all alone.'

But Beuno was immovable. 'When I do die, it's going to be in my mam's bedroom, looking out at the sea like I always have.'

'You can look out at the sea from Tan-yr-Allt.'

'Not my sea, I can't. Red Wharf Bay is my place. I'm staying.'

Isabel had known he would say this. She was ready for him. 'All right. So am I.'

'Don't be so daft, girl. You've got your own road to follow.'

'Yes, and you're on it. I'm staying, Beuno.'

'But what about your plans?'

'Perhaps this is really what I need. You're far more important than any of that. I'll leave it to take care of itself for the present, and see how I feel in a few months' time.'

He argued, denied his illness, even tried to tell her he did not want her in his house, but Isabel was adamant. Finally, he agreed gracefully.

'I must admit, it would be lovely having you here.'

'Well, there you are, then. I'll go back over to Tan-yr-Allt by boat this afternoon, tell Kate what I'm up to, and she can hold the fort over there. I only wish I could get a telephone put in here.'

That made him hoot with laughter. 'What for? To tell old Nick when to expect me?'

Beuno had plenty of life left in him after all. He recognised a need in Isabel to set aside the wide world for a while and retreat where no one could reach her. In the

591

warmth of her presence he bloomed again, and so did she. Robert Beynon wrote to her to ask if she had made a decision, but she put him off. Richmond's had survived three years of war; it could hang on a little longer.

Robin was a bigger problem. He bombarded her with letters, travelled to North Wales every time he had a long enough leave, and demanded at least twice a week that she should marry him. At first the old panic started swelling inside Isabel every time he raised the matter. But Beuno became a sort of spiritual shield for her. She began to realise that she could not live her whole life in isolation, as he had. She was not quite that self-sufficient. Given enough time, she knew she would marry Robin. She only hoped that he would accept the delay, but he seemed determined not to.

For more than two years, she divided her time between Tan-yr-Allt and Llanddona, never going to London and only visiting Chester three times when Robin had week-end passes which enabled him to get that far. Gradually the gaping wounds of her troubled past began to heal. Reality was a wide, windy seascape with meadows full of wild flowers sweeping down to it. Emotional warfare had no place in Beuno's world and she absorbed from him the secret of living for the moment.

In the summer of 1944, Robert Beynon came to see her again. 'I've given up trying to tempt you down to London,' he said, 'but I must still try to persuade you not to stay up here forever. Apart from anything else, I don't think you'll have the opportunity once the war is over.'

'Why not? No one can order me about any longer. I can please myself.'

'You can as long as the money holds out – now wait a

minute, I know you're hardly a spendthrift! It's not that. It's just that once the lid comes off business, there isn't going to be anything worth having left of Richmond's. You haven't seen your sister since 1942. She's beyond all reason now, living in a world of her own. Government restrictions on our competitors are all that's keeping us afloat. When they go, so do we.'

She had gone back to Tan-yr-Allt to meet Beynon. Kate Ashley had taken over out at Beuno's house for four days. Isabel said: 'You know I'm taking care of my father's half-brother?'

'Yes. Mrs Ashley told me. How is he?'

'Remarkable – but he knows better than I do that his time has almost come. I'll make you a promise, Robert. When he dies, I'll come back. I'll be ready for it then. D'you think there's a chance of the war keeping going just a bit longer?'

He smiled somewhat reluctantly. 'Depends on how long your uncle lasts. You're sure no one else can take care of him?'

'Out of the question. He's a debt I have to pay. I don't know why I think that – he'd deny it if he heard me – but it's true. In any case, I want to do it. Sometimes I think I love him far more than I loved my own father.'

Beynon reached out and took her hand. 'We'll keep things going, don't worry. All I wanted was a firm commitment from you.'

'You've got it. But God knows how I'll persuade Marianne to move over!'

'I've got enough faith in you to be sure you'll do it, Isabel. Try not to be too long.'

'That's up to Beuno.'

* * *

Beuno was troubled. For the first time in years, he was
dreaming about his mother. Waking, he scolded himself.
Of course she's not coming for me – there's just something I know I've left undone, that's all, and she's in my
mind because of it . . . It was some time before he
remembered. Of course! Mam's books. It was time to
tell Isabel . . .

She was somewhat preoccupied these days, her mind
constantly swinging back to Richmond International,
wondering whether she would have the talent to succeed
when she finally took over. Otherwise she might have
noticed sooner how restless Beuno was becoming.

They were outside, on his favourite patch of sunlit
grass overlooking the bay, when he told her what was on
his mind.

'I'm all ready to go, now, Isabel. My will is made, and
I'm feeling a bit tired. But there's something I've got to
ask you.'

'Why are you so determined to see yourself off? You
look good for five years.'

'Don't be so daft. I'm not complaining. But there's
something I want you to look at. The shop have got to be
cleared out.'

'Oh, no, Beuno! It'll take a month of Sundays!'

'Please yourself, but I've left it all to you, so you've
got to do something with it sooner or later. All I ask is
that you do it yourself when the time do come.'

'Of course I will. It won't be for ages yet, so stop
worrying.'

'There's something else. Go in the house and open the
second drawer in my old desk. Bring them books out.'

594

The notebooks were solid affairs with marbled end-papers. Isabel returned with them and started to hand them over.

'No, they're for you. First time they've gone out of the direct line. Use them well.'

'But what are they?'

'They are my mam's recipe books – not cookery, it's all right! – and they're meant for you.'

She opened the first book, and momentarily a lingering aroma of spice and formaldehyde seemed to perfume the air. Then it faded. 'Myfanwy Owen: her receipt book', said the inscription, the latest in a line of other names, the only one which was not Irish.

'I never added my name,' said Beuno. 'Always felt, somehow, that I was just looking after them for the next one. But I'd like you to put your name in. She would have liked it, too.'

'I'd prefer you to do it for me.'

'All right, then. Fetch me my pen and ink.'

He put her name in all the three books. 'There's lots of old papers and things in the shop, stuff to go with this,' he said. 'But you won't want them until you've gone through the books.'

Isabel was still perplexed. 'But what d'you expect me to do with them, Beuno?'

'Use them, girl. The fortune Marged Richmond started is almost spent. I think our mam would have liked the idea that her wisdom would make it all over again. In a way it would mean she'd won after all.'

'I still don't know what they are.'

'You will. You're a trained chemist. You know enough to get going on developing some of that lot. I spent half a lifetime adding my four penn'orth to it. It's all laid out in the herbalist's style, but it's much more than a herbal. It's a little step along the way to the Elixir of Life.'

That made her laugh, and he smiled with her. 'It's all right, Isabel, I'm not quite in my dotage yet! I know there's really no such thing. But some of them recipes, if they're used all the time, will make any woman look twenty when she's thirty, and thirty when she's fifty. I'd say that do come close, wouldn't you?'

'There are an awful lot of charlatans who claim they can do that sort of thing already – they advertise in all the women's magazines.'

'Yes, but the difference is that them recipes of Mam's do work. There's five generations of Llanddona witch-craft there to make sure of it.'

That was when Isabel realised there was something in the idea. Whatever the merits of the recipes – and Beuno had always looked years younger than he was – their source was what would sell them. Already, her fertile imagination was conjuring with phrases about enchant-ment from the sea to give timeless beauty. What a mar-keting prospect! Perhaps she wouldn't need Richmond International after all . . .

Beuno was watching her closely. 'You understand, girl? You promise you'll use them?'

'I promise – and Beuno, I can also promise you that no one will ever forget your mam by the time I've finished!'

'Good girl – I can let go now, then.'

It was a little while before he did. He died in his sleep a month after their conversation. Isabel entered his room as the first rays of September sunshine stole in. The casement window was wide open, the white muslin curtains quivered in the light breeze, and for a brief moment Isabel had an extraordinarily vivid mental picture of two figures swimming out to sea. She shook her head, and bent to feel for Beuno's pulse. There was a smile on his face, but no sign of life. Without quite knowing whence the thought came, she murmured, 'Swim to the moon, Beuno, love – swim to the moon.'

By late 1944, everyone was agreed that the Nazis were beaten, but somehow that made the terrifying new rocket bomb attacks on London even harder to endure. Air raid shelters no longer guaranteed protection – the rockets could pierce them effortlessly – and, worst of all, there was no advance warning. The terrible missiles simply erupted out of an empty sky at any time of day or night.

Marianne Richmond was oblivious to the danger. All she ever thought of these days was how the business would survive the war. It could not be long now before she found out. She was sick of discussing it with Robert Beynon and Edward Moore-Ross. They were convinced she did not know what she was doing. But she'd show them all. Peacetime would prove the wisdom of her harsh economies and closure of bomb-damaged premises. When the labour market was flooded with unemployed ex-servicemen, like after the last war, they would be able to recruit new sales staff for next to nothing. All she had to do was hold on, work hard and ignore the pessimists.

The trouble was that when she finished work, there

was nothing to fill her life any more. Heinrich was little more than a blurred memory now. She had even resumed her maiden name early in the war, when she experienced hostility from people who resented her German connections. Marianne had never been surrounded by friends, and the few she had were scattered around the world now. If she did not take the office home with her, she had nothing at all.

So it was that one November week-end she set off on what she called one of her little research trips. Recently she had taken to spending Saturdays in one or other of the London suburbs, wandering in and out of shops, watching how people spent their money, and, she told herself, seeking ideas for future development. One of the departmental heads at Richmond's had been extolling Woolworths' trading methods recently, and she was eager to see how they organised their branches. Who knew? Perhaps the large Richmond's shops could be developed as general stores once things were back to normal. It was an indication of Marianne's total lack of feeling for the trade that she could even have considered such a change, but for the moment it served to absorb her energies. This week she had decided to look at New Cross. She always travelled by bus on these outings. It made her feel virtuous about saving petrol, and she felt she was listening to the voice of the people when she eavesdropped on the conversations in the seats around her.

Marianne got off the bus outside New Cross Woolworths just after noon. The store and the street outside were packed with shoppers, jostling to get the best bargains in anything and everything before the restricted stocks ran out. She stood around for a while, looking at the jumble of cheap merchandise in the windows, the bright price tags beckoning the shoppers to spend their wages to maximum effect. It was a humid day, and people were sweating inside their heavy winter clothes. Marianne's lips curled in distaste. Perhaps this expedition wasn't such a good idea after all. She dithered between entering the store, where the smell of unwashed bodies would be that much worse, or going back to the clean loneliness of Eaton Place. In the end she decided to brave the store.

As she got to the half-open double doors, a middle-aged couple laden with packages jostled past her, almost knocking her down. Already irritable, Marianne turned and snapped at them.

'Ah, get out of the way, Lady Muck! Get back to Bond Street where you belong,' said the man, and made as if to push her even harder. But his shoulder never made contact with hers. As she watched, he seemed to rise in the air in slow motion. Marianne put out her hand, convinced he would cannon into her, but suddenly she was airborne, too. She felt the world begin to cartwheel around her, and as she cried out in fear, an incomparably louder noise drowned everything else. For a ridiculous split second, she became part of the window display, already a tangled mass of collapsed cardboard and broken glass. Then there was a second rumbling explosion, and an instant of unspeakable pain, before the falling building wiped out all awareness.

When the smoke cleared after the V2 explosion, there was nothing but a vast hole where the Woolworths branch had stood. Marianne Richmond was only one of the one hundred and sixty people who died in the blast. It was five days before her remains were positively identified.

In Tan-yr-Allt, Isabel replaced the telephone receiver with exaggerated care, then raised her eyes and stared at her reflection in the mirror over the hall table. She stood thus for a full minute, trying and failing to digest the reality of what she had just heard. Then, a vast shout of exhilaration began to bubble inside her, so huge she felt that the house would not contain it.

She rushed out across the lawn that overlooked the Menai Straits, down to the shrubbery where the ground fell away towards the landing stage, and yelled at the top of her lungs, 'Beuno! I'm free, she's gone – they're all gone!'

Moments later, Kate Ashley came out to see what was going on. Isabel, still light-headed, swung her around like a playful child. 'We're going back – the witch is dead!'

Kate tried to observe the proprieties. 'Isabel – do you mean it? Marianne, dead? Is she really?'

'Bombed out, squashed to a pulp! Robert Beynon just rang to tell me. They've only identified her by her teeth!' Then the reaction set in. Isabel's jubilation faded, at least for the moment, and she began to tremble. 'Oh, God, I don't mean that! Poor Marianne. What a terrible way to go . . . there's not even anyone to miss her.'

Kate Ashley shook her head sadly. 'Such a wasted life,' she said. 'Don't let that happen to you, will you, Isabel?'

The younger woman was taken by surprise. 'How

600

could I? We're nothing like one another.'

'Just a little, perhaps. She was a slave to her dreams. Don't lose control of yours, my darling.'

Isabel broke into a radiant smile. 'I've been waiting for this ever since Papa died,' she said, 'but I wasn't really sure I could succeed until now. I know exactly what I'm going to do. The funeral is next Monday, and on Tuesday they want me to attend a board meeting. Kate, we're in business at last – and it's not going to be a bankrupt business, if my ideas and Beuno's recipe books have anything to do with it!'

'And what about Robin Lester? What will you say to him?'

'Something I should have said years ago, Katie: "Rob, when will you marry me?" How's that for a brave new world?'


THE END

# A selection of bestsellers from Headline

**FICTION**

| | | |
|---|---|---|
| SUCCESSION | Andrew MacAllan | £4.50 ☐ |
| DECLARED DEAD | John Francome & | |
| | James MacGregor | £3.50 ☐ |
| WINNERS | Penelope Karageorge | £3.99 ☐ |
| BRIDIE | Christine Thomas | £3.50 ☐ |
| THE BROTHERS OF | | |
| GWYNEDD QUARTET | Edith Pargeter | £6.95 ☐ |
| DAUGHTER OF LIR | Diana Norman | £3.99 ☐ |

**NON-FICTION**

| | | |
|---|---|---|
| IT'S ONLY A MOVIE, INGRID | Alexander Walker | £4.99 ☐ |
| THE NEW MURDERERS' | J H H Gaute & | |
| WHO'S WHO | Robin Odell | £4.99 ☐ |

**SCIENCE FICTION AND FANTASY**

| | | |
|---|---|---|
| SLAVES OF THE VOLCANO | | |
| GOD | | |
| Cineverse Cycle Book 1 | Craig Shaw Gardner | £2.99 ☐ |
| THE ARGONAUT AFFAIR | | |
| Time Wars VII | Simon Hawke | £2.99 ☐ |
| THE CRYSTAL SWORD | Adrienne | |
| | Martine-Barnes | £3.99 ☐ |
| DRUID'S BLOOD | Esther Friesner | £3.50 ☐ |

*All Headline books are available at your local bookshop or newsagent, or can be ordered direct from the publisher. Just tick the titles you want and fill in the form below. Prices and availability subject to change without notice.*

Headline Book Publishing PLC, Cash Sales Department, PO Box 11, Falmouth, Cornwall, TR10 9EN, England.

Please enclose a cheque or postal order to the value of the cover price and allow the following for postage and packing:
UK: 60p for the first book, 25p for the second book and 15p for each additional book ordered up to a maximum charge of £1.90
BFPO: 60p for the first book, 25p for the second book and 15p per copy for the next seven books, thereafter 9p per book
OVERSEAS & EIRE: £1.25 for the first book, 75p for the second book and 28p for each subsequent book.

Name ..................................................................................

Address ..............................................................................

............................................................................................

............................................................................................